T0359920

WESTERN

Small towns. Rugged ranchers. Big hearts.

Faking It With A Fortune
Michelle Major

Her New Year's Wish List
Makenna Lee

MILLS & BOON

Michelle Major is acknowledged as the author of this work
FAKING IT WITH A FORTUNE
© 2025 by Harlequin Enterprises ULC
Philippine Copyright 2025
Australian Copyright 2025
New Zealand Copyright 2025

First Published 2025
First Australian Paperback Edition 2025
ISBN 978 1 038 94062 9

HER NEW YEAR'S WISH LIST
© 2025 by Margaret Culver
Philippine Copyright 2025
Australian Copyright 2025
New Zealand Copyright 2025

First Published 2025
First Australian Paperback Edition 2025
ISBN 978 1 038 94062 9

This is a work of fiction. Names, characters, places, and incidents are either the
product of the author's imagination or are used fictitiously, and any resemblance to
actual persons, living or dead, business establishments, events, or locales is entirely
coincidental.

MIX
Paper | Supporting
responsible forestry
FSC® C001695
www.fsc.org
FSC

Published by
Harlequin Mills & Boon
An imprint of Harlequin Enterprises (Australia) Pty Limited
(ABN 47 001 180 918), a subsidiary of HarperCollins
Publishers Australia Pty Limited
(ABN 36 009 913 517)
Level 19, 201 Elizabeth Street
SYDNEY NSW 2000 AUSTRALIA

Cover art used by arrangement with Harlequin Books S.A.. All rights reserved.

Printed and bound in Australia by McPherson's Printing Group

Faking It With A Fortune

Michelle Major

MILLS & BOON

Michelle Major grew up in Ohio but dreamed of living in the mountains. Soon after graduating with a degree in journalism, she pointed her car west and settled in Colorado. Her life and house are filled with one great husband, two beautiful kids, a few furry pets and several well-behaved reptiles. She's grateful to have found her passion writing stories with happy endings. Michelle loves to hear from her readers at michellemajor.com.

Books by Michelle Major

The Fortunes of Texas: Digging for Secrets

Fortune's Baby Claim

The Fortunes of Texas: Secrets of Fortune's Gold Ranch

Faking It with a Fortune

Welcome to Starlight

The Best Intentions
The Last Man She Expected
His Secret Starlight Baby
Starlight and the Single Dad

Crimson, Colorado

Anything for His Baby
A Baby and a Betrothal
Always the Best Man
Christmas on Crimson Mountain
Romancing the Wallflower

For additional books by Michelle Major,
visit her website, michellemajor.com

Dear Reader,

I'm so excited to be part of the Fortunes of Texas family once again this year. We have such a talented group of authors bringing you fun, emotional, heartwarming stories with a deliciously complicated new family and setting in the series.

Welcome to Emerald Ridge, Texas, and the Fortune's Gold Ranch! My story starts off with a bang—or more specifically with a sweet baby left on the front porch of the Fortune family. Newly certified foster parent Poppy Fortune might not be lucky in love, but she's committed to loving the boy named Joey until they discover the mystery of his parents' identity.

Turns out being a single mom is more of a challenge than Poppy expects, and when her former boyfriend Leo Leonetti steps up to help, she finds herself forging a partnership she never expected.

Leo admires Poppy's dedication but gets involved with baby Joey to make his beloved grandfather happy. However, Leo and Poppy quickly discover that playing at being a family feels far too real when their hearts get involved.

I hope you love this journey to happily-ever-after as much as I loved writing it!

Big hugs,

Michelle

To the authors and readers of the Fortunes of Texas family.
Everything's bigger and better in Texas!

CHAPTER ONE

POPPY FORTUNE BLINKED back tears as she read the words needlepointed into the square throw pillow she'd just unwrapped. "'Love lives here,'" she whispered as she met her mother's gaze across the kitchen table. "It's perfect. Thank you, Mom."

Shelley Fortune swiped a hand across her cheek. "I'm so proud of you, sweetie. I hope the pillow reminds you who you are and what an amazing thing you've done."

"I haven't done anything yet," Poppy countered with a smile. "The real accomplishment will be when I have a child placed with me. Laura, my caseworker, said it could take anywhere from two days to two months now that I'm official."

It had taken several months for her to become approved as a foster parent. She had to balance the hours needed to complete the training with her demanding job running the spa at Fortune's Gold Ranch, the property her family had owned for decades in the upscale town of Emerald Ridge, Texas. The spa was always busy over the holidays. Clients wanted preparty pampering or to unwind during the busy season. Bookings had remained steady through the first couple weeks of January, but it was Februrary now, and the winter lull was officially upon them.

The social service caseworker had completed Poppy's home visit earlier in the week, and she'd received word today that she'd been approved. Her mom, the only member of her family who seemed to take her desire to be a foster parent seriously, had insisted on a congratulatory dinner.

Poppy's father, Garth, was out of town until the following morning. Her brothers, Rafe and Shane, were busy with their own lives, so it was a girls' night, which she and her mom didn't have nearly enough of anymore.

"We're celebrating your decision and dedication to helping kids who need a safe place to stay." Shelley rose from her chair and went to stir the mushroom risotto, Poppy's favorite, simmering on the stove.

She adored her dad and brothers, but they didn't understand or appreciate her desire to become a foster parent. Maybe the same could be said for her mom, but at least Shelley made her feel supported no matter what path she took.

That was something she wanted to offer the children who came into her life through this endeavor. Growing up in Emerald Ridge as part of the illustrious Fortune family and one of the heirs to land that included a famed cattle ranch and a flourishing guest ranch and spa, Poppy had been blessed with an abundance of privilege. More importantly, she'd been shown unconditional love by her parents. In their happy marriage, she had an example of the best kind of relationship goals. Never mind that at thirty, she was nowhere close to establishing the family she knew would make her happy.

After a failed engagement and a string of less-than-successful relationships, Poppy was almost convinced that the white-picket-fence future she'd envisioned wasn't actually in the cards for her. And after all these years, one man still stood out in her mind and heart when she let herself go there.

Leo Leonetti—the one that got away.

They'd only dated a short time, but he remained the yard-stick by which she measured her attraction to every other guy. Sadly, they all came up short and even more pathetic, the secret torch she still carried was for a guy who'd told her outright he didn't want a relationship. She'd moved on but the memory of how happy she'd felt with him still lingered.

That said, her doubts about finding her dream man didn't change the amount of love she held in her heart and wanted to give freely. Being a foster parent would allow her to make a difference in the world beyond the boundaries of the land on which she'd been born and raised.

She knew the role would offer challenges and potential heartbreak but was committed to doing her best. Her heart filled with the knowledge that she would create a safe and nurturing environment for whoever entered her house, just like she'd always had at her childhood home.

As her mother continued to stir the pot, the scent of earthy mushrooms and rich cream filled the kitchen. Her parents shared the massive house that anchored the ranch with her uncle Hayden and aunt Darla. The Fortune brothers of her father's generation living together had been a stipulation of her grandfather's will. Although her dad and uncle didn't always get along, they each managed to raise their respective three kids under the same roof.

There had been plenty of room for all of them, and the families had primarily lived in separate wings, distance keeping the arguments between the brothers somewhat at bay. It had only been in recent years that Poppy and her siblings had formed close relationships with their cousins. It started when her cousin Drake and brother Rafe developed the Gift of Fortune, an initiative sponsored by the family that allowed deserving recipients to be invited to the ranch for a complimentary week of pampering.

Her dad and uncle had become friendlier after Garth and Hayden retired from the daily running of the ranch, but the two older Fortune couples still mainly lived separate lives in the same house. Poppy appreciated that there were two big kitchens thanks to renovations her father and uncle had done years earlier. Her family typically used the kitchen original to the homestead, and she loved the vibe of the weathered beams that ran across the ceiling, the rich granite of the countertops, the professional-grade appliances her father had installed for his wife, along with distressed cabinets and a wide plank floor.

Even with state-of-the-art accessories, the kitchen had a homey feel, beckoning people to settle in for a cup of tea or a home-cooked meal at the round oak table that could easily seat ten. Poppy had modeled her own kitchen on this same aesthetic, albeit on a much smaller scale.

"I'll get bowls and toss the salad," she told her mother, getting up from the table.

"And grab champagne glasses from the dining room while you're at it," Shelley added. "We're going to toast to your new role."

The doorbell rang at that moment. Both Poppy and her mother turned toward the unfamiliar sound. Fortune's Gold Ranch was an easy ten-minute drive from downtown Emerald Ridge, but most visitors went straight to the ranch office or the spa. It was rare to have people stop by the big house unannounced.

"Who'd drop in at supper time?" Shelley asked. She turned off the heat and covered the pot once more.

"No clue." Poppy headed toward the front of the house. "I'll go answer it."

The sun had already set, but darkness hadn't entirely swallowed up the last bit of the day's light, so she could see the outline of a woman through one of the windows flanking the tall front door. Poppy suppressed a groan as she got closer and made sure to "fix her face," as her mother would advise, before opening the door to greet Courtney Wellington, one of their closest neighbors and a fellow ranch owner in town.

"Hello, Courtney."

"I thought that was your Bronco in the driveway," the woman said by way of hello. "It's hard to miss."

Poppy looked past Courtney, who was dressed in bright pink slacks, a bedazzled T-shirt and a denim blazer. A distinctive outfit for Emerald Ridge, a town where most people wore casual or cowboy chic clothing. She smiled at her beloved Ladybug, as she'd named her bright red SUV. "Poppy red is my favorite color."

Courtney made a noncommittal sound. Her caterpillar-thick lashes lowered as she gave Poppy a quick once-over. "It's nice that something about you stands out. Is your mother home? I suppose she is since you're here." She offered a smile that reminded Poppy of a coyote baring its teeth. "I'm surprised to see a youngish, single girl like yourself hanging out at home on the weekend. You certainly aren't going to attract a man that way."

Poppy blinked and forgot all about fixing her face. She did her best to limit her interactions with the catty blonde who had booked a full day at the spa shortly after marrying her late husband. As the story went, Courtney and Mr. Wellington met in Dallas and had a whirlwind courtship that ended in marriage a mere month after their first encounter. Most of the locals in Emerald Ridge assumed Courtney had been the pursuer in the relationship, given that she'd been fresh off her second divorce when she met the wealthy rancher two decades her senior.

Like her mother, Poppy wanted to give people the benefit of the doubt. However, on her first and only visit to the spa, Courtney had left one of Poppy's best aestheticians in tears and skimped on tips for every one of her service providers, loudly complaining between appointments about the quality of the facilities and products.

Fortune's Gold Ranch Spa was regularly featured on the crème de la crème of luxury spa best-of lists in various high-end travel magazines. Their clients ranged from devoted locals to A-list celebrities to the wives of influential dignitaries as well as members of several European royal families who liked the idea of being pampered while experiencing a taste of what they might consider the Wild West.

Poppy could handle the jabs Courtney threw, but she'd never forgive the woman for dissing the spa staff.

She opened her mouth to offer a scathing comeback, but at that moment, she felt her mother's gentle hand on her shoulder.

"Hello, Courtney," Shelley said, her tone welcoming. "What brings you here tonight?"

"I was heading home from town, and since you'd mentioned that Garth was out of town until tomorrow, I figured I'd stop by for a friendly visit. You can be a bit of a homebody, Shelley."

Her mom's fingers gripped Poppy's shoulder when she would have lunged forward. Of course, Courtney didn't notice the effect her words were having on Poppy.

"I stopped by the liquor store," she continued, holding up one hand. Poppy hadn't noticed before that she had a bottle of white wine in it. "I thought we could have a drink to celebrate getting through January. I'm a bit restless with the short days and cooler temperatures. But now we have one winter month behind us. That calls for a toast."

"Actually, you can join the celebration we're having for my daughter," Shelley offered, stepping back and drawing Poppy with her so Courtney could enter the house.

She winked at Poppy as she entered. "I chose something from the Leonetti Vineyards. Didn't you date Leo at one point? Talk about a catch. That is one handsome hunk of a man. Too bad you couldn't keep him on the hook."

Poppy resisted the urge to stomp her foot. She didn't want Courtney anywhere near her, let alone crashing the celebratory dinner with her mother or reminding her of her past romantic failures.

"New job?" Courtney handed the wine to Poppy and then followed Shelley through the house, leaving Poppy to trail behind. "New boyfriend?" She chuckled as if she'd made some riotous joke.

"Poppy is going to be a foster parent." Shelley's voice was filled with pride, and an answering swell of it filled her heart. She loved the sound of that sentence.

"Wow," Courtney murmured. "That's really something."

Poppy forced a smile. "I'm excited to make a difference in the lives of children who temporarily need a stable home."

Her mom grabbed the bottle of champagne from the fridge, placed it on the counter and then disappeared into the dining room, where the crystal was kept.

"You must be okay with your nonexistent dating life," Courtney mused as she sat at one of the leather swivel chairs tucked under the overhang of the center island.

Once again, Poppy felt her mouth drop open. "I'm not sure one has anything to do with the other."

"Oh, yeah," Courtney retorted, reaching into her purse and pulling out her cell phone. "Because eligible single men are known to be into women with random kids hanging off them like barnacles."

There was a beat of silence while Shelley placed the glasses on the counter. She seemed as nonplussed as Poppy by their intrusive neighbor's rudeness.

"I mean, it's a selfless and admirable thing you're doing," Courtney quickly added as if realizing she'd gone too far. "Kudos to you for being a good person. That's something to celebrate."

"Thank you." Poppy had a hard time making her lips curve into another smile.

"Especially if your own biological clock isn't ticktocking."

"Let's open the champagne," Shelley said.

"Three cheers for Saint Poppy," Courtney agreed, which didn't sound like a compliment. "Actually, I'm glad you're here." She reached into her purse again. "I was going to give these to your mother, but you can take a look for yourself."

"A look at...?" Poppy couldn't imagine wanting to see anything Courtney Wellington had to offer.

"Products from Annelise's skincare line, AW GlowCare." Courtney set three small tubes on the counter. "These are sample sizes, of course, but you'll see the sublime quality after just one use. My stepdaughter is super talented. I told her the spa should carry her products and use them in all their services. It would be a big improvement over—"

She broke off when her phone began to ring. "Excuse me, I need to take this. Ranch owner business." Without batting an eye, Courtney accepted the call. "Hello? This is Mrs. Wellington..." She hopped off the chair with the phone at her ear and walked out of the kitchen. "Tell me exactly what you think I'm supposed to do about your problem."

Her words trailed off as she disappeared around the corner. Poppy allowed herself to both silently sympathize with whomever Courtney was reaming a new one and to feel a waterfall of relief that it wasn't her for a few minutes.

"She means well," Shelley offered with a wan smile.

Poppy burst out laughing. "So does a rattler when it strikes. The snake is just doing what snakes do."

Shelley rolled her lips together in an apparent attempt to keep from laughing as well, then popped the cork on the champagne. "You can't compare our closest neighbor to a venomous reptile."

"If the fangs fit," Poppy murmured as she unscrewed one of the lids from Annelise's sample tubes. She had no issue with either of Courtney's stepchildren. Jax was a year older than her and Annelise a few years younger. They hadn't run in the same circles, but she'd always gotten a good feeling about the other woman.

"I wonder why Annelise didn't come to you directly about her skincare line?" Shelley mused as she poured the bubbly liquid into the three flutes.

"Maybe because she isn't pushy and manipulative like some people I know." Poppy rubbed the thick cream into the back of her hand. "Wow. It smells amazing."

"Would you consider carrying the line at the spa?"

"Absolutely. We already source most of our products from Texas-based companies. Finding a quality line from a local business, especially one that's female-owned, would be even better. I'll call Annelise next week to set up a meeting to learn more about the ingredients and production. I like the idea of it."

"Maybe Courtney stopping by is a good thing after all," her mom remarked.

Poppy rolled her eyes.

"Why are ranch hands *so* difficult to deal with?" Courtney asked with an exasperated sigh as she returned to the kitchen. "Make sure to fill my glass to the rim, Shelley darling."

Courtney didn't seem to want or expect a response to most of her words. She was a woman who was clearly enamored with the sound of her own voice. Poppy exchanged a look with her mother and then moved toward the stove to scoop up a bowl of risotto. The doorbell rang again just as she grabbed a ladle from the utensil jar next to the stovetop.

"I'll get it." She dropped the ladle and hurried toward the front of the house. One visitor on a chilly winter night was odd enough, but two felt like some kind of sign. At least Poppy chose to take it as a sign that she would have an excuse not to focus on that awful woman.

But no one stood on the other side when she opened the door. Even odder. She glanced toward the darkness that had overtaken everything past the glow of the porch light and was about to close the door again when something made her look down.

"What the…?" A white wicker laundry basket sat on the porch. In it, wrapped in a pale blue blanket, was a baby.

CHAPTER TWO

POPPY SCOOPED UP the basket, kicked the door closed with the heel of her boot and then rushed back toward the kitchen. She didn't want to shout and risk disturbing the sleeping infant. A newborn by the size of his tiny features. She assumed the baby was a boy based on the blue blanket and the little cotton cap with airplanes that fit snugly around his head.

"I started toasting without you," Courtney announced, holding her half-drank champagne flute.

Poppy ignored her. "Mom, call 911! Someone left a baby on the porch."

The two older women let out matching gasps of shock, and Poppy realized she was also having trouble catching her breath. She forced air in and out of her lungs as she set the basket on the kitchen table. She needed to keep her wits about her. This was no time to freak out, at least outwardly.

"Hello, sweetheart," she cooed to the baby as she unfolded the blanket. He wore a blue-footed one-piece, and her gaze snagged on the name crookedly embroidered on the front. "Your name is Joey," she told the baby as she lifted him from the basket.

"How did that thing get here?" Courtney demanded.

"He's a *baby*," Poppy said through gritted teeth. "I don't know how he ended up on your front porch." She could hear her mother, who had walked to the room's far end, speaking with the emergency services operator. "There was no one out there when I opened the door."

"An ambulance is on the way," Shelley reported as she lowered the phone and moved toward them. "Is he cold?"

Poppy shook her head, staring with wonder at the tiny form cradled in her arms. Joey's mouth worked for a few seconds, but he remained asleep.

Courtney backed away a few steps like Poppy held a porcupine. "I should go," she whispered to no one in particular, her voice hollow like she was in shock.

"There's a note," Poppy told her mother, pointing to the basket and ignoring Courtney.

Shelley picked up the piece of paper, the edges ragged like it had hastily been ripped from a notebook. "'This baby is a Fortune,'" Shelley read slowly, her eyes widening. "'Please care for him since I can't.'"

Courtney gasped again, the sound grating on Poppy's last nerve. "Some poor girl must have felt incredibly desperate to leave her baby on a stranger's porch. Although someone in this house apparently isn't a stranger to her."

Poppy's gut tightened at the implications of Courtney's words, then soured as she continued, "Which of your boys do you think is to blame? Or maybe one of your nephews?" Courtney gripped the phone in her hand more tightly. "Or..."

Poppy and Shelley both stared at the other woman.

"Or what?" Poppy demanded.

"A man can father a child well past his prime." Courtney shrugged when Shelley's mouth dropped open. "I'm just saying—"

"Weren't you *just saying* you need to go?" Poppy shifted so that the baby was no longer in Courtney's direct line of sight, the immediate surge of protectiveness she felt for the abandoned child almost overwhelming.

"I'll walk you out." Her mom gripped Courtney's elbow. "Please don't tell anyone about the baby until we have more information on him."

"Your secret is safe with me," Poppy heard Courtney promise as Shelley led her toward the front door.

"Whose secret *are* you, little man?" she asked the bundle in her arms when she was alone in the kitchen. As if responding to her voice, the baby blinked and stared up at her with the clearest blue-gray eyes she'd ever seen.

"You're safe now," she promised Joey like he could understand her. "Nothing and no one will hurt you while I'm around."

The baby drew a deep breath before his heavy eyelids drooped and closed again.

"The EMTs should be here soon," her mother said as she returned to Poppy's side. She studied the baby for a long moment, then rummaged through the basket. "A few diapers, a plastic bottle and a container of powder formula," she reported, then looked at her daughter with concern. "I don't understand this, Poppy."

"Me neither, Mom, but if I can get approval from social services, I'm going to take care of Joey until we figure it out." Her gaze drifted to the note on the table. "Do you really think—"

A pounding at the front door interrupted her question. Not that she needed to ask it out loud. Her mom had to be wondering the same thing as Poppy. Could one of her brothers, or *heaven forbid*, her father, be responsible for this baby? It was difficult to imagine a world where any of the men related to her would make a woman feel like she had no options other than to abandon a newborn.

The EMTs, a young woman with a thick braid and a gray-haired man, entered the kitchen. Poppy reluctantly handed over Joey and watched as they did an initial exam. According to the woman, whose badge identified her as Monica, his vitals were all in the normal range. Her partner was called Stan, and they were efficient in their care but not particularly loving—at least not enough for Poppy.

They also refused to allow her to ride to the county hospital in the ambulance with Joey, and as they left with him, longing split Poppy's chest, a burning physical ache.

She turned to her mother after closing the front door. "I'm going to the hospital."

"We need a family meeting," Shelley said simultaneously.

"Not until I make sure he's okay."

"The doctors and nurses will take care of him."

"Not like I can." Poppy reached for her mother's hands and squeezed. "I don't understand this any more than you, but the fact that he was left on your doorstep the night after I received my approval is a sign, Mom. I'm supposed to be a part of Joey's life, at least temporarily."

Shelley looked like she wanted to argue, and Poppy understood the fear she saw in her mother's blue eyes. The mystery of the identity of Joey's mother and father would eventually be solved, but whatever they discovered could rock the Emerald Ridge Fortune family to its core.

Still, nothing was more important at this point than the baby.

She'd once dreamed of having her own baby, and maybe she'd even imagined a child with Leo Leonetti's soulful brown eyes. But she'd given up that girlish fantasy along with her belief in true love yet knew caring for a baby who needed someone was the kind of love she could offer in spades.

"Keep me updated." Shelley pulled her in for a long hug. "I'll call your father and uncle and let them know what's happened. The EMTs said the police would also come to the house to investigate. We'll figure out where Joey belongs sooner than later."

Poppy nodded, and after grabbing her purse and jacket from the coat rack near the front door, she hurried to her car. County Hospital was a twenty-minute drive from the ranch, but she had every intention of making it in fifteen. On the way, she would call her caseworker to start the process of being designated as the child's foster parent if he needed someone. Despite her mother's words, Poppy had the strangest feeling that the place sweet Joey belonged was with her.

ACROSS TOWN, LEO LEONETTI drained his wineglass and then immediately regretted his hasty swallow. Or, more specifically, he rued his promise to himself to enjoy only one glass of wine with dinner each night.

As one of the owners and CEO of Leonetti Vineyards, the oldest and most prestigious winery in Texas, Leo had an entire cellar of exceptional varietals. He allowed himself to imbibe more freely on a special occasion or the rare instance when he led a personal tour of his family's operations.

But typically, one glass suited his taste and personality.

"You're thirty-four, Leonardo," his grandfather Enzo reminded him as if Leo might have forgotten his age. "A man in his prime should have a wife and family. You don't want to end up a shriveled raisin trying to chase little ones through the grapes."

"Papa, I don't think I'll be hitting raisin status anytime soon." Leo twirled the stem of the empty glass between two fingers. "For now, the grapes *are* my children."

Leo had been at the helm of the vineyard for nearly ten years since his father's death from a fatal heart attack, a shocking loss that still left an ache in his soul. Leo had been in the Alps, indulging his love of travel and new adventures, when the call came from his mother.

All that wanderlust had been snuffed out in an instant, and he'd returned to Texas to take his place as a steward of the land his family had owned for generations.

He loved everything about the process of making wine, and under his leadership, the vineyard and winery were thriving. His younger sisters, Bella, Antonia and Gia, were equal partners in running the operation. While Enzo and Leo's mother, Martina, had retired from any formal role in the business, Leo appreciated having them close for guidance and support.

More recently, it became his turn to support Enzo. His grandfather, who enjoyed splitting his time between Emerald Ridge and Italy, had been diagnosed a few years ago with stage-three liver cancer.

Although the first round of chemo and radiation had taken a toll on the eighty-two-year-old man, they also believed the treatments had driven the insidious disease into remission.

Just before Christmas, Enzo had called a family meeting and shared that the cancer had returned. The proud and stubborn man had initially planned to forgo additional medical interventions to concentrate on enjoying his life and whatever time he had left with his family.

However, with encouragement from Leo, his mom and sisters, Enzo had decided on another round of treatment, determined to kick cancer's butt one more time. Leo had been grateful to the point of tears, unable to imagine the vineyard or their family without his larger-than-life grandfather. And he knew enough now to appreciate every precious moment they had together.

Other than the moments where he was being lectured on settling down. He might not have a wife—or girlfriend—but he wasn't exaggerating when he said his most intense relationship was with his work. His grandfather remained strong and in good spirits, but there was no guarantee how long that would last. Leo wanted to continue building on the success of Leonetti Vineyards so that Enzo would know his legacy was in good hands.

"Grapes will not keep you warm at night." Enzo shook his head. "They will not celebrate your joys and comfort you in times of sorrow. My beautiful Ella was the light of my life for many years, Leo. I only want that same thing for you."

Leo's grandparents had enjoyed the most picture-perfect relationship he could imagine, a flawless match in every way, until his grandmother's death in a tragic car accident when Leo was a boy. However, it hadn't been the same with his own parents. His father had loved his mother and been a devoted parent, if sometimes harsh and impatient.

Franco hadn't loved the vineyard the way Enzo did. The way *Leo* did, even when he felt the weight of responsibility he carried like a boulder on his back.

How could he settle down with a woman, and even more so, a family, when he knew he could never live up to the example his nana and papa set?

Maybe if his parents hadn't been rushed into marriage, thanks to a surprise pregnancy, his dad could have taken more time to figure out who he was and who he wanted to be in the world. Leo couldn't imagine balancing his focus on both work and a romantic relationship. He'd have to potentially sacrifice one or both parts of his life due to what was expected of him within the family business and the demands a relationship might put on him.

Suddenly a vision of Poppy Fortune with her blond hair and gentle green eyes appeared in his mind. She'd been the one woman who'd ever made him want to reconsider his refusal to open his heart.

If he was being honest, the time they'd dated had been the best and worst of his life. The best because spending time with Poppy felt like being bathed in sunshine on the most perfect summer day. She was beautiful, smart, funny and made him practically forget his own name because he'd been so infatuated with her.

Which had led to the worst part. The idea of losing control of his emotions had terrified Leo, leading him to spew out some verbal garbage about how he had no intention of settling down or getting serious with one woman. On their third date. It was like he'd shoved his own foot straight down his throat. And Poppy had dumped him like a sack of rotten potatoes in return.

He'd deserved it and that moment proved that Leo wasn't equipped to succeed at both love and work. With the pressure of generations of Leonettis on his shoulders, failing at the vineyard wasn't an option. Maybe his father had understood that, and the pressure had taken a toll until his heart couldn't withstand it.

"I'll get there, Papa," he promised, even though he had no idea if that was true.

Enzo stabbed a piece of plump gnocchi and popped it into his mouth, chewing with gusto as he stared at his grandson. Martina had made dinner before she and Leo's sisters left for their monthly book club meeting. "You can't keep hiding in the rows of vines, my boy. You are no longer a child, and this isn't a game. There's a time for everything, but time is finite. I want to see you happy."

Leo's throat burned. He could tell by the color rising in his grandfather's cheeks that this conversation upset the old man.

He hated not being able to offer the reassurance his grandfather wanted. "I'm happy, Papa. Work makes me happy. Spending time with you makes me happy." Another glass of wine would make him happy.

"Nothing makes a man happier than love," Enzo insisted.

Leo couldn't argue because he wasn't sure he'd ever been

in love. He didn't know if he was even capable of feeling that depth of emotion for another person. Maybe he'd inherited the trait from his father and that inability to love had contributed to Franco's discontent. Leo might have been able to fall in love with Poppy if he'd let himself, but he wouldn't. He couldn't. All he knew for sure was that he wasn't enough to be the man his grandpa saw in him.

He forced a smile and sopped up a generous amount of oil with a piece of the crusty bread his mother had baked earlier. "Valentine's Day is right around the corner," he said with a lightness he didn't feel. "Who knows what might happen?"

But Leo knew. He had more work on his plate than he could handle in a month of eighty-hour work weeks. There was no time for romance, even if he was interested in it. Which he wasn't.

Still, if it made Enzo happy, Leo would pretend. Wasn't that what his father had done as well? Smooth the waters and pretend like everything was okay.

Enzo let out a raspy sigh. "You speak the right words, my boy, but your heart isn't in them." The older man held up a hand when Leo would've argued. "But now you've put it out there, and it's up to fate to pick up your challenge. Love can happen in an instant. That was how it was with your grandmother and me on our family's trip to Italy when I was only sixteen. I saw her, and everything else fell away. She was the answer to a question I didn't even know enough to ask. If it can happen to me…"

"A toast to Nana, rest her soul." Leo held up his water glass, and Enzo clinked it with his wine goblet.

"To my darling Ella."

"Tell me again about your courtship with Nana and how you swept her off her feet."

Enzo's features relaxed as he smiled and sat back in his chair. He never tired of speaking about his wife. The memories, bittersweet as they must be in some ways, always put him in a good mood.

Leo took another bite of the potato pasta and settled into his chair. He would much rather hear about his grandparents' beautiful love story than think about the work involved to create one of his own.

That was work he had no intention of pursuing in the near future.

CHAPTER THREE

LEO FINISHED HIS run at his mother's front porch the next morning. He wanted to check in on Enzo after their dinner last night.

Sleep had been elusive as he'd been plagued with dreams of driving his truck down a washed-out dirt road to reach his family, but the wheels continually got stuck in ruts. Did the frustrating dream have anything to do with his guilt over not being able to give his grandfather what the older man wanted?

Enzo hadn't pushed any further about Leo settling down once he'd started reminiscing about his own love story. Still, Leo couldn't shake the nagging sense that his unwillingness to get on board the dating train made him a disappointment to the man who meant the most to him in the world.

Truth be told, he was a regular passenger on the dating train but only for short-term trips. He loved everything about women—the way they looked and smelled, how their bodies were soft in places his was hard. He'd never had any complaints in the bedroom department, and he kept their expectations in check as far as what he could and couldn't offer.

Usually, his dates cut him more slack than he deserved, thanks to his charm. It wouldn't be an exaggeration to say that Leo had charisma for days. But Poppy Fortune had seemed to look directly into his soul, bypassing his megawatt smile and twinkling brown eyes, and found him lacking in all the ways that counted.

Leo used the hem of his T-shirt to wipe the sweat off his brow as he took the front porch steps two at a time. Why was he thinking of Poppy so much lately? He'd dated plenty of women since, and no one cared about his inability to commit. Not when he was so damn much fun, or so he'd been told.

His papa, who'd also seen through Leo's attempt to sweet-talk his way out of answering difficult questions, would probably appreciate Poppy. She'd been a straight shooter in addition to being gorgeous, but Leo hadn't had more than a chance encounter with her in half a decade.

Emerald Ridge might be a small town, but it was easy enough to avoid a person who, with one glance, could make him uncomfortably aware of the ways he came up short.

He reached for the door the same time his mother opened it, her eyes red-rimmed and her lips turned down into a trembling frown.

"Mom, what's wrong?" He reached out and gripped her arm. "Is it Papa?"

Martina closed her eyes as she nodded. "He started having trouble breathing at about four this morning. We couldn't get his oxygen levels right, so I called 911. He argued with me, saying he was fine but looked real bad, Leo. They took him to the hospital twenty minutes ago."

"Why didn't you call me?" he demanded, his mind reeling. "Are Bella, Antonia and Gia there?"

"Not yet." His mom stepped forward, and Leo wrapped his arms around her. Enzo had moved into one of the guest rooms in the main house after his most recent diagnosis. His grandfather balked at being coddled and didn't want to be a burden for his daughter-in-law, but Martina had insisted.

It gave Leo a measure of relief to know his mom was there if Enzo needed anything, but he tried to stop by at least once a day to give her a break. His sisters did the same, and in some ways, their grandfather's illness had brought the four of them even closer. It was truly life-changing to deal with the mortality of a loved one.

"He made me promise not to wake any of you." Martina leaned back and looked up into his face, her gentle eyes filling with tears. "I knew you'd be by this morning because you're such a good son and grandson."

Was he? "What do they think caused the breathing issues?" Leo asked softly. He couldn't help but think it might have to do with his grandfather's agitation during their dinner conversation last night.

His mom shook her head. "They don't know. I'm going to shower and head to the hospital. The doctor called a few minutes ago and said Enzo is stable but weak. He doesn't think this is…" She placed a hand to her mouth and stifled a sob.

"It's going to be okay, Mom. I'll head there now." He turned away then paused as he realized he'd have to jog back to his house, which was only a quarter mile away on the fifty acres the vineyard encompassed, but it felt too far.

"Take the field truck," his mother suggested, nodding toward the storage barn. "The keys are inside."

Leo nodded. "I'll see you there."

By the time he exited the elevator on the third floor, his mind was a jumble of regret and worry. Martina would never accuse him, but how could it be a coincidence that Enzo had suffered this sort of setback after the conversation with Leo?

He spoke with the nurse at the desk, who gave him a strange look before asking if he'd run the whole way to the hospital in the wind. Leo quickly smoothed a hand over his rumpled hair—he'd been pulling at the ends for most of the drive over, a nervous habit he couldn't seem to break. "I came as soon as I heard my grandfather was here," he explained.

The woman's gaze became more understanding. "Your grandpa is sleeping, but he's stable. The morning took a lot out of him. Rest is the best thing right now."

"Can I see him?" Leo didn't bother to hide the desperation in his voice.

She looked like she wanted to deny him, but eventually nodded. "Room 301, down the hall to your right. You can stop in, but please don't wake him. His body is dealing with a lot."

"I know. Thank you." The words came out a croak as the ball of emotion in his throat threatened to overtake him.

He glanced at his watch as he headed toward Enzo's room. His mom would have called his sisters by now, and they'd be there soon. He didn't want to see or speak to anyone until he got his emotions under control.

Leo liked being in control, and he felt the opposite of that as he studied his grandfather asleep in the hospital room, the machine next to him displaying his vital signs.

Enzo's eyes were closed and his once-broad chest rose and fell in what looked like labored breaths. Clear tubes led from a tank to his nose, supplying the oxygen he couldn't seem to take in on his own. Because of his explicit instructions, there would be no CPR performed if his breathing stopped, which meant that Enzo had to recover on his own.

Although Leo was at loss for how to help, he'd find a way. He would not lose another man he loved...not yet.

His stomach grumbled loudly and he backed out of the room. Like his grandfather, he was a three-square-meals-a-day kind of guy and didn't function well in the morning before coffee or breakfast.

Now that he'd seen for himself that Enzo was stable, his earlier adrenaline rush began to wear off. He thanked the woman at the nurse's station again, then took the stairs at the end of the hall to the first-floor cafeteria.

He wasn't ready to go home and shower, but some food and caffeine might help clear his head. After paying for the coffee and an egg-and-chorizo burrito, he headed to the two-person tables in front of the bank of windows that looked out over the hospital parking lot then did a double take as he recognized the woman sitting nearby.

"Poppy?"

Poppy Fortune, staring out the window, looked up at Leo with those big sea-foam-green eyes that had captivated him when they'd first met.

Her mouth formed a small O before she flashed a self-conscious smile. "Hey, Leo, this is a surprise." She ran a hand through her shiny blond hair, which fell nearly to the middle of her back. It had been shoulder-length when they'd gone on their few memorable dates. "I didn't expect to see anyone I knew here."

"Me neither," he agreed, resisting the urge to lift his arm and take a sniff under it. Maybe he should have made time to shower after all. "Is everything okay?"

She took a few seconds to respond as if uncertain how to answer. "It will be. I'll make sure of it."

That piqued his curiosity. "Anything I can help with?"

The question prompted a choked laugh from her. "Definitely not. What about you?" She glanced behind him like she was looking for his mom or one of his sisters. "I hope you aren't here because of your grandfather."

Leo's grip tightened on the coffee cup. Of course, most people in Emerald Ridge knew about Enzo and his cancer battle. If memory served, Shelley Fortune had delivered a home-cooked meal or two during the months Leo's mother cared for Enzo during chemo and radiation. "He had trouble breathing early this morning, so he's been admitted until that's under control."

"Oh, no! Sorry to hear that." Poppy reached out and squeezed his arm. "I'll keep him in my prayers and hope for a fast recovery. Your grandfather is quite a character."

Leo wasn't prepared for the wave of emotion her touch elicited from him and gave a sharp nod. "He is that. I should eat so I can get back up there." For some reason, he didn't want to walk away but...

"Would you like to join me?" She gestured to the empty chair across from her. "I've been here all night, so fair warning, I might not be great company."

"I can't imagine an instance when you aren't great company," Leo told her as he sat down. "Not to pry, but your reason for being here was cryptic. Care to elaborate?"

She stared at him for so long he wondered if she'd fallen asleep with her eyes open. "I suppose a situation like the one I'm in won't stay quiet around here. Not for long."

The little hairs on the back of his neck rose to attention. "What kind of situation?"

She took a breath and said quietly, "A baby was left on my parents' doorstep last night."

Midbite of burrito, Leo nearly spit the thing across the table at her. "Say *what*?"

The words came out louder than he meant, and after making sure no one had overheard him, she continued, "Keep your voice down, please."

"Sorry, you just caught me off guard," he said quietly. "Whose baby is it?"

"We don't know. His name is Joey, and according to the note left with him, his father is a Fortune."

"One of the FGR Fortunes?" Leo's mind was racing, and it had nothing to do with the half cup of coffee he'd gulped down a few minutes earlier.

Poppy shrugged and looked down at her phone. Suddenly, the pallor of her complexion and the tight line of her lips took on a different meaning. He could tell she was not only exhausted but worried, both about the baby and what this could mean for her family.

"Neither of my brothers or cousins believe he could be theirs. No one is claiming him." She squeezed shut her eyes briefly then raised her gaze to Leo's. "Except me."

"You?" He placed the burrito back on the plate, his hunger wholly forgotten.

"A caseworker I've grown close to at social services helped me get assigned as his foster parent right away." She touched her phone's home screen then lifted it in Leo's direction. "This is Joey. The pediatrician on call wanted him to stay the night to be monitored. They don't think he's more than a few days old. But I'm taking him home as soon as he's discharged."

Leo looked at the photo of the infant swaddled like a baby burrito and sleeping soundly. His heart turned over uncomfortably. "For how long?"

"As long as he needs me," she said, almost defensively.

"Don't you have to be certified or something to foster a kid, let alone an infant?"

"I am." Her eyes blazed with flecks of gold as if daring him to challenge her. "I've been through all the training and background checks and received my final approval this week. Just in time to give this sweet baby a home."

"You're a foster mom," he murmured. "You decided to do this on your own?"

She bristled. "No doubt you heard that Michael and I called things off."

"Yeah. Bella mentioned it. He always seemed like a tool to me, so good riddance on that count."

Poppy laughed, covering her mouth to stifle it. "Only you could find a way to lighten the mood at a time like this, Leo."

He wasn't sure if it was meant as a compliment, but he damn sure intended to take it as one.

"Do you think I can't handle this by myself?" Her smile faded.

"I think you can do whatever you set your mind to." He lifted the coffee cup to his lips then lowered it again. "I admire the hell out of you for it, Poppy. That baby is lucky to have you, and so is your family, whether or not one of the Fortune guys is responsible."

Poppy bit down on her lower lip as a tear fell from the corner of one eye. She dashed it away and offered him a watery smile. "I wasn't expecting that."

Leo was horrified. He hated to see any woman crying.

"But thank you," she told him. "It means a lot, especially coming from you."

He lifted a brow. "Why coming from me?"

"Your feelings about commitment were abundantly clear and..." She made a face. "From how the ladies talk at the spa, your stance hasn't changed."

"The ladies talk about me? That's scary as hell." He leaned in closer, curiosity piqued. "Wait. Do *you* talk about me, Poppy?"

She huffed out a laugh. "Not to disappoint, Leo, but I have more important things to think *and* talk about than you."

Ouch. "That's fair," he conceded. "Especially now."

"To be honest," she told him with a grimace, "I'm not sure I fully grasped the responsibility I was signing up for as a foster parent until my caseworker approved me as Joey's guardian. Being in charge of such a helpless baby is intimidating to say the least. Things in real life feel a lot more..." She shrugged again. "It's a lot of responsibility."

Leo forced himself to concentrate on what she was saying, even though his thoughts snagged on the comment about his reputation.

He supposed he shouldn't be surprised that women around town gossiped about him and his unwillingness to commit. He also should have guessed his grandfather wouldn't be so easily swayed by his vague promises of eventually settling down.

Poppy's phone vibrated, and she quickly pushed back from the table. "Joey is being discharged," she said, looking both excited and nervous. "Here I go. Wish me luck."

"You don't need luck." Leo also stood. "You're going to be fantastic at this. I hope everything works out for that baby, although there's no doubt it will with you in his corner."

"I hope your grandfather feels better soon." To his surprise, she leaned in and gave him a tight hug.

Her sweet scent and the feel of her curves pressed against him jumbled his brain, not to mention other parts of his body. Where the hell had that reaction come from?

He also wished he'd changed out of his workout clothes almost as much as he wished he could hold on to Poppy for longer, but she released him a second later. "Your family is lucky to have you as well, Leo. You're a fine man. Better than you give yourself credit for."

She hurried away before he could respond, which was a blessing because he had no idea what to say. Poppy was such a good person. They were practically strangers at this point. Yet in the midst of dealing with something highly overwhelming in her own life, she'd managed to make Leo feel better about himself than he had in a long time.

If Poppy believed he was a better man, maybe he could become one. If not for himself, then for his grandfather. There was no doubt Enzo would like her. Leo certainly did.

Even though she'd broken up with him, there were no hard feelings. In fact, seeing her again made him remember how drawn he'd been to her. He wanted to see her succeed in this foster care venture.

As he tossed the remainder of his burrito and the empty coffee cup into the trash on his way out of the cafeteria, he realized, to his surprise, he not only wanted her to succeed—he wanted to *help* her succeed. And he knew a way that might benefit them both.

It was ridiculous and far-fetched and would put him galaxies away from his comfort zone. But it also might make his grandpa happy and relieve some of the pressure Leo felt from the women in his family, who wanted him to settle down as much as Enzo did. The more he thought about his potential solution, the more he thought it might work. All he needed was to convince Poppy to agree. How hard could that be?

CHAPTER FOUR

POPPY WANTED TO cry as she swept up the last shards of her shattered coffeepot, her nerves and resolve feeling just as ruined.

She could hear Joey, who she'd put down in his crib only moments before, crying through the video monitor on the counter.

After checking the time, she left the dustpan on the counter and hurried toward the spare bedroom, where she'd spent most of the night with the baby in her arms.

Joey had barely made a peep from the time Poppy found him on her parents' front porch to his day in the hospital to the errands they'd run yesterday for the items she'd need to care for a newborn baby.

Instead of asking her mother or one of her brothers to watch him, she'd taken him with her, because the child was her responsibility.

Not theirs.

She'd also driven past the shops in Emerald Ridge's downtown and headed to the next town over so the busybodies and lookie-loos wouldn't have her family's private business to discuss. At least not while she was right in front of them.

Her mother had invited her to dinner last night. Although Poppy had declined that invitation, she couldn't deny Shelley's request that she attend a mandatory family meeting with both sets of the Fortune cousins this morning at the main house.

She hadn't expected to sleep well with everything on her mind, but she'd expected to sleep more than an hour. Unfortunately, Joey had started fussing about an hour after she'd put him down.

Neither of them had enjoyed a restful night. Between rocking him, feeding him, checking for whether his diaper needed changing and swaddling him in hopes that he might finally settle, Poppy had scoured the internet searching for tips on the care of infants. She knew as a foster parent, she would be looking after children that ranged in age and experience, but this was trial by fire for her first case, and already she felt a little singed.

She'd knocked the coffeepot off the counter before pouring a drop into her cup, which had been the cherry on the top of her crap sundae. There was no time to make another cup, but she knew she could get some liquid sustenance at her parents' house.

Hopefully, her family wouldn't see how much she was already failing at her role as a foster mom. If she had a husband and kids of her own, she might be experienced enough to know how to soothe a fussy baby.

Her mom would be able to tell her, but Poppy hated the thought of revealing even to Shelley how ill-equipped she felt for the job she wanted to succeed at more than anything.

The doorbell rang as she carried the still-fussy baby from the bedroom as her rescue mutt, Humphrey, gave a woof of welcome and trotted to the door. Maybe it was one of her brothers. They lived in houses similar to Poppy's in the same area on the ranch. Each of the Fortunes of her generation had homes built on the ranch when they'd been ready to leave the main house.

All of the lots consisted of five acres, which meant she had privacy while still being close enough to feel like they had a small cousin community. She bounced Joey gently in her arms as she padded to the door.

Hopefully, it was Rafe and not Shane. Her older brother might not want anything to do with kids after losing his wife and daughter in a tragic car accident, but at least he had experience with babies.

Except Leo Leonetti, not her brothers, stood smiling at her on the other side of the door. Instead of the sweaty workout garb he'd worn at the hospital, he looked crisp and dapper in dark gray pressed pants and a white button-down that contrasted in a toe-curling way with his olive-toned skin. Yesterday, she'd wanted to smooth her hand through his finger-tousled hair, but today, not one strand on the man's dark head was out of place.

She'd purposely avoided looking in the mirror this morning but could imagine what he saw as he studied her face after two sleepless nights. He didn't give any indication if he thought she looked as bad as she felt. Instead, he bent to scratch Humphrey behind the ears when the dog head-butted his leg.

Then, to her eternal gratitude, he held up a steaming cup of coffee from the local shop in town. "I asked if you had a standing order, and they said sugar-free caramel latte. I hope you haven't already had your fill of caffeine this morning."

Once again, Poppy was brought to the verge of tears in front of Leo, the last man on earth she wanted to see her cry.

"Yes, please, coffee." She adjusted her hold on Joey, who was still whimpering, and stepped back. "You are my hero."

Leo startled at the comment. "I highly doubt that. You look like you're on your way out. I hope I'm not here at a bad time."

"My mom called a family meeting to discuss the situation with Joey." She glanced at her watch again. "I've got a few minutes until we're supposed to be there but planned to leave early because my coffeepot had an unfortunate meet with the tile floor this morning. But now that you've saved me, I'm good."

"And how's the baby?" Leo asked, eyeing Joey somewhat dubiously.

"I don't think he likes me," Poppy admitted thickly.

"I doubt that."

She swallowed, then said, "Despite my training, taking care of a baby in real life is way more of a challenge than I realized. Pretty sure Joey knows I'm in over my head."

Leo's jaw tightened as he studied her. Why had she admitted the worry that picked at the edge of her deepest fear about herself to this man? He undoubtedly had no interest in hearing about her troubles.

"Why are you here?" she blurted, too frazzled and sleep-deprived to care whether or not she sounded rude.

Leo smiled. "In addition to my sixth sense about when some-one needs a coffee fix, I have a proposition for you." To Poppy's surprise, he looked almost nervous saying the words.

"Do I look like a woman who's in the market to be propo-sitioned?"

For whatever reason that seemed to drain some of the ten-sion from his body.

"Maybe you'll be willing to entertain my idea because it also has to do with Joey. Our conversation in the hospital yesterday got me thinking about my contribution to the world and what's expected of me."

She quirked a brow. "Beyond running your family's vine-yard and helping to care for your grandfather?"

Leo might not be willing to commit to a woman, but he wasn't precisely irresponsible in the rest of his life. She knew how much the winery had expanded under his leadership. His mom and sisters and almost every woman Poppy could name adored him.

"More specifically, the *expectation* my grandfather has for me. He wants me to settle down, and we had a somewhat heated conversation about it the night before he had his setback."

Joey quieted like he was listening intently to Leo's words. He had a great voice, deep and soothing and just a touch gravelly.

"Any update on your grandfather?" she asked, trying not to get sidetracked by Leo's handsomeness or his voice or how good he smelled—like clean laundry and some kind of male spice she couldn't name.

"He hasn't woken up enough for us to talk to him, but the doctors say he's stable, so that's good." Leo cleared his throat. "When he does, I want him to know that he doesn't have to worry about me or my stability or how I'm going to honor his legacy."

Her heart pinched at the pain in his voice.

"You aren't alone at the vineyard," she reminded Leo gen-tly. "Your sisters have just as much invested in the Leonetti legacy that you do. It's not fully on your shoulders, capable as they might be."

His jaw tightened again, and his shoulders went ramrod stiff.

"My grandfather… The point is, I don't know how much time we have with him, and I don't want to give him any reason to worry."

"I get that." Poppy nodded. "But what does that have to do with Joey and me?"

"I'd like to help you take care of him."

She started to laugh because he had to be joking then stopped herself. His expression was completely serious, earnest even.

"If I have zero experience caring for a baby, then I would guess you have less than zero."

He shot her an affronted look. "I'm a great uncle to Antonia's baby, or at least I will be when she's old enough to appreciate me."

"I don't doubt it. You'll be the perfect fun uncle. But have you changed a diaper?" she challenged.

"I watched a video on YouTube," Leo said without missing a beat. "The most important thing with a boy is that you cover everything while cleaning them so you don't get sprayed in the face."

Poppy had to admit she was impressed and also *had* been sprayed in the face last night. One more moment that added insult to injury. Leo Leonetti, a confirmed bachelor who avoided commitment at all costs, had the forethought to educate himself on diaper changing. Her foster parent classes had handled a lot. She was certified in infant CPR but had still managed to be sprayed in the face.

Joey squirmed in her arms and let out a wail, and she began to rock him back and forth in a vain attempt to quiet him.

"Okay. Let's cut to the chase. What exactly are you proposing here, Leo?"

"I want to co-parent Joey with you. I could even stay here if that would help."

He held up a hand when she would have argued. "Give me a chance, Poppy. I'll help out in whatever way you need. It would mean a lot to me, but not because you can't do it alone. I think it would mean a lot to my grandfather."

Poppy's heart pounded, and her limbs felt heavy. How could she handle everything that was expected of her right now and cope with her overwhelming exhaustion at the same time? Of course, she'd figure out a way. It's what mothers—and in her case, foster mothers—did. She didn't want Leo or anyone to think she couldn't handle this because she could. There was no doubt in her mind she would take care of Joey, but would she always feel this tired?

Stifling a yawn, she managed a smile. "I need to get to the family meeting."

Leo nodded. Disappointment flashed in his eyes but he took a step away. Joey continued to cry. "What if we did a test run?"

She frowned at him. "Like a test drive of a car?"

He shook his head. "No, like you give me a chance to prove I can handle helping with Joey. I know you have no reason to trust me, Poppy."

Yet somehow she believed she could, not that she was going to admit as much to him in this moment.

"I can watch Joey while you go to the meeting. You'll be close if we need anything, and I'd really like to help you."

"I'm not sure this is a good idea, Leo. Knowing how much everyone in my family talks, I could be at my parents' for a couple of hours."

"Take as long as you need. I'll call the office and tell them I won't be in until lunchtime."

She knew Joey would have a better chance of actually taking a nap if he was at her quiet house versus in the middle of what would undoubtedly be an emotional and loud scene at her parents'. Nerves flickered through her at the idea of letting someone else watch over the baby, but she couldn't deny that Leo's offer would make the morning a lot easier.

"Are you sure?" She searched his dark gaze for any sign of reluctance, but he looked relieved that she was considering his offer.

He reached for Joey and plucked him out of her arms like it was the most natural thing in the world. "I've got this, Poppy. I promise I won't let you down."

"Thank you," Poppy said, surprised both to find herself agreeing and also that, so far, Leo had offered her the most support with Joey. Not that her mother wouldn't if she asked.

But Shelley was distracted, worrying about who might be revealed as Joey's father.

"Thanks for giving me a chance," Leo said as she picked up her purse from the kitchen table.

It felt like he knew she didn't trust his resolve to see through his sudden willingness to help. She didn't and fully expected to return to her house and never see Leo again after today—at least until they ran into each other in town.

But he was bailing her out at a precious moment, and she appreciated it.

He didn't bat an eye as she reviewed Joey's feeding and nap schedule, not that the baby was currently following any set schedule.

"Are you sure about this?" she asked one more time before heading to the meeting.

Leo flashed a smile so sincere it made her weak in the knees. *Get a hold of yourself,* she ordered.

"We'll be fine," he promised, then ran a hand over the top of Humphrey's furry head. "I've got my trusty helper, too."

Her dog pressed closer to Leo's side. She wasn't the only one susceptible to the man's charms.

"Call if you need anything. I can be back here in minutes."

"Take your time." Leo's smile widened. "Trust me, Poppy."

Sure. Trust a man who strolled back into her life like offering to raise a baby was no biggie.

Still, she appreciated the time this gave her. And if nothing else, it would make clear that Leo was not interested in getting involved with her and Joey the way he claimed. Better to find that out now before she let herself rely on him. This morning would prove something to them both.

TWO HOURS LATER, Poppy reached for her car door handle. She wanted to blame her trembling fingers on too much caffeine and not enough food in her belly, even though she knew her muddled emotions caused it. Her mom and aunt Darla put out quite the spread for breakfast, and her brothers and cousins had dug in with gusto as they talked and argued about what Joey's appearance on the doorstep and the accompanying note would mean for the family.

Poppy hadn't been able to eat a thing. Trying to balance the upset she felt over the way they discussed Joey—like he was an unwanted overnight package delivered to the wrong address—with the understanding that the rests of her relatives were as confounded by the mystery surrounding him as her, and everyone processed that shock in their own way.

"Poppy."

She turned at the sound of her cousin's voice. Although her long blond hair was pulled back into a high ponytail and she wore scuffed boots, faded jeans and a denim shirt, Vivienne looked more like a ranch-style fashion influencer than the forewoman of the entire FGR cattle operation.

She jogged a few yards from the porch to Poppy's parked car and hugged her. "How are you really? We talked about a lot of things during that meeting, but none of them were the fact that you've been the one to step forward in such a huge way to care for that baby."

Tears pricked the back of Poppy's eyes. She really needed to eat something and get a hold of herself. One night caring for the boy and she was wearing her heart on her sleeve. "I'm fine and grateful my approval as a foster parent came through in time for me to provide a safe haven for Joey."

She looked past her cousin to the Texas hill country–style mansion that still felt like home to her even after years of living in her cozy house on the property. "This isn't his fault," she said quietly. "I'm not sure people are keeping that at the forefront of their minds. He's innocent."

Vivienne squeezed her arms and nodded. "They know, but when we all get together, it's a lot of Fortune energy in one room and emotions are running high. The DNA tests will prove that no one in my immediate family or yours is involved. That will make things easier."

Poppy didn't argue with her cousin, although she wasn't sure she agreed. Even if the results proved none of the Fortune men had fathered Joey, it wouldn't change the fact that he'd been left on their doorstep for a reason. She wanted to get to the bottom of that mystery no matter who his parents turned out to be.

"I hope you're right," she said.

"We've got your back, Pop, so if you need anything, just holler."

"That means the world to me," she told her cousin. Even though she knew Vivienne meant the words, Poppy felt a strange sort of protectiveness toward Joey, like she wanted to keep him safe from judgment even if he was too young to know it was happening. "I should get back to him," she said. "Thanks for checking on me, Viv."

The other woman started to take a step away, then paused. "You know you could have brought him to the meeting. My mom would have been thrilled."

Poppy nodded. Her Aunt Darla had been the only one to seem disappointed when Poppy had walked in without a baby in her arms.

"He didn't sleep well last night." She repeated the excuse she'd given her family for why Joey wasn't with her. Her parents had glanced at each other with visible relief, and Poppy had tried not to feel a pang of disappointment.

"Did someone from the spa daycare come over to watch him?" Vivienne asked. Poppy's staff was loyal to a fault and would help out in any way she needed, so it was a logical assumption, but she shook her head.

"No, I didn't want to get anyone from the spa involved before all of us met. The gossip will spread through town quickly enough. Better to keep things quiet for now."

"So who stayed with him?"

Poppy thought about ignoring the question, but that would only make her cousin more curious.

"I ran into an old friend at the hospital yesterday," she said, doing her best to sound casual. "Leo Leonetti was there visiting his grandfather."

"I didn't realize Enzo was back in the hospital," Vivienne said as her delicate brows drew together. "I thought his cancer treatments were going well."

"I don't know the details…" And what she did know wasn't hers to share. "But he's back home now."

"Which of the Leonetti sisters is watching him. My guess is Bella because—"

"Leo offered to help with Joey," Poppy interrupted. "I took him up on it."

Vivienne's jaw dropped. "The same Leo Leonetti who avoids any type of commitment that doesn't have to do with winemaking like he's sidestepping a fire ant mound? The same Leo who broke your heart five years ago?"

So much for playing this off as casual.

"His sister has a baby, so I think he likes kids, and I'm not asking him for any sort of commitment." Poppy felt color rise on her cheeks. "He didn't exactly break my heart. We dated a few weeks, and it didn't work out." She pointed at her cousin. "You know I was the one to break it off."

Vivienne made a noncommittal sound in her throat. "Because he flat out told you he wasn't ever going to settle down, and you're all about settling down."

"I was back then," Poppy said. "A couple of failed relationships and a broken engagement have changed me. The only commitment I'm making at the moment is to Joey. Leo wants to help, so I'm going to let him. I know he'll keep quiet because he doesn't want single women around here getting the idea that he's changed."

"What if he has changed? Maybe he has." Vivienne's eyes were bright with possibility.

Possibilities weren't something Poppy could allow herself to entertain when it came to Leo.

"I got over him a long time ago. I was engaged six months after he and I broke up."

"You know what they say about the one who got away." Vivienne did an awkward little dance move back. "Now he's back."

"Don't do this, Viv," Poppy implored. "I'm not going to lie. I appreciate the help with Joey. I know you and your mom would support me, but until the DNA comes back, it feels like it's better if I keep Joey away from the family. There are so many implications to that note that was pinned to him and…"

Vivienne held up a hand. "I get it, and the baby is lucky to have you. Obviously, I'm here to help with anything, but I'm also kind of intrigued by the idea of Leo stepping in."

"It doesn't mean anything." Poppy wasn't going to share what Leo had said about his grandfather and his reasons for wanting to help care for Joey.

"You keep telling yourself that, but for the record, Leo made a huge mistake letting you go once."

"He isn't going to have to let me go now," Poppy insisted. "Because there isn't anything going on between us."

Vivienne shrugged. "Whatever you say, Poppy. Call or text if you need me. And give Leo a big hug for me. Or maybe a kiss. A really wet, sloppy kiss."

Poppy laughed and hugged her cousin one more time before climbing into her car. Vivienne could make all the jokes she wanted. No way would Poppy be fool enough to fall for Leo again.

After parking in her garage, she opened the door to the laundry room, wondering if she'd ever been so exhausted.

"How was the meeting?" Leo asked from where he sat cross-legged on the tile floor; two of the six-week-old kittens in her care snuggled on the towel draped across his lap while the other two attacked the plastic toy with the bell inside he flicked back and forth with one hand.

"Where's Joey?" she exclaimed as she tried to get over her shock at the scene before her. Leo did not strike her as a cat person.

"Sleeping." He nodded his head toward the monitor that sat on the dryer.

She grabbed it and studied the black-and-white screen with disbelief. The swaddled baby slept peacefully in his crib.

"He's been down for about twenty minutes." Leo carefully moved the towel with the sleeping kittens to the cat bed and stood. "That baby likes to be held. He barely fussed as long as he was in my arms and I was moving. I might have worn a path around your first floor," he added ruefully.

"You did it," she said in wonder, more to herself than him. "You got him to sleep."

"Don't give me too much credit. I think he eventually wore himself out."

He followed her out of the laundry room. Poppy noticed the few dishes she'd left in the sink were gone, and the broom and dustpan had been put away.

"You also cleaned up and played with the kittens?" She let out a small laugh as she turned to face Leo. "You're like a mash-up of Mrs. Doubtfire and Dr. Doolittle."

His answering grin made her stomach feel like butterflies were flitting through it. "Beginner's luck," he told her with a shrug. "Tell me about the meeting."

She led the way to the family room and sat on the overstuffed leather sofa. Leo lowered himself into the matching chair on the other side of the coffee table.

"The meeting was intense, to say the least," she admitted, glancing at the monitor she held. "It's kind of difficult to believe that one sweet baby can cause so much upheaval."

"Joey didn't cause anything," Leo reminded her, and her heart pinched at his insightful words.

"True, and of course no one in my family is upset with him. Aunt Darla wanted me to come back here and pick him up to bring him to the house. She and Vivienne are excited to meet him."

"What about your other cousins and your brothers?" Leo asked quietly as if he already knew the answer.

"Micah and Drake are as adamant as my brothers that they aren't Joey's father. All the guys, my dad and uncle Hayden in-cluded, seemed relieved that someone was watching the baby so they didn't come face-to-face with him yet. They're all on edge."

"Did you tell them that someone was me?"

"Not exactly."

Disappointment flashed in his dark gaze but was gone in an instant.

"So if none of the Fortune men are claiming him..."

She shrugged. "They all agree on DNA testing. My mom insisted it's the only way to know for sure. There are a lot of Fortunes in this state. I think she's hoping the results will con-firm that no one in my family is involved."

"Makes sense." He leaned forward, placing his elbows on his knees. "Did you get the sense that any of them was hiding something?"

"I'm not much of an investigator, but they were convincing in their denials. Of course, it wouldn't be my dad. He's way too old and he and Mom are happy. I don't think Uncle Hayden would have cheated on my aunt, and Rafe is still grieving the deaths of his wife and daughter."

"That leaves Shane and your cousins…"

"I guess," she agreed with a sigh. "It would be helpful if the police had any leads on Joey's mother. I spoke with my case-worker on the drive over. She said they checked with the hospitals in the surrounding area, and there are no recorded births at any of them in the past week that could be a fit for his situation."

"Do you think he was born at home?" He frowned. "Could the cops check sales on inflatable swimming pools? Isn't that how home births work?"

Poppy made a face. "I don't honestly know, but I can't imagine any local stores are selling pools this time of year." She placed the monitor on the coffee table. "I wish there was a way I could tell Joey's mother that he's safe and being cared for. She went through the effort to leave him at my parents' house instead of…" She shook her head. "In my heart, I believe she cares about his welfare."

"There's no doubt she knows he's being cared for since she left him with your family. Despite how confusing this situation is, the Fortunes are good people." He steepled his fingers and pointed at her. "You're the best of the bunch."

Her heart leaped and butterflies flitted across her stomach at his compliment. She silently commanded herself to get a grip. The last thing needed was to let her dormant crush on Leo to rear its silly head.

"I became a foster parent to help children who needed it. It's not a big deal."

"It's a big deal, Poppy. You're a big deal."

"Your grandfather must really be having an effect," she told him before she did something pathetic like burst into tears or ask for a hug, "because you are not the same Leo Leonetti who sat across from me at dinner trying to convince both of us that he was a selfish jerk who could only prioritize himself and his work."

Harsh words, but she couldn't help it. She needed some defense against this gentle and supportive version of Leo. Otherwise, it would be too easy to put aside her commitment to guard her heart and fall for him again.

Instead of looking offended, he smiled once more. "You might be right. I want to be the kind of man Enzo would be proud to call his grandson." One thick black brow rose. "I'm not trying to rush you but seeing me help with Joey would make him happy."

He rubbed a hand along the back of his neck, and she could see the muscles in his arm bunch underneath his tailored shirt. "I'm heading to the hospital later, and it would be great to tell Papa that I'm taking his advice to heart and focusing on something besides work."

She widened her eyes at that last part.

"Someone besides myself," he added with a chuckle, "as you so eloquently pointed out."

Poppy stifled a yawn. Despite her wariness, it would be a relief to share the responsibility of caring for an infant. It might save future coffeepots from the state of the one this morning. "Okay." She swallowed back the doubts that crowded her throat.

"But this is about *Joey*," she clarified. "And if it ever gets to be too much, you need to promise to talk to me. I can't take being ghosted like…"

Of course, Leo would've heard about Michael breaking up with her. Just like he was probably well aware that her entire track record of dating was littered with relationships that hadn't worked. She didn't want him to think she'd accept his help with Joey because she hoped it would turn into something more. There wasn't room for anything more in her life at the moment, especially nothing with a man who couldn't offer her the kind of love she wanted.

"It's about Joey," he agreed. "We're friends."

"But not the kind with benefits." Poppy felt her face turn bright red but didn't lower her gaze from Leo's. His eyes darkened even more like he was imagining the two of them engaging in a mutually beneficial—

"You should go now." She stood quickly, knocking over the monitor in her haste. "I'm going to take a quick nap while Joey is asleep." She reached for the monitor but snatched back her hand when Leo's covered it. His skin was warm and soft. Tingles of awareness danced up and down her arm.

"You go nap. I'll stay for a while longer in case the baby wakes up. I've got another hour or so before they expect me at the hospital. My sisters, mom and I are taking shifts to ensure Enzo isn't alone while he's there. If it's okay with you, I'll come back around dinnertime and bring some stuff so I can stay the night. We can take turns with the whole sleep thing."

Poppy didn't know how to respond, and Leo took her stunned silence as resistance.

"I can sleep on the couch."

"We can move the crib into my office so you can have the spare bedroom," she finally said. "There's plenty of room for it in there. You'll have to use the bathroom at the end of the hall, but I have an en suite, so we won't have to share a shower."

His mouth curved just a touch on one side. "Don't worry, Poppy. But truth be told, sharing a shower with you isn't the worst fate I can imagine."

She knew he was teasing, but her body reacted just the same. "I'm going to nap." Her voice came out sounding like a mouse on helium. She cleared her throat. "Thank you, Leo."

"Sweet dreams, Poppy."

His deep voice rumbled along her already-frayed nerve endings, and she hurried to her bedroom, wondering what in the world she'd gotten herself into.

CHAPTER FIVE

"I swear I had him on my shoulder for at least twenty minutes," Leo told his grandfather. His heart filled near to bursting as Enzo wiped tears of laughter from the corners of his eyes. "Somehow, Joey always manages to hold in his burps until he can aim his projectile spit up down the front of me."

"Babies are amazing creatures," his grandfather said with another chuckle, settling against the pillows propped behind him on the bed in his room at the family's house. "When do I get to meet little Joey? That's a nice, solid name for a lad. Short for Joseph, I assume?"

Leo shrugged. "I don't think anyone knows at this point. If you're up for a visitor, I'd love to introduce you to Poppy as well."

Enzo made a hum of approval. "I'd very much like to meet your new lady."

"Papa, we've been over this." It had been three days since he and Poppy agreed on their arrangement. As Leo had suspected, his grandfather was thrilled to hear about his involvement in caring for the abandoned baby. Joey's story had spread like wildfire through the Emerald Ridge community, although no one had come forward with any information on the little guy or his mother.

Leo couldn't be confident Enzo's rapid recovery from the setback was attributable to Leo's news. Still, the old man perked up every time he heard another story about Leo caring for the infant.

His mom and sisters also seemed shocked by his eagerness to help out and peppered him with questions about the nature of his relationship with Poppy. Leo didn't lie outright, but he didn't contradict them when they assumed there was more to it than his willingness to support an old friend.

"Poppy and I are *friends*." He shook his head and smiled at the exaggerated wink his grandfather gave him.

"Is that what the kids are calling it these days?"

"Lunch is served," his mother announced as she entered the room, holding a wooden tray with a plate of food and a glass of juice.

"Feeding me in bed like I'm an invalid," Enzo muttered, rolling his eyes. "The doctor said I'm fit as a fiddle."

"He also recommended that you take it easy for a few days." Martina never seemed to lose her patience or get flustered at how reluctant of a patient her father-in-law remained.

It reminded Leo of Poppy's unwavering patience with Joey. No matter how loudly the boy cried or how many diaper blowouts he managed, she remained gentle, nurturing and affectionate with him.

"It's warming up nicely today," Leo offered before his grandpa could argue further. "If you're feeling up to it, we could take the Polaris for a ride through the vineyards. Nothing like a bit of vitamin D to promote your healing."

"Don't you have to get back to help with the baby?" Martina asked as she placed the tray over Enzo's legs. She'd made a turkey sandwich with a caprese salad and slices of ripe apple.

"Poppy opened the spa this morning, then came home just before lunch so I could head over here," he explained. "She's going to work on promotional materials at home this afternoon while Joey naps." He held up his crossed fingers. "*Hopefully* naps."

"Where's my cookie?" Enzo asked as he dug into the sandwich.

Enzo had a legendary sweet tooth and proudly claimed that he'd enjoyed a cookie after lunch every day for the past fifty years. He'd even started baking his favorites—oatmeal raisin—after Enzo's grandmother died years earlier.

"I was thinking you might want to cut back on dessert." Martina sat at the edge of the bed.

"I have cancer. Why would I give up my cookies now?"

Leo grimaced at the matter-of-fact tone his grandfather used to describe his prognosis. They all knew it was true but hearing the future in such blunt terms made Leo's gut clench.

His mother's hands closed into fists, but she smiled. "You're right, of course. I'll bring up a cookie."

"Two," Enzo called after her. When she frowned over her shoulder, he pointed at Leo. "One for me and one for my best grandson. He's going to need all the sustenance he can get to have the energy to care for his baby."

"Not *my* baby," Leo gritted out. He suddenly felt overheated.

Martina nodded and waved a hand as she headed out of the room.

"It's difficult for her when you talk about dying," Leo told his grandfather, nipping an apple slice from the tray.

Enzo grunted. "We're all dying."

"Papa." Leo waited until his grandfather glanced up. "She worries about you. We all do."

"Okay, okay," Enzo agreed with a sigh. "I'm feeling much better now. Especially after hearing about your new lady."

Leo opened his mouth to explain to Enzo, once again, that Poppy was not *his*. But he couldn't force himself to say the words. His family understood that he was helping her as a friend—he'd been clear to make that distinction when he first told them about getting involved with Poppy and the baby. If assuming there was something more to the arrangement made his grandfather happy, who was Leo to burst that bubble?

"Poppy is amazing," he said instead, which was true. In the past few days, she'd impressed him in a myriad of ways that involved way more than simply infant care.

He'd overheard several conversations she'd had dealing with issues at the spa, and she remained calm and understanding as she offered guidance to her staff. Her brother Rafe had stopped by after dinner the previous evening.

He'd been a year younger than Leo in school, so they knew each other from playing youth sports and the close-knit Emerald Ridge social scene.

Rafe had been surprised to hear that Leo had moved into Poppy's to help with Joey. In turn, Leo hid his shock that she hadn't shared his part in caring for Joey with her family. There had been a few awkward minutes, then Poppy made a joke that eased the tension. She'd turned on the football game, and the three of them had settled in for an unexpectedly fun night of cheering on the Cowboys while Poppy and Leo took turns with Joey.

Rafe seemed vaguely interested in the baby but more curious about his sister's role as a foster parent. Poppy answered her brother's rapid-fire questions, blushing slightly when she confirmed that she was giving her romantic life a breather for now.

It wasn't fair that she had been repeatedly hurt by men and led astray by her own trusting heart. Was Leo any better than the other guys she'd dated?

Based on the mistrustful looks Rafe kept shooting him, it was evident her brother didn't think so. It was difficult to imagine the kind of loss Rafe had experienced. Leo assumed the other man's unwillingness to hold or interact with Joey had more to do with his personal history than a general dislike of babies.

Poppy didn't push her brother or make it weird. She had the innate ability to accept a person wherever they were in their life, evidenced by her willingness to allow Leo to insert himself into her orbit as if it were the most natural thing in the world. As if they were genuinely close friends, the way they pretended to be to make this arrangement seem more natural.

Even though they'd barely spoken in the past five years, Leo felt close to her. Being with Poppy and Joey made him feel part of something bigger than his work. Of course, his dedication to the winery wouldn't change, but it gave him a better understanding of why the Leonetti name and legacy were so important to his grandfather.

"Do they have any more of a clue as to the identity of the baby's mother or which Fortune is the dad?" Bella asked as she walked into the room, pulling his wandering mind back into the present moment.

"No DNA results yet," Leo told his sister.

Enzo shook his head as he finished the last bite of sandwich. "I had a friend in Italy once who had to take a paternity test. He had a reputation with the ladies but prided himself on being careful, if you know what I mean. It was the most terrifying couple days of his life until that test came back proving he wasn't a match."

"Terrifying," Bella repeated with an eye roll. "Imagine how terrified Joey's mom must have been to leave him on the Fortunes' front porch."

"You're right, of course," Enzo agreed. "I never took Garth or Hayden as the philandering type, so it must be one of those young guns."

Bella arched a delicate brow as she met Leo's gaze. "The question is which one?" she mused.

For some inexplicable reason, her pointed comment got his hackles up. He couldn't help feeling a surge of protectiveness at the thought of what this type of scandal would mean for the Fortune family and, more specifically, for Poppy.

The mystery around Joey's parents wasn't his to unravel but sharing what he knew might help quell some of the gossip around town if his sister shared the information.

"From what Poppy has told me, there's a backlog at the lab because they have so much evidence that needs to be tested with regard to the sabotage that Fortune's Gold Ranch and the other cattle operations in the area are experiencing."

Bella whistled under her breath as she stepped forward to lift the tray off the bed. "This is more drama than Emerald Ridge has seen in years."

"Why would someone want to damage the cattle ranches?" Enzo threw his hands in the air. "Those families are an integral part of this community."

"Maybe it's someone outside the community," she suggested. "It could be hired thugs from a different area of the state who want to hurt the success of the ranches around here. Particularly FGR, since they're the biggest and most profitable."

"You're watching too much true-crime TV," Leo told his sister, hoping her supposition wasn't true. "Likely they're going to find out it's high school kids carrying out pranks that have gone too far."

"Don't be naive," Bella said, her tone sharp. "Whoever is behind the sabotage could come after our vineyard next. What if someone has general beef with the town and everyone in it?"

"Beef. Cattle ranches." Enzo chuckled. "I see what you did there."

"I'm serious, Papa. Leo needs to take a potential threat seriously, too. As *CEO*—" she placed a particular emphasis on that word "—you need to look out for the vineyard's safety. Maybe hire an outside firm to watch the vines at night?"

It was a bone of contention when Leo had been named the head of the company after their father's death. Bella had always been the most interested in the vineyard. Since Leo was the eldest of his siblings, it made sense as far as a line of succession, but he knew his sister believed his getting the title—which he hadn't necessarily wanted—had more to do with his gender than birth order.

She'd become an expert on the grapes, and he'd named her head vintner for the operation when his late father's right-hand man retired. At this point, they all worked in concert, each with autonomy in their specific area of expertise—Leo as the head of the company, Bella overseeing the winemaking, Antonia in charge of finances, and the extroverted baby of the family, Gia, handling the marketing and PR. Sometimes, however, the past grievance popped up like a headstrong weed in a garden.

"I'll look into it," he promised. If Bella thought extra security measures were important, he took it seriously.

"So what about the Fortunes and their DNA?" Placated, she turned the topic back to one Leo did not want to discuss.

"Like I said, the lab is backed up. Only two results have come back so far. Shane and Rafe are not Joey's father."

Both his grandfather and sister seemed to consider that.

"Two down, four to go." Bella picked up the tray from the dresser. "I need to head over to the barrel room and check on the fermentation. If you bring Papa around for a drive, stop by." She smiled at the old man. "I have a new blend I want you to sample."

"Can't wait." Enzo beamed at his granddaughter, who'd inherited her love of tending the vines from him.

She left the room and Enzo turned his gaze to Leo. "I might take a short nap before we head out." The old man gave a wide yawn.

"If it's too much for you—"

"A nap will refresh me," Enzo interrupted. "Come back in an hour. It's been too long since I've felt the energy of the vines. It will do me good." He reached out and clasped Leo's hand. "Just like hearing stories of your new domestic adventure does. Plan a time to bring Poppy and the baby to see me, Leo. I don't want to miss a thing."

"You won't," he promised even as his heart ached knowing it was a vow he couldn't keep forever. His grandfather sank back again. His eyes drifted shut, and Leo silently walked out of the room. He owed Poppy Fortune big-time for fostering this new opportunity to connect with his grandfather.

Without overthinking it, he pulled his phone from the back pocket of his jeans and sent a quick text checking in on her day. She responded within seconds with a selfie of her smiling at the camera while holding Leo in her arms. Humphrey's fluffy head rested on her shoulder.

He *liked* the photograph and smiled as he headed out of the back of the house and toward the winery's main office. There were several ongoing initiatives he needed to check on. Typically, he had no problem working through lunch, dinner and late into the night. But now he had the urge to finish as quickly as possible and get back to Poppy and Joey. Oddly, he missed them even though he'd only been away for a few hours.

AT THE SOUND of the doorbell, Humphrey let out a barrage of excited woofs, and Poppy jumped up from the sofa where she was working on her laptop. She shushed the dog as she rushed toward the front door. Joey had been asleep for only ten minutes after another afternoon of on-and-off crying, so Poppy sent up a silent prayer the dog wouldn't wake him.

Annoyance flickered through her as she opened the door, already admonishing Leo. "You can come in. I told you that you didn't have to knock, especially—"

She paused midsentence as Courtney Wellington gave her a dubious look, the late-afternoon sky dusky purple behind her. "It's not smart for a single lady to allow unannounced guests to simply walk into your house." However, the woman seemed to have no problem striding past without being invited.

"That's not what this is." Poppy slowly closed the door behind her. "I was expecting someone else."

Courtney's eyes gleamed. "And who would that be?"

Poppy fidgeted and tried to come up with an answer that would be evasive but not an outright lie. She wasn't trying to keep the fact that Leo was staying with her a secret. Yet she didn't feel like advertising it either, especially to Courtney, who could make something sordid out of even the most innocent arrangement.

Even though Poppy's family knew about Leo, none of them seemed inclined to question her decision. They were consumed with both the rash of vandalism being committed against local ranches and the mystery surrounding the abandoned baby, so no one had time to worry about her situation. She hoped the same could be said for Courtney, although that seemed like a stretch.

"What can I do for you?" Poppy gestured toward the laptop and stack of papers on the coffee table. "I'm trying to get through some work while Joey's napping, so this isn't the best time for a visit."

"I brought you a baby gift," Courtney said with a sniff. Poppy immediately felt guilty for her rudeness. "It's a blanket with his name embroidered on it." She handed over the shopping bag. "It will help him always know who he is."

Poppy pulled out a fleece blanket with an appliquéd illustration of a horse and the name Joey Fortune embroidered below it in a bold font.

"He's going to be first of the next generation in line to inherit FGR," Courtney pointed out. "Although I suppose depending on which generation of men is responsible, he could be your new baby brother."

Poppy refolded the blanket and tried not to grit her teeth too obviously. "My father is not Joey's father," she said, unsure why she felt so certain about it but unwilling to show any doubt in front of the other woman, who tsked in response.

"I suppose that remains to be seen. I texted your mother to see if more DNA results had come back. I didn't get a response from her. She must be beside herself and the implications this scandal could have for her family's good name."

"Why do you sound happy about that?"

Courtney blinked her heavily shadowed eyes. "Isn't that a cheeky thing to say? I want to support your mother and aunt. You as well, if you need me."

"I don't," Poppy said without missing a beat. "Thank you for the gift, Courtney, but I have plenty of support so—"

At that moment, the front door opened, and Leo walked in. While Poppy was relieved to see him, she was not thrilled at the shocked gasp Courtney let out.

"*This* is who you were expecting?" Courtney rolled her lips together as if trying to hold back a comment. Poppy could imagine what the woman would say to her: What was she thinking to let a man like Leo back into her life?

She could deny it all she wanted, but he had the power to hurt her. Yes, they were becoming friends and she appreciated his help but none of that changed the fact that she'd have to work hard to keep her heart out of the mix where Leo was concerned.

"Hello, Mrs. Wellington," he said as he walked toward them.

"Oh, honey, please call me Courtney. Mrs. Wellington makes me feel ancient."

There was a predatory glint in Courtney's eyes as she gave Leo a thorough once-over. Poppy had the urge to step in front of him like a shield, although he didn't need her protection. He was an experienced man. Maybe he was into older women. At the realization that his love life was none of her business, Poppy's mouth felt coated in sawdust.

"Leo and I are old friends," she said, sounding prim even to her own ears. "He's helping me with Joey since the placement was so sudden."

Courtney didn't take her eyes off Leo. "I'm sure he could help you with any number of things…"

Leo visibly blanched. "I think I hear Joey fussing. I'll go check on him."

"I don't hear anything," Courtney cooed. "I've been meaning to pay a visit to your winery, Leo. Perhaps we could arrange a private tour."

"My sister Gia handles the tours, and I'm sure she can set something up. I really need to check on Joey." As if on cue, the video monitor crackled, and they heard the sound of a baby's cry.

Leo looked visibly relieved. "Nice to see you, Mrs. Welling— Nice to see you again, Courtney."

Poppy almost laughed at the speed with which Leo hightailed it out of the family room.

She turned back to Courtney. "I should probably get dinner started."

If the woman hadn't been Botoxed within an inch of her life, her eyebrows likely would have hit the top of her forehead. Instead, she conveyed her shock with a gaping open mouth. "Are you shacking up with Leo Leonetti?" she asked.

Poppy pressed her lips together. "Such a crude phrase, but no. As I said, Leo is a friend, and he's helping with Joey."

"And whatever other kind of late-night assistance you might need." Courtney winked, and it was a wonder her eyelashes didn't stick together.

"Bottle-feeding and diaper changes," Poppy muttered. She didn't owe their nosy neighbor an explanation but felt compelled to clarify again that nothing was happening between her and Leo. It was a good reminder for herself as well.

"Thanks again for stopping by," she said, moving to the front door. "I'll let my mom know you were asking after her."

Courtney glanced at the baby monitor. Leo was singing an old Johnny Cash song as he danced around the room with Joey in his arms. "That's unexpected." She sounded awestruck.

Poppy quickly scooped up the monitor, turned it off and then placed her hand on Courtney's lower back to give her a gentle push toward the door.

"Whatever it takes to soothe a baby," Poppy said cheerily.

Courtney allowed herself to be shown out the door but turned back and gripped Poppy's wrist. "Watch out for that one, girl. He's got a reputation that a woman like you might not want to invite into her life." She paused, then added in a low whisper, "Into her *bed*."

Poppy's face flamed, but she kept her features neutral. "Bottle-feedings and diaper changes," she repeated. "Have a good night, Courtney."

Leo appeared with Joey in his arms just as she turned from the closed door.

"Is it weird to say I feel violated?" He gave a mock shudder. "I've heard stories about Mr. Wellington's widow, but this is the first time I've had that close an interaction with her. Next time, I'm renting a shark cage."

She shook her head but smiled. "For your sake, I hope there won't be a next time. How's our best boy?"

"Pretty sure he's hungry. I'll make a bottle."

"That would be great," Poppy said, grateful for Leo's constant willingness to pitch in. She wasn't sure what she'd do without him. Obviously, she shouldn't get used to it. After all, she'd known what she was getting into as a single foster parent but hadn't expected her first placement to be an infant.

Having Leo around made everything easier, and she doubted he even realized what a huge impact he was having on her. Despite what had happened between them in the past, it was easy to believe this arrangement could develop into something more—that the three of them might make a real family.

But was she just setting herself up for more heartbreak?

"Everything okay?"

She blinked to find Leo staring at her from the edge of the open-concept kitchen.

"What? I mean, yes." She gave him a quick thumbs-up. "Just a bit tired."

"I can take overnight duty," Leo offered as he balanced Joey in one arm and measured scoops of powdered formula with his free hand.

"It's fine," she assured him. "I'm fine. I'll start dinner."

"About that…" Leo glanced over his shoulder at her, and Poppy's stomach did that annoying pitch and tingle again. "My mom made us a lasagna. I forgot to bring it in, so it's still in the back seat of my car."

"You feed babies, take overnight shifts and provide dinner." She forced out a laugh. "Better not let this get out, Leo Leonetti, or there will be no level of commitment phobia that will keep the women around here from descending on you."

She expected him to crack a joke in response, but his gaze was serious as he turned to face her fully. "But you'll protect me, Poppy. You'll keep me safe, right?"

In a way, that was its own kind of joke, but she also felt something shift deep in her heart. Leo didn't need her protection—not with Courtney or any other woman—except what if he did? What if this man, who was so guarded and yet possessed a generous heart, needed to feel safe and cared for just for being him?

Poppy couldn't offer him much in return for his help with Joey, but she could give him refuge from whatever feelings and worries weighed on him.

"I've got you, Leo," she said softly.

His eyes flared like he hadn't expected her to take his request seriously. The air between them changed in that moment. It grew heavy and charged. She could practically see sparks flickering between them.

Joey squirmed and whimpered, and the invisible tether that connected them broke apart. "I'll grab the lasagna," she offered, turning for the door.

"Thanks," Leo called but she didn't answer.

Poppy hurried down the porch steps, then stopped and looked up at the stars blanketing the February night sky. She needed to be reminded that there was a big universe beyond the cozy walls of her house. Her attraction to Leo—her emotions—were tiny in comparison. Tiny and insignificant, even if it didn't feel that way in her heart.

CHAPTER SIX

LEO WALKED INTO Coffee Connection, the popular coffee shop and bakery in downtown Emerald Ridge later that week. He paused as he noticed all three of his sisters sitting at the table in front of the window waiting for him. Gia had invited him to meet, and she guiltily dropped her gaze when he glared. He had half a mind to turn on his heel and walk back out. He loved his sisters, but this was clearly an ambush.

"Don't even think about it," Bella, the oldest of the sisters, commanded, pointing a finger at him. She'd always been the bossiest of the trio.

"We ordered you a chocolate chip scone," Gia told him. "Your favorite." Her smile was coaxing, which, despite his affection for her, didn't give him the slightest bit of encouragement.

"And a double-shot espresso," Antonia added. "We figured you could use all the caffeine you can get right now."

It must be serious if the three of them were being so accommodating—two out of the three, anyway. Things would be end-of-the-world dire if Bella ever became accommodating.

Yet even with his disrupted sleep schedule, Leo felt more energized than he had in a long time. He also knew little Joey wasn't entirely to blame for his wonky sleep patterns. He and Poppy took turns keeping the baby's monitor overnight, but

even when she was responsible for late-night feedings and diaper changes, Leo seemed to be attuned to Joey's cycles.

Not to mention the dreams he had on a regular basis star-
ring Poppy—the not-in-any-way-platonic dreams that woke
him. Seeing her selfless heart on display with Joey made her
even more alluring than she'd been when during that short time
they'd dated. Last night, he'd blinked awake just in time to hear
her opening the door to the baby's bedroom. He knew she'd be
wearing one of the sets of quirky pajama pants and T-shirts
from her collection of cartoon characters and animal prints.

Leo had never considered himself a connoisseur of women's
sleepwear. He was typically too preoccupied with taking it off
to pay much attention to lacy camisoles or complicated linge-
rie with straps and clasps. Getting worked up over shapeless
cat-print pajamas that showed nothing of Poppy's trim curves
bordered on pathetic. He cleared his throat as he slid into the
chair across from Gia.

"Are you getting sick?" Antonia asked. "Your face is flushed."

Bella, who occupied the chair beside him, reached over and
placed her cool hand on his forehead. "I don't think he's fe-
verish."

Gia was already pushing back from the table. "I'll order you
a cup of their medicinal tea blend. It'll wipe out any cold or flu
nasties you have coming on."

"I'm not sick," Leo muttered. He couldn't exactly share with
his sisters what had prompted the color to rise to his cheeks. "I
don't need to be coddled by the three of you. Save it for Papa."

"He's not a cooperative patient either." Bella reached over
and broke off the corner of his scone.

"Hey, that's the best part."

"I know." She elbowed him gently. "It's why I took it."

Leo couldn't help but smile. Bella had been nipping bites off
his plate since they were kids. "So what is the purpose behind
this unexpected tribunal?"

He lifted the cup to his lips and took a moment to savor the
nutty richness of the dark liquid, although it didn't offer the
same pleasure he usually derived from the shop's famous coffee.

Poppy's maker had a built-in timer, and since she'd replaced the broken pot, he awoke most mornings to the smell of freshly ground beans brewing in the kitchen. It was a vast improvement over the swill he typically made for himself.

No one in his family understood how Leo had never learned to make a decent cup of coffee. His father had prided himself on the espressos he turned out from the fancy Italian machine in Leo's parents' kitchen. One of Leo's most vivid memories as a kid was coming out of his room on weekends—he'd never been a late sleeper—and going to sit quietly with his father at the kitchen table.

Franco would sip his morning espresso while Leo poured orange juice into a matching cup. He knew better than to talk to his father before he finished that first cup, but he still missed those moments of companionable silence.

Growing up with three sisters, there was very little quiet, and he'd welcomed the day he finally moved out and into his own place, even if it was only a quarter mile from his childhood home. He enjoyed the solitude of coming home to a silent house. Yet when he'd stopped by this morning to pick up some items he wanted to bring to Poppy's, the stillness of the empty house struck him as sad. After a few days at Poppy's with her sunny presence, plus the noise from the dog and menagerie of cats, not to mention Joey's cries, his house seemed cold and uninviting.

He hated to admit that he didn't look forward to returning to it after Joey was placed in a permanent home, but a part of him couldn't deny it.

"We want to talk about you and Poppy Fortune," Antonia said after a moment.

Leo blinked. "What about us?" he forced himself to ask. Honestly, he didn't want to know what his siblings would have to say on the subject.

"Gia stopped by the spa yesterday," Bella explained.

Gia nodded. "I talked to Poppy."

"She works there." Leo frowned. "Did you come over to FGR to check up on me?"

His youngest sister rolled her yes. "Of course not. I wanted to book a Galentine's Day treatment for the three of us and Mom. We thought we'd treat her to—"

"What is *Galentine's* Day?"

"Get with the program, bro." Bella nabbed another bite of scone. "It's a holiday that celebrates female friendships."

"The day before Valentine's Day," Gia clarified, then leaned across the table. "You do remember that next week is Valentine's Day?"

He tried not to fidget under her scrutiny. "February 14. I know the date. But I'm not dating anyone."

"You're *living* with a woman," Antonia said.

"We're friends," he muttered.

"That's what Poppy told me, too." Gia shook her head. "It doesn't make sense."

"You aren't some kind of generous, always-do-the-right-thing type of guy," Bella told him.

Leo rubbed two fingers against his chest. "Ouch."

"No offense." Bella lifted her palms in the air. "You're great, bro, but we figured you spouted out the line about being friends to protect your privacy. Rude, by the way, when we're your family. We don't have secrets. So there must be something more to it. It's a big thing you're doing, Leo."

"Maybe I'm a better man than you three give me credit for." He crossed his arms over his chest, irritation pulsing through him even though his sisters were right.

Antonia made a tsking sound that reminded Leo of their mother. "You're not romantically involved with Poppy?"

"She's got a lot on her plate right now," he said.

"Which is a nonanswer," his middle sister pointed out.

"Poppy and I tried dating a few years ago. We weren't a match."

Bella scoffed. "Back then, you weren't the type of guy who would have offered to help her raise an abandoned child."

"We do think you're a great guy," Gia said with a smile. "And we like Poppy a lot. She said the nicest things about you."

He clamped his jaw shut so he wouldn't ask *what things*. "She wants something different than I can give her. She deserves someone who can provide that."

His sisters exchanged looks among themselves.

"Don't do that silent-female-conversation thing right in front of me," he complained.

Gia smiled. "Poppy looked smitten when she talked about you."

"I'm helping her out with Joey. She's grateful."

"She *likes* you," Antonia said. "Not just because you change diapers."

"Although a man willing to change diapers is hot," Bella said with a laugh. "Do you load and unload the dishwasher, too?"

"Um...sure...if it needs it."

"Also hot."

"Loading dishes is not hot," Leo argued. "I haven't even taken Poppy out on a date since we've reconnected."

"Maybe you should change that," Antonia suggested.

"We'll babysit," Gia offered. "Mom would be over the moon. Papa, too, to have a baby around again. Especially one that's yours."

"You're the favorite," Bella grumbled but there was a smile in her voice.

"Joey isn't mine." Leo forced himself to say the words even though the statement made his chest ache. "Poppy either."

"But she could be," Gia countered. "If you aren't a dum-dum."

"Dum-dum. Is that a technical term?" Leo shot back.

"She likes you," Antonia said again. "We think you like her, too."

"A lot," Bella added.

Leo glared at her. "You don't know that."

His opinionated eldest sister nodded, confirming the opinions of the other two like she was their queen. "We know."

He felt his face go hot again like he did have a fever. If only this *were* a fever dream and one he could wake up from quickly. "I don't do commitment," he argued. "Everyone knows that. Poppy knows that."

Gia shrugged. "You haven't until now, but things change."

"Nothing has changed," he practically shouted then counted to ten in his head when several customers at the tables nearby looked his way. Everything had changed, but he wasn't willing to admit it, not even to himself. He'd only been staying with Poppy a week, but their routine felt natural in a way he hadn't expected.

Nothing would come of it. He had too much to handle running the winery, wrangling his sisters and helping his mom take care of Enzo. A relationship was out of the question, and Joey was temporary. What would he and Poppy have without the baby to bind them together?

A chance at a future together, an annoying voice inside his heart whispered. He shook his head to loosen the grip of those fanciful thoughts. Even if he gave them a chance, he'd likely mess it up. Again. He couldn't risk it. He *wouldn't* risk the kind of pain that would cause them both.

"I asked Poppy to let me help," he told his sisters. "Not because I'm kind or generous or anywhere near the unselfish person she is. Papa and I had a heated conversation the night before his oxygen levels dropped."

Leo kept his gaze on the crumbs scattered across the empty plate. He couldn't watch his sisters' faces go from hopeful to disappointed. "He was nagging me to settle down or at least put more emphasis on having a life outside of work."

"Not terrible advice," Gia said quietly.

"There's nothing wrong with being dedicated to work," Bella countered.

"I don't want to upset him again," Leo continued, wrapping one hand around the now-cooled coffee mug. "He's been in such good spirits lately, but things went sideways when we had dinner. The next morning, he'd had the setback." He swallowed around the lump in this throat. "Then I saw Poppy in the hospital cafeteria, and she told me about Joey. She's the best person I know, exactly the kind of woman Papa would want for me. I asked her—*begged* practically—if I could help with the baby because it would make him happy."

Silence met his revelation, and he finally glanced up. "It worked. He loves hearing my stories about taking care of Joey."

Gia smiled, but it looked forced. "You're lying to him."

"You're lying to all of us," Antonia added. "Are you and Poppy even friends?"

"We are now." Leo tried not to flinch under his middle sister's scrutiny. "I really like her, and I think she likes me." He shrugged. "I'm pretty likable, you know."

"Oh, Leo." Bella's sigh was one for the ages. "The truth is you're lying to yourself most of all. It doesn't matter how this arrangement came to be."

"It doesn't?" Antonia demanded.

"What matters," Gia continued, "is what you're going to do now. You like her. She likes you. Don't mess it up."

"I'm not," he protested, hands up. "I won't."

None of the women looked convinced.

"There's nothing to mess up. We aren't together." Leo wasn't sure why he insisted on arguing for a fact that made his gut twist. Poppy might not have had the best luck with men, but that was bound to change. She was too fantastic to remain alone forever. She had so much love to give and whatever man was on the receiving end of it would be lucky indeed.

Why couldn't it be him? At least temporarily.

"It's a good thing we're here to knock some sense into you." Gia reached across the table and rapped her knuckles on his forehead. "You're living with her. You're taking care of a baby with her. You are together in all the ways that count."

"Not *all* the ways," Bella said with a laugh.

"You can change that, Leo," Antonia advised him. "Bella's right. Do more than not mess it up. Step up and make something more happen. Poppy deserves a man who makes her feel special."

"She *is* special."

"Then it shouldn't be hard," Bella said.

Right. It would be easy to take his relationship with Poppy to a new level. Hell, sometimes it felt like he wanted to kiss her more than he wanted his next breath.

"What if she says no?"

"You've got charm for days," Gia told him. "Put it to good use."

He nodded and pushed back from the table. "Charming. I can do that. Thanks for the coffee and scone." He grinned at the three of them. "And the advice."

"We give great advice," Gia confirmed.

"Because we love you," Antonia added.

Bella smirked. "Also, we don't want you to be a dum-dum."

"I think I can handle that," he promised. Could he handle it? He'd certainly try his best. How hard could it be when he already cared for Poppy? Wanted to kiss her. Nope, no kissing. Not unless they could agree to new terms involving no-strings-attached benefits. She might be willing. If he was able to convince her it would be fun for them both. It would be his great pleasure to make it fun for her.

Time to turn on the patented Leonetti charm.

"Do you have something in your eye?" Poppy asked Leo as they stood at the bend on the nature trail. "Want me to take a look?"

He went absolutely still as he stared at her. "I'm winking at you."

"Oh." She glanced down at the top of Joey's round head covered by another soft cap. The baby was fast asleep, lulled by the rhythmic motion of the two-mile hike Leo had suggested they take Saturday morning.

Poppy had been surprised at first. She assumed Leo would use the weekend as an excuse to get some space from her and Joey. Not that he ever acted like staying with her was cramping his style. But it had to be, right?

Based on how the women talked at the spa, Leo was one of Emerald Ridge's most eligible and elusive bachelors. Poppy knew this from personal experience and also understood the motivation behind why he'd offered to help with Joey. Neither changed the fact that his dedication and care felt real. He seemed as happy to be a part of her life as she was to have him there.

She figured that was a part of the deal. Leo's commitment to a goal he set for himself left no room for doubt. The growth and success of Leonetti Vineyards under his leadership proved that. Spending a quiet Saturday with Joey and her felt like extra credit. And the winking…

"*Why* are you winking?"

"Because it's charming?" He laughed, sounding embarrassed at being called out. "I was trying to flirt with you, Poppy."

"Oh." She repeated the word on an exhalation. Her mind reeled as she tried to come up with a reason *why* he'd be flirting with her. That went above and beyond the parameters of their arrangement.

"I guess my skills in the charm department are a little rusty." He seemed as befuddled as she felt.

She shifted as an abrupt breeze blew up from the nearby creek, barely a trickle of water at this time of year. She shielded Joey from the gust. "I'm sure your skills are as sharp as ever, Leo. It's me. I didn't expect to be on the receiving end of your..." She shook her head. "Of any of this."

He stepped closer and, whether on purpose or instinctual, shifted his body so that he sheltered *her* from the wind. It had been a long time since someone—a man in particular—had acted the least bit protective of Poppy. She had a type, and it was men who let her do the caregiving as if she should feel privileged to dote on them and cater to their needs.

Leo's intuitive ability to make her feel special in little ways was a much more powerful aphrodisiac than all the winking in the world.

"Why not?" he asked, genuinely curious. "I like you, Poppy. I always have."

He reached out and tucked a stray lock of hair behind her ear, his finger skimming her sensitive skin. Goose bumps erupted, and she had trouble remembering to breathe.

"I like you, too." Her voice was husky, and she should have been embarrassed, but Leo's mouth crooked into a grin.

"I'm going to kiss you now." He spoke softly as if he didn't want to startle her. "If that's okay with you?"

No, no, no. She'd told herself she was taking a break from romantic entanglements, and her heart was already half lost to Leo and his unexpected thoughtfulness. The only thing keeping her safe was knowing their arrangement included only friendship. A kiss would change everything.

"Yes," she said, ignoring all the warning bells clanging in her brain. Because more than being safe, at the moment, she wanted Leo's mouth on hers.

She knew how it felt to kiss Leo. They may have gone on

only a few dates two years ago, but they also shared several passionate kisses. Those kisses had muddled her resolve when it came time to end things after he told her he had no interest in the future she wanted.

Now he pressed his lips to hers with a tenderness she didn't expect. He cupped her cheeks with his hands and wasn't she a sucker for that gesture?

Leo's kiss felt brand-new, a reintroduction of sorts. Like he wanted to know her in a different way than he had before. But he already knew how to make her feel wanted. It simply wasn't enough. He could be holding back out of respect for her or a healthy dose of caution, but she wanted to forget about smart and throw caution to the wind.

Poppy wasn't inexperienced, but she'd never been assertive. This felt like a new version of her—one she wanted to discover with Leo. She traced her tongue across the seam of his lips, and he let out a barely audible groan as he opened for her.

A wave of lust-filled power rushed through her. She went along for the ride without thinking about the crash that might come on the other side. He moved in closer, as close as he could get with a baby between them. Poppy lost herself in the feel of Leo's warmth, his strength and the heady intoxication of knowing that he was just as affected as her.

He seemed content to savor their kisses without pushing for more, not that anything more could occur in this setting.

When Joey fidgeted and let out a tiny cry, Poppy would have jumped away like she'd been caught making out in the basement by her father. Instead, Leo lowered his hands to her shoulders and eased her back slowly.

"I like you." His eyes were dark with passion. "I like kissing you. I'd like more, but only if you want it."

Poppy wanted more…more than was prudent for either of them. The type that could put her guarded heart at risk if she wasn't careful. She opened her mouth to answer, but he placed a finger against her lips, then bent down and dropped a gentle kiss on Joey's head. He adjusted the hat the boy wore to cover his ears more fully.

"Don't answer now," Leo told her gruffly. "I want you to

think about it. I want you to be certain. I'm not going any-where, Poppy, so you'll know where to find me. For as long as you need me." The words sounded like a promise, then he pointed to the western sky. "But we should head back before those clouds get any closer."

"Right." Poppy nodded and started down the trail toward the parking lot. It was good that he'd told her not to answer. She needed time to figure out how much she could give Leo with-out losing herself in the process.

CHAPTER SEVEN

POPPY UNSTRAPPED JOEY from his infant seat, picked him up and walked toward the main barn of the FGR guest ranch later that afternoon.

Although Leo had planned to spend the entire day with her after the hike, he'd gotten called to the winery to deal with a personnel issue that couldn't wait. He promised to return before dinner, but she felt restless in the house without him.

Perhaps her inability to settle had more to do with the nerves tingling along her spine every time she thought about the kiss she and Leo had shared and his comment about wanting more.

Now that the moment had passed, she should file it away as a fantastic but one-and-done situation. Getting more involved romantically—or at least intimately—with Leo could only end in disaster.

She couldn't seem to convince her heart or body. She'd always been one for commitment and knew full well Leo wasn't interested in the same thing. But that had gotten her nowhere. It might be time to try something different.

Her feelings for him didn't necessarily change her opinion about relationships. It was much easier to concentrate on work and Joey than think about trying to find love again. So if she wasn't worried about falling in love or having her heart broken, being with Leo wouldn't be as big of a deal as she feared.

She'd been unable to stand pacing back and forth in the house. Going to her parents' didn't seem like a decent option, as seeing Joey was still difficult for her mother. There'd been a delay in getting some of the DNA results returned, and the tension within the family kept ramping up.

So Poppy headed for her second-favorite place on the ranch after her beloved spa, the FGR horse barn.

While the temperature had reached the midfifties today, Joey was bundled up in a hooded one-piece in a dusty periwinkle color. She hadn't wanted to take a chance on him catching a chill in the sometimes-drafty barn. Maybe an experienced mother wouldn't worry about that, but she preferred to err on the side of caution where the baby was concerned.

Although she was well aware her time as his foster mother could end at any point, it hadn't stopped her from falling deeply in love with him. There were so many things about the baby that were easy to adore...

The way he smiled and the tiny gurgling noises he made after a feeding was just one example. How his little legs kicked during diaper changes like he was happy to have them free. And he seemed so content when she or Leo bathed him, glad to stay in the warm water until the skin on his little fingers turned pruny. She had a feeling Joey would grow into a kid who loved summers and swimming. It hurt her heart, knowing she would likely not witness that joy.

Unless, of course, her cousin Micah turned out to be his father. That was the DNA test that had yet to come back, along with her father and uncle Hayden. She couldn't even consider that either of the older men might be Joey's father.

She forced herself to draw in a deep breath and then exhaled her worries about the identity of Joey's mother and father—for the moment, anyway. She'd come to the barn to clear her head, and that's what she intended to do.

The horses she wanted to visit were standing in a group in the pasture behind the reclaimed wood structure, so she walked to the fence line. Balancing the baby in one arm, she pulled a handful of cut carrots out of her jacket pocket. She kissed the air, and immediately Pecan, a chestnut mare and one of Poppy's personal favorites of the trail horses at the ranch, ambled over to her.

"Hey, sweetheart," she cooed, holding out her open palm. The large horse whinnied and gently took the carrots from her hand with a snuffle.

The noise startled Joey, who scrunched up his face as if he might let out a wail, but when Pecan leaned over to sniff his belly with her soft nose, he immediately calmed. One of his hands shot up as if to pet the big animal.

Tears sprang to Poppy's eyes as she witnessed the sweet interaction between the baby and the horse. There were so many moments and milestones she wanted to share with Joey. In her secret heart of hearts, she wondered what would happen if they couldn't locate his mother, and the DNA tests proved that no one in her family had fathered him. He could still be a Fortune, just like the note said. He could be *hers. Poppy's.*

"You're such a good girl," she told Pecan, her voice trembling.

She'd been warned about getting too close to any child assigned to her but wasn't sure how to help it. Could she talk to Leo about all this, or would that scare him away?

"Hey, Pop-Tart."

She glanced over her shoulder, keeping one hand on Pecan's head, to see Shane ambling toward her from the ranch's business office. It overlooked this part of the paddock so she imagined he'd seen her through his office window. Her brothers had a million nicknames for her. Pop-Tart. Popsicle. Popcorn. As a kid, it had annoyed her to no end, but now she smiled at the silly term of endearment.

"To what do I owe the pleasure of this visit? Are you looking to go for a ride? I could saddle up—"

He broke off as Poppy turned to him fully, and his gaze settled on Joey.

Other than the women in her family and Rafe when he'd briefly stopped over, no one else had met the baby.

"I needed to get out of the house. It's such a nice day... I thought I'd bring him to meet some of the horses. It's never too early for a Fortune to be introduced to life on the ranch, right?"

Shane ran a hand through his dark hair and seemed to consider her question even though she'd posed it rhetorically.

"Do you really think one of us is his father?"

"If I'm being honest, I hope none of you is Joey's father."

Shane nodded. "I get it. Brady is a bundle of energy at six, but it's fun energy. It's a lot tougher when they're babies, and I imagine the foster parent gig is a tough one and probably already getting to be a drag. If he's not part of our family then..."

"It's not that." Poppy couldn't believe her brother would suggest such a thing and swatted him on the arm. She knew how much he loved his son and maintained a cordial relationship with his ex-wife for Brady's benefit. "I hope none of you is the father because I can't imagine somebody in our family treating a woman so poorly that she would resort to leaving her baby on someone's front porch step."

"Of course." Shane cringed. "I spoke without thinking." Pecan snorted as if she couldn't believe the comment either. She shook her head then moseyed back toward the other horses since snack time was over.

"Maybe you should have a big glass of water to wash down the foot lodged firmly in your mouth." Poppy continued to glare at her brother. "I love Joey already. I would love for him to be part of this family—for him to be part of *my* family. I just..."

Shane's jaw went slack, and she realized she'd just given voice to her most secret wish, the one she couldn't share with anyone. So much for keeping her emotions to herself since she'd blurted them right out. "I know being a foster parent is a temporary arrangement." She licked her dry lips.

"Not always, Pop Rocks. If they can't track down the mom or figure out who the father is through DNA testing, this baby is going to need a permanent home." He offered a tentative smile. "You would be an excellent mother."

"I'm on my own," she whispered because along with her deepest desire came her deepest fear. "They might think I'm unfit to adopt a baby because I don't have a partner."

Shane gripped the fence post as he looked out over the pasture. Other than Brady, he spent more time with the herd of ranch horses than people most weeks, and he seemed to like it that way.

To her surprise, he reached forward and lifted Joey from her arms. "You aren't alone. Not that you couldn't handle raising a child if you were, but no matter what those DNA test results show, if you want this baby to be a Fortune, we've got your back. Plus, Brady would be over the moon."

She leaned in and hugged her brother. He was tall like Rafe, both of them over six feet, and she took comfort in his strength and the words that reminded her how lucky she was to be a part of this family.

"He's a cute kid." Shane ruffled her hair as she pulled back from the hug. "Although I wouldn't say he looks like any of us."

"He's not even a month old." Poppy smoothed a finger over Joey's soft cheek. The baby was wide-eyed, like he wanted to check out everything around him. "Leo says he looks like a grumpy old man, especially when his face scrunches up to make a poo."

Shane barked out a laugh. "I never thought I'd hear the day when Leo Leonetti was making jokes about baby poo."

"He's been a huge help," Poppy said, that annoying protectiveness where Leo was concerned rising to the surface again.

Her brother seemed to consider that as he lifted his head to take in the open fields again. "I like the guy. It's just a surprise that he's stepped in to be there for you and the baby in this way."

"I don't know what I'd do without him."

Shane's gaze met hers. "Because of Joey or because you're falling for him?"

It was a good thing Poppy wasn't a gambler since she seemed to have no poker face. Still, she offered a bland smile. "We're friends." The words threatened to stick in her throat, but she forced them out. "When Joey no longer needs me, Leo and I will return to our regularly scheduled lives."

Her brother didn't look like he believed her. One of the ranch hands stepped out of the barn and called Shane's name. "I've got to get back to work." He deposited Joey back into her arms. "You're doing a good thing, Pop. Just remember you aren't doing it alone."

Poppy nodded, tears stinging the backs of her eyes. It felt like her heart had opened in a different way since Joey entered her life. All of her resolve to guard it could be struck down with a kind word or one of the baby's sweet smiles.

Not ready to return home, she walked into the barn, pointing out the equipment and tack to the baby like he could understand her. Her mind wandered to Leo and the heated kiss they'd shared. Did she truly want more? Could she handle it?

Yes, her body whispered. *A thousand times yes.*

She knew better than to let desire lead. Or love for that matter. A broken engagement had at least taught her that.

But she also wasn't naive and believed what she'd told her brother. This arrangement with Leo was temporary, and she simply needed to keep her feelings that way, too.

IT WAS NEARLY TEN, the night sky dotted with sparkling stars, before Leo let himself into Poppy's house. The personnel issue had taken far too long to handle, and then his grandfather insisted he stay for dinner and a few rounds of cards with him and Leo's mother.

He understood that the old man, claiming to feel totally back to normal, was chafing under the doctor's orders to continue taking it easy for a few weeks. Thin lines of tension bracketed Martina's mouth as she worked to keep her father-in-law compliant with his schedule of rest-and-modified-activity.

Leo had texted Poppy to explain, and of course, she hadn't pushed back. She never seemed to demand more of him than he was willing to freely give.

But it rankled him that their romantic interlude had been cut short, and their kiss now felt like a whole world away instead of something that had occurred a few hours ago. Did his leaving give her time to reconsider? Leo wouldn't blame her, but he sure as hell hoped nothing had changed.

He let himself into the darkened house, disappointment flaring that Poppy hadn't waited up. As if she owed him anything. Maybe he should have stayed at his own house for the night so he didn't bother her.

That would have given him the distance to try to loosen

the bond he felt with her—the need that pounded through him whenever they were together. If he was being honest, it wasn't just when they were together.

This house had cast a spell on him. He felt pulled back any time he was away and the welcoming interior had quickly become a haven from the pressure of the outside world. Or maybe it wasn't the house at all but the woman who occupied it.

For a man who prided himself on his ability to have relationships with women without committing to anything more than a good time, all of his resolve dissipated when he was here with Poppy and Joey.

The closeness and something of their enmeshed lives filled his heart in a way he hadn't known he needed or could experience. And he could no more stay away than a magnet could resist the pull of its mate. He'd return as long as she let him, and he would force himself to be satisfied with whatever she was willing to give, whether or not it differed from what he wanted.

Quietly walking down the hall toward the spare bedroom, he felt his pulse leap as he noticed the light spilling out from the partially closed door of Poppy's room.

He knocked softly, and she beckoned him in, much to his relief. He'd never been in her bedroom before and she kept the door closed most of the time. Her citrusy scent filled the house, but it was stronger here. He wanted to rush to her bed and bury his nose in the pillow beside her. Bury himself in Poppy as the desire he'd falsely believed he could control pounded through him in another wave.

"A good night?" she asked, and something in her tone made his gaze sharpen on her. Her pajama shirt buttoned down the front with little panda faces covering it. Pandas were *not* sexy, he reminded himself, but his body was not getting the message. She sat propped up on overstuffed pillows, a book in her lap, but the smile she gave him didn't reach her eyes.

"I'm sorry I'm home so late," he said automatically, out of character for him. Leo made a habit of not apologizing, but he didn't like to think that the evening he'd spent at his mother's house was upsetting to Poppy.

"You don't owe me anything." There was an edge of disappointment in her voice. "I know you have your own life."

"My grandfather was in a restless mood, and I can tell it's taking a toll on my mom." He took a tentative step forward, almost expecting her to send him away.

She looked like a sleepy golden queen on a king-size throne. He wondered how many times a man had shared that bed with her, then mentally shook his head. None of his business, but he couldn't seem to tamp down the part of him that wanted it to be.

"I'm sure she appreciated you staying to take some of the weight off her shoulders. I know I do." She nodded toward the baby monitor on the dresser. "Leave yours off tonight," she told him. "I'll listen for the baby."

"It's my turn."

"Everybody gets a night off sometimes."

Why did she have to be so damn easygoing? Effortless to appreciate, like the first bite of a perfectly baked birthday cake.

"How was the night here?" He continued approaching the bed until he could sit down on the edge of it. She shifted her legs to make room for him. Always so accommodating.

"He took a full bottle, had a blowout diaper and several man-size burps."

Her smile widened as he chuckled. "I'm taking that as a sign it's going to be a restful night for all of us."

She nodded, then glanced down at the lavender duvet cover. Placing a hand on her covered leg, he gently traced the outline of her delicate ankle bone. "We started something earlier…"

"We did." She sounded breathless, and his body grew heavy, but he continued the light touch through the soft fabric without meeting her gaze.

"Then I got called away, which might be for the best." He forced a smile. "I'm sure it gave you time to change your mind about anything more."

"It did," she agreed, and it felt like his heart stopped. He glanced up at her, and the heat in her sea-green eyes stole his breath. "But I didn't change my mind."

"Poppy," he rasped. "Do you mean that?"

She nodded and sat forward, pressing a tentative kiss to his mouth. "More than you know."

It felt like his birthday and Christmas and the Fourth of July all rolled into one. Leo didn't understand his reaction. They were agreeing to sex, nothing more, but it was difficult to pull his thoughts together when his need for this woman overwhelmed everything else.

He placed his hands on either side of her face and angled her head to deepen the kiss, but she broke away.

"Is that a move?" she demanded, her voice trembling slightly.

"Excuse me?" He tried to make sense of her question.

"You cupping my cheeks like that. Do you do that with all the women you kiss?"

It was the strangest question he'd ever been asked, but he didn't say that. "No," he told her, which wasn't a lie. As experienced as he was with women, Leo couldn't remember ever wanting to simply hold and touch anyone other than Poppy. Hell, he'd be satisfied to spend all night kissing her.

"What happens between us is only about us, Poppy. You do something to me I can't explain, but it's undeniable. You are so special."

"*We* are special," she countered, and he wanted to believe her.

Leo didn't argue, although he was still convinced Poppy held the magic. He kissed her again, and when he couldn't seem to get close enough, he shifted until he was kneeling over her on the bed. She lay back against the pillow and wrapped her arms around his shoulders, her fingers tickling the hair at the nape of his neck.

Then she tugged on the hem of his sweater, and he happily yanked it over his head, feeling satisfaction rush through him at the way her eyes dilated as she splayed her open palms across his bare chest. He still wanted more. He wanted to feel her skin. She must have read his mind because she reached for her own shirt, leaning up to pull it over her head.

Heaven help him, she wasn't wearing a bra. It wasn't as if he'd never seen breasts before but viewing Poppy's body after spending an embarrassing amount of hours imagining it felt like a revelation.

He leaned in and licked the tip of one pink peak, gratified at her answering moan. Then forced himself to focus on the moment and not on the fact that it felt like he was floating on a cloud of desire he'd never before experienced.

It was a joy to take his time exploring her delectable body despite the need of his own. Her skin was soft and smelled like summer, fresh and vibrant but mixed with a sinfully salty musk he knew came from her center.

He was both terrified he would lose control and determined to make this night the best she'd ever had.

She responded to every touch, every lick and tug, like they were exactly how she wanted to be ravished.

Her hands kneaded his back as she drew him closer, and he reached between them under the covers, expecting to find the hem of her pajama pants, and thrilled when the lacy corner of her panties was the only material to greet him. He groaned her name as he dipped two fingers inside her, finding her as ready for him as he felt.

Still, he took his time, mimicking with his tongue the movements of his fingers until Poppy gasped and broke apart underneath him. It was the most satisfying moment of Leo's life.

After one long, lingering kiss, he climbed off the bed. Shock registered in Poppy's eyes, but he held up a hand.

"I'm not going anywhere, sweetheart," he told her. "Unless you're finished with me?"

Her eyes tracked to the obvious erection straining the front of his jeans. "Nowhere near finished," she reassured him.

He got undressed and took a condom from his wallet and stretched it over his length. He joined Poppy on the bed again, rolling the two of them so that she was on top.

"Are you sure?" she whispered.

"Absolutely," he answered without hesitation. "This is the best view I could imagine." He just about died of happiness when she lowered herself onto him, taking every inch like she might never let go.

Her hips began to move, and he gripped her, a groan escaping his mouth. She was perfect, and he loved witnessing this new facet of her personality. Wild, free and not self-conscious about setting a pace that would ensure her pleasure was just as much of a priority as his.

Release found her again, and as she slumped forward on top of him, he flipped her so that her back was against the mattress. Then he plunged deep within her. She let out a muffled cry of satisfaction and met him thrust for thrust until he followed her over the edge.

Normally, this was where things got awkward for Leo. He didn't do the afterglow part so well. But just like everything else, being with Poppy made it different. Better.

Perfect.

He forced himself to disentangle himself from her long enough to clean up and dispose of the condom before returning to the bed. She was just leaning over the side to reach for her pajama shirt.

"You won't need that." He lifted the covers on the other side and scooted toward her. "I'll keep you warm tonight."

For all the nights she would have him, he realized with a start. Even that awareness didn't scare him. Nothing could burst the bubble of contentment he was reveling in at the moment. Poppy snuggled closer, and he drew her tight into his embrace, drifting off with a smile on his face.

CHAPTER EIGHT

LEO WOKE THE following day to the scent of coffee brewing and a cold, empty place in the bed beside him. Joey had only cried once during the night, and when Poppy started to get up, Leo had dropped a kiss on her forehead and told her to stay put.

He'd fed the sleepy baby a bottle, burped him and changed a wet diaper, re-swaddled the little guy, then put him down again. When Joey sighed and dropped back to sleep, Leo had the sensation of doing something remarkable with his life.

Although this arrangement had started out as a way to appease his grandfather's doubt about his character, Leo truly enjoyed taking care of Joey. And he felt like a good partner to Poppy, something that would have his previous girlfriends cackling in disbelief.

Wait. Was Poppy his *girlfriend*? Did he want her to be?

He hadn't put a label on a relationship since high school, and back then, it hadn't meant anything to him.

But what happened between them last night seemed significant. As if it meant more than he usually allowed sex to represent. It felt as though they'd made love.

No, no, no. Leo was not a naive teenager. He knew one didn't equal the other. That was why he'd implemented a rule as soon as he'd moved to his house: he never invited a woman to spend the night and didn't allow himself to sleep in someone else's bed.

Rules kept him safe. Especially his no relationship rule—the one that had wrecked his relationship with Poppy the first time around before they'd even gotten to the good stuff. But he was different now, or at least this arrangement felt different. Because he couldn't truly change, could he?

He needed to stop overthinking things. Otherwise, he'd do something stupid like bolt out the door and ruin everything. They'd made no promises to each other, and that's how it would stay. Without promises, he wouldn't risk hurting her. Or being hurt in return.

He'd put on his boxers at some point in the night after making lo—nope, *having sex* with Poppy for the second time. And while he should be sated, need rose in him again. Padding down the hall to his bedroom, he focused on the image of his third-grade math teacher, a terrifying woman with bony cheeks, a hooked nose and the scent of sauerkraut constantly wafting from her pores like she'd bathed in the stuff.

Okay, that helped get him under control. He pulled on sweatpants and a T-shirt and made his way to the kitchen. Joey sat in his bouncy chair on the counter, staring at the toy bar above him. Humphrey got up from his bed in front of the window and greeted Leo with an enthusiastic head butt.

Poppy came around the corner from the laundry room, buttoning up a pair of jeans as she walked, then stopped at the sight of Leo.

"Why do you look guilty?" he blurted.

"I don't."

She definitely did.

She grabbed a ponytail holder from the catchall basket on the counter and tied back her hair. "What would I have to be guilty about? Do *you* feel guilty?"

"I feel fantastic," he said honestly. "Or at least I did. Where are you going?"

"I got a text a few minutes ago. My mom called another emergency family meeting."

He moved toward her for a good-morning kiss but seeing her tense up, changed course and headed for the coffee maker. What the hell was going on?

Never in a million years would he have guessed Poppy to be the one to put the postcoital distance between them. That was his role.

"She didn't give you any indication why?"

Poppy shook her head and then placed a hand on her stomach. "The message was vague and went out to my brothers and me, but there was something in the tone of it. I have a bad feeling."

Leo poured himself a cup and reached into the refrigerator for the creamer. "Do you think the rest of the DNA results came in?"

She looked sick at the thought, and he felt the same. A positive match would mean they'd know more—not only the identity of Joey's father but who his mother might be based on his dad's dating history. It also meant that this little interlude of playing house with no repercussions for the future might end just when it was getting really good.

"It's going to be okay, Poppy. No matter what happens."

She dashed a hand across her cheek as she stared at Joey. "I wish I could believe that."

Leo placed his mug on the counter and moved toward her. He barely recognized this version of himself—the one who wanted to comfort someone to ease their worry and pain. He didn't like complicated anything but especially emotions.

Ignoring all of his normal instincts, he wrapped his arms around her. She stood ramrod straight for a few seconds, then melted against him. His heart pinched with emotion, and he wanted to stay like this for as long as she'd have him.

"You must regret getting involved in this." She sniffed. "With me."

"Not for a second." He pulled back and kissed the center of her forehead, much as he had before falling asleep last night, tangled in each other's arms. "Go to your meeting. Joey and I will be here when you get back."

She shook her head. "You need to get to the vineyard. I'm sure yesterday's issues didn't disappear like a miracle."

"They can wait." He kissed her again. "Go ahead, Poppy. Trust me. I've got you."

"Thank you again," she said softly, her cheeks coloring as she added, "For last night, too."

His heart swelled, and he forced his features to remain neutral even though he wanted to jump for joy. "Anytime," he said with a wink. "I aim to please."

She frowned slightly but didn't comment on how much he sounded like a wanker.

After she left, Leo downed his coffee then lifted Joey into his arms. "You might not realize this," he told the boy, "but I used to be chill when it came to women. Any tips on how to reclaim it?"

The baby shoved his fist into his mouth.

"A man of few words." Leo nodded and poured himself another cup. "Good advice, kid. I'll remember it."

To Poppy's surprise, she was the last member of her family to enter the kitchen. Her mom and dad stood on opposite ends of the large island like they were facing off in some sort of high-noon shoot-out. The winter sun poured in through the bank of bay windows behind the table, but a heavy shadow seemed to hang over the room.

She'd never seen her parents at odds this way, and her stomach tightened painfully.

"You don't even recognize the number," Garth shouted.

"Don't raise your voice to me," Shelley answered in a harsh whisper.

Rafe and Shane stood just inside the doorway to the kitchen, both dressed for work in jeans, denim shirts and well-worn boots, watching their parents with twin looks of consternation.

"What's going on?" Poppy asked.

Her mother turned and Poppy had to stifle a gasp. Shelley's eyes were bloodshot and red-rimmed, her usual rosy complexion devoid of color. She looked absolutely miserable.

"I received a text early this morning," Shelley said, her voice hollow.

"From an anonymous number," Garth grumbled.

"It said your dad is Joey's father."

Rafe let out a string of curses while Shane shook his head. "How is that possible?" he asked no one in particular.

"That's what I want your father to explain." Shelley jabbed a finger in Garth's direction.

"It's *not* possible," their father said simply, but Poppy could see the lines of tension bracketing his mouth.

"What about the DNA test results?" Rafe stepped forward, hands fisting at his sides. "What is the holdup? Have you—"

Garth ran a shaking hand through his thick salt-and-pepper hair. "I called the supervisor of the testing lab this morning. I woke him up only to have him tell me they discovered late yesterday that the samples from me, your uncle and Micah haven't been reported because they're missing."

"They *lost* them?" Poppy moved toward her mother's side, but Shelley flinched away as if she couldn't stand to be touched.

"He gave me some line about the vandalism and theft and how crowded the lab is. His staff is scouring the place but..." Her father frowned and then met Poppy's gaze across the island. "I'm not that boy's father."

Shane strode toward their dad and placed a firm hand on his shoulder. "Keep it together. The three of you can give new DNA samples. We know you aren't—"

"We don't know anything." The words left Shelley's mouth in a staccato rhythm like bullets raining down on their close-knit family.

Growing up, Poppy had heard stories about other branches of the illustrious Fortune family and the scandals and drama that had plagued certain members. As a girl, she'd lamented the boring normalcy of her own family. Even though her dad and uncle didn't get along, there had never been anything more than petty squabbles or veiled barbs thrown back and forth.

Now she realized a person should never wish for excitement in the form of scandal. It might be entertaining to an outsider but living it and dealing with the raw emotion made her chest feel like it was about to rip open. Her mother's anger, sadness and devastation were almost tangible, a bubble of upset surrounding Shelley that Poppy didn't know how to pierce.

Like her brothers, she never imagined her father would be

associated with the baby in her care, even if some anonymous tipster offered up the unproven revelation. It must be some sort of mistake or misunderstanding. She had to believe her parents would get through this. They were strong. They loved each other.

"I'm moving out." Shelley audibly swallowed like the words left a sickening taste in her mouth.

"No." Garth shook his head and started around the island, but Shane held him fast. "You can't leave, Shel."

"Mom, you don't mean that!" Poppy lifted a hand toward her mother and then pulled it back because when Shelley turned to Poppy, she could see the resolve in her mother's gaze. The eyes that were usually filled with kindness and understanding had taken on a hard, bright glint.

"You can stay with me for a couple of days," Rafe offered, and they all ignored the hiss of displeasure that elicited from their father.

"I'm going to the Emerald Ridge Hotel in town." Shelley made a sharp movement with her hand when her husband would have protested. "I need space, Garth. I need time and I need answers. Until I get them, I'm staying at Emerald Ridge."

Poppy waited for her father to rage or argue. He wasn't a violent man, but he also didn't exactly have an inside voice at the best of times. His jaw remained clenched as he stared, devastated, at his wife of over three decades. He gripped his forehead between his thumb and index finger.

Poppy could imagine the pounding headache he must be trying to massage away. If it rivaled hers, no painkiller in the world would alleviate it.

Without a word, he turned on his heel and stomped out of the kitchen toward the back of the house.

Shane and Rafe exchanged a look then turned toward their mother. "Go on," Shelley told them. "I'm fine."

Neither brother looked like he believed her, but they followed Garth out of the room.

Shelley immediately sank onto one of the plush leather barstools. "I'm *not* fine," she whispered and Poppy enveloped her mom in a tight hug.

"It's not Dad," Poppy insisted. "He wouldn't do that to you. He loves you so much, Mom."

Shelley's shoulders trembled as she cried softly against Poppy's chest. Could a heart break in sympathy for someone else's pain? If so, hers was close to cracking in two. She didn't allow herself to cry, however, knowing she needed to be strong for her mom at that moment.

She didn't say anything else but held Shelley tight. The kitchen looked the same as it always did: bright, warm and welcoming, except for the cloud of sorrow that hung in the air. How was it possible that the baby who brought so much joy into Poppy's life was also the catalyst for this overwhelming pain that threatened to rip her family apart? Not that anyone blamed sweet Joey. He was innocent but still a reminder of a potential betrayal that would change all of them going forward.

It took several minutes before her mother's tears ebbed. Shelley pulled back and offered her a watery smile. "Where did you learn to hug like that?"

"My mom taught me." Poppy grabbed a wad of tissues from the box on the counter. "She's the best."

Shelley drew in a shaky breath and blew her nose. "Where's the baby?" she asked as if just now realizing Poppy didn't have him with her.

"Leo offered to stay home with him."

Her mother's lips thinned. "I'm still not sure how I feel about him staying with you."

"He's a huge help."

"He's also not a man who wants commitment."

"I know that," Poppy insisted. Despite the pleasure they'd shared last night, she also knew a roll in the sheets—even an amazing one—wouldn't change who a man was on the inside.

"Be careful," her mom said. "Look at me. I'm proof you're never too old for a broken heart."

"Let me see the text." Poppy held out her hand. Shelley unlocked the home screen then gave the phone to her.

"It's a Dallas area code," Poppy murmured, unnerved by the cryptic message.

"Your father tried to trace the number. Apparently, whoever sent it used a burner phone."

Poppy blinked. She would never have expected to hear her mother use the term *burner phone* except when talking about the details of a crime podcast she was bingeing.

"Mom, you don't have to go to the hotel. This house is plenty big enough if you need space."

"I don't want to be in the same house as your father right now."

"Then stay with me," Poppy suggested. "Leo would probably be thrilled at a break from baby duty." She didn't necessarily believe that and hoped it wasn't true. He'd never given her a reason to think he wanted out of their arrangement. If last night and this morning were any indication, he was all in—at least temporarily. But if her mom needed a place to stay…

Shelley rose from the chair and plucked a tall glass out of the cabinet, filling it with water then taking a long drink. "Your father and I wanted to shield you kids from this, but I've been contemplating a temporary separation for a while now."

Poppy felt her mouth drop open. If her mother had said she was running off to join the circus, it couldn't have been more of a surprise.

"Why?" she demanded, trying not to sound like a petulant kid. "You and Dad are happy. You love each other."

She sank into the chair her mother had just vacated as Shelley traced a finger around the rim of her glass, refusing to look up. "We do love each other, but it's more complicated. At least it is after all these years."

Poppy gripped the edge of the granite counter. "Did he cheat on you? Do you have proof?"

Her mother's delicate brows furrowed as a quiver ran through her. Poppy hated everything about this conversation. Hated this morning that tipped the stability of her family like a toddler knocking over a stack of blocks.

"I have no proof he's cheating on me, and he denies it just like he denies the truth of the anonymous text." Shelley placed the now empty glass into the sink. "I hope time proves he's telling the truth, but your dad and I have hit a rough patch. Sometimes it happens, sweetheart. We've been together for a long time. It's not exactly fair that men are seen as distinguished and more attractive as they age and women..." She lifted her shoulders in a resigned shrug. "We just get old."

"Mom, no." Poppy climbed off the stool and went to hug her mother again. "You are beautiful. More beautiful than you were when you were young."

Her mother laughed and kissed Poppy's cheek. "My darling girl, I'm not complaining. I wouldn't trade my age for youth if someone offered to pay me, but there's no denying the truth." She released a quavering breath. "Please don't worry about me. Things will work out as they are meant to. Your father and I love you and your brothers. Even though it would be an adjustment, if the new test results show that Joey is a part of this family, I'll welcome him into it."

Poppy blinked away the tears that flooded her eyes. "I'm so sorry. I never thought having Joey here would be so difficult for you." She forced herself to continue, "If you need me to call the caseworker and find him a diff—"

"Of course the baby will stay with you. He's innocent, and more than anything, he deserves to be taken care of. No one can care for him better than my daughter. I know that."

There was a crash from the back of the house and Shelley winced. "I'm going to pack. I know this is hard on you in particular. The hopeless romantic in the family." She blew out a breath. "But it's what I need to do. I hope you'll support me."

"I'll always support you, Mom, just like you support me. Do you want help packing?"

"I can manage it. Go be with Joey. Give him an extra tight hug. Tell that Leonetti boy we appreciate his help. You can leave out the part where I have my doubts about him. It's more important to know that you aren't alone."

"Neither are you, Mom." After one final hug, Shelley went upstairs, and Poppy returned to her house.

She parked in the garage but walked outside to look up at the pale blue sky and the clouds floating on the breeze like they didn't have a care in the world.

Lucky clouds.

She turned at the sound of a door shutting. Leo stepped out of the garage. "I heard you come back and wanted to make sure everything was okay since you didn't come in right away." His face darkened as he studied hers. "Everything is not okay." The words were a statement rather than a question.

"It's terrible." A sob escaped her mouth. Her knees gave way and she started to crumple to the ground, but Leo caught her before she did.

"I think my parents are splitting up," she managed through her tears. It was stupid to react this way. She wasn't a kid anymore, and this separation might be temporary. But knowing her mom and dad didn't have the perfect marriage she'd believed rocked Poppy to her core.

If her parents couldn't make it work, what chance did anyone else have?

"They'll be all right," Leo said as he carried her into the house. "You'll be all right, Poppy."

She buried her head in his shoulder and inhaled the spicy, sexy scent of him. "I can walk," she protested but didn't make any move to wiggle out of his arms.

"I know, but this is an excuse to get my hands on you again."

His teasing helped to calm the chaotic emotions still coursing through her. He didn't stop until he was at the sofa. Even when he sat, he continued to cradle her in his arms. She didn't try to move away but took the comfort he offered.

"Tell me as much or as little as you want," he said. "If you want to be left alone, I understand that, too, and—"

"I don't," she quickly replied. The thought of being alone at the moment felt unbearable. She explained the text, her father's reaction and her mother's insistence on moving to town. Leo seemed shocked by this new development.

"It will work out," he assured her. Even though he had no way of knowing that, his words soothed her.

"The worst part is the lab losing the DNA samples." She squeezed shut her eyes. "My father can't prove his innocence without them."

Leo considered that for a few weighted seconds before he answered. "Are you still convinced he's innocent?"

She started to nod, offended that he'd make the suggestion then stopped. At this point, she couldn't be certain of anything.

"It's what I want to believe that counts."

He pulled her close again, but she could hear his phone buzzing from the counter.

"You need to go," she whispered.

He nodded. "I wish I could spend the whole day just holding you."

She sighed and climbed off his lap. "It's okay. I appreciate everything you've done already."

He didn't release her hand. "Come with me," he said.

"To the vineyard?"

She'd heard amazing things about the property Leo and his family owned on the other side of town and had recommended it to clients looking for a local winery experience, but he'd hadn't taken her there when they'd dated years earlier. And then after it ended she didn't want to run into him and take the chance of it being awkward. And speaking of awkward...

"Won't it be weird with your mom and grandfather?"

Leo chuckled and kissed her knuckles. "My grandfather has been begging me to bring you to see him. Mom will love it. She adores babies. My nieces are the light of her life."

Poppy swallowed as emotion caught in her throat. "My mom loves babies, too. She's such a good grandmother to Brady and also Rafe's daughter before the accident. It's hard for her with Joey and everything we don't know about him. The possibility that..." She broke off.

"It's understandable." He stood and wrapped an arm around her shoulder. "This is a difficult situation for your family and the missing test results only make it more so. Can they spare you at the spa today?"

"I think so. It's busy this week but I can make the time."

Leo gave her a grin so boyishly pleased she couldn't help but return it. "Prepare to be dazzled by your own private vineyard tour, Poppy."

"What about Joey?"

"He'll come with us. There are photos of me in my father's arms in the field the day I came home from the hospital."

Poppy nodded, even though it wasn't the same. As much as she wanted to pretend they were family, Leo wasn't Joey's father. She might not be the baby's foster mother for much longer. That made her even more committed to relishing the time she did have with the two of them.

"I'll head over now and finish up the work I can't put off. Joey's been down for about a half hour so he shouldn't sleep much longer. Text when you're on your way and we'll meet at the winery office."

He leaned in to give her another long, lingering kiss before grabbing his wallet and phone from the counter.

Poppy listened to the sound of his car driving away as she snuggled Humphrey, who'd ambled over to keep her company in Leo's absence.

It might not be the most prudent decision, but she intended to enjoy everything Leo was willing to give her before their time together ended. She might not know what her future held, but she'd savor all the happiness she could manage along the journey.

CHAPTER NINE

"ARE YOU NERVOUS about your girlfriend coming for a visit?"

Leo tried to ignore his youngest sister, much as he would a gnat flying near his face.

But Gia wouldn't be snubbed so easily. She danced around him in the winery's tasting room, chanting "Leo's got a girlfriend" like she was an annoying little kid.

Deep down he hoped Poppy would love the tasting room the way he did. Leo had always found the interior to be warm and welcoming to visitors, with rich wood trim and tall windows that allowed the tasting tables and counter to be bathed in light for hours each day. The shelves and glass cases showcased the winery's chosen varietals, while cushioned chairs and sofas invited guests to enjoy their visit. He wanted Poppy to appreciate every aspect.

"Poppy is a *friend*," he said when he couldn't take the chorus any longer. He was standing near the front window so he'd see when she pulled up. His mom and grandpa were at the main house as far as he knew but he had no intention of taking the chance that they might walk over to greet her on their own.

"You've never brought a *friend* who's a girl to the vineyard," Gia pointed out as if that meant something.

"Have you always been this irritating?"

"Yes," she answered without hesitation. "It's my role as the baby of the family."

"At least I only have you to deal with today." He blew out a breath, still surprised by the nerves flitting through his gut. Bella and Antonia had driven down to Dallas with Bella's kids for the day.

"Trust me, I have orders to report back on everything." She patted him on the arm. "We're taking credit for this, you know."

"For what?"

She grinned. "For you and Poppy. You clearly took our advice and figured out how to put all of that Leo Leonetti charisma to good use for once. Rizzing up Poppy Fortune."

"That's not what's happening," he said through gritted teeth. It would be much easier to understand if it was just a matter of charm or charisma. He knew how to wield both, but things with Poppy felt different in a way that confounded him.

Mostly because his actions with her came from his heart, which seemed intent on leading him to places his brain warned were dangerous.

"She's dealing with a lot right now, and I'm trying to support her." He shrugged at the skeptical look his sister leveled at him. "I'm not thinking about *rizzing up* anyone."

Gia surprised him by wrapping her arms around his waist. "I'm so proud of you," she said against his chest. "I can't wait to get to know Poppy. She always seems so nice, but I've only talked to her briefly at the FGR spa. She must be special for you to change so much."

"I haven't changed that much," he grumbled. "It's not like I was some womanizing ogre before this."

Gia released him and chuckled. "No one would describe you as an ogre."

He noticed she failed to address his womanizing comment and didn't like what that said about him or the prevailing opinion he knew most people, including his family, had about his character.

What would they think when his time with Poppy came to an end? What would *he* feel?

She pulled into the gravel parking lot, and he pushed aside those disturbing thoughts. Leo preferred to concentrate on *not* feeling. His attention was best left dedicated to the family business.

"Don't make this weird," he commanded his sister. "You stay here and…"

Gia was already rushing from the tasting room toward the winery's front entrance. Leo hustled to catch up with her. He exited the building and met Poppy's gaze over Gia's shoulder as his sister embraced her like they were long-lost friends.

Even though he'd instructed his sister not to make things weird, it was—as always—Poppy's ability to adapt to any situation that ensured the encounter didn't become awkward.

She accepted the youngest Leonetti's enthusiastic embrace and happily answered Gia's rapid-fire questions about Joey, the latest specials at the spa and the foster kittens Leo had told his family about over dinner last week.

He had to give Gia credit. For all of her inability to employ personal boundaries, the one subject she didn't go near was the mystery surrounding Joey's parents.

His sister gleefully took Joey from Poppy's arms. After cooing over the baby and peppering his forehead with kisses for several minutes, she handed him to Leo and excused herself to return to the tasting room, where a tour was scheduled to begin.

"I'm sorry for that," Leo said when they were alone again. "To be honest, I was more worried about my grandfather overwhelming you. But Gia ripped the too-much-too-soon bandage right off."

Poppy squeezed his hand, and he took the opportunity to link their fingers together. "She's adorable. I already feel ten times lighter than I did this morning. Thank you for inviting me into your world for a little bit."

For as long as you want in, he wanted to tell her but didn't because that was an emotional check he didn't think his heart could cash.

"The most impressive part of this place is the vines," he said, leading her toward the Polaris Ranger ATV. "Bella is the vintner. She has a gift with the grapes, but everyone in my family loves them in our own way."

Poppy let out a sigh. "That's how my brothers, cousins and I feel about the ranch. My cousins might run the cattle operation, but we all take part at different times. At least once a year, we do a family night at the spa."

Leo laughed. "Somehow, I can't see Rafe getting a facial."

"You'd be surprised." Poppy adjusted Joey's cap. "My brother rocks the clay mask like nobody's business."

"No way."

"Don't knock it." Poppy turned to him, pretending to examine his skin. "One of these nights, I'll give you a facial. I got my aesthetician's license a few years ago so I can fill in during the busier times."

"I would love that."

Her eyes sparkled at his response like he'd surprised her. It shocked the hell out of him, but Poppy's dedication to work and family and their legacy was another thing he loved about—no, *admired* about her, he amended silently.

He'd already moved the baby's car seat base and infant carrier from his truck to the back seat of the off-road vehicle, and the boy fell asleep as soon as the engine revved.

Poppy glanced toward Joey and then at Leo. "I worried the noise and vibration would upset him."

Leo put the vehicle into gear and started toward the vineyard. "Gia was like that as a baby. The motion and noise put her right to sleep every time. I remember Mom piling us into one of the old vineyard four-wheelers to drive up and down all over the property so my baby sister would take a nap."

Poppy looked around the vehicle's interior then rapped her knuckles on her head. "Knock on wood that Joey stays a good sleeper."

"We'll deal with whatever he throws our way," he told her. Leo felt like he could do anything with this incredible woman beside him, driving on the lush, fertile land that had been in his family for generations.

"This is already the best day I've had in a long time." Poppy placed her hand on top of his on the gearshift, and Leo's heart swelled.

"You're going to love the vineyard," he promised and to his surprise the word *love* rolled right off of his tongue.

To his relief, Poppy didn't react like it meant something more, and he settled in to share with her the part of his life he'd never shown to anyone else.

POPPY KNEW HER family was unique. The fact that two generations of Emerald Ridge Fortunes lived and worked on the ranch that had been a part of their family for nearly a century made them noteworthy in this part of the state.

However, the Leonettis took close-knit to a new level, their pride in the vineyard and their Italian heritage on full display around the property and in the family home.

At FGR, the two families had always remained somewhat separate as they went about daily life. Poppy and her brothers had only grown closer to their cousins since Rafe and Drake had conceived and launched the Gift of Fortune program. However, the love and affection between the members of Leo's family felt natural and long-standing.

It was inspiring to tour the property with Leo; his passion for both winemaking and running the business side of the operation was infectious. Every employee greeted him with a mix of affection and admiration, a testament to how much he meant to his staff. She'd had no idea the amount of planning, strategy and cooperation from Mother Nature it took to make a vineyard successful.

After the tour, they'd returned to the tasting room, where she'd expected his youngest sister to join them as Leo poured samples of some of his favorite vintages. The depth of his knowledge astonished her even though she understood his family history with the vineyard. During their talks, Leo typically gave more credit to his family for the winery's success and took little for himself. Poppy understood his dedication in a deeper way and was thrilled by his encouragement as she attempted to identify the different notes in the vintages.

Gia joined them again, and to Poppy's surprise, reported that the other two sisters had returned home. Along with Leo's mom and grandfather and Antonia's baby, they were waiting at the main house. She looked a little sheepish explaining that as much as they wanted to visit with Poppy, all of them, including Bella's two kids, were most excited to get their hands on little Joey. She'd asked if she could take the bundled-up boy who'd woken from his nap to the house while they took their time with the tasting.

Poppy's face flushed when Gia made a point of telling Leo that the rest of the staff had been sent home for the night, and she was locking the door on her way out.

"Does your sister think you need help getting lucky?"

"That would be a first," Leo had answered with a wink. "But she's currently my favorite sister because of it."

Without another word, he picked her up and carried her into his office, where they made love on the leather sofa. He'd proved himself as attentive and thorough in worshipping her body as he'd been the night before.

The time before her mom had received that awful text felt like a world away, but this afternoon gave her the distance she needed to regain her composure after the events of this morning. She once again felt certain her family would be okay—just like her mother said.

"You have a fine boy here, Poppy," Leo's grandfather said as he cradled the baby. Martina set out a delicious charcuterie for the group to snack on.

The Leonettis took turns holding Joey, all of them doting on the baby, and it made her once again wish that whoever Joey's parents were, they wouldn't be related to her. In truth, she hoped the mystery might remain unsolved and that she'd eventually be allowed to adopt the baby, who already felt like hers.

"I couldn't have managed so well without Leo," she admitted, and his grandfather beamed.

"I told him there's more to life than work," Enzo said, "but it took you and this tiny man to prove it."

Poppy glanced at Leo, who was sipping a glass of wine, his hip resting against the kitchen counter.

"Papa always knows best," he said lightly, although his gaze looked troubled.

Was it too much having them here with his family? She hoped the Leonettis wouldn't be too disappointed when things between them came to their inevitable end. As sad as that would make her, she knew she shouldn't allow herself to believe there was any other way. She'd opened her heart and had it broken on more than one occasion. Life had taught her that hope was a treacherous thing when it came to love.

Apparently, the lesson hadn't stuck because each day she spent with Leo, her heart opened to him more and more. It didn't feel like she had any power to stop it, and she was lying to herself if she believed otherwise. Lying to all of them—her family and his, which was a hard pill to swallow.

Poppy didn't like feeling as though they were deceiving people who cared about them, especially Enzo. But would it be so wrong for her to hold out hope that this time it could be different? Leo wasn't the same man he'd been during their first try at a relationship. Maybe he just needed someone to make him see that. She couldn't be that someone if she let herself.

"What are you guys doing for Valentine's Day?" Antonia, the quietest of three sisters, asked.

"Nothing," Poppy answered truthfully, realizing the holiday was in a few days.

Leo's mother gasped in dismay and pointed the fork she held in Leo's direction. "I raised you better than that. You must take a woman out on this important day that celebrates your love."

Leo looked like he wanted the floor to swallow him whole, which was exactly how Poppy felt.

"It's not a big deal," she told the group. "Dinner out isn't exactly an option with an infant."

"Of course not," his mother agreed. "Leo's grandfather and I will watch the baby."

"Do you hear that?" Enzo gently jiggled the boy, who continued to gaze up at him. "You and I will have another night together."

"A sleepover if you'd like," Martina offered.

Poppy held up her hands. "Oh, no. That's too much. You don't have to…"

She met Leo's gaze across the room, unable to read his expression.

"Poppy's right," he agreed after a moment. "It's a big ask

and too late to make reservations. Valentine's Day is a fake holiday, anyway."

Gia and Antonia let out twin groans of disgust.

"That's something only an idiot would say." Bella reached across the center island and pinched her brother's arm. "Don't be an idiot."

He looked so discombobulated that Poppy almost laughed. Leo warned her his family had assumed that they were a couple because of his willingness to participate so fully in caring for Joey.

At first, she thought it was funny and knew certain members of her family probably believed the same, but now his shoulders slumped as his sisters and mother glared at him. She understood that he'd given up so much to be the man his family needed him to after his father died. The last thing she wanted was for their ruse to put more pressure on him or give his family false hope that more would come of their arrangement.

Except they could make it more. It would take time, but she had that and enough patience to allow Leo to see that they were good together. And it could be so much better if they opened their hearts. If she led by example on that front.

Enzo continued to stare down at the baby, even though Poppy had a feeling he was trying to refrain from laughing at the predicament his grandson faced.

That odd protectiveness she felt for Leo rose to the surface. "Leo and I agreed not to celebrate Valentine's Day." She made her tone firm as she met Bella's gaze. "I don't need a special holiday or night on the town to feel special. Your brother does that every day with how he supports me and cares for Joey."

She placed her hands on her hips. "Heck, he even scoops the litter box, and when you're dealing with foster kittens, that can be a messy job."

There was a beat of stunned silence in the kitchen, then Bella asked, "Are you saying scooping poop is romantic?"

Poppy laughed. "I'm saying there are more-important ways to show you care about someone than a heart-shaped box of chocolates or overpriced roses."

She still couldn't read Leo's expression, but at least he stood a little bit taller. She'd done that for him. Given how much he'd helped her in the past few weeks, it was the least she could offer.

Before she knew what was happening, Martina wrapped her in a tight embrace. "You are a treasure," she told Poppy. "And you…"

Still gripping Poppy's arm, she pulled her toward Leo and gave her son a loud, smacking kiss on the cheek. "You make me so proud, Leonardo."

Poppy hadn't expected such an emotional reaction from Leo's mother and hoped he didn't mind her unprompted defense. He could handle himself, but for some reason, he didn't. Something held him back from owning who he was and the choices he made.

Maybe it was the pressure of being the oldest and only son. Poppy had been judged plenty over the years. Most people in town thought she was a silly romantic who must have some fatal flaw that made her incapable of keeping a man. Was she too needy? Too vulnerable? Too ordinary for anyone to truly cherish?

Any or all of those things might be true, but she'd decided she was also satisfied with who she was as a person on the inside. None of her doubts or fears or other people's judgments would control her life.

If she could give Leo one thing during their time together, it would be the ability to accept himself, and that would start with convincing his family to accept him and where he was in life.

Although if that were the case, letting them believe he had more interest in Poppy than was true wouldn't help matters He might be different than the man she'd dated, but that only meant he had more power to break her heart if she gave it to him.

But when he wrapped an arm around her waist and pulled her close and out of his mother's grasp, all she could do was enjoy the feel of his warmth against her body. For something that she knew wasn't real, it certainly felt that way.

"Will you be my valentine?" Leo asked, his breath tickling the hair around her ear. Her mouth went dry as desire sparked along her skin.

"Yes," she answered, kissing the edge of his jaw. His mom

and sisters let out cheers of delight and Poppy blushed. She'd forgotten they had an audience because that's what Leo did to her. He made her forget everything, including her determination to keep her heart guarded.

CHAPTER TEN

A FEW DAYS LATER, Leo dropped Joey off at his mother and grandfather's before returning to Poppy's house to pick her up for their evening of dinner and dancing in the ballroom at the Emerald Ridge Hotel. Leonetti Vineyards supplied much of the wine for the hotel so he'd called in a favor from the owner.

He'd never taken a woman out on Valentine's Day. All part of his determination not to set expectations he couldn't live up to. Deep in his cynical soul, a voice whispered that this was a huge mistake.

It didn't matter that he and Poppy both knew the terms of their arrangement, and she had never pushed or even hinted that she wanted more.

The problem originated inside him because, to his continued shock, he wanted to push. Over the years, he'd seen more than one friend worn down by a girlfriend only to end up in a long-term relationship, and in some cases, even marriage. Those poor fools seemed happy enough.

Maybe if Poppy forced him, he could commit without really capitulating, the way he did so often in his family. He bent to what they wanted and expected of him without having to take full responsibility for those decisions.

Yeah. That would be okay. Not forever. He wasn't marriage material even though he had trouble imagining his life without her. He'd learned from his father what committing to forever if you weren't ready would do to a person, but Leo couldn't imagine his life without Poppy and Joey in it so...

He gripped the bouquet he held in his hand—not overpriced roses—more tightly and walked into the house with a new sense of purpose.

Then came up short at the sight of Poppy standing in the entryway, shoving a tube of lipstick into the compact velvet purse she held.

"I haven't worn lipstick for weeks," she said. "I almost forgot how to apply the stuff." She pressed her lips together, drawing Leo's gaze. They were shaded in a soft plum color, darker than her natural pink and almost the same hue as they took on after he thoroughly kissed her.

His body urged him to chuck the flowers over his shoulder, forget about their dinner reservation and carry her back to the bedroom and peel that gorgeous dress right off her even more beautiful body.

The dress was amazing, or more accurately, she *looked* amazing in it. It was deep burgundy with a low V-neck that sorely tempted him to dip his tongue into the crevice between her breasts. The fabric clung to her hips and shimmered as she fidgeted in front of him.

"Is it too much? You're staring at me like it's too much."

He shook his head and opened his mouth, but no words came out. He couldn't breathe, let alone formulate a sentence.

A crease formed between her brows, and she drew that plum-colored bottom lip between her upper teeth. "Too much," she whispered, possibly more to herself than him.

When she started to turn away, Leo got ahold of himself. He stepped forward and took her hand, linking their fingers together. She'd painted her nails. They reminded him of tiny rubies sparkling in the light from the fixture overhead. "You are never too much for me, Poppy."

One corner of her mouth lifted in an almost smile, but she didn't look convinced.

"You're so beautiful I lost my ability to speak. You take my breath away. There aren't words for what I feel when I look at you."

At least not words Leo would ever utter.

Thankfully, she didn't seem to need him to. Because of her heels, they were nearly the same height. She leaned in and brushed a featherlight kiss against his mouth. When he tried to deepen it, she pulled away.

"The disadvantage of lipstick." She used the pad of her thumb to wipe his lip. "You'll end up with more of it on your face than mine if we aren't careful."

"Worth it," he told her. "We won't need to worry if we skip dinner and—"

"Oh, no." She took another step back. "We're taking advantage of our babysitters and going out."

He saw the moment her doubts about the night crept in because a shadow entered her green eyes, turning them the color of the ocean just before a storm.

"Unless you're having second thoughts about—"

"Not one," he assured her. "I'm excited for no dish duty and even more to share a first dance with you."

The shadow cleared at his words, but she wrinkled her nose. "I'm not the best dancer."

"Sweetheart…" He leaned in like they were sharing a secret. "Dancing is an excuse to get my hands on you *in* that dress before I get my hands on you *out* of that dress. You'll do fine."

He was rewarded with an adorable blush and took her hand as he led her out the front door. Leo couldn't remember ever anticipating an evening so eagerly, especially not one that called for him to wear a sports coat and tie. But Poppy was exceptional, and he'd been an oaf when they'd tried dating a decade ago. This time it would be different. He'd do his best to make amends for the past and ensure this night was perfect for them both.

"ARE PEOPLE STILL STARING?" Poppy asked, trying not to be obvious as she turned to glance at the patrons seated at the tables around them.

They'd been at Captains, the fancy restaurant on the top floor of the Emerald Ridge Hotel, for nearly two hours, and Poppy had enjoyed a delectable three-course meal of fresh ceviche, a perfectly blackened serving of Chilean sea bass and the most amazing crème brûlée she'd ever tasted for dessert.

Leo reached across the table and grasped her fingers. She started to tug them away, but he held fast, his smile never wavering.

"If they are, it's because you look as beautiful as you did when we walked in." He lifted her hand to his mouth, but she yanked it away.

"You can't do that here."

"Why not?" His voice was a low rumble.

"Everyone will think we're together."

He picked up the wineglass and swirled the dark liquid that complemented the color of her dress. It was a rich Syrah from his family's vineyard. "We *are* together. It's Valentine's Day, and we're on a date, in case you've forgotten. You also happen to look so gorgeous I *still* can't stop staring. Why would I care if people think we are together?"

Why would she expect him to understand? Leo didn't have the reputation in town that Poppy did. The polar opposite reputation, which meant no one would think twice about Leo on the date but Poppy...

"I told you I'm not doing relationships at the moment."

"And I'm okay with that," he agreed, although his eyes narrowed like he didn't like it.

"So when this ends, everyone will think I was a fool to give my heart again. They'll feel sorry for me. I'm tired of being pitied because I'm a failure at love."

She gripped the napkin tightly and ordered herself not to run from the table as embarrassment washed over her. Why was it so easy to share her most secret and humiliating thoughts with this man?

"We should have gone to dinner in the next town over," she muttered.

Leo studied her for what felt like hours, but it probably took only seconds before he said, "You aren't a failure at love. You have more love in your life, Poppy Fortune, than almost any person I know. The people you love are so lucky."

He shrugged, looking almost boyishly embarrassed. "I can hardly believe anyone would think I'm the kind of man who deserves you, but I'm proud as hell if they do. I'm grateful to be here, and I don't care what anybody assumes or what they say. When this ends, we can play it however you want. I'll be the one who's brokenhearted if that makes you happy. Please don't let what other people think or assume ruin this night."

Her heart first expanded at his words and then caved in on itself because amid all the flattery directed her way, he'd also used the phrase *when this ends.*

She didn't want it to end. Most of her worry was directed at her own heart because she couldn't stop falling for him. Leo had become the man she'd always wished him to be. A man who could fully capture her heart.

He might be willing to play at being crushed when they broke up, but Poppy knew she'd never be the same after this ended.

"You've changed," she murmured, and his wide-eyed expression told her he was as surprised as her that she'd made the observation out loud.

"Everyone changes," he answered, his voice tight.

"I like this version of you." Her voice sounded husky to her own ears and she cleared her throat. "I mean, I liked you five years ago but it's...different now."

An emotion flashed in his eyes that she couldn't name, but it made her pulse quicken. "Maybe we're both different."

"Maybe," she agreed, although one thing that hadn't changed is her attraction to Leo. It was only growing stronger the more time they spent together, and she was tired of resisting the way he pulled her in so effortlessly.

The waiter cleared their dinner plates just as the band took the stage. When the music started, a pretty decent cover of a popular love song by Adele, Leo stood. With a smile, he held his hand out to her.

"Ms. Fortune, may I have this dance?"

She hesitated, and his smile faltered. "Poppy?"

She shook off her worries, a task becoming more frequent and difficult each day. But it wasn't Leo's fault that she couldn't control her feelings. Tonight she'd find a way to enjoy how special he made her feel without worrying about the future. Or at least not worrying too much. That became easier as he led her to the dance floor, where a few couples were already swaying to the music.

"The moment I've been waiting for all night," he said as he pulled her close. He held her right hand, and she rested her left one on his shoulder as he began to lead her around the dance floor.

The first song was awkward. Poppy hadn't exaggerated when she'd told him she wasn't a good dancer, but Leo didn't so much as wince when she trod upon his toes. He simply pulled her closer and whispered, "Relax," against her ear.

To her shock, her body overrode her brain's swirling anxiety and did just that. Once she stopped thinking, she found it easier to enjoy the moment.

When was the last time she'd danced with a man? It had been at Rafe's wedding, with Poppy fresh off another breakup. She'd been chosen as a pity partner by her brothers and cousins. Eventually, she'd slunk into the shadows—hiding behind a potted palm—and watched the actual couples glide across the floor, wondering why relationships or even casual dating came so easy for other people but never for her.

Her parents had spent most of the evening dancing to everything from romantic ballads to country line dances. To Poppy, they'd seemed like the epitome of happiness, two people who'd found their perfect partner. Her chest pinched at the thought of what the future might hold for them and the role the baby who she loved with her whole heart would play in it.

As Leo smiled then twirled her so expertly, she felt as though their next stop was a standing ovation from the *Dancing with the Stars* judges. Poppy understood how deceiving looks could be. She and Leo might appear to fit together but their reality and eventual ending had the power to devastate her.

"You okay?" he asked, attuned to her emotions in a way that should be alarming but caused a thrill of happiness to flare in her heart.

She opened her mouth to tell him no. She *wasn't* okay. He couldn't come home with her again. There was no way she could continue to play the part of friends given how much she was coming to care for him. It went way beyond attraction, intoxicating as their physical connection could be. Her feelings far transcended gratitude for his help with Joey.

Leo was the crux of her emotions. She cared too deeply for him—for how he made her feel cherished and special. Like he saw her as something more than dependable, easygoing Poppy. He asked questions about her day like the answers mattered. Often, he solicited her opinion about issues he was dealing with at the winery, as if her ideas and suggestions offered a unique perspective, one that he respected and honored.

Although Poppy took her role in the FGR organization seriously, she often wondered if her parents, brothers and cousins did the same. She ran the spa and it made money and contributed to the reputation and success of the guest ranch arm of the business. But dealing with skincare products and pampering didn't often seem as significant as guest relations or supervising the cattle operation.

However, Leo helped her see that she mattered, and even though it might lead to heartbreak, she wasn't willing to give that up just yet. As this potential scandal with her parents proved, life had no guarantees. So even though her feelings became more tangled each day, she wanted to continue to enjoy whatever moments she and Leo had left. Despite the challenges, was it too much to hope this could be their second chance? And was she a fool for wanting it so badly?

"I'm fine." She lifted her hand to the back of his neck, loving his warm skin under her palm. Let people watch and talk. Poppy would savor the contentment that came with knowing she was the only woman this enigmatic man had let in. "Just a little tired."

His eyes closed when her nails grazed the skin above his starched collar. "Tired," he repeated in a whisper.

"Well, not exactly *tired* tired." His gaze felt like it pierced her soul with its intensity when he opened his eyes to stare into hers.

"What kind of tired?" He sounded hoarse like he had trouble forming the question. Another song had started, a fast dance number, but they stood still in the center of the dance floor, ignoring the couples who spun and whirled around them.

"Tired of not being alone with you." She flashed a cheeky smile and added, "Tired of not being naked."

Leo gave a choked response, then grabbed her hand and dragged her toward the ballroom's exit.

"My purse," she reminded him with a laugh.

"Don't move." He released her hand and sprinted to their table to retrieve her sparkly clutch, holding it tight to his chest like a football as he raced back to her and led her out into the quiet night.

"Heels," she protested when he started to pick up speed across the parking lot.

Barely breaking stride, Leo scooped her into his arms. He moved like a man possessed, and some of Poppy's doubts melted away with the intoxicating knowledge that this strong, handsome, confounding man might be as affected by her as she was by him.

Despite his frantic rush to the truck, Leo deposited her on the front seat like she was as delicate as a porcelain doll. He pulled the seat belt across her chest and lap, leaning in for a deep, soulful kiss as the buckle clicked.

Then he climbed in and started for her house, his knuckles white around the steering wheel.

He didn't speak, but Poppy could feel the desire pulsing between them. It glimmered in the air like diamonds. Her body throbbed with need, and it felt as though the ten-minute drive would be too much to bear. She'd explode with longing if they didn't...

"Leo?"

"Need to concentrate," he rasped.

"Leo, please." She reached out and placed a hand on his leg. He let out a hiss as his muscles bunched and then quivered.

"Poppy, I'm not sure I can."

"Take a right," she told him. "Now."

He didn't question her as he turned the truck onto the unmarked dirt road at the edge of the FGR property.

The truck's brights showed the open fields of sagebrush before them.

"There's a gate up ahead. No one except the ranch hands uses this entrance and only when they need to access one of the outer pastures. It's private."

His gaze flicked to hers, the question in them evident even in the dim glow from the dash.

"And close." She squeezed his leg. "Closer than home, and I can't wait." She wanted his hands on her skin, his mouth fused to hers.

The air sizzled between them as he turned off the engine, killed the lights and reached for her.

"That's the nicest thing anyone has ever said to me."

He threaded his fingers through her hair and leaned over the console to kiss her. Although the taste of him was familiar by now, she lost herself in the pleasure of it. Her body hummed with need and desire, and when he tugged her closer, she maneuvered herself onto his lap, straddling him. He moved the seat back, and they both laughed when she leaned into the horn.

"I feel like I'm back in high school," Leo confessed, trailing kisses along her neck. Her dress bunched around her hips, and he kneaded her bare skin with his fingers.

"I never did this in high school." She laughed self-consciously. "Clearly, I was missing out."

She'd never been confident enough to tell a man to pull over because she couldn't wait. Leo made her feel bold, and she wanted to revel in it.

"Tell me what you want." His voice was low and seemed to offer all sorts of wicked promises Poppy could barely acknowledge.

But she'd for sure try. "Touch me," she said, grateful for the darkness because she could feel the heat in her cheeks.

He gripped her legs, thumbs grazing the sensitive skin on the inside of her thighs. "Here?"

A moan escaped her lips.

"And here?" He leaned forward to run his tongue along her collarbone.

"No, not there," she managed, her breath coming in rasps.

His right hand scraped the fabric of her panties.

"Yes," she whispered.

Humming with approval, he dipped one finger inside her.

The horn blared again when she bucked backward. Leo chuckled and wrapped an arm around her.

"Easy," he told her then kissed her again.

It was easy to give herself over to the pleasure of his touch, the rhythm he set with his fingers and his mouth.

"So beautiful," he murmured against her mouth.

"More," she answered and barely recognized her own voice. Poppy had never demanded anything of anyone.

Leo didn't seem to mind. He deepened the kiss and his touch until she was mindless with sensation. Too much. It was *too much,* but he didn't stop. Her hips writhed in time with his fingers until she reached the peak and tumbled over the edge.

The darkness had no hold over her because her entire body felt like it was bathed in light. She threw back her head and called out his name, her voice echoing in the truck's cab.

And then the lights from the approaching truck hit her. She scrambled off Leo like she'd been electrocuted.

"Oh, my gosh." She twisted her dress into place as she turned to stare out the truck's back window. "No one comes down this road." She glanced at Leo. "Why are you grinning?"

"You're cute about being caught fooling around."

"Because I've never been caught!" She drew in a sharp breath. "Wait. What if whoever's in that truck is the person who's been sabotaging the ranches? It could be the villain."

Leo's smile dimmed. "Then we'll deal with it. I'll take care of you, Poppy. I promise."

She believed him, and her heart seemed to skip a beat. Leo reached out and linked their fingers as Poppy continued to watch the truck draw closer, exhaling in relief when she recognized the Fortune's Gold Ranch logo on the side. "It's one of our vehicles."

As the truck parked behind them, Leo turned on the engine. A man got out and approached the driver's side. Leo rolled down the window as Micah shone a flashlight into the cab.

"Poppy? Leo?" Her cousin frowned.

"What the hell are you two doing out here?"

Poppy's face flamed, but Leo remained cool. "Stargazing."

Micah looked between the two of them, and Poppy shrugged. "I've always loved the night sky, and it's so clear with no lights around. How did you know we were here?"

Her cousin flipped off the flashlight. "I installed game cams around the perimeter of the property. Can't take any more chances with the bad stuff happening lately."

"Sorry we bothered you," Leo said smoothly.

"I was just watching TV," Micah answered easily. "You won't find me venturing out on Valentine's Day."

Poppy rolled her eyes at that. "You sound like my brothers."

"Smart guys." Micah reached in to pat Leo's shoulder. "Not as smart as you taking out our Poppy. She's one of a kind."

"Yes, she is," Leo agreed brusquely. "And she's mine."

Micah grinned then winked at Poppy before heading back to his truck. "Enjoy the rest of the night."

"Let's go home, sweetheart." Leo grabbed her hand again and lifted it to his mouth. Instead of kissing her knuckles, he turned it over and pressed his mouth to the inside of her wrist. "We have a little time before we need to pick up Joey..."

She grinned. "Then let's make the most of it."

CHAPTER ELEVEN

POPPY ENTERED COFFEE CONNECTION, her favorite coffee spot in town, two mornings later with Joey's infant carrier tucked under her arm.

It was the first time since the baby had come to live with her that she'd brought him into town on her own. Her staff and some of the regular clients at the spa had met him as he came to work with her if Leo was at the winery.

But the spa felt different than being in public for real. It was Poppy's happy place, her work haven, and she knew her close-knit staff supported her endeavor as a foster parent. If any of them made assumptions about her rocky romantic track record, they kept their opinions to themselves, unlike some of her friends, neighbors and former classmates, who seemed happy to offer unsolicited advice.

She waved to Annelise Wellington, Courtney's stepdaughter, who sat at a table in a somewhat private corner of the coffee shop. Poppy had told Annelise she'd be bringing Joey to their meeting and appreciated the other woman's discretion.

Courtney likely would have picked a table that put Poppy on display for all the world to see and judge. She shook off her insecurities as she approached the counter and ordered a caramel latte. She had to get over caring what other people thought. Part of being a foster parent would involve potentially helping older children navigate challenging situations where they might be subject to questions or criticisms from classmates.

Poppy didn't doubt her ability to offer unconditional love and support no matter the circumstance but also knew modeling self-confidence was more powerful than simply giving lip service to it.

Poppy recognized the manager on duty from her high school days. She might have even briefly dated Shane if Poppy remembered things correctly.

When the woman raised a questioning brow at the car seat, Poppy smiled and gestured her closer. "I'm sure you heard I'm fostering the baby left on my parents' porch at the beginning of the month." She kept her features neutral. "I'm so grateful the timing worked out so I could be a part of his life until we track down his mother and father." Her former classmate, whose name tag read Dawn, which Poppy hadn't remembered, offered a tight smile. "It's hard to tell if he looks like he belongs to one of the men in your family. Babies all look like grumpy old men when they're so young."

Poppy traced a finger over Joey's cheek while waiting for her order. "A little old man with the softest skin I've ever felt. No matter who he belongs to, I'm going to make sure this sweet boy ends up with a family who loves him."

Dawn stared at her for so long it became awkward. Finally, the barista at the coffee maker handed Poppy her drink.

"Well, nice talking to you." Poppy offered a smile then started to turn away.

"Wait." Dawn pulled a small plate from the stack on the counter behind her and used a pair of tongs to pull a blueberry muffin from the display case. She offered it to Poppy.

"I didn't order—"

"On the house," the woman said. "I'll carry it to your table since you've got your hands full."

"Thanks, but you don't have to do that." Poppy assumed that Dawn pitied her the way most of the town did. *Poor Poppy can't catch a man and has to resort to taking care of other people's children since she has none of her own.* "I feel lucky to have Joey in my life."

She thought about Leo and the way he'd slipped into her bed after Joey's final feeding last night and held her until she drifted off to sleep. "I'm happy."

Dawn walked around the edge of the counter. "You seem happy," she agreed, then glanced at Joey. "That baby is the lucky one. My husband, Jared, spent a few months in the foster care system when he was a toddler before being adopted by a couple down in Chatelaine. You're doing an admirable thing. Not many people are so selfless. A blueberry muffin is the least I can offer, but hopefully, it reminds you of what a difference you're making."

"Oh." Poppy's throat suddenly stung, and she swallowed back the emotion lodged there. "I appreciate you saying that."

"Everyone's talking about how amazing you are."

Poppy gave a quiet snort as she led the way to Annelise's table in the back. "I thought they were talking about the scandal Joey means for my family."

Dawn wrinkled her nose. "That, too. It's a small town. But they also admire you." She placed the muffin on the table. "*I* admire you."

"Thanks," Poppy repeated and set Joey's carrier in the infant carrier high chair Annelise had situated at the table as Dawn walked away.

"I don't know what that was about," Annelise said as Poppy slipped into the seat across from her after the woman walked off. "But I admire you, too. Not many people would step up for a baby like you have."

"Plenty of people are foster parents," Poppy countered. "I'm not special."

"I think you are," Annelise told her with a smile. "Other people do, too."

"I appreciate that." She tore off a bite of muffin and popped it in her mouth. The flavor was sweet, with the perfect amount of blueberry tanginess. "Honestly, I figured most people think I'm odd and possibly pathetic because I don't have a family of my own." She frowned then added, "Your stepmother certainly thinks so."

"I wouldn't put much stock in my *stepmonster's* opinion."

It made Poppy wonder if she'd been doing herself a disservice for longer than she realized. She assumed that her friends, family and people she knew in town considered her a failure at love and a bit of a bad luck charm when it came to relationships because that's how she'd seen herself. Had she simply been projecting her own fears onto other people?

Dawn didn't seem to believe that Poppy's desire to be a foster parent and her dedication to Joey was anything other than altruistic. Of course, the baby situation hit close to home given that the new DNA results still hadn't been processed for her father, Micah and her uncle Hayden.

But Poppy couldn't control that. Whatever people thought about the mystery of Joey's parents, it didn't reflect on her. So what if she hadn't found love despite her many attempts at relationships? She led with her heart, which wasn't the worst offense in the world. Especially if she was her own harshest critic.

Poppy smiled at Annelise's nickname for Courtney. "Let's talk about your skincare line. I took the samples Courtney gave me to the spa. Everybody who tried them has been very impressed with the quality. How did you get started in this business?"

Annelise smiled, but it looked pained. "Let me start by saying I'm embarrassed if my stepmother pressured you into this meeting or anything. I'm proud of the line and would never want the FGR spa to feel obligated to carry any products. Your reputation is impeccable."

Poppy held up a hand. "And let *me* start by saying I was a bit put off initially. Courtney isn't exactly my favorite person."

Annelise's smile faded. "We have that in common, although the fact that she mentioned the line to you—"

"Oh, she did more than mention. She brought samples and talked you up quite a bit," Poppy explained. "To be honest, she seemed legitimately impressed by what you've created. She's a great hype person."

Annelise laughed softly. "I appreciate her support. Maybe I've been wrong about Courtney and need to try harder to mend our relationship."

Poppy inclined her head in agreement. "I think a lot of Fortunes and Wellingtons have been wrong about each other over the years. It's never too late to try something new. But regardless of how I was introduced to your products, I would never carry anything or ask my staff to use or recommend products to clients that I don't believe in a hundred percent. As I told Courtney, most of the products we carry are from Texas-based companies. That's important to me and to the whole operation. The guest ranch sources as many items as possible from local or regional businesses. In fact, we just did a Valentine's Day special partnering with Abuela Rosa's chocolates. It was a big hit with the guests who came in for the weekend."

"I went to school with her granddaughter," Annelise murmured. "They are an amazing family, and those chocolates are to die for!"

"My staff would argue that your products are also to die for. If we can work something out, I think it would be great to carry AW GlowCare as part of our product line. Because you're local and a small operation, I'm hoping you might have some flexibility so that we could develop some products or packaging that will be unique for the spa. I love for our clients to be reminded of their experience at FGR once they get home."

She saw the moment Annelise forgot to be nervous or self-conscious about making a pitch. Her eyes lit up as she explained the origins of her interest in skincare and beauty products. Poppy loved the enthusiasm and appreciated that Annelise was dedicated but not overly boastful when discussing her talent and products.

As Annelise answered questions about the various aspects of the line's production, sourcing ingredients and her vision for the future, she became more animated, her earlier self-doubt forgotten.

"I love everything you've just told me." Poppy took the final bite of the muffin and savored not only the sweetness but also the reason Dawn had offered it to her in the first place. "I'd like you to meet a few of my staff members, particularly the aestheticians. Then we can discuss an initial order and potentially a long-term partnership."

"Really?" Annelise beamed. "It would be a dream come true

to work with you and have AW GlowCare affiliated with the spa. Thank you, Poppy."

"It's a win-win," Poppy assured the other woman.

The family supported Rafe and Drake when they'd first come up with the Gift of Fortune initiative. Poppy had no reason—other than her own nagging doubt—to believe her brothers and cousins wouldn't support her in developing formal partnerships with local Emerald Ridge business owners.

She simply needed to take the risk to step out of her comfort zone. It was time she stopped hiding her light. If she didn't take risks or make her desires known, her dreams and goals would remain out of reach.

Joey, who'd been sleeping peacefully throughout the meeting, blinked awake and whimpered quietly.

"He's adorable," Annelise said as Poppy unstrapped the baby and lifted him from his carrier.

Poppy kissed the boy's forehead as she arranged him in her arms. "It's only been a few weeks, but sometimes I can't remember my life before him." Or imagine her future without him and Leo, she added silently.

"Babies are easy to fall in love with."

"Very true," Poppy agreed, reaching for the premade bottle she'd packed in the diaper bag. "Don't feel like you have to keep us company. I'm going to feed him before heading out again."

Annelise checked her watch and then pushed back from the table. "I do need to get to a meeting with my chemists. They'll be so excited about this opportunity. Thanks again, Poppy."

"You should be thanking *me*," a shrill voice said from behind Poppy's shoulder. Joey startled. Poppy couldn't blame him, but she plastered a smile on her face as Courtney came to stand next to her.

"Hey, Courtney." Annelise's smile looked just as forced as Poppy's felt. "Yes, thank you for dropping off the samples, although you knew I had a plan for approaching Poppy."

The older woman waved away the comment. "You move too slow on opportunities, just like your father did. Sometimes a person has to take the proverbial bull by the horns to get what they want. Coming out on top is the end goal and the ends justify whatever means it takes to get there."

"Dad was a good man," Annelise said tightly. "His sense of honor never hurt his success, and he could feel proud at the end of the day about not only what he accomplished, but how he achieved his goals."

Courtney feigned a yawn. "Perhaps that was true for the men of your father's generation when life moved at a slower pace, especially out here in an insignificant cow town," the woman said.

Annelise had grown up in Emerald Ridge the same way Poppy had and seemed just as put off by her stepmother's assessment of the town and her late father. Poppy sat forward still cradling Joey, who was now happily taking down his bottle. "The FGR spa focuses on the history and legacy of the land my family owns. I think our customers will appreciate Annelise's products, not just because they're fabulous—which they are— but because of the ties she has to this community. Legacy is important."

Annelise shot her a grateful nod. "I'm honored by the opportunity. But now I really have to go. Courtney, lovely to see you as always. Poppy, I'm excited for a visit to the spa."

Poppy wasn't sure if Courtney had stopped by to insert herself into their meeting or if she wanted an opportunity to visit with her stepdaughter.

"I actually need to head to another meeting," Annelise said as she stood. She placed a hand on Courtney's arm. "Let's grab dinner later this week."

Courtney blinked several times, clearly shocked by the overture from her stepdaughter. "I'll have to check my calendar, but I could probably fit you in."

Poppy hid her grin as Annelise nodded. Mending her relationship with Courtney might be like trying to cuddle up to a porcupine, but at least Annelise was trying. She picked up her empty mug and Poppy's plate, then hurried to the front of the shop. Poppy would have liked to follow her out the front door. But she was stuck in place until Joey finished his feeding.

"I won't keep you," she said, hoping Courtney would take the hint. "I'm on the way to visit my mother when Joey's done." As soon as the words were out of her mouth, she regretted them. Courtney's gaze sharpened with interest.

"Is poor, sweet Shelley still hiding out at the hotel?"

Poppy tried not to growl. Thankfully Courtney didn't seem inclined to occupy Annelise's vacated chair. On the other hand, that would have made it more convenient for Poppy to *accidentally* kick her in the shin.

"I wouldn't call it hiding out. Everyone knows my mother's there."

"Yes, it's the talk of the town after your little situation." She waved a hand toward Joey.

"He's a baby, not a situation," Poppy clarified.

"Potato, potahto," Courtney chirped.

Poppy considered arguing, but that would only prolong this conversation, which she desperately wanted to end. "I'll tell her you said hello."

"Please do," Courtney cooed. "Send my apologies for not reaching out in her time of need." She heaved a dramatic sigh. "I understand what it's like to be a woman of a certain age on her own. Although, your mother is quite a few years older than me."

"She's also *not* alone," Poppy ground out.

"I'm just saying that it might be good to have a bit of space from your father at the moment. She'll have plenty of time to be there for you."

"My mother has always made time for me, my brothers and whoever needs her support."

"A regular *angel*," Courtney agreed. "Being so perfect all the time must get tiresome." She tsked quietly. "Or boring."

Poppy had never in her life wanted to inflict physical harm on another person, but Courtney brought out the worst in her, especially when she aimed her comments at Shelley.

Joey finished the bottle, and Poppy placed a burp cloth over her shoulder, lifted the boy and gently patted his back. "I have things to do, Courtney, and I'm certain you do as well. I appreciate you introducing me to Annelise's skincare line. She's extremely talented, and I look forward to working with her. If there's anything else you want to say, please just spit it out. I have too much going on right now to deal in games or puzzles."

Dawn, who'd been wiping down the table behind Courtney, leaned around the woman and gave Poppy a thumbs-up.

Maybe it wasn't so hard to stand up for herself and the people she loved after all. A couple of weeks with Joey had taught her so much about her life and what she wanted from it. One thing she wanted was to stop playing small.

Naturally, Courtney jumped at the chance to get more jabs in. "Well, I did hear you and Leo Leonetti made quite the dashing couple at the hotel ballroom on Valentine's Day…"

Poppy winced. Of course, people were talking. She reminded herself that other people's opinions about her were none of her business but deep down it still stung. "Did you want to ask where I got my dress because you heard it was so pretty or was there a specific question?"

"I tried to warn you about him."

Joey let out a burp, the most beautiful sound Poppy had heard in a long time because it meant she could pack the diaper bag, put the baby in his carrier and walk away.

"You warned me, and he took me to a nice dinner and dancing." She certainly hoped no one had heard about her cousin catching them in the far pasture. No way Micah would have gossiped about her.

"You should listen to me. Leo reminds me of Garth in a lot of ways. I've known men like your father. I *enjoy* men like your father. But I'm not at all certain Leo is the right man for a woman like you."

Courtney's suddenly silky tone made Poppy's skin crawl. The woman wouldn't dare make a play for her father, at least not during her parents' temporary separation. But what if things didn't work out? Would Courtney consider him fair game?

She scrambled to her feet, knocking over her empty coffee cup in the process.

"I need to go." She grabbed Joey's car seat and lifted him off the high chair.

Courtney grabbed her arm. "Your mom should be careful," she said in a hushed tone, as if sharing a secret. "I believe the text she received about your dad is true, and I think she does, too. I've also heard that some of the samples went missing.

Garth is a powerful man and if he has a reason for those results to be delayed, you never know what he might do."

Ice clogged Poppy's veins. She yanked her arm free. "I know my dad. He wouldn't cheat on my mother or tamper with the DNA samples. He's a good man. Leo is, too, for that matter. He's a good friend to help me with Joey."

"It's sweet you think that, but be careful, Poppy. Leo is also a handsome man who likes women—*lots of women*, based on his reputation. You don't want to get hurt. Again."

No. This couldn't be happening. Poppy's concern for her own reputation and people talking about her felt ridiculously petty given Courtney's veiled accusation. How must her mother feel?

"I've got to go," she repeated, then rushed out of the coffee shop. She didn't bother returning to her parked car, too jittery to think about driving.

The hotel was only a couple blocks away, the February day unseasonably warm. She adjusted the cover on the infant carrier to protect Joey from direct sunlight as she hurried along the sidewalk.

By the time she knocked at her mother's room, sweat trickled between her shoulder blades, although she guessed nerves had more to do with it than the heat.

Shelley opened the door with a smile that quickly faded as she took in her appearance. "What happened, sweetie? What's wrong? How can I help?"

Poppy placed Joey's carrier on the coffee table in the small sitting room of the hotel suite. She busied herself with unstrapping and lifting him from the car seat. Otherwise, she might burst into tears if she met her mother's gaze. How was it possible that Shelley could be going through so much, yet her first concern remained her daughter's well-being?

Maybe she could take comfort in that. Even if her parents' marriage wasn't the model relationship she'd always thought, Shelley was still the perfect mother.

"Poppy?"

Cradling Joey to her chest, she sank onto the damask sofa. "Do you have water? It's warmer out than I expected." Her mother gave her a quizzical look but nodded and pulled a bottle from the minifridge under the walnut cabinet.

"Did you run all the way here?"

Poppy blinked, then realized her mom was making a joke and smiled. "I was at the coffee shop meeting with Annelise about her skincare line. Courtney showed up."

"What glad tidings did Courtney Wellington bring to you today?" Shelley lowered herself to the sofa next to Poppy. She seemed intent on looking anywhere but at Joey.

Poppy thought about lying to her mother, but she hated secrets. Hated the way the one involving the baby in her arms had the power to potentially tear apart her family.

"She said the text about Dad being Joey's father is probably true."

Shelley sucked in a harsh breath. "I didn't think anyone knew about that."

"Courtney said she heard it around town. That it's hard to keep secrets in Emerald Ridge."

"How ironic since no one seems to be able to unravel the mystery of Joey's mom and dad." Her mother leaned back against the sofa cushion and rolled her shoulders. "It doesn't matter. If it's true, everyone will eventually know."

"It might not be," Poppy insisted. "I refuse to believe Dad cheated on you." She waited for her mom to agree, but Shelley remained silent. "Mom, you know Dad loves you, right?"

"I do." Shelley sighed. "Like I told you before, sweetheart, it's not that simple."

"I'm worried about you," Poppy admitted thickly.

"I'll be okay." Shelley reached out a hand and tentatively placed it on Joey's back. The baby was sleeping peacefully, unaware of the tumultuous emotions surrounding him. Poppy took comfort in the soft sound of his breathing and the warmth of his little body against hers. "He's adorable and innocent."

"I love him so much, Mom." Poppy's voice cracked, and she squeezed her eyes shut.

"It's obvious. I felt the same way when you and your brothers were little. Babies are easy to fall in love with."

Just what Annelise told her. But so were men with dark eyes

and a smile that made her knees go weak. Unfortunately, neither Joey nor Leo truly belonged to Poppy. But she wouldn't share those fears with her mother. She wanted to be the one to offer support, not take it.

"Would you like to hold him?" Poppy's heart tightened as she waited for her mother's answer. "Like you said, Joey is innocent in all of this."

Eventually, her mother nodded, hands trembling as she took the baby. Shelley's gaze softened when Joey made a soft gurgling noise and then burrowed his head in the crook of her neck.

"He's a snuggler," Poppy told her mom.

"I hope you know that the difficulties of this situation don't detract from my admiration for you. I'm glad Joey has you in his life." Shelley cradled the back of the baby's head with one hand and looked at Poppy. "Is it going to be difficult to eventually let him go?"

Poppy swallowed and dashed a tear from the corner of her eye. "Yes, but I knew that going in. Difficult things don't scare me anymore. I can deal with feeling my emotions even when they hurt."

"That's a gift, Poppy." Her mom reached out to hold her hand. "I hope it's one you never lose."

"You taught me." Poppy's voice cracked, but she continued, "You taught me how to love unconditionally, and I know that's how you love Dad. It's hard to see the two of you apart when you love each other so much."

Tears shimmered in her mother's soft blue eyes. "I'm trying to deal with the hard things, too."

"Why not together?" Poppy asked quietly.

"I do love your father." Shelley rested her chin on the top of Joey's head, something Poppy often did when she was holding him because his sweetness brought her a sense of comfort that nothing else offered. "But I let myself get lost in the role of wife and mother. That's on me, not him, but neither of us can deny the distance between us. Maybe we've become too comfortable in our marriage, but the situation with Joey made me see I don't want to settle anymore. I deserve a partner who treasures me, even if I'm not young, exciting or new."

"*Of course* you deserve that," Poppy agreed.

Shelley smiled, although it didn't reach her eyes. "You deserve that, too, sweetie. I might have taught you more than I meant to by devoting myself to your dad so fully. You need to know that you're special for who you are. Don't settle for anything less than a man who makes you feel that every day."

Poppy bit down on her lower lip to keep herself from saying that Leo made her feel special. He valued her and respected her. She'd seen for herself how much he'd changed over the years, but the fact remained that their relationship was based on a convenient arrangement. Convenient for both of them, perhaps, but he wanted it because being with her made his grandfather happy. Not necessarily because it made *him* happy.

"How are things with Leo?" Shelley asked as if she could read Poppy's mind.

"Temporary," Poppy answered before thinking better of it. Their date on Valentine's Day felt like a lifetime ago.

Shelley frowned. "Is that what you want?"

"It's all he's able to give." Her voice sounded sad and resigned even to her own ears.

"Not an answer to my question," her mother said. "Let me teach you something I'm learning only now, my sweet daughter. You are stronger than you know. Strong enough to put your needs and desires out there."

"Look at where that's gotten me in the past. Alone with a string of failed relationships littering the road behind me."

"It's gotten you to a place where those relationships ended because they weren't right. And now you're doing this beautiful, amazing thing for kids who need someone to love them. You have so much love to give. If Leo can't see that, he's a fool. If you make yourself smaller for him, well…"

"I'm the fool," Poppy whispered.

"And I didn't raise a fool." Shelley shifted Joey so she could place an arm around Poppy's shoulder.

Poppy leaned against her mother and took comfort in the warmth of the familiar embrace. It was time she did as her mom said and made her desires known. Maybe Leo would surprise her and be the man she needed him to. Perhaps Poppy would finally get that happily-ever-after she'd always wanted.

CHAPTER TWELVE

"I THOUGHT IT was just a burp, but there was projectile spit-up at the same time he had a blowout diaper. The kittens were prancing through the mess, and Humphrey looked as horrified as I felt."

Leo grinned as he watched his grandfather wipe tears of laughter from his eyes. He loved how much Enzo enjoyed the stories of Leo's escapades in parenting. *Not parenting,* he corrected silently.

Helping Poppy parent.

He was just the helper, not truly committed the way she was. Although if he was capable of commitment, it would be to Poppy and Joey. He'd always told himself he didn't want a serious relation and certainly not marriage. Never marriage. Except a lifetime with Poppy...well, any man would be lucky to have that.

"And you thought grapes could make a mess," Enzo said with another chuckle.

They sat at the farmhouse table in his mother's kitchen while she stood at the counter chopping vegetables for the minestrone soup she was making. Some of the color had returned to his grandfather's cheeks. Although Enzo still seemed to tire more quickly than before the setback, Leo's mother reported that the doctor had been satisfied with his progress during his most recent checkup.

Leo glanced down at his phone, which had remained stubbornly silent for the entire duration of his visit. Poppy had left hours earlier for her meeting with Annelise Wellington, and Leo had expected her to let him know how things went when she returned to the house.

Not that she owed him a play-by-play on her daily movements, but they'd gotten into the habit of keeping each other informed under the guise of coordinating Joey's schedule.

The truth was he liked having somebody to check in with. More importantly, he liked *Poppy* being that somebody.

Enzo finished his last bite of the tomato-and-hummus sandwich Martina had served for lunch and pushed back from the table. Leo also stood and picked up his grandfather's empty plate before Enzo could.

"I'll clean up for you, Papa," Leo offered. The old man had taken the last few bites around a series of yawns. "Why don't you head to your room for a rest?"

"I'm not an invalid," he grumbled. "I can put my own plate in the dishwasher."

Before Leo could answer, his mother snorted. "Everyone knows you're capable of clearing your plate, but you should never reject an offer of help, especially from my beloved son. Leo has been an expert at avoiding the dishwasher until recently—one more thing to credit to Poppy, I presume." His mother raised a brow.

It was Leo's turn to grumble. "I knew how to load an empty dishwasher before Poppy."

"Knowing and doing are two different things," his mother retorted, making Enzo smile again.

"I'm proud of you, Leo," his grandfather said.

While the words should have made Leo happy, his gut twisted. He appreciated his grandfather's pride but felt undeserving of it in some deep part of his soul. Especially given that his whole motivation for helping with Poppy had been contrived to do exactly that.

"I think I will take a little rest after all," Enzo said as he shuffled toward the back staircase that led to the second-floor bedrooms from the kitchen. "Bring Poppy and the baby to see me again. Little Joey makes me feel younger than I am, and that's always a good thing."

"I will, Papa, very soon. I should get back to the office," he told his mother after loading the dishwasher. "Unless you need help here?"

"No, I've got it handled." She wiped her hands on a dish towel and patted his cheek the way she used to when he was a kid. "But can you stay and talk for a minute?"

"Sure, Mom, what's up? Is it about the new label redesign? Gia said you had some thoughts on that."

"It's about you and Poppy Fortune."

Leo tried not to react, but something serious in his mother's gaze made him wary.

"I promise I'm even more helpful at her place, and we had a great time on Valentine's Day. Thank you again for watching Joey. You were right, as always. She deserves to be treated like a queen."

"And that's what you're doing?" He heard the doubt in his mother's tone, which grated at his pride.

"I hope so."

"She's special," his mother said, as if that would explain the reason for this conversation, one he definitely hadn't bargained for.

He held his hands up high and wiggled them. "Preaching to the choir." His mother didn't laugh at the lame joke.

"What are your intentions when it comes to Poppy Fortune?"

Leo tried not to cringe at the bluntness of the question and the fact that he didn't know how to answer it. "Isn't that something her parents should be asking?"

Once again, his mother didn't smile at his attempt at humor. "Her parents are dealing with a lot. Otherwise, I'm sure they would have asked you that question long before now. But *I'm* asking it now. Your previous relationship with her was short lived, but I know she meant something to you. This is a second chance if you're smart enough to take it, Leo."

She reached for his arm, but he stepped away, in no mood to pretend this wasn't a gently worded interrogation.

"My intention is to help her with the baby. Don't you think I'm doing a good job of it?"

"I've seen you with Joey." His mother smiled almost wistfully. "It's obvious you care about him, and I know you, Leo. You're fantastic at meeting a goal when you set your mind to it. But I'm not talking about your mind right now. I'm talking about your heart *and* Poppy's heart."

"Poppy loves Joey," he said, as if she needed him to defend her.

"Yes." Martina nodded. "I think it's quite possible that she also loves you."

His heart felt like it was seizing in his chest. The words were thrilling and terrifying in equal measure.

"We're friends, Mom. We agreed on that."

"You're a lot of things, Leo. You are smart, passionate and committed to this family. I appreciate all of those. But I never took you to be a coward."

"Ouch."

"You need to hear this," his mother insisted. "If you can't be the man Poppy needs, and not just when it comes to Joey, but as a true partner, you have to let her go."

He felt his head snap back like his mother had slapped him. And he couldn't even be angry with her because he deserved her doubt. He didn't want to hurt Poppy, but he also wasn't ready to let her go. Nowhere near ready.

"Come on, Mom. It isn't as if I kidnapped her. We both understand the arrangement."

Martina's lips rolled together as if she was holding back for his benefit. Finally, she blew out a breath. "It isn't as simple as you're making it out to be. Emotions are complicated—*people* are complicated. When a woman opens her heart and lets a man in, he has a responsibility to either meet her halfway or admit that he can't. Pretending only leads to heartbreak for everyone, whether or not your intentions are honorable."

His mother's grip tightened on the dish towel, her knuckles as white as tiny snowballs.

"Mom, is this about Poppy and me, or are you talking about Dad? You know he loved you."

"I'm not speaking ill of your father. He was a good man. He did the best he could with a life he didn't necessarily want."

"What do you mean? Of course Dad wanted this life. He wanted you." He hated the way his stomach twisted in response to her words. Hated that despite his denial, a part of him knew it was true.

"He wanted freedom. He wanted to travel and see the world, just like you did before he died and you took over."

"I had plenty of time to travel after college," he argued. "I always understood I'd come back. I'm fine with it. What does any of this have to do with Poppy?"

"I know you care about her, but sometimes that isn't enough. Don't commit to something to make your grandfather happy. It isn't fair to you or her."

"She's Joey's foster parent. It's temporary, just like…"

His mother sighed. "Just like your relationship. I know what I see when I look at her. When she looks at the baby and you, how things started might have been temporary, but it could be more if you want it to."

Did he want that? Leo's heart began to beat an unsteady rhythm. Sure, he'd considered what might happen between him and Poppy, but having his mother question him felt different. It felt real, and he wasn't sure he could deal with it. But could he let her and Joey go at this point? He'd messed up his chance with her five years earlier and the regret had never fully faded. Now he was so much more invested and it terrified him.

"Am I like Dad?" he asked, unsure whether he wanted to hear the answer. "I know I look like him, but is it more than that?"

"There are parts of you that remind me of your father, just like there are ways your sisters take after him. He had a gift with the grapes and your leadership capabilities. Antonia's financial acumen." She smiled and shook her head. "Gia embodies his way of charming the customers. Franco had everything, but he didn't appreciate this life. It wasn't the one that filled his soul."

"I'm sorry, Mom," he said, but she waved away his apology.

"We muddled through, and there were aspects of our life

together that he loved desperately. Being a father was on that list. I can't tell you what you want, Leo, but whatever it is, I want you to have it. Of course, it would make me happy if you chose Poppy, but I also understand if you don't want all the responsibility that comes with her. I think she will as well, but you can't pretend."

Leo's chest burned with longing, but he couldn't name what he yearned for.

"If this place starts to make you feel confined, we'll find a way to give you space and freedom."

Never before had anyone acknowledged that he'd taken on the mantle of CEO without being given the chance to decide if that was the role he truly wanted.

His mother seemed to take his lack of an answer as a sign. "Is that what you want?" she asked. "More freedom?"

"I'm involved with a woman whose life is the opposite of what I thought I wanted," he admitted, more to himself than his mother. Then he looked at her. "I don't want to hurt her."

"I know, son, but if you act like someone you're not to make other people happy, then you're the one who's going to be hurt. I don't want that."

His phone trilled, breaking the tense heaviness of emotion that hung in the air with a series of rapid-fire chimes. "Must be something important," Martina said as he moved toward the kitchen table where he'd left it.

He muttered a curse and then glanced up at his mom. "Joey's sick." He pocketed the phone, already heading toward the door.

Her eyes widening in concern, his mother took a step toward him. "What's wrong?"

"I'm not sure," he replied. "Poppy texted that he seemed drowsy this morning and lethargic when she left her mom's, but he'd spiked a fever by the time she got home. She called the pediatrician, and they told her to head to the ER. I'm meeting her there."

Martina pressed a hand to her heart. "Babies get sick, Leo," she said reassuringly. "The doctors will take care of him. He'll be fine."

"Of course, he will," Leo agreed. "I'll call you later, Mom."

He dashed from the house to his truck, and gravel spit up behind him as he peeled out of the driveway. Joey would be fine. He had to be because Leo couldn't imagine his life if something happened to the boy.

POPPY DISCONNECTED THE call and leaned back against the uncomfortable chair in the small pediatric unit at the county hospital. She could see the doorway to Joey's room from where she sat. He was being monitored so if anything happened while she was out of the room, she'd know.

Her mother had offered to drive over and keep Poppy company, but it was already nearly nine at night, so there'd be no point. As soon as Leo returned from gathering a few things for her overnight stay with Joey, Poppy would climb into the reclining chair next to his bassinet and settle in for what promised to be a restless few hours of sleep.

Her phone pinged with messages from both her brothers and her dad, sending good thoughts for the baby. She closed her eyes and willed herself not to cry. Tears wouldn't do any good, and Joey's fever had finally broken an hour earlier, so the on-call pediatrician hoped he'd be discharged in the morning.

It was difficult to believe how much had changed from a couple weeks earlier when she'd spent the night at this same hospital waiting to take Joey home. At that point, she'd felt sympathy for the abandoned baby and a call to help care for him.

Now she loved the boy with her whole heart.

And speaking of love…she watched Leo exit the elevator and walk down the hall toward her. There'd been no hesitation in her decision to text him first after talking to the pediatrician, and he'd been waiting at the entrance of the ER when she arrived with Joey.

Leo Leonetti continued to blow her away with the way he'd gone all in with her and Joey. It still felt somewhat baffling that a man who professed to be almost allergic to relationships so easily gave her what she needed, both in his support of Joey and the way he made Poppy feel.

She didn't think that kind of dedication could be faked, and although he hadn't spoken the words aloud, she couldn't help but believe his stance on commitment and romantic love might be changing. Their time together had certainly transformed Poppy, or at least made her rethink her views on dating.

Yes, she'd had some failures when it came to men, but she realized now she still believed in love. She wanted love, even with the scandal surrounding her family and learning that her parents' relationship wasn't perfect.

She had been working from an ideal in her mind that maybe no one could live up to, even herself. Leo might not say the words, but his actions, the way he looked at her, held and touched her body—all of those spoke to their growing bond.

But Poppy also understood after the conversation with her mother that she wanted the words, too. Not flowery sonnets or grand gestures, but she wanted to know that the man she cared about loved her.

She deserved someone who would put her first, not just let her do the heavy lifting. She knew Leo could be that man, even if he didn't realize it yet. The conversation with her mother had been a light-bulb moment for Poppy, pushing her out of her comfort zone and into admitting she *did* want more. Maybe Leo needed the same thing.

She stood as he entered the room. He didn't hesitate to wrap his arms around her after he deposited her bag on the carpeted floor. Who was she kidding?

Poppy had already fallen hard and fast. She wanted a real romance with Leo, at least once they were certain Joey would be okay.

But at the moment, she couldn't focus on any future other than Joey's and the baby getting better.

"It's going to be okay," Leo said, able to read her thoughts again. "His fever's gone, and he's getting good care."

She let out a little sob, her worry coalescing into tears after holding them back for the baby's sake. "I know, and I'm so grateful for the doctors and nurses. But why, Leo? Why did he get that fever? We don't have an answer, and what if it's my fault?"

"It's not your fault," he assured her in that deep, rumbly tone.

She pulled back to look into his deep brown eyes, searching them for some inkling of the doubt swirling through her.

"You don't know that. I had him out in that coffee shop, and who knows what kind of germs other customers were breathing on him? Maybe the guy we shared an elevator with at the hotel had some kind of virus—"

"Sometimes babies get sick."

"But why did *my* baby get sick?" she demanded like Leo could give her a satisfying answer.

"*Our* baby," he responded, with an emphasis that made her heart lurch, "is going to be okay. You noticed it right away and called the doctor. You took care of him."

"I hated that night he spent in the hospital after being left on my parents' porch, and I hate this even more."

"But you're here with him." He smoothed her hair away from her face. "And you have me if you want."

"They said only one person could stay in the room."

He didn't miss a beat in offering, "I'll sleep on one of these chairs. If you want me to stay, I will."

It was tempting to accept the offer. Even before Leo had started spending every night in her bed, the fact that he was asleep down the hall gave her so much comfort.

"But what about tomorrow? One of us needs to be awake. Plus, Humphrey and the kittens will be nervous without me there. You don't mind staying at my house on your own?"

"Of course I'll stay," he replied gruffly.

He hugged her again, and they stood together for several minutes in companionable silence. Poppy didn't need him to speak. As she was coming to rely on, his actions told her everything she needed to know.

Leo held her hand as they returned to Joey's room, and while she washed her face and brushed her teeth in the connecting bathroom, he conferred with the nurse, then fed Joey and changed his diaper. Ready for bed, Poppy ran a hand over the boy's forehead, which remained blessedly cool.

The nurse checked the output in his diaper, and instead of returning him to the bassinet, Leo sat on the chair next to the bassinet as if he wasn't ready to let the baby go.

Poppy's heart felt like it was bursting with a myriad of emotions. This incident reminded her about the uncertainty of life and how important it was not to let fear stop her from living the way she wanted.

After Leo gently tucked Joey and her into their respective beds, Poppy watched the door close behind him, staring at the acoustic tiles on the hospital room ceiling for a long time before drifting off to sleep.

Leo cared for her. Deeply. She knew it in her gut.

Once things were back to normal with Joey, she would tell him her feelings and hopefully give him the confidence to acknowledge his. No matter what happened with the DNA tests and how long she got to keep Joey, his presence in her life would always be a blessing because it had taught her that some things were truly worth fighting for.

CHAPTER THIRTEEN

As Leo opened the door to Poppy's house the following evening, he was greeted by an incredible smell, along with music from the kitchen.

He turned the corner from the entryway to see Poppy dancing around the island with Joey in her arms. The day had been a rough one with production delays and frustrated retail outlets. Plus, there was the constant worry in the back of his mind about how the baby was doing, even though she sent him some pics of Joey cooing and kicking on his activity blanket. The baby seemed to have made a quick and complete recovery from his scary fever the previous night, but Leo had trouble shaking his anxiety.

His dad had seemed fine when he said goodbye to him before that last trip to Italy, and he'd been dead two days after Leo landed. His grandfather had been agitated at their dinner, but not alarmingly so, and then he'd wound up in the hospital. This was part of the reason Leo didn't trust himself to focus on other areas of his life besides work. He could leave stressful tasks at the office overnight. No matter how bad things were, they'd still be waiting the following morning.

People, however, weren't the same. They could get hurt—or die—and there was nothing he could do about it if he wasn't there to protect them, and maybe not even then.

Loving people simply wasn't safe, and his heart expanded in his chest watching Poppy twirl the baby. She had no rhythm, making her staccato dance moves even more charming.

Leo couldn't continue to ignore how he felt about her, not when they were together playing house and family each night. The way to save himself from being hurt again was to keep his heart out of the mix. As much as it killed him to admit it, doing that meant not letting himself fall in love with her.

He just hoped it wasn't already too late...

Poppy gave a startled cry that quickly turned into laughter as she noticed him standing in the doorway.

"Care to join us?" She held out a hand. It was all he could do to keep himself from reaching for her, to refrain from dropping to his knees and begging her never to leave. Never to put herself at any risk...never to break his heart.

But that was a promise no one could make. He gave a slight shake of his head. "I left my dancing shoes at the office."

She scrunched up her nose. "You're just trying to avoid me tromping all over your feet again."

He wanted to avoid a lot of things, and what a stupid coward he was for all of it.

She gave the Bluetooth speaker the command to turn off, then approached him. "How about a quieter greeting?" She leaned in to kiss him.

He wanted to freeze this moment and memorize everything about it. The warmth of her, this kitchen and the way he felt at home every time he walked into it.

Poppy's beautiful green eyes, the color of the soft shoots of the first leaves growing on the grapevines. The way she always smelled like sunshine. Even on a dark February night. The baby nestled in her arms and the way he'd captured Leo's heart from the first time he'd held him...

"It smells delicious," he said, grasping for some neutral subject to help him find purchase when it felt like he was free-falling off an emotional cliff. "I was planning on takeout. I thought you'd be exhausted after last night."

Poppy grinned, her eyes sparkling. "Actually, I feel energized with relief that Joey is himself again. That fever freaked me out, you know?"

He nodded and took a step away from her. "Still, you didn't have to make dinner." It was a stupid thing to say. Poppy made supper most nights when she was at the house, just like he did if he was taking a turn with the baby in the afternoon.

It doesn't mean anything, he reminded himself. *It's food. People have to eat, typically three times a day.*

She handed Joey to him, and Leo tried not to notice the baby's familiar weight, warmth or the milky smell that radiated from him along with the scent of lavender.

Poppy must have bathed him, which always made the boy kick and coo delightedly. Leo loved bath time. He was going to miss bath time. If someone would have suggested a few years ago that such a simple task would mean so much to him, he would have laughed in their face. He'd been so sure he wasn't built for anything other than his work and having fun. No-strings-attached fun. But maybe there was more to him than he thought and he could be that man for Poppy and Joey.

She grabbed two potholders sitting on the counter and opened the oven door.

"It's three-cheese baked manicotti," she said. "Your mom called earlier to check on Joey, and I asked her about your favorite meal. She gave me the recipe along with instructions for making tiramisu."

Beads of sweat popped out on Leo's forehead. "You made tiramisu?"

She placed the red casserole dish on top of the stove and shrugged, her smile still wide and trusting. "I thought we could both use a home-cooked meal, and I wanted to do something for you."

He shook his head but didn't move, rooted in place. "You don't owe me anything, Poppy."

"You've been so supportive and helpful. I couldn't have managed this without you, Leo. I wouldn't have wanted to either. This is my way of thanking you for it."

"We have an arrangement." His voice sounded hollow. "I'm

helping you because it makes me look good to my grandfather. It makes him happy."

She inclined her head. "Enzo is the best. I love watching him with Joey but impressing him was how this started. It's become more now, hasn't it?"

He forced himself not to smile even though it killed him. "Sure," he relented. "We're friends. We'll continue to be friends."

A crease appeared between her brows. "You have to know it's more than that for me, Leo. I—"

"Don't say it, Poppy. You can't say it. We had an arrangement. Eventually, those DNA tests will come back, and you'll know the identity of Joey's father. From there, you can track down his mother and this—" he waved a hand in the general direction of her house "—will be over."

She stared at him for a long moment and said, "This is my life. My home. It's not going to be over, and I don't want it to."

"You know what I mean."

"I do," she agreed. A chill entered her tone, a cold completely at odds with the warmth she'd exuded moments earlier. His fault. *Always* his fault.

"We're friends," he repeated. "Nothing has to change if we don't make it."

"I love you," she said simply.

The words hung between them like dandelion fluff floating on the air in the heat of summer.

"You love the idea of us," he answered. "Caring for a newborn was overwhelming at first, and I relieved some of that pressure. But it's different now. You don't need me."

She walked toward him, her features stripped of emotion. The only tell that revealed the control she struggled with was her fists clenched at her sides.

"Don't mansplain my feelings to me, Leo. That's low, even for you."

He didn't argue with her accusation because he felt so low it was like his stomach scraped the floor.

"I'm sorry, Poppy."

"For what?" she demanded, lifting Joey from his arms like

he no longer had a right to hold the baby. No, she wouldn't do that. They had an agreement. They were a team.

"I'm not the one changing things." He ran a hand through his hair, grasping for a way to make her understand. "I can't be the white-picket-fence partner you want."

"I don't *want* a fence," she shot back.

"You know what I mean." He blew out a frustrated breath. How had things gone to hell so quickly?

"I want *you*."

Damn it. Why did she have to keep going? Was she trying to wreck them both?

"Please, Poppy." He crossed his arms over his chest to keep from reaching for her. "Things are fine the way they are. If you could just—"

"Fine isn't good enough." She rubbed a hand over Joey's back when the boy began to fuss, likely attuned to the tension between the only caregivers he knew. "I told you I love you. I'm not lowering my expectations or what I want from our relationship because you can't handle it."

"We had an *arrangement*," he repeated through clenched teeth, willing her to understand what this was doing to him. To both of them. "Love wasn't part of it."

"I can't tell whether you're lying on purpose or you really believe the lines you're trying to feed me." She backed away, and he wanted to shout in protest. "It doesn't matter. I'm not settling. This isn't me asking for too much—it's about what you can't give. You've been a huge help, and I appreciate that. I'm glad your grandfather has enjoyed watching you in this role with Joey. You're a natural, Leo."

She spoke the words sincerely and he wanted to be grateful, but the compliment lodged between his ribs like a knife. "Why do I feel like there's a *but* coming?"

She shrugged. "But you missed your calling as an actor because you sure had me fooled. I thought you cared about me and not just because of the baby."

"I *do* care."

"Not in the way I need you to."

He didn't argue. What could he say? That she deserved better...more than he could give. Weren't his track record and his father's unhappiness proof of that?

"You should go." Those three words felt like a round of bullets to his heart.

"It doesn't have to be this way."

"What other way would you have it?" She posed the question like she was asking about the weather. Leo scrambled for an answer, but he had nothing to offer. Nothing that would make her feel better or ease the pain piercing his gut.

He took a step toward the hallway leading to the bedrooms, but Poppy held up a hand.

"I need you to go now. I'll pack your stuff, and you can pick it up from the porch tomorrow morning. Thank you again for your help. I wasn't lying when I said I couldn't have done this without you."

Her green eyes were sad when they met his. "I wasn't lying about any of it."

Something about the sentence felt unfinished, as if insinuating that *he* was the liar. And maybe he had been lying to both of them, acting as if he could handle more. Pretending he could be the man she said she saw in him. The one his grandpa so desperately wanted him to be.

He should fight or argue. A bigger man would. A better man.

Leo only turned and walked out of the house into the dark, cold night, feeling more alone than he ever had. He understood, even if Poppy didn't, that she could have done everything without him. He hadn't been the hero to step in and rescue her.

She was plenty capable of that on her own, and she'd done her best to save him. But a person could only be saved if they wanted to. Although anyone would tell him his logic was twisted, it seemed safer to remain in the solitary confinement he'd sentenced his heart to. Because as much as that treacherous organ ached as he drove away, he knew the risk of opening it fully would be so much worse.

"I KNOW IT sucks for you, Pop-Tart, but I have to say, this is the best meal I've had in a long time. I should text Leo Leonetti and thank him for being a doofus."

Poppy offered Rafe a weak smile across the table. The baked manicotti she'd made had gone cold on the stove while she sat with Joey in her arms and cried her eyes out after Leo left.

Her tears weren't because she'd been a fool to let Leo in, the way she'd felt after almost every one of her other breakups. This time, she didn't regret loving Leo. The only way to claim the future she wanted was to keep her heart open, no matter how many times it got crushed in the process.

Somehow, she couldn't imagine getting over this one. Yet, her tears had been as much for Leo as for herself. He loved her. Despite all the stupid things he'd said and the ways he'd denied his feelings, she *knew* he loved her.

How sad was it that he was too scared to admit it? Too committed to staying safe that he couldn't take what she offered and reciprocate those emotions.

Rafe had texted her about a half hour after Leo walked out. On his way home, he'd seen the truck speeding away from the ranch and had been concerned about another potential issue with Joey.

Poppy'd started to return her brother's message with a vague everything is fine text of her own.

But no. Part of being true to herself was acknowledging the good with the bad and asking for support. Being willing to accept it instead of feeling like her role—the only way she could add value—was offering it to the people in her life.

So she'd dashed off the truth to her brother.

I told him I loved him. He drove away like the devil was chasing him.

Rafe's response had been immediate.

I'll be there in five.

She had just enough time to splash cold water on her face and dry her cheeks before her brother burst through the front door. He'd been spitting mad and admitted he'd been unsure whether to start at her house or chase after Leo and knock his lights out.

"No lights knocking," Poppy'd told him, then instructed him to reheat portions of the manicotti while she put Joey down for bed.

She was happy Rafe enjoyed the meal because her first bite tasted like sawdust in her mouth.

She sipped on a glass of wine, a pinot grigio Leo had brought over at some point, special from his private collection. She'd expected to share the bottle with him, but they wouldn't be sharing anything.

Not anymore.

"Maybe I came on too strong," she murmured, even though she didn't believe it.

One of her brother's thick brows rose. "You're perfect, sis, and I'm sure however you treated Leo was also perfect."

"You're right. It wasn't too strong. The truth is, I didn't come on to him at all. I just fell in love."

"Oh, Pop Rocks." Rafe sighed like he was disappointed but not surprised.

"He loves me, too," she said because that's what she believed to her core.

"Then what's the problem?"

"Men are dumb."

Her brother laughed as he stabbed a piece of pasta. "I won't argue that point. It seemed like Leo was having a good time with you and Joey. Any man who willingly changes diapers and scoops cat litter is either a masochist or in love."

He paused with the fork almost to his mouth. "They might be one and the same."

She dipped her fork into the sauce and tasted it. "This is good."

"Delicious," Rafe confirmed. "You said it's Leo's favorite?"

"According to his mom."

"Then he must have been extra spooked to walk away before eating."

Poppy rolled her eyes. "I didn't give him a choice. I kicked him out."

Rafe stopped chewing and stared at her. "*You* ended it?"

"Yes. Why do you sound shocked? I told him I loved him, and he told me not to."

"Rough." Rafe cringed then placed his fork on the table. "I'm surprised because you typically hang on until the bitter end. Good for you. It's about time you started owning what a catch you are. I didn't think Leo was as big of an idiot as some of the other guys you've dated, but maybe I was wrong."

"My previous boyfriends weren't idiots."

Rafe definitely thought they had been by the look on his face. A wistful smile played in the corners of his mouth. "Bridget used to get so mad at how you'd let them walk all over you."

Poppy's face burned, but so did her heart. Rafe very rarely spoke about the wife and daughter he lost in that accident.

"I should have listened to her. Although you could argue that Leo and I never officially dated, so maybe he can't be considered a boyfriend."

"He helped to raise a baby, lived with you, took you out for the big V Day. I assume there were benefits between friends?"

"Oh, my gosh, we can't talk about *benefits*. You are my brother."

"I guess you don't need to answer because your voice is reaching decibels I didn't even know were possible for a human to hear. That tells me everything."

She pushed back from the table and picked up their bowls to take them to the sink. "Enough about the pathetic state of my life. Tell me something about you."

"Not much to tell." Rafe crossed the kitchen and leaned one hip against the counter. "I've been working on the Gift of Fortune program, but things are stalled because one of the recipients is ghosting me."

"Not interested?" Poppy asked, hiding her smile. Rafe wasn't used to being ignored.

"Hard to tell since she won't return my calls." He shrugged. "I don't get it. The woman, Heidi, is a single mom with twins. She has to need a break."

Poppy laughed. "I'm taking care of one baby so I can only imagine the effort two takes on your own."

"Right. So why won't she respond to the invitation? It's a free week at the ranch."

The frustration in his tone chased away her smile. This was important to her brother, and she admired what he was trying to do with the generous program.

"You never know what's going on in another person's life, Rafe."

"Tell me about it," he muttered.

"But it's amazing that you're working so hard to bring happiness to people who might not find it on their own. Give it some time."

"Thanks, Pop." Rafe blew out a breath then gently grabbed her arm and circled her wrist with his big hand. "You deserve to be happy, too."

"That makes two of us," she told him quietly. His lips thinned as he released her to stand.

Her brother processed grief in his solitary way, but she didn't like to see anyone in her family sad. Rafe hadn't been happy for a long time.

"You want a piece of tiramisu for the road?" she asked. "I'm going to take some to Dad tomorrow."

"I want a bigger piece than you give him. I might take a selfie of me eating it and send it to Leo with the one-finger salute."

Poppy sighed then smiled, as her brother expected her to. Her family members were experts at changing the subject and lightening the mood. "Do you think Dad could be Joey's father?"

She took the glass dish of tiramisu out of the refrigerator, then grabbed plastic to-go containers from under the island, her brother silent at that question.

"I want to say no and believe it. Dad is very convincing in his denials."

"But how do we explain the text? That's pretty damning."

Rafe shrugged. "Sure, but if a person was so determined for the truth to come out, why would they send the message anonymously?"

Poppy loaded a generous square of the dessert into a to-go container, then placed the lid on it, licking a bit of cream off her thumb. "Good point. Mom says the separation isn't just about Joey. It's hard to fathom that when they always seemed to get along."

Rafe placed his hands over hers. "Maybe that's the lesson. Things might seem okay on the surface, but that doesn't mean they are."

She hugged her brother. "One of these days, everything will be okay again."

Rafe nodded. "You'll be okay, Pop."

She locked the door behind him, and Poppy leaned her back against it. The tears had dried, but her heart felt empty and hollow.

Humphrey climbed off the couch and with a soft whine, trotted over to her, head butting her thigh. "I miss him, too," she told the dog, "but the good news for you is that the empty space in my bed is available again."

His tail wagged as if he understood her words. Poppy walked to her bedroom, brokenhearted but proud of herself for staying true to the woman she wanted to be. If Leo Leonetti couldn't give it to her, she'd find it on her own. Maybe that was the lesson all along.

CHAPTER FOURTEEN

THE NEXT MORNING, Poppy's emptiness had shifted into a fiery ball of anger. She was trying her best to be brave, take risks and not worry about what other people thought as long as she followed her heart. Yet she was surrounded by people, men in particular, who refused to show that kind of courage.

She might not be happy that her mother had moved out but admired Shelley's willingness to ignore potential gossip and be true to herself.

Leo wasn't doing that. She no longer knew if the man she'd fallen in love with over these weeks together was the true Leo. Did fear prevent him from becoming the man she saw when she looked at him?

Or maybe she had it backward, and he truly didn't want a commitment but was too afraid to admit that and disappoint his grandfather.

Then there was her oldest brother, who'd loved with all of his heart but wore his grief at the tragic loss he'd suffered like a badge of honor. Poppy knew his late wife wouldn't have wanted that for him. Bridget would have given him a kick in the butt to get back on that horse and open his heart again.

Poppy hoped he eventually met a woman who could convince him to do that.

And as for her father...

She entered her childhood home without bothering to knock and let the door slam shut behind her.

"I'm in the study," Garth called out.

Poppy practically stomped down the hallway to the wood-paneled room, her father's inner sanctum. As a kid, she'd sneak into the library to sit at the chair behind his desk. She and her brothers weren't allowed to play in this room, but Poppy hadn't been playing. Even as an eight-year-old girl, she'd been thinking about family and the future.

She knew what she wanted, and while a few failed relationships had forced her off course, she was back and not in the mood to listen to any more excuses, rationalizations—or God forbid—gaslighting.

"Hello, my beautiful girl," her father said, studying her over the top of his tortoiseshell readers. "What's all that?"

In addition to Joey's car seat slung over one arm, Poppy held a plate of manicotti and half the leftover tiramisu. The rest would go to the staff lounge at the spa, but her father had a big sweet tooth. Poppy might be angry, but she still loved the guy.

"I brought you leftovers. I'll put them in the fridge in a minute." Poppy placed Joey's infant carrier on the round work table that sat in one corner.

"A visit from my best girl and homemade lunch." Garth raised his hands in the air. "Am I a lucky man or what?"

Poppy stared at him for several long seconds, waiting for him to recant that bit of tomfoolery. When he didn't, she shook her head in exasperation. "Seriously, Dad? Right now, we are going with door number two, which is *or what.*"

He blinked at her, clearly shocked at being called out on his pretend joviality. His face crumpled, shoulders slumping as he took off the reading glasses and placed them on the desk.

"Before this month, that statement would have been true. I've always been lucky." He stared at the black blotter covering the walnut wood like he was studying tea leaves. "Lucky to live on this ranch with your mother. Lucky to have three amazing kids. I don't know how it all went so wrong so fast."

Poppy stepped closer. "Do you mean that? Do you truly have no idea what happened between you and Mom?"

Her father's head snapped up, and he jabbed a finger in the direction of the carrier. "I know for damn sure I'm not that boy's father."

At the sound of shouting, Joey let out a weak cry. Poppy flashed her father a quelling glare, then went to unstrap the boy and lifted him into her arms.

"He isn't the only reason she left."

"She hadn't packed her bags before then."

Poppy came forward and lowered herself into one of the leather chairs in front of her father's desk. She'd been allowed into his lair upon invitation as a kid and had loved sitting across from him doing her homework while he managed the guest ranch from the same seat his father had. The same chair where her great-grandfather before him had sat. So much history in this house, and yet some of the things that needed to be said were kept silent.

"Mom says the two of you have been having problems for a while."

Garth frowned like the words were hard to acknowledge but eventually nodded.

"I didn't cheat on her," he repeated in a solemn tone.

It might be naivety or wishful thinking, but Poppy believed him.

"Then how did it get to this point, and why aren't you fighting for her?"

Her questions registered slowly on her father's face, a slight pull at the corners of his mouth and a flash of uncertainty in his dark eyes. "I'm not sure I know how on either count," he admitted finally.

"Dad."

"It's true. Your mom and I have had an easy go of it. Sure, we've dealt with issues over the years. Everyone does, but..." He pulled at his thick salt-and-pepper hair with one hand. "It's embarrassing to admit, especially to my daughter, but I've let her do the heavy lifting on the relationship side. Your mom is the glue that keeps this family and our marriage together."

Poppy swallowed back the emotion that swelled in her throat. "She's the glue, but she has needs, too, Dad."

"I appreciate that." He shook his head. "I'm just not sure I know how to meet them."

How odd to be in the position of offering relationship advice to her father, a turn of events neither of them likely had expected.

Yet, in some ways, this was another example of Poppy stepping out of her comfort zone to be brave. She wanted to make a difference, not only in the world but in the lives of her family. That couldn't happen if she didn't speak up. Secrets and assumptions wouldn't help anyone.

"You might be terrible at it," she told her father, earning a disbelieving snort. "But you won't know if you don't try, Dad. If I've learned anything from taking care of Joey this month and the way things turned out with Leo, it's that being willing to fail is the only path to success. It makes the journey that much sweeter. If you love Mom, you've got to try to find a way to make her believe it again. Not just for your sake but for hers. Trust me when I tell you that relationships are way more satisfying when both people put in the effort."

"Is that what you and Leo have?"

Poppy breathed out a sigh of relief, realizing her brother hadn't left her house and immediately shared her latest failure with the rest of the family.

She shook her head. "I thought so, but he didn't feel the same, so I ended things."

"Oh, honey, I'm sorry. The right guy is out there for you. I know that."

Her heart still rebelled against the idea that Leo wasn't that man, but she nodded. "I don't have regrets, Dad, because I tried. I refuse to compromise what I value. Not anymore."

She cradled the back of Joey's head with her hand, the feel of his downy-soft hair soothing her the way it always did.

"Joey might have been the catalyst to our current upheaval, but maybe that's also a blessing. No matter who his father turns out to be, this situation has forced us to reevaluate our lives and behavior. It's allowed us to put the focus back on what matters."

"So what you're telling me is that I managed to raise a daughter—" Garth rose from his chair and walked around the side of the desk "—who is not only beautiful, sweet and funny but also way smarter than her father."

Poppy grinned at him then stood. He wrapped his big arms around her, the way he'd been doing for as long as she could remember.

Her dad was a good man, not perfect, but *perfect for her* and, hopefully, for her mother. He drew back slightly and placed a hand on Joey's back.

"May I hold him?"

Nodding, she shifted the baby to Garth's arms. "It's going to be so difficult to say goodbye when the time comes."

"Maybe it won't come to that." Garth supported Joey's head and neck as he lifted him to eye level. "This little fella couldn't find a better mother. Although I still don't think he resembles any of us, I sense the Fortune spirit in him. He's been through more in a month of life than he should have, but he's going to be strong like you and your mother are."

He drew the baby close again and met Poppy's gaze. "You mentioned loving Joey. How do your feelings stand with Leo? Do I need to shake some sense into that boy?"

Poppy laughed softly. "You sound like Rafe. I didn't fall in love with Leo on purpose, but it happened just the same."

"Because of the time the two of you spent together caring for the baby?"

Poppy thought about the question then shook her head. "Joey brought us together, and the proximity moved things along faster, but I fell in love with the man Leo is now all on my own. I like who he is and who I am with him. He makes me believe I'm capable of so much. I love how he sees me. I love…him."

"Like I said, Poppy-girl, you're a smart kid. But to fall for a man who can't give you what you need…" Garth trailed off.

"And you're the smartest man I know, Dad, so don't let Mom go."

She watched his chest rise and fall with the long breath. "I'll do my best, sweetheart." Poppy's phone dinged, and she took it out of her back pocket, secretly hoping Leo had reached out.

Nope. She read the text from the spa's manager, Benita, and glanced back at her dad. "Can you hold him for a minute while

I put the leftovers in your fridge? Then I need to go. We're debuting a new skincare line at the spa, and the products were supposed to arrive tomorrow, but they were delivered this morning. I want to be there to organize things."

"What about Joey?" Dad bounced the baby in his arms. "Are you and Leo still caring for him together given how things stand with you?"

"Leo and I aren't anything. I'll take him with me. Everyone loves Joey at the spa, so I'll leave him in the daycare room for a bit. I'm on my own again."

"You're never on your own as long as I'm around. Joey is a cutie, and I'm here by myself right now. He can stay with me for a couple of hours."

"Did you just offer to babysit?" Poppy tried not to gape.

Garth flashed a sheepish grin. "Your mom isn't the only person I should be treating with more care. I've been focused on what this baby means to our family from a DNA standpoint. But there's still the matter of you, Poppy, and the huge thing you've done by taking him into your home and heart."

"It wasn't hard."

"Because you are something special. I haven't recognized that as much as I should, and it's not simply about Joey. The staff at the spa adore you. You support every single person in this family without fail. The whole fact that you are willing to be a foster parent says so much about your character. I don't know what's going through Leo's mind. But it's about him. Not you. *You* are amazing."

She bit down on the inside of her cheek to keep the tears from leaking once again. Stupid tears. Leo had told her she was amazing, but in the end it hadn't mattered.

"Thanks, Dad."

"Thank you for being a better daughter to me than I probably deserve."

"That isn't how love works." She lifted up on her toes to kiss his cheek. "You don't have to earn or do something to deserve my love. I'm happy to give it freely."

"I don't take that for granted," he said gruffly. "No one should."

She grabbed the to-go containers and then picked up the diaper bag from the thick wool rug to place it on the table. "Clean diapers and a ready-made bottle are in here. If you need anything, call or text me. I'll keep my phone close."

Her father smiled. "Don't worry about us. I may be out of practice, but I changed plenty of diapers with you and your brothers. We'll be fine."

"Thanks, Dad. I love you."

"Love you, too," he said.

She placed the leftovers in the stainless steel refrigerator then retraced her steps, pausing at the study's doorway. Her father stood in front of the bookcases, lined with books and framed photos of their family and past generations of Fortunes. He balanced Joey in one arm as he picked up each of the frames and introduced the baby to members of the Fortune clan.

It warmed Poppy's heart and defused the residual anger she'd felt upon waking, filling her heart with a sweetness she hadn't expected.

She missed Leo like she missed the sun on a cloudy day but knew if she waited long enough, the light would find her again. Eventually.

"HEY, PAPA. HOW about a game of chess before dinner?"

Enzo looked up from the book he was reading in the sun-drenched living room that afternoon. "What are we having for dinner?"

Leo shrugged. "I thought we could order a pizza. The Cowboys are playing tonight, and with Mom and the girls in town for their monthly night out, it's just us."

It had been just over two weeks since the dinner that led to Enzo's setback, and Leo couldn't help but frown as he thought about how much his life had changed. And how he was right back to where he'd started.

Only nothing felt the same because he knew what he was missing. It had been his idea to get involved with Poppy Fortune, but he never would have guessed the way she'd change everything.

"What about Joey and Poppy?" Enzo closed the book and

placed it on the table next to his recliner. "Does she like pizza and football?"

Leo thought about her shouting at the refs on the TV when they made a bad call and smiled. "She likes football and sausage and mushroom pizza."

"Let's order that and get her and the baby over here."

"Sausage is too spicy for you right now, Papa."

Enzo slapped a palm on the recliner's armrest. "I'm not a toddler. I can handle some spice, Leo."

"I can't," Leo admitted with a laugh, appreciating his grandfather's instinct to retain his self-respect, even if it meant advocating for sausage pizza. "I can't call Poppy to come over."

"Why not?" Enzo asked, tone softening from his previous outburst.

Leo thought about how to explain the current state of his relationship with Poppy to his grandfather. Although making excuses or talking around the subject would be easier, he wasn't going to do that.

"Poppy and I..." He massaged a hand over the back of his neck, trying to figure out how to explain something he barely understood. "She doesn't need me anymore."

Enzo looked confused. "Why? Did they find the baby's mom and dad? Is it one of the Fortunes?"

"No. Or I should say no one knows. Her dad, uncle and cousin resubmitted DNA results but still haven't heard anything because of the backup at the lab."

"You'd think a family like the Fortunes could figure out how to expedite some results."

"I'm not sure they want to know that badly. The test results have the power to change everything."

Enzo flicked his hand in the air, brushing aside that excuse. "Then those men are cowards, and right now, they're letting Poppy do the heavy lifting. She deserves better."

"She does," Leo agreed. "She deserves better in so many areas..."

"So she *does* still need you. And even if she didn't, you want to be there with her. With Joey."

"Yes." Leo said the word slowly, testing the weight of it on his tongue. Then he shook his head. "It isn't that simple, Papa."

"Why the hell not?"

Enzo's cheeks were flushed by now, and Leo stepped forward. "Don't worry about it. I've got things under control. It's all fine."

"Don't treat me like an invalid. You look like a dog someone has just kicked in the ribs. I know you aren't fine."

"I will be."

"Don't lie to me, boy." Enzo straightened his shoulders and sat forward in the chair. "The cancer has addled my body, not my mind."

Leo moved toward the cabinet under the bookshelf that held the board games. "I don't want to worry you. Seeing you in the hospital a couple weeks ago after you'd been so upset with me at dinner..."

"Upset with you? What are you talking about?"

Leo turned and clutched the chessboard to his chest like a shield. "You were agitated when we had dinner a couple weeks ago, just the two of us. I came to check on you the next morning, and you'd been rushed to the hospital."

"You thought that was because of our conversation?" his grandfather asked.

"I know the fact that I'm still single and have no plans for that to change is disappointing. So maybe it's a topic best left alone for a while."

"You aren't single. You're with Poppy."

"No," Leo whispered.

"You broke up with her?"

"Papa, please. I don't want to talk about this."

Enzo rose and took a step toward Leo. He no longer used a cane or walker and appeared strong and stable. But that could change in an instant. Joey's sudden fever was a great example of that, and the heart attack Leo's father had suffered...

"The doctors determined that the B vitamin I was taking messed with my electrolyte balance and caused my oxygen levels to dip. It might have happened after our dinner, but that conversation wasn't the cause, Leo. You weren't at fault. I'm sorry you thought otherwise."

"You *were* upset with me."

"I have no inside voice. Your grandmother was always shouting at me to modulate my tone. I shout because that's what we do. I'm a passionate person, Leo, and I'm passionate about my family and love. Cancer doesn't change that. I won't turn myself into some mealymouthed mouse in the time I have left."

"You could never be a mouse." Despite the burning in his chest, Leo smiled at the thought. "You're the least mouselike person I know."

Enzo reached out and took the chessboard, leaving Leo feeling strangely exposed.

"And I'm wondering if *you're* a coward," his grandfather said as he arranged the pieces on the board. "It's a surprise, Leo. Not a good one."

"Ouch. That's harsh, Papa."

Enzo rolled his eyes. "You say you didn't end things with Poppy, which means she gave you the boot."

"It was more like a soft kick in the pants, but she doesn't want to see me anymore."

"Why? It was obvious how much she cared about you, and I thought you felt the same about her and the baby."

That much was true. He cared about Poppy. *Intensely.* But still not in the way she needed. Not in a way that would allow him to risk his heart.

Leo's mind whirled with explanations and rationalizations he could offer, but in the end, he stayed with his commitment to speak the truth. "She told me she loved me."

Enzo slapped a hand on the table, causing the black knight to topple over. Leo set it to rights without a word.

"That's wonderful."

"It's not. I haven't been honest with you."

"Then I think it's time to start." His grandfather sank into one of the club chairs surrounding the game table. He held up a hand before Leo could speak. "Don't even think about sugarcoating it. I can handle whatever you're going to tell me."

Sighing, Leo took his seat as well, twirling one of the chess pieces between two fingers. "Poppy was in the cafeteria when I came to visit you that morning in the hospital. She told me about Joey being left on her parents' doorstep and the fact that she'd been certified as a foster parent. I knew you'd be impressed by that."

Enzo nodded. "She's an impressive young woman."

"So much more than me," he murmured, trying not to sound petulant. Based on his grandfather's cocked brow, he failed.

"I was inspired by her. I wanted to do something that would make you happy. Make you proud."

"I'm *always* proud of you," Enzo countered.

"You also worry. You worry that I give too much to my job. You and Mom think I need to have a more well-rounded life. I need to not make the winery my only priority."

"Is it wrong that I want—"

"Not wrong. But I'm not sure it's possible. I tried because I wanted to make you happy."

"You took on the responsibility of an abandoned baby because of me?" Enzo leaned back against the leather, clearly dumbstruck.

"I know all of you worry about me, concerned I'm unhappy the same way Dad was. I love the vineyard. It's a responsibility I take seriously. I don't want to let you down the way he did."

"Your father had no head for business and even less heart for it," Enzo said. "Yes, I was disappointed, but not in him. I was disappointed *for* him because he was never satisfied when he had so much to be grateful for."

"I'm grateful and I appreciate it," Leo insisted. "Anyway, the whole arrangement between Poppy and me wasn't real."

"Maybe it didn't start that way, but I don't believe you were faking your feelings for her."

"Why does everyone insist on discussing feelings?" he grumbled.

"Now you *do* sound like your father." Enzo chuckled. "But you aren't him, Leo. You are your own man. We put a lot of pressure on you, maybe before you were ready. Maybe in a way you didn't want then and don't want now. It's to be expected." He exhaled slowly and waited a beat before continuing. "This vineyard has always been helmed by the oldest in the next generation. It could be time to think more about what the children of that generation want."

"I *want* to run the vineyard. But I can't help thinking if I had been more involved before Dad died and he hadn't felt so much pressure, that maybe his heart wouldn't have given out."

"You're a strong, smart man, Leo, but you are not God. I'm sorry if I made you feel like I wasn't proud of you for who you are. I didn't want you to play small in other areas of life because you were so busy taking care of his family. If Poppy Fortune isn't the woman you want—"

"I didn't say that," Leo interrupted, his fingers knotting together. "But at the moment, she doesn't want anything to do with me."

"She's not a damsel in distress. What does she want from you that you can't give her?"

"Aside from my heart?"

Enzo lifted a brow. "Someone else got dibs on it?"

"Of course not. No one makes me feel the way I do about Poppy, not even close."

"I'm a simple man, and I've got to admit I'm having trouble understanding. Do you love her?"

"Yes."

"Have you told her?"

"No, I can't tell her."

"Because…"

"Because I don't think I have it in me to love her, not like she needs."

"What are you so scared of? The girl has her own career. Her family has a business as steeped in legacy and success as ours. I don't think she's going to hold you back."

"Of course she wouldn't hold me back. She does the opposite. She challenges me to be a better person, but…"

"But what?" Enzo prodded. "Is it the baby…the fact that he's not yours biologically? Because I got the feeling that if they can't solve the mystery surrounding him, Poppy would be more than happy to become his official mommy. That's a lot for a man to take on."

"I love Joey. I would love to be his father but…"

"You keep saying *but*. I need more of an explanation."

"I'm afraid of hurting her."

"It seems to me that Poppy should be allowed to decide for herself what she's willing to risk."

"That's the problem. She's a lot braver than me." Leo gripped the white queen tightly in one hand. "I'm afraid of not measuring up. What if she realizes I'm not the man she thinks I am?"

"Become him."

Leo felt his mouth go dry. His grandfather didn't understand how hard this was on him. How much he secretly feared he could never measure up to Enzo's example. And if he tried and failed, everyone would know he wasn't enough. The idea of disappointing the people he loved—or cared about in Poppy's case—had his gut churning. "Even if I could, I don't have time for love right now."

"Make time, Leo, because nothing's more important." Enzo's smile looked wistful. "It's the one thing I can guarantee is finite."

Leo frowned. "I don't want to think about that."

"No one wants to think about it, but you have to. I'm not necessarily talking about myself, so don't start grieving me just yet. My time on this earthly plane is limited, but so is yours. No one can predict the future. I didn't expect to lose your grandmother when I did. There were times after her death I thought I would have rather followed her into the unknown than live without her."

Enzo drew in a steady breath. "But I kept living and gradually learned to love life again. We don't get to decide how much time we have. We only get to decide what we do with it while we're here. This is the only life you have, Leo. I don't know if you'll get over Poppy or she'll find someone else…"

Leo growled low in his throat. He hated the thought of her with *anyone* else.

"But if you love her, the joy of every day you have with her will be worth the potential pain of risking your heart."

"There's a chance she won't even take me back. But I do love her—" he admitted quietly.

"Then what are you going to do about it?"

His grandfather asked the question so matter-of-factly it made Leo smile despite the nerves pulsing through him.

"I'm going to convince her we belong together." He felt lightheaded and dizzy but somehow free as he said the words out loud. "No matter what. Poppy and I belong together."

"Do you want to spend the rest of your life with her?"

Leo swallowed then nodded. "So much it scares the hell out of me."

"Then you need to stop wasting time. Make the most of every moment you have."

Enzo stood and walked to the small writing desk in one corner, opened a drawer and returned to the table with a small black box clutched in his hand.

"I knew the moment I met your grandmother that I wanted to spend my life with her."

He opened the box to reveal a familiar emerald-cut diamond set in a white-gold band with filagree on either side of the stone. "It took a few years before her feelings caught up to mine, but the day I slipped this ring on her finger was one of the happiest of my life. I hope it brings you the same sort of joy with Poppy."

"Nana's ring?" Leo stood and embraced his grandfather. "Papa, it's too much. I can't—"

"It would make your grandmother so happy, Leo," Enzo rasped, then pulled back and placed the ring box in Leo's hand, wrapping his fingers around it.

"Yes, it's a risk to let yourself love with your whole heart, but I believe the two of you are the real deal. I'd be honored if your intended wife wore this ring."

"Thank you, Papa. It means the world to me." Leo grinned and dropped the box into his pocket. "Now I just have to convince Poppy she still loves me as much as she did before I messed things up."

Enzo shrugged. "You have the Leonetti charm. It shouldn't be that difficult."

Leo hoped his grandfather was right. He took a step toward the door, then stopped and glanced at the game table. "Would it be okay to take a rain check on our chess game?"

"Anytime, my boy." Enzo winked. "Go claim your queen."

"I plan to do exactly that," Leo promised as he hurried out of the room, determined to tell Poppy what was in his heart.

CHAPTER FIFTEEN

LEO TRIED NOT to fidget as he waited on the porch after knocking. It took a few minutes for the door to swing open, and he couldn't hide his shock as Garth Fortune stood on the other side with Joey in his arms.

"Joey," Leo whispered.

"Hello, son," Garth said coolly. "What can I do for you?"

"Is Poppy here?" He tried to look beyond Garth's shoulder, but the older man wasn't budging an inch. He made a better door than a window.

"Pretty sure you're aware she doesn't live here." Garth frowned. "Were you expecting to find her?"

Leo shook his head. "No, sir. I wanted to talk to you. I just…" He reached out to touch Joey's cheek, but Garth stepped back. "I didn't expect to see you holding my…the baby."

"I'm watching him while Poppy's at work. She was going to bring him to daycare at the spa since her regular child-rearing partner flew the coop, if you know what I mean."

So Poppy had talked to her father about the two of them. He shouldn't be surprised. She was close to her family in the same way as him. He wanted her to have that support.

"Do you have time to talk for a few minutes?" he asked. It seemed prudent to ignore Garth's not-so-subtle jabs.

As his grandfather had recommended, Leo was willing to

beg to earn the right to get down on one knee and ask Poppy to forgive him and be his wife.

"Who's there, Dad?"

Garth chose that moment to turn to one side and reveal both Rafe and Shane approaching behind him. Based on the glares they sent Leo, they knew what had happened as well.

"You have a lot of nerve showing up here looking for my sister," Rafe barked.

"I was looking for your father. I'd like to talk to you about Poppy and my intentions toward her," Leo told Garth.

"Oh, hell no." Shane shook his head. "You keep my sister's name out of your mouth, Leonetti."

Garth shifted the baby to one arm and held up a hand. "I'll talk to him," he said, and although both sons looked pained by the thought, they didn't argue. Leo wondered if anyone other than Shelley dared to argue with Garth.

"Can I hold him?" Leo asked, gesturing toward Joey. "I miss him so damn much."

"I'll hold the baby for now," Garth said.

Leo realized that although the head of the Fortune family had agreed to speak to him, he wasn't going to make the conversation an easy one.

That was okay. Leo had done hard things before, and nothing compared to how difficult it had been to walk away from Poppy. He'd been a fool and was determined to make things right, whatever it took.

He could handle whatever these three Fortunes threw at him. Eyes on the prize, he reminded himself. And there was no greater prize than Poppy.

He followed her brothers and dad down the hall and into Garth's office. It fit the distinguished man, with wood accents, heavy furniture and walls lined with books and framed photographs.

He wanted to take a closer look because he could see a blonde girl at various ages smiling from many of the pictures. There would be time for that, he hoped. Time to learn everything about Poppy.

"Tell me what you're doing here and why we shouldn't kick your butt," Shane interjected.

"I know I made some mistakes." Leo grimaced as he looked between the two brothers.

"Putting it mildly," Rafe muttered.

"Can Leo speak without the two of you interjecting every three words? Otherwise, we'll be here all afternoon." Garth's serious, steadfast gaze focused on Leo.

Joey, who had an uncanny ability to pick up on the mood of a situation, shoved his fist into his mouth and quietly sucked on it while staring at Leo.

Suddenly, the rehearsed explanations and rationalizations Leo had devised on the way over seemed trite and ridiculous. The thought that Poppy would consider taking him back was absurd and so out of reach that he might as well fashion wings and try flying to the sun.

"I'm an idiot," he said, remembering what his sisters had told him not to be. "I love your daughter, Mr. Fortune, and the baby you're holding like he's my own. Both of those things scare the hell out of me because I'm not a man who expected to fall this hard. Or at all."

"For someone who professes to love my daughter, you have a funny way of showing it."

"That was fear," Leo admitted. "I'll regret hurting her until the day I die, but if she'll give me another chance, I also promise you that I will love her forever and beyond."

"Talk is cheap, Leonetti," Rafe said, and his father nodded in agreement.

"Why should any of us believe you now? Poppy has been hurt too often, but it's never been like this. She sees something in you—"

"It's the hair," Shane said, tousling his own dark locks. "He's got good hair. He may be a tool, but he's got good hair."

Leo wasn't sure how to take that, but Garth smiled slightly, so that was a step in the right direction, even if it was at Leo's expense.

"I hope it's more than my hair. I love her, and I have a ring in my pocket that I plan to ask her to wear. But first, she has to forgive me, and I want your permission before I talk to her. I've made mistakes, and I know Poppy is surrounded by a family that adores her. She loves all of you very much. I don't want to go forward on the wrong foot."

Garth lifted Joey onto his shoulder and then gave a small nod. "Okay."

Leo waited for more, but the older man offered nothing else. He glanced over his shoulder again at Poppy's brothers. Their attention was also focused on their father as if something more would be coming.

"So you believe me when I tell you I love her?"

Garth gently drummed his fingers on Joey's back as he considered the question.

"The question is whether my daughter will believe you," he replied. "I appreciate the nerve it took to come here and speak to me, given what a mess you've made of things. But Poppy is the one you'll have to convince, and I hope you do. If my daughter chooses you despite the mistakes you've made…"

He looked over Leo's head once again to his two sons. "You have the blessing of everyone in this family."

"Yeah, but if you hurt her again, all bets are off," Shane added brusquely.

Garth smiled but his dark eyes were hard. "That's true. Hurt her again, and you're finished."

Leo probably should have been offended at the veiled threat, but he felt just that protective over every one of his sisters, so he understood the sentiment.

He was glad Poppy was surrounded by people who had her back. That said, he had no intention of getting into a predicament where he would have to face any of these Fortunes again. If she gave him another chance, and he prayed she did, he wouldn't take her for granted for one moment.

"Are you going to wait until she gets home from work?" Rafe asked, stepping forward and patting Leo on the back. "Because if you think we're protective of her, her staff makes us look like one of those litters of foster kittens she raises."

Leo did not relish taking up another gauntlet or publicly acknowledging how much of a fool he'd been. But he also didn't want to wait, and Poppy deserved a public apology. He wanted everyone to know how much he valued her. If telling her at the spa would convince people, that's what he'd do.

"I'm going to the spa," he said, and her father nodded again, this time in obvious approval. "Good for you, son. I think you'll be a nice addition to this family."

"Yeah, we'll put you in charge of the wine at holiday dinners," Rafe said.

"Gladly," Leo agreed. "But there's one more favor I have to ask. Because as much as my feelings for Poppy are about her, I plan for a life that includes more than just the two of us. I want to give her the world because she's mine. The whole of it."

"Then let's talk about how you prove that to her," Garth said, and suddenly Leo felt hopeful that he might have a chance to win Poppy back and claim the happily-ever-after he wanted more than anything.

POPPY WALKED OUT of her small office at the end of the spa's long hallway and paused. She heard loud voices coming from the reception area and quickly moved in that direction, unsure about the source of the commotion and wanting to deal with it before the bridal party scheduled to come in for an afternoon of prewedding pampering arrived.

Clients needed to be greeted with a calm, peaceful vibe as soon as they walked through the door. She liked to think of the spa as an oasis from stress and hoped it would also work its magic on her.

At the moment, she felt less than blissed out, but the morning of keeping busy made time go by faster. Her boots clicked on the marble floor as she walked, and she plastered on a smile that froze in place as she saw Leo standing with Joey in his arms in the center of the reception area.

Benita, the spa's manager, and several aestheticians stood before him, looking for all intents and purposes like a white-smocked firing squad.

"What happened?" she demanded as she pushed through the line of staff. "Why do you have Joey? Is my dad okay?"

Leo visibly swallowed, then nodded. "Everything is fine. I'm sorry, I didn't mean to frighten you. I stopped by your dad's house and asked him if I could have Joey for a while."

Poppy's heart lurched at his words. As devastated as she felt that Leo had walked out, the fact that he still cared enough about Joey to want to be a part of the baby's life tempered her anger ever so slightly.

"You can't," she said, despite her feelings.

"Damn straight," someone behind her muttered under their breath. "This fella's messing with your head, girl."

Leo flinched at the words, which were not exactly said in a hushed tone.

"Do you want to go back to my office and talk?" she offered. "It might be easier."

Joey fit so perfectly into the crook of Leo's arm, and the boy cooed happily. Poppy understood how comforting it was to be held in Leo's strong embrace.

But seeing them together was making this so much worse for her.

Because whether fact or fiction, she *wanted* to believe the process of getting over him would be easier if she avoided going into town or any place she might run into him.

So as much as it hurt, she had to make him understand they couldn't see each other. He needed to let go of Joey so Poppy's heart could release him.

He started to nod, then held up a hand. "No. I'm going to do this here."

"Do what?"

"Your dad and brothers agreed that it might be my only chance of convincing you."

"What are you trying to convince me to do?" Poppy's mind whirled in confusion. "And why are you talking to my dad and brothers?"

"I'm making a mess of this." Leo ran a hand over his jaw, his gaze slightly panicked until he looked down into Joey's sweet face and his features relaxed.

"Help me out here, kid." The baby's mouth worked, but then his eyes drifted shut. Leo smiled ruefully at the boy then raised his gaze to Poppy. "I guess I'm on my own."

Behind Poppy, someone snorted. "I thought this guy was supposed to be smooth and charming. He looks like my son when he got caught sneaking out."

Leo nodded and pointed to the spa manager. "Exactly. I'm in trouble and completely out of my element."

"I don't understand *any* of this," Poppy murmured.

"Yeah, I know I'm mucking this all up, but..." He took a deep breath then blurted, "I'm scared to death I've lost you forever." He shifted closer and lowered his voice, looking so sincere that Poppy's heart fluttered in response. "I'm terrified I won't find the right words to persuade you to give me another chance."

"You want another chance?" Poppy pressed her palm to her chest, where her heart had started beating an erratic thump. "Another chance at what?"

"To convince you that I understand you are the best thing that's ever happened to me, Poppy Fortune. The morning I saw you in that hospital cafeteria will go down as one of the best days of my life because it brought you back to me. Please forgive me for being the biggest idiot on the planet...

"And the truth is, I never should have let you go the first time." He placed a hand on Joey's stomach. "This baby gave me a second chance to get things right. I owe him my heart for that. My life. Because *you* are my heart and my life."

"That's a darn good apology," Benita said.

"Next level," someone else murmured.

Poppy spun on a heel to face her staff. "Don't you all have someplace to be or work to do?"

Only to be met with a row of shaking heads.

She turned back around when the bells over the door chimed, and four boisterous young women filed into the spa. Their voices trailed off as they took in the scene before them.

"Welcome," Poppy told them. "You must be our afternoon bridal party?"

The woman in front sported a bedazzled Future Mrs. Travis T-shirt. She lifted a pair of oversize sunglasses to the top of her head. "Are we early?"

Leo didn't move, and Benita took a step forward before Poppy could answer. "No, ladies, you are right on time. Come on in. We'll get you checked in momentarily, but right now, we're witnessing something magical. Have a seat on the couch over there, and you can join in the fun."

Poppy rolled her eyes, her cheeks heating with embarrassment. "Leo and I can continue this discussion in my office."

"Not a chance," Benita told her with a bright smile.

"We're always up for fun," one of the bridesmaids offered. "Especially if it's juicy!"

Benita nodded and gave them a thumbs-up. "The best kind. Let me bring you up to speed. Poppy and Leo are fostering this sweet little baby…"

The bride nodded. "The abandoned Fortune baby. I heard about that."

Poppy suppressed a groan as Benita continued, "Yes, well, things got a little rocky between Leo and our Poppy. He made some bad choices."

"We've all made bad choices at one point or another," a petite redhead told Leo, looking sympathetic. "It's how you deal with them that counts."

"Now, Leo, tell Poppy what we're all waiting to hear."

The bridal party quickly moved to the leather couch on one end of the reception area and sat close together, clearly ready for the show.

Leo's intense gaze hadn't left Poppy. "I love you and I want to spend the rest of our lives proving how much. Please don't make me wait, sweetheart. I have to know whether I've got a chance with you."

Poppy had trouble getting the words out, the lump caught in her throat, making it difficult to speak.

"What's changed from yesterday?" she asked softly. "If this is just about Joey… I know how much you care for him, and I appreciate that, but…"

Leo studied her, visibly struggling to articulate his thoughts. "Yes, I love him but you will forever hold my heart, Poppy. You have to believe me. You are courageous and beautiful. Brilliant and strong. You inspire me to be a better man. I'm already a better man with you in my life."

She smiled and shook her head. The problem was she didn't

know how to play hard to get. She didn't know how to do anything but give him her heart. But as much as she wanted to believe him, she couldn't do that if he couldn't give her what she needed.

"I love Joey so much it hurts," he continued. "If no one comes forward to claim him and the DNA tests prove he isn't part of the Fortune family, I want to raise him with you. But the most important thing to me is being with you, Poppy. It's loving you."

"But what's changed?" she insisted, refusing to settle for anything less than how she knew she deserved to be cherished.

"I have. You've shown me how valuable it is to be vulnerable, which I never thought I could be. I thought I didn't have time for love or family. That if I opened my heart, I'd be hurt. The thought of living without you is so much worse than anything else. I'm not sure I'll ever deserve the way you love so openly and how you give your heart so freely, but I'll try every day to make you happy."

His voice cracked and he drew in a shaky breath. "Any storm that comes our way, we'll weather it together. I don't know how much time we have, but I want to spend all of it with you."

"That was a darn good speech." Poppy spoke the words around the tears that she couldn't stop from streaming down her cheeks. "I love you, Leo," she whispered. "I love how you make me feel special just for being me."

"You still love me," he repeated as tears filled his dark eyes. "Even though, as my sisters would remind us both, I've been an idiot."

"My idiot," Poppy said and took a step toward him.

At the same time, Leo pulled a box out of his jacket pocket. With Joey still in his arms, he dropped to one knee. "I will love you forever, Poppy Fortune. I don't want to wait or waste another moment without you. Will you make the dreams I didn't even know I had come true and agree to be my wife?"

There was a collective gasp from the peanut gallery.

"Girl, that's a way better proposal than the one I received," the bride on the couch called out. "You *have* to say yes."

"Yes," Poppy murmured. "Of course I say yes!"

Leo slipped the beautiful vintage diamond ring onto her finger. "This is the ring my grandmother wore, and it's a perfect fit for you. I plan to love you the way my grandfather loved her—with his whole heart."

"And I plan to love you right back, Leo."

Holding her hand in his, he stood and kissed her.

The happiness Poppy found in Leo's arms filled her heart in a way she knew would last a lifetime. As her staff crowded around her and Leo for congratulations and to admire the ring, pure joy washed over Poppy like a warm wave.

She'd taken a risk to be herself and found love in the process. Life might bring challenges along with the good times, but with Leo at her side she'd make the most of every moment.

* * * * *

Don't miss the stories in this mini series!

THE FORTUNES OF TEXAS: SECRETS OF FORTUNE'S GOLD RANCH

Welcome to Fortune's Gold Ranch...where the vistas of Emerald Ridge are as expansive as the romantic entanglements that beckon its visitors!

Faking It With A Fortune
MICHELLE MAJOR
January 2025

A Fortune's Redemption
STELLA BAGWELL
February 2025

A Fortune With Benefits
JENNIFER WILCK
March 2025

MILLS & BOON

Her New Year's Wish List

Makenna Lee

MILLS & BOON

Dear Reader,

Welcome back to Channing, Texas! *Her New Year's Wish List* is the third book in my miniseries, The Women of Dalton Ranch. In this story, the second Dalton twin gets to live out her greatest romance. I had a lot of fun writing this book because Daisy and Finn have such a playful and passionate relationship.

When Daisy and Finn—best friends and neighboring Texas ranchers—spend the days between Christmas and New Year's snowed in together, Finn sees her wish list. He can't fulfill her desire for a brief romance. Or can he? He doesn't do forever, but he can do temporary. He discovers that unexpected challenges can lead to a beautiful life he never dreamed possible.

I hope you enjoy *Her New Year's Wish List*. As always, thank you for reading!

Best wishes,

Makenna Lee

Makenna Lee is an award-winning romance author living in the Texas Hill Country with her real-life hero and their two children, one of whom has Down syndrome and inspired her first Harlequin book, *A Sheriff's Star*. She writes heartwarming contemporary romance that celebrates real-life challenges and the power of love and acceptance. She has been known to make people laugh and cry in the same book. Makenna is often drinking coffee with a cat on her lap while writing, reading or plotting a new story. Her wish is to write stories that touch your heart, making you feel, think and dream.

Books by Makenna Lee

The Women of Dalton Ranch

The Rancher's Love Song
Her Secret to Keep
Her New Year's Wish List

Home to Oak Hollow

A Sheriff's Star
In the Key of Family
A Child's Christmas Wish
A Marriage of Benefits
Lessons in Fatherhood
The Bookstore's Secret

Visit the Author Profile page
at millsandboon.com.au for more titles.

To Kitty.
Thank you for cheering me along on my writing journey.

CHAPTER ONE

"Is THAT A baby goat in your rowboat?"

With a hip bump, Daisy Dalton closed the door of her new sapphire-blue truck, zipped up her heaviest winter coat and looked past the three cowboys standing at the edge of the pond. Their arms were crossed over broad chests, and their heads were tilted in what she recognized as their thinking pose.

"Yep. That is in fact a baby goat." Finn Murphy glanced over his shoulder with a shrug and a half grin. He was the tallest and blondest of the brothers, with wavy strands brushing the tops of his ears below a black cowboy hat.

The ice-tipped blades of grass crunched under Daisy's boots as she joined them at the edge of the oval-shaped pond. This wasn't the first time she'd found them involved in something unexpected. "She's so tiny. Where in the world did you get a goat?"

"You'll have to ask our big brother about that," Jake said, and punched Finn's shoulder. Jake was the youngest Murphy brother, always quick with a comment and very outgoing.

"I didn't have a choice." Finn rubbed his fingers through his blond beard, which had grown thicker over the winter months. "Someone abandoned the goat at the feed store. The second we got home, she sprinted down the hill, hopped into the rowboat, and it slid down the frosty bank and launched into the pond before I could catch her. I've decided to name her Rascal."

"Seems like an appropriate choice." Daisy smiled at the man who had become one of her best friends. He was a tough as they come cowboy, but it didn't surprise her that Finn was the one who'd brought home the orphaned animal.

A gust of wind rustled the cluster of bare-branched trees that grew along the edge of the water, and the musical sound of tiny ice shards tinkled onto the rocks below. Sleet began to fall from the gray sky as the tiny brown-and-white goat jumped up onto the center bench seat, making the boat rock in the frigid water.

Daisy's heart sprang into her throat. "What if she falls into the water?"

"That's what I'm worried about," Finn said. "I'm hoping the wind will blow the boat to the edge of the pond."

As if the universe was laughing in his face, another gust blew the boat farther into the middle, but at least Rascal hopped down from the seat into the center of the boat and propped her chin on the side. The little animal was bleating excitedly and looking around as pleased as could be with her grand adventure.

"So...how are you going to get her back to shore?" Daisy asked the three brothers.

"I guess we need another boat," said Riley, the quiet middle brother who only talked when necessary. His extra deep voice was a low rumble in contrast to the goat's high-pitched bleating.

Daisy's long hair blew across her face, and she tugged her red stocking cap lower to cover more of her ears. As she watched Finn pace along the bank, an idea took shape. The two of them were always on the lookout for a challenge to issue to the other, and this was something he wouldn't be able to do. In one of his recent dares, she'd ended up with her butt in the mud, and it was payback time for Finn.

"Too bad there isn't anyone brave enough to swim out there and tow the boat back to shore," she said.

Three sets of blue eyes snapped in her direction.

"Are you offering?" Jake sat on the open tailgate of an old black truck and lifted his hat to brush back his dark blond hair.

"Absolutely not." She shivered at the mere idea of torturing herself in such a way. "You know I don't do cold water, but your big brother is always bragging about how he used to jump into the river in the middle of a Montana winter." Finn's playful scowl made her grin. He hated it when she came up with a dare that he couldn't complete.

"You don't think I'll do it?" Finn asked.

"Nope. I think you're going to drive next door to my ranch and borrow my boat."

He shrugged off his coat, tossed it over the truck bed and then started unbuttoning his flannel shirt. "Shows how much you know, Daisy Maisy," he said, using the nickname he'd given her.

This was a dare she would've refused and assumed he'd do the same, but she was getting a bad feeling. "You cannot actually mean to jump into that ice cold water."

"Sure I can." Now bare chested, he walked out onto the wooden dock, hung his shirt and his hat on one of the posts and pulled off his cowboy boots and socks.

Heat blossomed in her belly. She'd learned to think of Finn as a close friend who just happened to be good-looking, and her initial lust had been safely tucked away, but when he paraded his perfect male body like this... She sighed and shook her head.

I really need to start dating again.

Every once in a while, he did something that re-sparked her libido. He'd say something that made butterflies dance or he'd touch her in an innocent way, completely unaware of the tingles rippling across her skin.

His full-body shiver snapped her back to the danger of what he was doing. This could go wrong in a hurry, and it would be all her fault. Who was going to rescue him when he cramped up in the middle of the pond?

"Okay, you win. You don't have to turn yourself into a human Popsicle to prove how tough you are. I believe you swam in the ice-cold river as a kid."

"It's the quickest option to get the goat back to shore before she falls in." He started working on the top button of his jeans.

She spun to face Riley and Jake. "Guys, tell him not to do it."

They both shrugged, not appearing the least bit concerned.

When she turned back to Finn, he was standing at the end of the dock in a pair of black boxer briefs—his powerful physique framed by the gray winter sky. And it was quite glorious.

He glanced over his shoulder with a mischievous grin and then dove into the water.

"Finn!" She gasped and rushed out onto the dock, holding her breath until he surfaced and began swimming with long powerful strokes toward the boat. "Is he going to be all right?"

"He'll be fine." Riley stepped up beside her and handed her a heavy wool blanket. "We always keep a few of these in the truck."

"Now I understand why." She'd always wondered if Finn kept the blankets there so he could take his dates out "stargazing" in the bed of his truck.

Finn grabbed the front of the rowboat and began towing it in. The goat peeked over the side, bleating noisily in-between attempts at trying to eat his hair.

As he reached the shallows, each step revealed chilled skin so taut across his muscular body that he resembled a marble statue. And with water droplets clinging to his blond beard and his breath pluming into the icy air with each huffed breath, he looked like a painting of a Viking warrior of old.

Shivering and scolding the noisy goat, he pulled the small boat onto dry land. "This is the thanks I get for saving your scrawny little butt?"

Daisy rushed forward with the blanket held open and wrapped it around his shoulders. "Crazy fool. I can't believe you did that."

His teeth chattered behind lips that were tinged blue. "Payback is g-going to be a b-b-bitch."

There was no doubt that she'd set herself up for something awful.

Riley scooped up the tiny animal before she could bolt again and tucked her into the front of his coat. "I'll take her back to the house." He started walking up the hill while Jake pulled the rowboat farther up the bank.

"Get in my truck. The heater is already running full blast." Daisy put a hand on Finn's back and urged him forward and was relieved when he didn't argue. "I'll grab your clothes."

Jake handed over Finn's coat. "Tell my brothers that I'm

driving down to the barn to put out a couple more bales of hay for the cattle."

"Be careful. It's icier than you think," she told him.

Daisy followed the path of Finn's striptease and put his hat on her head, her stocking cap making it fit and not slide down over her eyebrows like it normally did. Lifting his black flannel shirt, she caught the scent of his soap and cologne and brought it closer to her nose before she could stop herself. Why did he have to smell as good as he looked? Stepping around icy patches on the dock, she made her way carefully to his discarded jeans.

At least I don't have to pick up his underwear.

With her arms loaded, she made it back to her truck without incident, until she reached for the door handle. Her feet slipped in two different directions and his clothes tumbled to the ground. The only thing that saved her from going down completely was her one-handed grip on the door frame.

"Graceful as always," Finn said with a chuckle.

"Shut up, Jack Frost." Daisy still had a hold of one boot, and once she righted herself, she tossed it his way before collecting the rest of his belongings.

"Sorry I laughed. Are you okay?" he asked.

She scoffed. "You're not the least bit sorry about laughing at me."

"That might be true." He put the boot on the floorboard and leaned his face close to a heater vent. "Why did you come over this evening? I thought you were excited to have the house all to yourself while your niece and sister's families are away for the week."

"I am, but some of your mail was in my box again." She flicked an unpolished fingernail across an envelope sticking up from a cup holder. "It's postmarked from Montana. Maybe it's from one of your family members?"

"We don't have any relatives left in that part of the country." He scrubbed a hand roughly over his face.

Daisy wasn't sure if it was to warm up his skin or to brush away his past. He didn't like talking about his life in Montana, and she regretted bringing it up. "What are your plans for New Year's Eve? Hot date?"

"Jake wants to have a party and invite everyone we know, and not surprisingly, Riley wholeheartedly objects to a house full of people. But the bad weather and icy roads might prevent any kind of big celebration." He wiped water droplets from his hair with the blanket. "What about you? Got any big plans?"

"No. It will be a chill New Year's Eve for me." She didn't want to admit her lack of a date, and since he hadn't answered her question, maybe he didn't have one either. But that seemed so unlikely, and he'd no doubt have his choice of gorgeous dates by New Year's Eve. A hint of melancholy settled over her, and she sighed. She'd been looking forward to her time alone, but now…the idea of ringing in the new year all by herself wasn't as exciting as it had been only a few hours ago.

IT ONLY TOOK a minute to drive up the hill from the pond to his house, and Finn Murphy's skin was prickling painfully as the heater began to thaw him from the outside in. He'd never been this cold. Ever. But letting Daisy know the extent of his misery after plunging into glacial water was out of the question.

When she grinned at him, he playfully scowled. "You lost. I took your dare and did what you thought I wouldn't. So, you're enjoying this more than you should be."

"Not as much as I would have if you'd kept your clothes *on*. Now I have to wash my eyes out."

He barked a laugh. "I've never had a woman wish I'd keep my clothes on."

"Okay, Casanova." She angled another heater vent in his direction. "I had such big plans to endlessly tease you when you refused to swim in an ice bath, but you foiled my evil plan."

"Don't mess with the master. My brothers learned that lesson years ago."

She parked beside the row of hawthorn bushes and turned off the engine. "I'll bring in your clothes and boots, so you don't drop your blanket."

"Good idea. We can't risk you getting another look at me without my clothes on," he said. "It's too cold to have you fainting like a wilting flower."

"Hey, my name might be flowery, but I'm…" Her voice trailed off as her brow crumpled. "Not."

Why had that made her good mood fall away? Did she wish she was more…flowery? She was pretty, but not turn-your-head-gorgeous. He'd only seen her in a dress a few times, and her face was usually free of makeup. She was more tomboy than feminine. But did she want to be seen differently? For some reason, anytime Daisy was sad, it made his chest tight.

It's just because I'm protective of her like I am with Riley and Jake.

He grimaced and instantly knew that was not the reason. She might not be some party girl he was dating, but he definitely did not put her in the sister category.

She moved his cowboy hat from her head to his. "Maybe this will keep you warm."

"You're such a giver." He grabbed the mail, took a deep breath and stepped from the warmth of the truck's cab. "Holy hell." He hissed as his feet touched the ice-cold gravel and every step was like walking on a pile of Lego bricks.

Why the hell didn't I put my boots back on? This was yet another time he wasn't willing to admit a weakness. All that did was give people an invitation to use it against you.

The sounds of chaos met them before he'd even opened the front door of the sprawling one-story log ranch house he shared with his brothers. When the front door swung open, the scene that greeted them was his own doing. He'd been the one who brought another animal home. Their black dog was barking his head off at the baby goat who was bouncing across the back of their old sectional sofa. They seemed to be competing to see who was louder.

"Enough, Astro!" Riley knelt beside the dog. His deep voice could bring a rowdy room to attention, but he rarely used it at full power.

Daisy dropped Finn's things onto one of the recliners and scooped up the miniature goat. "You really do live up to your new name, don't you?" She laughed when Rascal headbutted her shoulder and then snuggled into her arms like it was nap time. When the animal was curled up, she was no bigger than a puppy.

Finn rushed across the cold hardwood floor of their living room to stand on the rug in front of the fireplace. Flames blazed in the stone hearth, and he flung open the wool blanket to let in the heat, but in his haste, he forgot he was holding the letter from Montana. The envelope slipped from his cold fingers and sailed right into the fire. The center blackened immediately, and the edges curled as they were caught in a flash of flames.

"Damn. I hope that wasn't important."

Daisy came up beside him with Rascal curled up in her arms. "Did you just burn that letter?"

"Not on purpose. For some reason, my fingers are too numb, and I couldn't hold on to it."

She winced. "I feel partially responsible for your discomfort, and I know you're—"

"A hero?" he suggested.

She smiled wide enough to show her one dimple, which was low on her right cheek. "I was going to say freezing, but now that you mention it, yes. I'm sure the goat will agree with your hero status." She snuggled the animal under her chin. "Do you have any idea what kind of goat she is? She seems smaller than other baby goats I've seen."

"She's an African Pygmy goat. The old farmer who brought her to the feed store said she was orphaned, and he didn't have time to supplement her food with bottle feeding." He shivered.

"Want me to start a hot bath for you? A long bubble bath can be so relaxing, and I'm planning to have one when I get home. It's the least I can do for you before I leave."

When she licked her lips, which were red from the cold, an image flashed in his mind. Daisy in the bathtub, wet and surrounded by a mound of bubbles. He squeezed his eyes closed. A flash like this had happened once before. His brain needed to get it together and knock it off.

Back when she'd been their boss, he'd had no choice but to keep things completely chill because he and his two brothers had needed the job on her horse ranch. Once they saved enough and bought Four Star Ranch next door, he briefly considered asking her out for a bit of fun, but Daisy Dalton was the girl next door type—both figuratively and literally—and his tastes ran more toward party girls who had no interest in anything serious. Plus Daisy was his first female friend, and she meant a lot to him. If he let his mind go down a dangerous path, it could ruin everything.

Daisy expected—and deserved—a committed relationship, and that's something that was not part of his DNA. He never did it on purpose, but he always ended up breaking hearts. He wasn't the kind of guy who settled down with one woman.

He cleared his throat. "I think I'll just get in the shower. Seems faster."

And safer.

CHAPTER TWO

THE WINTER ICE storm raged across the whole Dallas Fort Worth area, but Daisy was safe inside the white farmhouse that had been in the Dalton family since it was built by her great-great-grandparents.

"Brrr. Thank heavens for central heating." Daisy sat on the wooden bench right inside of her front door and slipped off her boots. They were wet from the sleet that was quickly forming into slick sheets of ice, and her toes were numb from the below freezing temperature. She set them on a mat to protect the narrow-plank oak floor.

The walls of the wide entryway were eggshell white with an eclectic mix of artwork. Watercolor landscapes, black-and-white family photos in antique frames and a collection of McCoy pottery wall pockets holding dried flowers. The entryway led from the front door to the center of the house, where a staircase went up to the second floor. On each side of her were identical archways. To the left was a cozy living room with a fireplace. To the right was a dining room where she remembered family dinners and lively conversations with lots of laughter.

The jingle of the cat's collar reached her a moment before the white fluffball hopped onto her lap. "Hello, Lady. I hope you're ready for a cozy night indoors. There will be no sneaking out for a midnight hunt." Stroking Lady's long fur, Daisy stood with the purring animal in her arms and went down the center hallway past the stairs and into the kitchen for a hot drink.

She fed the cat and groaned at the stack of breakfast dishes in the sink. Instead of washing them right away, she opened a cabinet and moved aside her nephew's sippy cup to grab a mug. It was her sister's favorite pink one, but it was the biggest and Daisy often used it. While water heated for hot chocolate, she rinsed and put the dishes into the dishwasher. For the next five days she had the place all to herself.

Her identical twin and business partner, Sage Dalton DeLuca, was on a post-Christmas trip with her husband, their teenage daughter and baby girl. Her niece Lizzy, who also worked on the family horse ranch when she wasn't singing with the Fort Worth opera company, was with her husband and son visiting grandparents. Sage's family lived with her on the horse ranch when they weren't at their house in town, and her niece's new house was so close she could see it from the front windows. This led to the main farmhouse being a hub of activity with lots of people in and out on a regular basis, and she didn't mind a bit. It had once been just her and Sage on their ranch, and now having so much family around was wonderful, but she told herself that a few days alone was going to be good for her. A chance to recharge.

And she had big plans to start her evening with a long, hot bubble bath, and then complete control of the television remote and the freedom to eat junk food without judgment. She could even walk around the house in the nude if she wanted to—not that she'd ever do such a thing. But first, she wanted to make a list of goals, wishes and dreams for the new year. Lots of options had been spiraling around in her mind, and she wanted to get at least the important ones written down before her bath.

With her hot chocolate in hand, Daisy made her way to the living room and plugged in the Christmas tree lights so she could enjoy them for a little longer. The festive decorations they all loved so much would likely stay up until well into January, mostly because no one wanted to be the one to remove the decorations and pack it all up. The house was too quiet, so she also turned on the television. An old movie about a group of misfit cowboys was playing. She'd seen it many times but left it playing in the background.

Daisy grabbed a thick sheet of pale blue stationery and her favorite pen, then sat in her comfy blue velvet chair beside her sister's matching pink one to begin her list.

Daisy's New Year's Wish List

She'd been planning to make number one something really important, like donate to a children's charity or learn a new language, but after watching a few minutes of the movie and letting her mind drift into thoughts of real-life cowboys, she decided to start with things that were more fanciful and save the serious stuff for the end of her list. She glanced back at the TV just as one of the cowboys pulled his shirt over his head and revealed a killer physique, and she wrote down the first thing that came to her mind.

Sleep with a hot guy/Brief fun affair.

There was a tug low in her belly, but she rolled her eyes at her own line of thinking. She didn't just want some meaningless hookup. She wanted to fall in love and be loved in return.

On the TV screen, cowboys were stacking bales of hay, and it made her think of the Murphy brothers working around her ranch or theirs. The brothers had strikingly similar features, with big blue eyes, square jawlines and full mouths that smiled often. But none of them were dating options.

The thought of reentering the dating field once again came to mind. Her last date had been months ago and had been a disaster. A nice guy at the horse auction had asked her out, and she was starting to think she should stop giving him excuses and say yes.

Number two on her wish list really should be something with more substance, but before she could complete the thought about falling in love, the lights flickered, and she was plunged into darkness.

"Nooo." She groaned into the quiet, dark room. "Is this seriously happening?"

In the blink of an eye, all her plans disintegrated. Normally in a situation like this she could go out to the efficiency apartment behind the horse stable where a backup generator powered their high-tech horse facility, but the new to town and very cute veterinarian was temporarily living there until his new house was ready. Dr. Dillon Cameron was also a possible dating option, but going out with him while he was living on her property seemed like a recipe for trouble.

Maybe Lizzy's house, right across the fence, had electricity. She folded her list—that was something she didn't want anyone else to see—and slipped it into the back pocket of her comfy jeans and went to look out her front window. The outdoor security lights that usually shone across the metal roof of Travis and Lizzy's log home were dark. It was a good thing they had remained in Austin because having no electricity in an ice storm with a toddler would be no fun at all. But the lights at Finn's house glowed in the distance, sending out halos in the icy air.

Her phone rang, with the veterinarian's number appearing on the screen, and she answered. "Hi, Dillon."

"Is the electricity off up at the main house?" he asked.

"I'm afraid so. Do you know how to start the generator?"

"I do. I'll get it running and check all the horses."

"Thanks. I appreciate it."

"If it doesn't come back on soon, come stay out here in the apartment with me."

Her mouth dropped open. What was Dillon suggesting? Skipping a first date and going straight to sharing a bed, or an I'll-take-the-couch kind of thing? "I'll get back to you on that. I'm going to call the power company and see if I can get any answers. Let me know if you have any trouble with the generator."

"Will do, Daisy."

She got a recorded message about downed power lines, and because of the weather, they had no idea when they would be repaired. Her next call was to Finn.

He answered on the third ring. "Hey, Daisy. What's up?"

"I see that you have electricity on at your ranch."

"I take it this means that you don't."

"Sadly, I do not."

"At least you have a generator and an empty apartment behind the stable."

"It's not empty. Dillon moved into it yesterday. He'll be here until his house is ready."

"Dr. Cameron? You can't stay there with him," he said in a quick, sharp tone.

She held back a laugh. He sounded scandalized by the thought of her staying in the one-bedroom apartment with a man—even though she was in her midthirties. "Why not? It's a safe, warm option."

He was quiet for a few heartbeats. "Pack a bag and come over here. This isn't a night to be without power."

So much for a bubble bath and all her other leisurely plans. Instead of having a relaxing evening, she'd have three rowdy guys, a dog, a goat and the cat she'd have to take with her. "I guess you're right."

"Don't get out on the icy road. Come through the gate between our properties."

"Like I don't already know to do that? I always come that way even in good weather. First, I need to make sure everything is good in the stable and that Dillon has everything he needs." When you had horses that were worth as much as theirs, you had to take precautions.

"Dr. Cameron is a grown man. He'll be fine. Need my help with anything?"

"No, thanks. I'm a grown woman. I'll be fine," she said, mimicking his words with a chuckle. It was comforting to know he had her back, but his sudden papa bear protectiveness was also a bit entertaining. "I'll see you in a bit."

She packed a small suitcase, and tote bag of all the snacks she'd planned to hoard for herself. She'd be lucky if Finn, Jake and Riley didn't eat everything within an hour. She bundled up and rushed to her truck with first her bag and a litter box and then the cat inside a carrier. After double-checking that all was good at the stable, she drove over to Finn's.

When she arrived at Four Star Ranch, the sleet was coming down faster and the wind was whipping. The brothers kept the new truck in the garage, but there was no sign of their old black truck that was normally parked in front. Surely Jake wasn't still out working with the cattle. She walked in their front door to only the dim lighting of the fire, the television and the Christmas tree she'd helped them decorate. Finn was kicked back in one of the recliners with the dog at his feet and the goat asleep on his lap.

"Where are your brothers?"

He turned down the volume on the movie he was watching. "Both in town with women they're dating."

Warmth swirled inside her, and she pressed a hand to her stomach, willing away the butterflies caused by their seclusion. What was wrong with her? They were frequently alone. But something about this stormy-night setting made it feel like they were the only two people on earth. "So, it's just you and me here?"

"Plus a dog and a goat."

She lifted the cat carrier. "And one feline."

On cue, Astro got up and bounded over to sniff the cat. Lady hissed and made the carrier shake in Daisy's hand. The dog always wanted to play and never tried to hurt her, but the cat had other ideas. When Daisy opened the carrier, Lady hissed once more and then rapidly pranced away with her head held high and her fluffy tail swishing. Astro followed her into the kitchen.

She put her tote bag on the couch and opened it. "At least the snacks will last longer without Jake and Riley here."

"Please tell me you brought junk food?"

"I did." She put a bulging plastic grocery bag on the battered square coffee table.

Shifting the sleeping goat to the warm spot where he'd been sitting, Finn got up to rifle through the bag.

Daisy moved closer to his chair and laughed at the small animal wearing a child's diaper with a hole cut out for her little tail. "Where did you get a diaper?"

"We have a couple different sizes of them for when Rose and Davy are here with their fathers when y'all have your ladies' nights," he said about her niece and nephew. "I put one on the goat after cleaning up a puddle. I also looked it up, and apparently, you can potty train a goat."

"That's good news."

"I wrote down the important points, and I can start working on it tomorrow. But for tonight, I'm going to put Rascal in the big dog crate."

"Good idea." She sighed and flopped onto the threadbare couch.

He pulled out a bag of chips from the grocery bag and sat in the corner of the sectional couch. "What's wrong? Did you not get your bubble bath?"

"No, I didn't."

"I have that huge tub in my bathroom that I never use, but you can use it if you want to."

"Too bad I didn't bring any bubble bath."

"The best I can do is dish soap."

She laughed. "I think I'll pass, but I will take you up on using the tub."

"My bathroom door doesn't close all the way and needs to be fixed, but no one will bother you."

She paused on her way out of the room. "Don't eat all the food while I'm gone."

Finn sprawled across the couch with the chips and grinned. The bag crinkled as he opened it. "I'll try, but no promises."

"Remind me why were friends?"

"Because I'm so much fun and totally irresistible."

Daisy rolled her eyes—even though his assessment was true. "Says you."

His ego was big enough without her confirming it. Resisting Mr. Irresistible would remain at the top of her list.

Daisy rolled her suitcase down the hallway, the wheels softly bumping over the hand-scraped hardwood floor. She peeked into the youngest brother's room and shook her head. Jake was definitely the messy one of the bunch. Clothes, boots and random items were tossed across his bed and most pieces of furniture. The next bedroom was filled with workout equipment and the third was Riley's tidy room and the one she chose. She glanced toward the open door at the end of the hallway. Being the oldest, Finn had claimed the largest room with the attached bathroom.

In Riley's room, she put her suitcase on the navy spread of his neatly made bed and unzipped it. Her cosmetics bag was bulging and heavier than she remembered, and she was pleased to find the products her sister had added. And luckily, one of the little bottles was cherry blossom scented bubble bath.

"Thank you, Sage." Her twin was so good about restocking the travel-sized products for both of them.

She took what she needed into Finn's room, where there was not much more than the king-size bed without a headboard, one nightstand and a dresser that didn't match. One wall was made of logs that had been stripped of their bark and varnished with a satin finish and had a row of tall windows with an excellent view of the ranch. Instead of curtains, several sheets were tacked up above the windows and held back with string. He'd stripped off the floral wallpaper from the other three walls and left them in great need of paint.

The bathroom had a granite countertop in shades of gray around the double sinks, sage-colored walls and a large sunken Jacuzzi tub beside the walk-in shower. It was uncluttered with nothing more than a toothbrush and tube of paste in a plastic cup. She pulled the door, but as he'd warned, it wouldn't close all the way.

She started filling the large tub and poured a generous amount of bubble bath into the running water. After undressing and twisting her hair up into a knot on the top of her head so it wouldn't get wet, she eased into the deliciously scented hot water and sighed as her muscles began to relax. But every time she closed her eyes, she pictured Finn standing on the end of the dock in a pair of fitted boxers. He was perfectly formed. Not like a bodybuilder who spent all day in the gym, but rather sculpted from hard work and good genetics.

She'd only been in the tub for five minutes when the bathroom door squeaked open a crack and she sucked in a breath, but it was only her cat prancing into the room. It wasn't uncommon for Lady to sit with her or her sister as they bathed, but Daisy wasn't in her own bathroom and the thought of someone coming in made her jumpy.

What would she do if Finn opened the door? Yell at him to get out or… She shivered. Or invite him to join her?

She groaned and blew out a long slow breath. Starting her New Year's list had put foolish ideas into her head.

She reached out to let the cat bat at a pile of bubbles on the palm of her hand. "Are those other two rowdy animals getting on your nerves, Lady?"

Before the cat could even meow her irritation, the door burst all the way open and banged against the wall. Daisy gasped and sunk deeper into the mound of bubbles as the dog and goat bounded into the small space.

"Are you kidding me?"

The goat spotted her and kicked up her back hooves as she headed her way.

"No! Stop!" But it was too late. The goat gave one final hop and plunged into the tub. A wave of soapy water hit her in the face with a splat, but Daisy quickly scooped her up to make sure her head was above the water. Rascal had a mound of bubbles on her tan-and-white head, and if a goat could smile, that's exactly what this little girl was doing.

"Astro, get out here," Finn called from his bedroom. He appeared in the open doorway but came to a sudden halt, covered his eyes and turned around. "Sorry, Daisy. I promised no one would bother you, and you didn't get more than a few minutes to yourself."

She was too busy holding on to the wiggly creature. She was far enough under the bubbles that he couldn't see her, but she appreciated his discretion. She yelped as the goat attempted to jump from her arms up onto her shoulder. Daisy's butt slipped across the bottom of the tub, her head went under, and one leg curled beneath her as the other went straight up into the cool air above the bubbles. She came up sputtering and wiped her face with her free hand.

She met Finn's eyes right as her soggy topknot of hair flopped over her forehead, and he burst into laughter. With the wily animal clutched against her, she tossed her head to flip back her hair and laughed along with him when the goat sneezed.

"Get the dog out of here, and I'll deal with this one."

With his gaze averted but his chest still shaking with laughter, he picked up the dog and left her to her ruined bath.

With one arm curled around Rascal to keep the goat from

splashing her in the face, Daisy pulled the plug to let the water out. "You are on the naughty list, girlfriend."

Rascal nuzzled her cheek and tried to nibble on her ear. "Stop that, silly girl."

The water drained quickly, so she stood, grabbed a towel and wrapped it around herself before getting another and lifting the animal from the remaining water. She bundled her up so only her head was visible. When Rascal was basically dry, she carried her to the bathroom door.

"Finn," she yelled. "Come get this little beasty."

"Coming."

"Rascal, the next time you want a bath, I better not be in it." She kissed the top of her head that now smelled of cherry blossoms, put her on the bedroom floor and closed the bathroom door the best she could.

"Come here right now," Finn said from the other side of the door. "I couldn't figure out why anyone would leave you behind, but now I'm starting to suspect I know the reason. You're a handful and a half for someone who's smaller than Daisy's cat." The animal bleated in response. "But you do smell better now. Kind of like...flowers."

Daisy sniffed her own hair as she studied herself in the mirror. Even with her best intentions to keep it dry, it was dripping wet.

What does Finn see when he looks at me?

Her hair needed a trim, and she didn't pamper her skin like her sister did, but maybe she should start. She didn't wear a lot of makeup like most of his dates. Mascara and lip balm were her go-to items. She didn't wear the high heels or short skirts he favored. She wasn't Finn's type at all. But she had his true friendship, and that was worth protecting.

Finn might be good-looking, but he was not an option for the hot guy who could help fulfill number one on her list. He would laugh his head off if she suggested sleeping together and would probably think she was pulling a prank on him. It was clear that he wasn't into her in that way. Sure, he had a flirty nature, but he was that way with every adult female, even if they were ninety years old.

Lady came out from her hiding place behind a wicker laundry basket and brushed against her legs.

"It's been a very eventful day, hasn't it, girl?"

She dressed in the new pajamas her sister had given her for Christmas and brushed out her long blond hair. But when she picked up the tubes of pink lip gloss and mascara—also courtesy of Sage—she stopped herself. There was absolutely no reason to put on makeup for Finn Murphy. It was clear that he thought of her as a buddy, or worse, like a family member.

She tossed the tubes back into her cosmetics bag and marched toward the living room.

CHAPTER THREE

WHEN DAISY CAME into the living room dressed in a black tank top and a pair of fuzzy red pajama pants covered with pink hearts and lip prints, Finn smiled and grabbed the bag of chocolate candy from the coffee table. He leaned back against the couch cushions. With her wet hair and bare feet, she looked way younger than midthirties. Sometimes he forgot she was five years older than him.

"That was way more entertaining than when you almost slipped getting into the truck." He flashed her a wide grin.

She held out her arms and curtsied. "Happy to be the evening's entertainment."

"Somehow...that's not what I pictured you sleeping in."

"Well, now I have to know. What *did* you picture?"

An image popped into his head. Daisy naked with her long limbs stretched out on soft sheets. Heat surged through his body. Although the moment had been brief, when she'd popped up in the water after being dunked, he'd seen most of her breasts. Only clinging bubbles had preserved some of her modesty. He rubbed his eyes and hoped his beard would hide the heat creeping onto his cheeks.

He had to say something before she guessed where his wayward thoughts had gone. "I'm thinking you wear one of those head-to-toe, long-sleeved granny nightgowns."

"For your information, those are very comfortable." She snatched the chocolate candy out of his hand and fished around in the bag.

She was no doubt looking for her favorite dark chocolates and was going to be so irritated when she discovered that he'd hidden all of them. "I gave Rascal a bottle and put her in the dog crate." He motioned toward the fireplace where the dog was stretched out alongside the crate.

"Wow. You got that done fast. I put my things in Riley's room because he's the neat freak." She sat on the couch, tucked up one foot and put the other on the coffee table.

"Good call. Picking up after himself is not one of Jake's strong points. When we interrupted you, I couldn't help but notice the bubbles. Did you end up using dish soap?"

"No. I found a bottle my sister put in my suitcase. Hey, where are all the dark chocolates?" She shot him a thunderous glare that made her look like a disgruntled little girl.

He grabbed his drink from the side table and took a sip to keep from laughing. "You know I don't eat the dark ones. Maybe they messed up at the candy factory and forgot to put any in this bag."

"What did you do, Finnigan?"

"You know that's not my name. It's just plain old Finn."

"You're trying to change the subject. Where'd you put them?"

"They're around." He circled his hand to encompass the whole room. "Somewhere."

Her sigh was long and overly dramatic. "I guess this is payback for your cold swim. At least I won't eat them all at once. Aha." She leaned forward to grab a foil-wrapped chocolate that he'd hidden under a remote control.

"Want to watch a movie?"

"Sure. Let's watch that classic holiday movie we started the other day."

Daisy fell asleep thirty minutes into the movie. She was curled up on one end of the couch with her head on a green pillow. He'd always considered her pretty in a girl-next-door kind of way. She wasn't all made up and pushed up and overtly sexy like most of the women he dated, but with firelight flickering on her ivory skin and her full lips relaxed in sleep, she was very attractive.

Daisy stretched out her legs and her feet pushed against his thigh. For a woman her height, her feet were small, high arched and narrow. For some reason he was surprised to see her toenails painted a shimmery red with silver snowflakes on her big toes. Her sister must have talked her into a holiday pedicure because he'd never seen them painted more than a barely there pink, and she never painted her short, neat fingernails.

He couldn't resist running the pad of his thumb back and forth across the sole of her foot.

Her toes spread, and then she jerked her foot away. "Sage, I don't want to wear high heels," she mumbled in her sleep.

He grinned, finding it unsurprising that she'd say that and fitting that she talked in her sleep. He had a thing for a pair of long legs in sky-high heels. He'd only seen Daisy in heels a few times, whereas her twin sister wore them often.

He yawned and turned off the TV. "Daisy, time to go to bed."

She tucked her hands under her cheek. "Later. I'm not hungry."

He chuckled. Her sleep talking was something he could have some fun with. There was no telling what information he might learn and be able to use later. He curled his fingers around her foot and used his thumb to knead the high arch, and this time, she didn't pull away. Daisy moaned and arched her back in a way that made his stomach flip.

"So-o-o good."

When she sighed, long and breathy and sweet, he was hit with an urge to discover what other spots gave her pleasure. He jerked his hand away before he could slide it under the leg of her fuzzy pants.

What is going on with me?

Daisy was his friend. The first real female friend he'd ever had. She was his next-door neighbor for life—not the next woman whose heart he'd no doubt break if anything happened between them.

Picking her up off the couch and carrying her to bed was completely out of the question. Especially if she made one of those moaning sounds that made his body tighten. Finn stood and linked his fingers behind his head, backing slowly away from the surprisingly tempting female curled up on his couch.

He never meant to make women cry, but it too often happened, usually when they discovered he was not kidding about never marrying or having kids. The revolving door of people in his childhood home, plus the times he and his brothers been left alone to fend for themselves, had taught him many hard-earned lessons. He'd seen too many examples of the many ways relationships went wrong.

His friendship with Daisy was important and had to be protected, because if he let romance enter the picture, she would want more than he had to give. It would end badly, and then he'd have to share a fence line with a woman who hated him. He shook his head, pulled a blanket off the recliner and covered her before heading to his room. She was the kind of woman who expected—and deserved—a committed relationship.

Continuing to think of her as a buddy was the only way to protect both of them.

SHADOWS MOVED IN a fitful dance across the ceiling every time the wind blew the trees outside Finn's bedroom window. His insides felt as rattled as the branches, and sleep wouldn't come because he couldn't stop thinking about his best friend Daisy. When he'd offered her dish soap for her bubble bath, his brain had created an image of her in the tub. Like a muted, fuzzy watercolor that left a lot to the imagination.

But getting a real-life glimpse of her in a mound of bubbles had put a clear, vibrant picture in his head. One he couldn't shake. He kept replaying the way that one long leg had popped up into the air when the naughty goat dunked her. She'd come up sputtering but had laughed along with him. Even with the splashing, noise and complete chaos, he'd seen enough to add the word sexy to a description of his best friend.

This is not good. Not good at all.

He considered stepping out into the freezing night air for a blast of cold to clear his thoughts, but he'd had enough of being frozen after his icy dip in the pond.

With his door cracked open, he'd heard Daisy go to bed shortly after him. She was probably once again sleeping soundly. But he couldn't. He got out of bed and went to check on the baby goat. Rascal saw him and headbutted the door of the crate.

"Are you hungry, little girl?"

He unlatched the door, and Rascal bounded out, bouncing in a circle around him and causing Astro to get up from his bed in a corner of the kitchen and join in on the fun. He tried to shush them before they woke Daisy but wasn't having much luck. He grabbed a bottle of the milk replacement he'd mixed up earlier, picked up the baby goat and carried her into the living room.

LOUD BARKING AND Rascal's answering high-pitched calls had awakened Daisy. For a couple of minutes, she'd stayed perfectly still, hoping they would settle down.

Lady had been asleep at her feet but was now trying to work her way under Daisy's pillow as if that would protect her from the chaos.

"All right, scaredy-cat, I'll go check it out." Before she could open the bedroom door, the noise died down. She was about to go back to bed, but Finn's voice stopped her. She tiptoed down the hallway and stood in the shadows to watch him kick back in a recliner with the goat.

Rascal bounced from one of Finn's thighs to the other, and he winced. He adjusted her on his lap, and she practically attacked the bottle. "I hope you plan to sleep through the rest of the night," he said to the goat.

Astro hopped onto the couch, turned in a few circles and then settled down to sleep.

"What am I going to do with you, Rascal? What are the chances that someone left you at the feed store right before I get there? I think they must've seen a sucker coming."

The tiny animal butted her head against his arm.

"We need to have a conversation about this potty training thing. Daisy brought a litter box for the cat, and tomorrow we are going to try the technique I read about. I'll make a deal with you. I'll wake up in the night to feed you if you promise to be easy to house-train."

Daisy stayed where she was and watched the tender scene. He claimed he didn't want to be a father, but from her point of view, he had the skills and instincts needed to be a really good parent. Now, he just needed to realize that for himself.

CHAPTER FOUR

THE BABY GOAT bounced around in a patch of morning sunlight that was streaming in across the terra-cotta tile floor, and then she hopped up onto the low kitchen windowsill.

Daisy followed her and looked out at the backyard. "Oh my gosh. Finn, come look. It's snowing. Everything is a sea of white."

He joined her at the window with a mug of steaming coffee. "It sure is."

She took the coffee from his hand and took a sip. "Why aren't you more excited? It's so beautiful."

"Because I grew up in Montana and have seen more than my share of snow."

"Well, for a Texas girl, even an inch is exciting." He barked a laugh, and she smacked his shoulder, sloshing a bit of coffee onto the floor. "Your mind is in the gutter."

"I'm a thirty-two-year-old single guy," he said in way of explanation.

She wasn't actually bothered by his humor. It was just fun to mess with him. "Guess it comes with having a guy as a best friend."

"Are you done with my coffee yet?"

"I suppose." She took one more sip and handed it over with

a grin. "It's your own fault for taking your coffee with heavy cream just like I do."

The cat ran over to lick the milky coffee off the floor, then hissed and ran away when the dog nosed in on her territory.

"I think you just enjoy taking my stuff," he said. "My coffee and my favorite T-shirt. And always my french fries."

"If I order my own, I'll eat too many of them."

The oven timer rang, and he crossed the room to pull biscuits from the oven. "Come eat your breakfast, and then I'll take you out to play in the snow, Daisy Maisy."

Once they'd fed themselves and the animals, they attempted the first suggested steps for house training a goat—with little success. Daisy dressed in layers, and they both bundled up before going out into the cold, crisp morning air. But Finn had refused her suggestion to wear a stocking cap and insisted his winter cowboy hat was enough.

Astro darted past them and barked at Rascal when she attempted to hop onto his back. Her cat tiptoed onto the snow and then darted back into the house, wanting no part of the unusual conditions.

Daisy tipped her face up and let snowflakes land on her cheeks. "You have to admit that this is beautiful."

"It's nice. This is the first time I've seen Four Star Ranch covered in snow."

"Over my lifetime, there have been a number of times it has snowed here, but it's rare enough to be special." Daisy stuck her finger down into the snow, then looked at the level of white on her red glove. "Looks like it's about an inch so far."

The goat and dog were darting back and forth across the yard and didn't seem the least bit concerned about the cold.

While she admired the snowy landscape, he scooped up enough snow to make a snowball. "Be careful walking. There's still ice under the snow."

"I will." She carefully lay down on the ground and swept out her arms and legs to make a snow angel.

"Enjoy it while you can. The temperature will be dropping again in the next few hours, and more ice is expected," he said. "With our horses in your stable during the storm, the cattle are the only animals that need tending on my ranch. Without my brothers here, I could use your help, if you don't mind."

"Of course I'll help you. Where do we start?"

"First, I have to get feed from the barn and drive it out to the pasture. And I'll probably have to break the ice on the water tanks, so remind me to grab the sledgehammer from the barn."

"After I help you with the cattle, I need to go over to my ranch. Dillon is there to watch over the horses, but I still want to check on him."

"You want to check on *him*? Shouldn't he be able to handle it?"

She bit her lip to hide a grin. If she wasn't mistaken, Finn sounded a little…jealous. But it had to be her imagination. "It's the first time Dillon has looked after my animals, and I want to make sure everything is good. And make sure he is comfortable in the apartment," she added just to get his reaction.

He made a sound in his throat. "Since my horses are there too, I should go with you."

After Astro and Rascal were back inside the warm house, they got into his truck and headed for the barn. To keep from sliding on any patches of ice, he drove slowly along the dirt road. When she opened the big sliding door, he backed inside the barn, and they put bags of feed into the bed of the vehicle.

"Daisy, will you drive so I can hop in the back when we get out there and pour the feed in the troughs?"

"Sure." She got in on the driver's side and drove out to the pasture where the cattle were wintering.

Wire fencing was stretched between cedar posts, and it had a large section of one corner walled off with corrugated metal walls. It blocked the cold north wind and had a roof to keep the rain off. Most of the Black Angus herd was gathered in that corner, munching on hay and waiting for their morning feeding. The mooing started the second they spotted the truck. Daisy drove very slowly beside the long metal feed trough that stretched across the front of the windbreak, and Finn poured in the feed.

She smiled when she saw Finn pulling his scarf up to cover his exposed ears. He was a tough as they come cowboy on the outside, but at the heart of him, more and more every day she was discovering a sensitive side. A part of himself he kept so carefully hidden around most people.

From what she had pieced together, she had a strong feeling he was guarding a wounded part of himself. Protecting it from more damage. The tough guy swagger was his armor.

He jumped down from the truck bed and got in on the passenger side. "Pull over there and wait for me while I break up the ice on top of their water."

She pulled forward. "I can help you."

"There's only one sledgehammer, and it won't take me long."

"If you insist, but don't say I ever shy away from the hard stuff." A tingle zipped across her skin as the words "hard stuff" made her think of his bare chest. She hadn't meant for it to sound sexual, but he'd no doubt be unable to pass up the opportunity for a comeback.

"No one can say that you shy away. It would be untrue to say that about Daisy Dalton." His smile was genuine, and his tone was serious, without a hint of teasing.

The sincerity of his comment was so unexpected that she didn't know what to say. She'd totally been expecting his usual style comment—as if she was one of the guys.

When she put the truck in Park, he got out and retrieved the sledgehammer from the back.

As he swung it high above his head and down to crack the ice, she was once again taken back to the moment he'd emerged from the pond. The Viking warrior moment. But today, dressed in flannel, denim and leather and wielding a hammer the size of an axe, it brought to mind lumberjacks.

Why does he have to be so damn good-looking?

She just needed to set her mind to other contenders, and everything would be fine. Dr. Dillon Cameron came to mind. He was tall and sturdily built with dark hair and structured features, and although he could look slightly intimidating, his frequent grin gave away his kindness and fun personality. And judging from his recent behavior, he certainly seemed interested in exploring what could be between them. She had to admit that she was intrigued.

More and more, she'd been thinking about asking the handsome veterinarian out to dinner, but something always stopped her. She hated the thought that somewhere deep inside she was holding herself back because of Finn. When they got to her place, she would pull Dillon aside and talk to him and see if he sparked anything inside her. Any little thing that could catch her attention enough to make her forget about something happening with Finn.

SMOKE CURLED FROM the little chimney off the rear of the apartment attached to the stable. Finn knew the veterinarian was staying there, and he hoped he would stay put and not come out to talk to them. He didn't dislike the man. There was just something about the way Dillon was extra attentive with Daisy that bothered him.

I'm being ridiculous.

As they went into the high-tech stable on Dalton Ranch, Finn blinked to adjust to the dim lighting that was necessary to save on the pull on the generator. The scent of hay and horses greeted them, and several horses stuck their heads out of their stalls and whickered.

"Hello, my beauties." Daisy grabbed the red treat bucket and stopped at Titan's stall to stroke his long sleek neck. The stallion was their sought-after stud horse whose breeding capabilities had financed this stable and led to Dalton Ranch becoming famous and extremely profitable.

The high ceiling was vaulted with heavy timber framing and lighted fans that were fancy enough to be in a house. The large stalls along one side of the barn had solid wooden walls of horizontal boards between them so the horses could not see one another. The opposite side's stalls had smooth, round metal bars on the top half of the walls so the horses could look across to see other horses.

The aisle down the middle was red bricks laid in a herringbone pattern that matched Daisy's patio at the back of the farmhouse. Most stalls had a door that led to an outdoor area that was half covered by a roof so the horses could choose sun or shade while getting fresh air. But with horses that were worth as much money as these, the danger of one of the animals slipping on ice was too risky to let them outside until the storm cleared.

Finn walked over to his horse, Maverick, and rubbed the heart-shaped white spot right in the center of his brown forehead. "We'll get you back to our place as soon as the storm is over, big guy. You're much better off here than in our drafty old barn."

While he was more than happy for the Dalton twins' success, he couldn't help but compare the way he and his brothers struggled to make ends meet on their own ranch. Daisy looked his way with her usual happy smile before moving to the next stall. Something weird shifted inside his chest. Why was her smile suddenly affecting him in an unusual way? He took a deep breath and glanced upward while counting to ten.

Daisy went farther down the aisle while he stayed at his horse's stall.

A door closed behind him, and Finn turned to see pretty boy veterinarian Dr. Dillon Cameron coming from the back door that led to the apartment. He walked past the tack room and raised a hand in greeting.

"Morning." Finn nodded. He had no problem with the other man. He'd never been anything but nice and respectful as far as he could see, but the way he looked at Daisy made his teeth ache.

Daisy came from the far end of the stable, past him and headed straight toward Dr. Cameron. "Good morning, Dillon. "How's everything going here?"

"Great. The stalls have been cleaned and everyone is fed according to the list you gave me. But I do have bad news about the electricity. I called and they said a bunch of lines are down along with other issues, so it will probably be a couple more days without power."

"That's a bummer."

For some reason, Finn wasn't upset by the news. No electricity meant Daisy would need to continue staying with him. At his house. But it was only because he'd be lonely with his brothers not there. At least that was the excuse he was going to stick with.

She spread her arms. "This building is insulated enough that the horses will be okay even if we run out of fuel for the generator, but what about you?"

Dillon braced a hand high up on the wall and grinned at her. "I'll be fine. The wood-burning stove in the apartment heats it up nicely, and it makes me feel like I'm at a secluded cabin in the mountains. And the offer to stay in the apartment with me still stands."

She blushed and nibbled one corner of her full lower lip. "I'll keep that in mind. I really appreciate you being here 24-7 with the horses."

"Not a problem. It's part of our agreement in lieu of rent."

Finn couldn't help but wonder what the rest of the agreement entailed. His stomach tightened without warning, and he had a strange urge to growl. He did *not* like his own reaction.

What is this feeling? Jealousy?

Maybe it was, because he didn't like the way the other man received her sexy smile. One that he did not. When it came to Daisy, this sudden shift of emotions was a new phenomenon.

I need to get out of here.

"Daisy, I'm going to go get the milk and other perishables from your refrigerator," he said on his way out the small side door where they'd come in. Cold wind hit him when he stepped outside, and snow was once again coming down in soft flurries. Daisy was going to love it.

"Finn, wait for me," she called after him, and promptly slid on a patch of ice but caught her balance just in time.

"Nice save. I thought maybe you'd decided to stay with the doc."

On her way to the passenger side, she ran her gloved hand across the snow-dusted hood of his truck. "Trying to get rid of me already?"

No! His brain answered, but thankfully he had better control of his mouth. "Not yet, Daisy Maisy."

CHAPTER FIVE

THE SECOND THEY got back inside the ranch house, Daisy built a fire while Finn worked on house-training the goat. She sat on the geometric patterned rug in front of the stone hearth, rubbed her hands together and shivered when the fire's heat reached her chilled body. Even with the central heating unit running, it was having trouble keeping up with the unusually cold conditions. The fireplace was a bonus, and the giant stack of logs on the back porch would last for weeks if necessary. Courtesy of a lumberjack cowboy who she knew looked good while swinging an axe.

She grinned at the mental image and wrapped her arms around her drawn-up knees, but then she frowned.

Her little experiment in the stable to see if she could create a spark with Dillon had been a failure. No lust or unbridled excitement had been generated by the handsome man with thick dark hair and moody brown eyes. Not even when he'd touched her arm and dropped his voice to a low rumble.

The whole time she'd been talking to Dillon and searching for something between them, she'd felt Finn's eyes on them. Returning to her over and over, the heat of his gaze making her blush. She'd also felt a little thrill because Finn had seemed—maybe jealous wasn't the right word—bothered by her full attention on another man. And she hadn't even been flirting.

The good-looking vet who appeared to want more than friendship with her was not the one who gave her tingles in all the right places. Not the one who gave her foolish fantasies about skinny-dipping in the summer and what it might be like to be in his arms and—

"I'm starving."

She jumped and clasped a hand to her heart at the sound of Finn's voice.

He quirked up an eyebrow. "What's got you so jumpy?"

She ignored his question. It's not like he knew what she was thinking about. "I'm hungry too. Let's go see what our options are."

Because it was suddenly too hot in front of the fireplace.

THEY REHEATED BOWLS of nine bean soup they'd grabbed from her refrigerator and sat at Finn's round kitchen table. It was a well-used chunky piece with four chairs from several different eras in time. A cane-back chair was older than the table, while a diner-style metal one across from it was flanked by two swivel chairs meant for an office. The mismatched grouping was positioned in front of a bay window that looked out over Four Star Ranch. Just looking at the snowy view made her happy.

"What should we do for the rest of the day?" he asked.

"Good question. Too bad we can't get out on the icy road."

"Where is it you want to go in weather like this?"

"Well, your bedroom is in serious need of painting, and a trip to the hardware store for supplies would have given us a project to work on."

"I already have paint. It's in the garage."

She put her spoon in her empty bowl. "No kidding?"

"I bought it a few weeks ago along with brushes and stuff."

"Excellent. I'm up for painting. What do you think?"

"I'm not turning down your help."

After they finished eating, she went with him to help get everything from the garage. A wooden workbench ran along one wall with large tools neatly lined up and smaller ones hung on the pegboard behind it.

"Does Riley organize your tools?"

"How did you know?" he said with a chuckle.

"Just an educated guess."

"If you'll grab those two bags of supplies, I'll get the paint." He carried a can of paint in each hand and a roll of plastic sheeting under one arm.

"What color did you pick?" she asked as she followed him back inside through the laundry room.

"I don't remember."

The outer log wall wouldn't need paint, but the other three walls were made of Sheetrock, and they were in desperate need of attention. He pried open a can and let paint drip off the lid and back into the can.

Her nose wrinkled. "Finn, you cannot paint your bedroom that color. It looks like mustard."

"I like mustard."

"On your walls? I'm sorry, but this is the color of a spoiled condiment. Did you pick it out?"

"Not exactly. You know that rack in the paint section where you can get really cheap paint that's been mixed but no one bought?"

She laughed. "That explains it. And you have two cans of this unfortunate color?"

"No, that one is different." He pointed at the other can by the bathroom door. "It's light gray."

"That sounds much better. You were planning to use two different colors in here?"

He shrugged. "A couple different colors sound better than the way it looks since I stripped off the wallpaper. And what's the worst that can happen? I have to repaint it? I have two more colors still in the garage. Want me to get them?"

"Yes, please. We'll see if we can salvage this project." While he was out of the room, she tuned the radio on his dresser to a country station and hummed along with the number one song of the week.

He came back into the room and put two more cans of paint on the bedroom floor beside the gray. "Check these out and see if any of them meet your strict standards, Daisy Maisy."

She knelt beside him and looked at the lids, which had a

smear of paint indicating the color. One was a blue that was a bit too bright for a man's bedroom. The other was a light shade of green. "These three are way better than the mustard. That's for sure."

"What color do you suggest?" he asked.

"I have an idea. One can isn't really enough to paint all three walls, but if we mix two colors, we might be able to make something nice. Do you have some disposable plastic cups we can use to test out a few different options?"

"I have red plastic cups in the pantry."

"Perfect."

Once they had several options mixed, they painted a swatch of each color on the wall, then stood back to look at them. She tilted her head to catch the light in different ways. "I like the gray mixed with the blue. It reminds me of the Texas sky right before a storm."

"I agree," he said. "But where can I use the mustard paint, Ms. Designer?"

"In very small doses. Maybe the barn or the back side of one of the wooden fences."

He laughed. "Damn. You really hate that color."

"Hey, I'm just being honest with you."

They scooted the furniture into the middle of the room and laid down plastic. He found a bucket, and they mixed the color they'd chosen. She started with a brush and painted around all the edges and in the corners, while he used a roller on the center of the walls.

"You already have paint in your hair," he said.

"Of course I do. Maybe I'll just claim it's the new fashion. That's the kind of daring thing Maleficent would do."

"The Angelina Jolie character in that movie you made me watch?" he asked.

She chuckled. "Yes. But it actually started with the animated version of *Sleeping Beauty*. You know how people talk about the angel on one shoulder giving good advice and the devil sitting on the other? Well, Sage and I saw that in a movie when we were about ten, and we were also really into *Sleep-*

ing Beauty at the time, so we named our angel and devil after the movie characters.

He dipped his roller into the paint tray. "That's pretty clever. I can't say that I've ever thought much about what mine would be."

"Probably a cowboy dressed in white and one in black."

"I wear a lot of black."

She pointed her brush at him. "What does that say about you?"

He let his smile grow. "That I'm the fun one."

A COUPLE OF hours later, Finn stood back to survey their work while Daisy was on her hands and knees touching up a spot above the baseboard. The way her curvy bottom swayed from side to side along with the beat of the music was very distracting—in a good way. His eyes moved to the tray of paint beside her, and he couldn't resist. The tight, faded denim stretched across her butt became an irresistible canvas. He quietly knelt beside the paint tray and dipped the palms of both hands into the blue-gray paint. In one swift movement, he pressed two handprints to the denim. One on each cheek.

She stiffened and froze, then shot a startled look over her shoulder. She gaped at his paint-covered palms. "Finn! What did you do?"

He shrugged and walked into the bathroom to wash his hands. "It had to be done."

"You're lucky these aren't my favorite pair." She followed him into the bathroom and gasped at her reflection. "Why didn't you tell me I have paint on my face too?"

"That part was not me." He held up his wet hands in surrender. "I swear."

"I think this is a good excuse to leave you with the cleanup while I get to take a shower."

"I suppose that's fair." His mouth trembled with the urge to laugh.

She shooed him out the second his hands were dry. The door shuddered against the frame as she tried to force it closed.

"Your next project should be to fix this door," she called from the other side.

"Hand out your jeans and I'll take care of them."

A minute later, the door opened enough that her arm slipped through, jeans dangling from two fingers by a belt loop.

Daisy was holding a towel across the front of her body, but obviously didn't realize he could see her reflection in the mirror behind her. The sight of her nicely proportioned bare backside made his mouth go dry.

Without his brain's permission, his eyes took in her beauty. Long blond hair trailed halfway down her back, almost to the graceful curve where her waist met her hips. She might have only one dimple on her face, but now he knew she had two more low on the small of her back. And long legs, toned from riding a horse.

He stood there like a dummy as she closed the door and cut off his view. All that feminine beauty had been hiding under the denim and T-shirts.

A very unhappy meow and hiss followed by barking pulled him from his thoughts, and he rushed out into the hallway and followed the cat and dog into the living room.

"You two, knock it off." He draped her jeans over a ladder back chair by the fireplace.

Astro trotted over to him and sat at his feet with his tongue lolling out of the side of his mouth. Finn rubbed his head. "You like having someone to play with, don't you? Let's go see if Rascal is awake from her nap."

After he let the goat out of the crate and got the animals settled down, he went back to the fireplace and saw a folded piece of paper on the floor below Daisy's jeans. Without thinking much about it, he picked it up and unfolded it.

Daisy's New Year's Wish List
1) Sleep with a hot guy/Brief, fun affair
2) Fall

His body started to awaken. He couldn't believe he was seeing this right after seeing her half naked. He shouldn't even consider it, but technically, he could grant her first wish. That's if he was willing to gamble with their current relationship. But if number two on her list was the start of what he thought it was, he could not help her with falling in love.

His head snapped up.

Was Dr. Dillon Cameron the guy she had in mind to fulfill her New Year's wishes?

CHAPTER SIX

Daisy had just put conditioner on her hair when the bathroom lights went off. She sighed and tipped her head under the water. Her first thought was that it was just Finn messing around with her, but the radio had gone silent as well as the small space heater she'd set up on the granite countertop. Only the dimmest of evening light came in through the long narrow window above the shower.

"Well, shoot. This can't be a good sign."

She quickly rinsed her hair and fumbled for her towel. It helped that she always stacked her clothes in the order she put them on, with her panties on top. She dressed in her pajamas and wrapped a towel around her head before opening the door.

In his bedroom, the large bank of windows gave her a view of the gray stormy night. The trees swayed like contemporary dancers in the strong wind as snow flurries swirled about like fairies. It felt like one of those nights that was made for ghost stories and warm drinks and snuggling with someone. But the only cuddling she was going to get tonight was from either a cat, a dog or a tiny goat.

She ran her hand along the wall until the flickering glow of firelight helped light her way into the living room.

Finn closed the fireplace screen and looked up. "Our luck

just ran out. I already checked and found out another power line was pulled down when an ice-covered tree fell."

"I was afraid it was something like that."

"I got a couple of lanterns out of our camping gear." He pointed to the green metal lanterns on the coffee table. "Tomorrow we'll probably have to move some of the things in the refrigerator to an ice chest and put it outside."

"Guess we won't be baking the lasagna and garlic bread we had planned for dinner."

"I have a cast-iron pot and know how to cook over a fire. But the easiest thing would be roasted hot dogs and s'mores."

"Yum. I could go for that. Do you actually have s'mores makings?"

He thought for a minute. "I do. But now that I think about it, I don't have any hot dogs."

"You're such a tease." She laughed. "If you provide dessert, I'll get out the stuff we brought from my house and put together a picnic style meal."

He gazed into the flames for a couple of seconds before answering. "Deal."

She sat on the stone hearth, pulled the towel from her hair and began to dry it. "Did the paint wash out of my jeans?"

"Um. I didn't wash them." He pointed to her pants still hanging over the chair.

"Finn! Do you expect me to walk around with your giant handprints on my butt?"

When his mischievous grin appeared, she knew she'd said the wrong thing.

FINN COULDN'T BELIEVE the great opportunity that was being handed to him on a big, shiny serving platter. "I dare you to wear those jeans with my handprints. In public."

"Oh, man. I walked right into that one." She dropped her head forward in a dramatized show of defeat. Firelight filtered through her curtain of golden hair, the drying strands swaying in the waves of heat from the flames.

"Told you I was the master."

"I'm not crowning you king of anything just yet."

With the goat in the lead, all three animals raced in a circle around the room and disappeared down the hallway.

"I suspect Lady is starting to enjoy the companionship." No sooner had she spoken than the cat bounded back in and jumped into Daisy's arms. The disgruntled feline looked over Daisy's shoulder and growled at the other Astro and Rascal. "Or maybe not so much."

"Your cat sure has got some sassy attitude, but at least she never uses her claws."

"She doesn't get the attitude from me," Daisy said.

"I don't know about that. I think you have your sassy moments." He could think of a few right away.

"What about my claws?" She raised her hand and curled her fingers. "Do these worry you?"

It had not taken him long to figure out that Daisy was a protective mama bear when it came to those she cared about. And he felt like he was lucky enough to be counted in that group. "I think for someone that you love you would use your claws to eviscerate the bad guy."

"You're right about that. It used to be just me and Sage, and we had to be tough."

"I remember." When he and his brothers had first arrived in Channing and started working on Dalton Ranch, the twins had both been single and living alone in their family farmhouse.

"It was such a wonderful surprise when Lizzy returned to us, and then fell in love with Travis and brought Davy into our lives."

"Your niece came in like a singing whirlwind." Travis, their business partner who owned half of the Four Star Ranch, had had his life upended by an opera singer and an orphaned baby with Down syndrome. Finn had to admit that his friend was happier than ever.

He just couldn't relate to being that happy about taking on the responsibility for other human lives.

He'd somehow gotten his brothers well into adulthood without major damage, and the memory of the overwhelming stress from when they were young was a big part of the reason that he'd chosen a bachelor life.

Daisy ran her fingers through her hair to untangle it. "And then Sage found her happily-ever-after with Grayson. Now, because of Lizzy and Sage, I have two beautiful nieces and an adorable grandnephew."

The sadness in her eyes and the longing in her voice kept him from teasing her about being old enough to have a grandnephew. He knew she wanted a child of her own. A family of her own.

The exact opposite of his goals.

She shivered and moved closer to the fire with Lady still on her lap. "Without electricity, it's going to get really cold in here fast."

"We'll both have to sleep in front of the fire." When her eyes widened and her lips parted, his gaze was drawn to her mouth. How had he never noticed how full her lips were?

Seeing her reflection in the bathroom mirror and then her handwritten wish, the idea of sleeping side by side in front of the fire was making him lose his grip on what was between them. Keeping some level of distance was the only safe choice. Sex wasn't worth ruining their friendship. "I should go have a shower before there's no hot water."

Don't be a dumbass and screw this up.

DAISY SET THE cat on the floor and got up. "Take your time. I'll work on our fireside picnic."

Finn's eyes widened, and he rushed from the room. She stood perfectly still. Something had made the fun-loving attitude disappear from his eyes, and then he'd bolted. Maybe it was the term fireside picnic? It sounded too romantic, and she'd probably freaked him out.

What she'd thought would be a relaxing but boring few days alone had certainly taken an interesting turn. First, Dillon had offered to share the one-bedroom apartment with her, and now, Finn was talking about both of them sleeping in front of his fireplace. Was this happening because she'd written down a New Year's wish and put the thought out there into the universe?

"I'm being ridiculous," she whispered, and shook her head.

She grabbed one of the lanterns and went into the kitchen to prepare their meal. She didn't want to have an awkward discussion while she was feeling so off-kilter. If he took a long shower, she'd have time for Sleeping Beauty on her right shoulder to give her a pep talk about being a good girl.

Why did her BFF have to be a Greek god? Being his friend was wonderful, but also confusing and sometimes difficult. Especially since she'd worked hard to overcome and put aside her initial attraction to him. At times like this, her dedication to stick to the smart choice was tested.

She opened the refrigerator and pulled out a variety of food. The Murphy brothers didn't own any fancy wooden charcuterie boards or pretty trays, so she got out a cookie sheet and covered it with foil. She sliced cheese and dried meats and added the fruit they'd grabbed from her house.

While she was standing at the kitchen island cutting an apple, she caught a glimpse of him as he walked past on his way to the living room with his arms piled high with sleeping bags and a stack of blankets. He hadn't been kidding about making a bed in front of the fire. The thought of sleeping beside her sexy, younger best friend was exhilarating and scary. And way too tempting.

"Don't even think about it," said Sleeping Beauty.

Finn Murphy had always been very clear about what he wanted in life. He was not at all a good choice for her in any romantic sense. He didn't plan to make any permanent commitments and had made no secret of it. He had no interest in a serious relationship and zero intentions of ever having a wife or child. Not to mention no romantic interest in *her*. Sure, he sometimes flirted with her in his usual way, but he did that with everyone.

Her cat pranced into the kitchen and rubbed against her leg. "Hello, Lady. How did you get away from the rowdy duo?" She'd spoken too soon. Her words were immediately followed by the clip-clopping of teeny-tiny hooves, dog paws clicking and cowboy boots making a familiar shuffle against the floor.

"Everyone wants to eat," Finn said. "Maybe if this crew is fed, they'll give us some peace."

"Here's hoping."

"Rascal ate a little of the goat feed earlier, but she is probably ready for another bottle."

"I'll make the bottle." While he fed the cat and dog—each on opposite sides of the kitchen—she mixed the milk replacement formula with the tiny goat perched on her foot.

"Come with me, little miss." Finn scooped up the goat and took the bottle Daisy held out. Rascal started sucking on it right away. "She's happy with this, but for us, wine, beer or hard liquor?"

"With the—" She bit her tongue. She'd almost used the words fireside picnic, again. "With the kind of food I'm putting together, I think red wine sounds best." She ducked her head to continue her work, unwilling to let him see any emotion her face might show. She was *not* setting up a romantic evening.

"Red wine. Got it. I'll take this one into the living room to feed her where it's quiet and see if she'll go to sleep."

It suddenly felt like they were playing house, and it was messing with her mind. Tending the ranches, painting a bedroom and now meals by the fire.

Why am I doing this to myself?

She had worked so hard to bury her attraction to him. She shook her head and pushed the thought away before turning back to her original task of food prep.

In the living room, he had spread out and layered everything in one bed that was big enough to sleep two, and she set the tray on the center of their bed.

"My brothers and I used to sleep in front of our fireplace when..." His voice trailed off.

The pinched look on his face hinted at a painful memory. She hoped he would someday share some of his past. But... she had secrets too, so she understood and had never pushed him to share.

"I forgot the wine. Be right back," he said, and hurried away.

Both of them seemed to be doing a lot of running away this evening. She sat on one side of the bed and got comfortable. He returned with a bottle of bourbon, an open bottle of wine, two mismatched glasses and a couple of shot glasses from their trip to the San Antonio Rodeo. He'd barely filled hers with bur-gundy liquid before she grabbed it and took a big sip.

"Better slow down or tonight's nickname will be Dizzy Daisy."

"Hey, you're the one who brought wine and hard liquor."

"I thought we might need it to keep warm."

This evening could go a couple of different ways, and she wasn't sure which one she was hoping for. Maleficent's red lips curled into a grin.

Finn put another log on the fire and adjusted it with a rustic poker that was topped with a star, kind of like the one they used as part of their Four Star Ranch cattle brand. "Do you know Tim, the new guy at the hardware store?"

"I've met him a few times," she said.

"He recently got a huge surprise. Fatherhood."

Daisy rolled onto her side and propped up on one elbow. The way he'd said it sounded like this was one of his worst fears. "He is going to be or already is a father?"

"The baby is two months old." He returned to his spot beside her on the sleeping bags.

"That would certainly be a big shock."

"No doubt. At least a woman knows for sure whether or not she has a kid."

Her heart was hit with a quick, sharp jab. "That's not always true." The second she said it, a knot formed in her belly.

"What do you mean? How can that be?"

"Never mind. You're right. The wine has already gone to my head."

Finn stretched out on his back beside her and tucked his laced fingers under his head. "Tell me a secret, Daisy Maisy."

The request startled her. But...this was her chance to learn more about him and his past. To get a deeper peek into that part of himself he kept shuttered behind layers of cockiness.

"If I tell you a secret, you have to do the same."

"Deal," he said.

Finn was a private guy, so his rapid agreement surprised her. But she'd forgotten how talkative he could get while drinking. She was right on the edge of grasping that nice, warm, fuzzy feeling that came with being tipsy, and one more drink would be just right.

And one more drink for him would make him even more talkative. "First, pour a couple of shots, please."

He did as she asked, they clinked shot glasses and drank. She shuddered as the bourbon burned its way down her throat and warmed her chest and belly. "Okay. My secret is that I like to eat ice cream right out of the carton. In bed."

He chuckled. "I could've guessed that. You also talk in your sleep."

"That's a well-known fact. Stop stalling. What's your secret?"

"I like to sleep in the nude."

"Not a surprise." She used this moment as an excuse to look him over from his head to his toes, possibly lingering longer than necessary on the black T-shirt pulling taught across his chest. "Thank you for being appropriately clothed this evening."

He grinned. "It's only because it's so cold."

"Rascal sure is cozy by the fire." At Finn's feet, the baby goat was tucked into the size of a football on their nest of sleeping bags. The firelight made the animal's white-and-tan hair glisten, and she looked more like a child's toy than a real live animal. Of course, Finn—the ladies' man that he was—would be adored even by a female goat.

"How old were you when you had your first kiss?" she asked him.

"I was thirteen. And I know for a fact that I'm a great kisser."

She chuckled. "I'm sure you think so, Casanova."

"I've been assured that it's true. Multiple times." He propped up on his side to face her. "Now tell me something real. Something few people know about."

Taking her own opportunity to stall for time, she bit into an apple slice and chewed. Only her sister knew about the sacrifice she'd made to save their ranch years ago. When she had given the gift of parenthood—to someone else without really thinking it through.

Over the last couple of years, she'd told Finn a lot about her life, but she didn't want to put a downward spin on tonight by bringing up something that made her sad. Reliving it aloud would make it all too real. So, she decided to tell him her second most regrettable decision.

"I was married."

"For real?"

"For six months. When I was eighteen years old. We spent a lot of our time together in high school and both thought it was love, but it was only lust that burned out way too quickly. We were a disaster in the bedroom and much better friends than lovers."

This important lesson was something she needed to keep at the forefront of her mind in her current situation. Friends didn't always translate into lovers.

"So, you just decided to split?"

"Well…he sped things along when he cheated. I think he lives in Houston now."

Finn bit into a cracker and studied her. "Is getting burned like that the reason you've never married again?"

"No. It sounds cliché, but I just haven't met the right one, I guess." She swirled her wine and took a sip. "Your turn. Tell me something about your childhood. You started to say something about you and your brothers sleeping by the fire."

"It's a long story."

"Do you have somewhere you need to be?"

He chuckled. "Well, no. I suppose I have time." He scratched his head as if choosing where to begin his story was hard work. "I had to start taking care of Riley and Jake when I was nine years old."

"Like babysitting?"

He plowed his hand through his hair. "It was more than that. Our mom was gone by then. She was in a boating accident with a group of her wild friends."

"Oh, no." She had known his mother died when he was young, but she hadn't known how tragic it had been.

"Our dad was rarely around. He was a long-haul trucker. Sometimes we didn't see him for days at a time."

Daisy's chest ached at the thought of three little boys all alone and scared. This was heartbreaking and explained why the three brothers were so close. "Did he leave you with enough food and money?"

"Most of the time, but not always. When the electric bill didn't get paid is when we slept by the fireplace to stay warm. I did odd jobs for neighbors. Raking leaves, walking dogs and stuff like that. Thankfully, it was enough for some food, and the grocery store was within walking distance. We ate a lot of sandwiches and cereal."

Daisy clasped her hands to keep from putting her arms around him to comfort him like she would do with Sage or Lizzy. "Did you have to move from place to place?"

"No. Thankfully we owned the house. It had been my grand-parents' house."

"It doesn't surprise me that you stepped up and took such good care of your little brothers."

"Somebody had to." His brow furrowed, making the faint lines of his early thirties more pronounced. "But I'm not so sure good describes it. I did the best I could. Getting us all to school on time was a challenge, but I couldn't let us be late all the time and have anyone discover we were alone. I couldn't stand the thought of us being separated."

This explained more about his in control personality. "That must have been so stressful. Especially for someone so young."

"It was. It's a big part of why I plan to remain childless."

That made her sad. "I'm sorry to hear that because you are naturally good with kids. You're wonderful with Rose and Davy when you babysit."

"It's not so bad when it's just for a few hours at a time. But anything longer than a day or so is too much. I'm not built to ever be a full-time father." He reached one hand across to his opposite shoulder and kneaded the muscle as if it was suddenly tight. "Give me one more secret," he requested.

He had shared some hard stuff, so maybe she could too. She was just tipsy enough and comfortable enough to consider letting someone other than her sister in on the secret that haunted her. Maybe it would be cathartic to talk about it.

"Well, there is something no one other than Sage knows. Remember when Loren announced that Sage was the surrogate who carried and gave birth to her and was now going to be her stepmom?"

"Who can forget something like that?" He sat up suddenly and looked at her waist. "Wait...were you a surrogate too?"

She shook her head as her pulse raced. "No. I was not a surrogate." The lump in her throat made it difficult to speak. Bringing this up was a mistake. She should have listened to her first gut instinct.

I should have chosen something embarrassing or funny. Think. What can I say instead?

Before she could think of something that would match up with what Loren had said, Finn sneezed, and the goat's head popped up a second before her whole body sprang into the air. She bounded up the space between their bodies.

Finn picked her up with one hand, and Rascal's little legs churned in the air like she was running. "Wish I could wake up this perky," he said.

"I'm surprised you don't."

He shot her a sexy smirk. "My brain takes longer than that to fire up and tell my body to get out of bed. But there are times when the mind and the body have different ideas."

That was certainly true. Her mind, body and heart, plus Maleficent and Sleeping Beauty, were all arguing about what to do with Finn Murphy. What box did he—or should he—fit into?

She reached out to rub the goat's soft ear between her fingers, and Rascal tried to suck on her pinkie. "Looks like someone is ready for another bottle."

"I'll go get it." Finn handed over the tiny animal and walked around the corner to the kitchen.

Daisy cuddled Rascal, rubbed her tummy and whispered, "Thanks for interrupting right when I needed you to."

Sharing too much while drinking had been a problem for her more than once. She crisscrossed her legs and closed her eyes.

When she and Sage had needed the money to save their horse ranch a little over fifteen years ago, she'd come up with her portion of the money before really thinking it through for the long-term. In desperation, she had donated her eggs so some other woman could have a baby. But even now, she too often wondered if she had a child out there somewhere in the world. A boy? A girl? More than one?

This was the reason she'd started going to hold babies in the NICU at the hospital. Even though she'd never know for sure, there was a chance she might've held her own baby.

CHAPTER SEVEN

IT WASN'T UNTIL Finn was moving around the kitchen and slightly off balance that he realized he had more than a buzz going. He put water and two scoops of powdered formula into the bottle, screwed on the top and shook it.

The kitchen was cold now that the central heat had been off for a few hours, and a chill was seeping through his socks, but he knew right where he could find some warmth. And he was feeling just relaxed and playful enough to be slightly dangerous.

Even though he knew he couldn't see Daisy, he glanced toward the living room. It wasn't the fire that was drawing him in. It was the woman he was having fun with. The woman he could be himself around. He waited for the panic to hit him... but it didn't come.

That's because there is nothing wrong with what we're doing.

It had felt good to share some of his childhood struggles with her after keeping it locked inside for so long, and he was glad she had encouraged him to talk about it. Daisy couldn't seem to understand why he wanted to remain an unencumbered bachelor. Knowing him better would help her understand.

Back in the living room, Daisy was sitting cross-legged, eyes closed and swaying from side to side with the goat in her arms. She looked ethereal in the flickering light. What Mother Nature must look like if she was young and beautiful.

He shook his head. *What is going on with me?*

She opened her eyes, smiled and held out her hand. "I'll feed her."

"Thanks. I'm going to let the dog out. Don't forget to set Rascal directly into the litter box when she finishes eating."

"I will. I think she is already making progress with her training."

"I certainly hope so. She's way too little to be outside or in the barn. I don't know what I was thinking when I offered to bring her home."

"Why did you?"

"Because if someone didn't take her before close of business, the feed store owner said he was going to take her to the pound."

"Do they even take goats at the pound?"

"I think he was just blustering, but I didn't want to find out. I swear I don't know how someone who owns a business that sells feed and supplies for animals can have such a dislike for them."

"He really is a grumpy old man. I'm glad you brought her home." She kissed the top of the animal's head as Rascal devoured her bottle.

By the front door, Finn pulled on his coat and boots and went outside. Astro whimpered. "I know, buddy. Do it quick and then we'll go back inside."

He remained on the front porch while the dog went to the very edge, gathered his courage and then went a couple of steps into the yard. A sudden gust of wind jerked at his coat and went right through the material of his black-and-gray-plaid pajama pants. He shivered, and it brought on a strong craving to live on the wild side. A craving for the woman he was snowed in with.

Astro didn't take long to do his business and then dashed back into the house the second the door was open enough to squeeze through.

"The conditions are not getting better out there." He stood on the hearth and held his hands out to the warmth.

Daisy pulled the bottle from the goat's mouth, then got up and took her over to the litter box by the front door. She put her in and said, "Okay, Rascal. Show us what a smart girl you are."

The little animal bleated happily and did exactly what she

was supposed to do, and they both praised her. But just to be safe, she put a diaper on her for the night.

"I'll go wash this bottle. Need anything?" she asked.

"No, thanks."

When she returned, he was sitting at the foot of their make-shift bed with his forearms braced across his drawn-up knees.

Rather than sitting beside him, she settled behind him. "I should've put my socks on. My feet are freezing."

That was all the warning he got before she slid her Popsicle feet up under the back of his T-shirt to the small of his back. He sucked in a sharp breath but remained as still as possible. "I charge extra for warming services." He looked over his shoulder and into her smiling face.

"I'm sure it will be worth every penny." She slid her feet up higher to torture a new spot on his back.

But he didn't really mind. She didn't know he was more than willing to warm her up for free. He was enjoying their playful, flirty banter. Having this closeness was helping him relax and let go of some of his worries—if only for a little while. Being with Daisy felt comfortable and...safe.

"Who said it's money that I want as payment?"

"I probably don't want the answer to that question. Do I? It's bound to be something embarrassing or cause me to need several showers." She moved to his side, stretched out her legs and propped herself up on her elbows to gaze into the flames like he was doing.

"It's nothing bad. Just a little bit of light housecleaning. Bathrooms, kitchen, bedrooms, living room and my laundry. And windows."

"I think that's where the shower part comes in. For maid services, we're going to have to spend a whole lot more time with my feet on your warm skin."

He opened his mouth to issue a witty comeback, but the image of any part of her against any part of his bare skin made him momentarily lose his words. He jerked his gaze back to the fire.

"I'm open to negotiations."

She shivered. "Let's talk about it under the covers."

He grinned at her soft gasp and horrified expression. It was right on brand for his Daisy Maisy. She often said something that she didn't mean to sound suggestive, but it did, and it presented a perfect opportunity for a comeback that would make her blush.

"Because I'm cold," she hurried to say in answer to his grin. "I need to stay warm until we can negotiate a reasonable exchange of services."

"I'll sleep on it and have it figured out by morning." He pulled the blankets up over them.

They'd never discussed boundaries between them. It had just always been understood as friendship, because that was safe. But they'd never stated any specific rules. At least none he could think of at the moment. He and Daisy were adults and deserved to enjoy themselves. But what exactly would that look like or mean for them? Flirting was one thing, but what was the point of no return?

He'd sleep on this as well and see if he found answers in the light of day. Or maybe in his dreams. In companionable silence, they fell asleep side by side.

A LOG SHIFTED and crackled in the fireplace, and Finn half-opened one eye, still hovering somewhere between that fuzzy dream state and reality. A soft, warm, sweet-smelling woman was spooned against the front of his body. The scent of flowers lingered in her hair, and he pulled her closer, letting his hand slide from her curvy hip up to a full—

He froze and his eyes popped open.

Daisy.

She sighed and arched her back, simultaneously pushing her breast into his palm while wiggling her bottom against him. He groaned and fought against the urge to pull her closer and touch every part of her.

He should roll away from her. He really should. Except that she was on his side of the bed, and if he rolled, he'd end up on the floor. But before he figured out a way to let her go, it wouldn't hurt to hold her for just a little while longer.

He slowly eased his hand down to her waist and breathed in

her scent. He would take this small moment in time. Just for himself. And he'd imagine what it would be like if he knew how to love a woman.

Daisy turned in his arms and snuggled against his chest with her head tucked under his chin. He once again froze. There was no way she could miss the physical effect she was having on his body. But she wasn't pushing him away. In fact, her hips shifted forward ever so slightly, but it was enough that he noticed. Inner heat built.

"Daisy, are you awake?"

CHAPTER EIGHT

THE DEEP RUMBLE of Finn's voice pulled Daisy from a deep sleep. Hovering in a dreamy state, his musky scent filled her head and swirls of stardust danced across her skin.

"Daisy?" he whispered.

She wasn't sure what made her do it, but she didn't want him to know she was awake. "I'll have the chocolate cake," she mumbled, hoping he would believe she was talking in her sleep.

His chest rose and fell with a deep breath, and he remained still, but his body was giving away his excitement about being pressed so closely together. He tightened his arm around her and smoothed a hand over her hair as he kissed the top of her head.

His tenderness made her heart do a cartwheel.

He seemed to like holding her as much as she was enjoying being in his arms, and their cozy cocoon was too good to give up. Everything felt right, and there was no harm in remaining right where she was.

Snuggling didn't cross a line. Not like kissing or making love would. If there was any fallout, she'd deal with that when she wasn't living out part of a fantasy.

Daisy needed this small haven of security. She closed her eyes and relaxed into his warm embrace.

A FEW HOURS LATER, the goat was making a racket in the dog crate and woke Daisy once again. It only took a few seconds to realize that her head was still on Finn's chest. She popped into a sitting position like a cork bobbing in the water.

He chuckled. "You wake up just like Rascal."

Not normally. She thought to herself. She was not a morning person. "Sorry about using you as a pillow. I've been told I'm a bed hog."

"No worries." His voice was still gravelly from sleep, but he was chuckling. "Hard times, desperate measures."

"Hard...what?" She was still too groggy to fully comprehend what he'd said, but his comment made something flutter in her belly.

He tried to hold back a smile but gave up. "The hard time was the freezing temperature. The desperate measure was you seeking my body heat."

"Oh." She chuckled. "Now I really owe you for your warming services."

"I have no doubt we can work something out that will make both of us happy."

She tried to smooth down her bedhead. "You know, I did return the favor of warmth last night, and now that I think about it, who is to say you weren't the one who pulled me over to keep you warm?"

"Fair point." He stretched and his T-shirt rode up to reveal his lower abs and the V of blond hair that disappeared into the waistband of his pajama pants. "I guess your tab is forgiven. This time."

She quickly got to her feet and pulled off the top blanket to wrap around herself. "I'll go start the coffee."

"No electricity," he said, reminding her.

"Shoot. I forgot about that."

"Never fear. I have a camping coffeepot and a small propane stove."

"Thank goodness. I'll make Rascal's bottle while you do that." She was smiling as she stepped over the cat and crossed the room to the front windows to pull back the curtains that they'd drawn to help keep out drafts. "There's a fresh layer of snow. My snow angel and all of our footprints are covered."

This meant they would likely be without electricity for even longer, but rather than being upset by the likelihood, it put an even bigger smile on her face.

The idea of extending their ice storm seclusion was very appealing.

THEY FOLLOWED MUCH of the same routine as the day before. But this time breakfast was by lantern light and the dim morning sun trying to make its way through the storm clouds. After tending to his cattle, they went over to her ranch.

In her stable, the familiar scents of molasses feed, hay and horses always made her smile. Ever since she was a toddler riding in the saddle with her dad, horses had been one of her favorite things in the world.

Dillon was walking up and down the aisle between the stalls with his cell phone to his ear.

He paused his conversation when he saw her. "Morning, Daisy. I'm talking someone through delivering a calf. But all of the horses are fed, and the stalls are mucked out."

"Thanks for keeping on top of that. Don't let me keep you from your important call."

He turned and headed toward the apartment. "Call me later," he said over his shoulder.

Finn was coming in the side door and the two men waved to one another.

"Phone date?" Finn asked her.

The idea of him being jealous was kind of fun. "We just didn't have a chance to catch up because he is being a virtual veterinarian. Since he can't get out on the road, he is walking someone through how to deliver a calf."

"I checked all the outdoor water faucets to make sure the weatherproofing is still in place, and they all look good." Finn's phone rang, and he pulled it out of his jacket pocket to look at the screen then started walking toward the tack room while answering. "Hi, Connie. What's going on with you?"

A twinge of jealousy stirred to life in her belly, and she hated it, especially since she'd just been enjoying the thought of him being the jealous one. Connie was a woman he'd gone out with several times, but Daisy didn't think she was right for him. She wasn't the least bit outdoorsy, and of all things, she was afraid of cows. That made her grin, wondering what Connie would think of a goat in the house.

The other woman's fear of animals was the kind of information she learned when she listened to him talk about his dates. She always listened, occasionally offered advice and never complained because she wanted to be a good friend. But she hated hearing about how this lady or that one couldn't keep her hands off him.

She grabbed the red treat bucket and started down the center aisle, giving each horse some attention along with their favorite treat. An apple for Titan, Lou, Zeus and Lizzy's horse, Misty, and carrots for the rest of them.

"Hello, handsome," she said to Titan. He nuzzled his nose against the red stocking cap on her head, then took the small apple from her hand. "I know it's hard being stuck indoors. I'll turn on the radio before I go so you can have some entertainment."

She moved along to the next stall to talk to their youngest stud horse, Cinder. He was a jumpy one and let few people other than herself touch him. It annoyed Finn that Dillon was one of the other people Cinder allowed near him. Was that another sign of jealousy?

Something small and light kept thumping against the back of her head and shoulders.

"What is that?" Not for the first time, she looked up to make sure it wasn't one of those spiders that drops down on a long strand of web to float in midair as if ready to land on her face. There was no sign of an arachnoid or any other critter such as a raccoon moving around in the rafters or running along the top rail of the stalls. She caught movement from the corner of her eye and spun to see the cause of it.

"Finnigan Murphy! I should've known it was you."

He stepped out of his horse's stall and dropped the pieces of feed he'd been tossing. "Took you long enough."

"You are such a man-child. A big man-child."

"I'm choosing to focus on the big man part."

"Of course you are." She turned to go—and to hide her grin.

"Daisy, freeze. Don't. Move."

His tone of voice hinted at danger and brought her to a sudden halt. Every muscle tensed. "Please, tell me it's not a spider."

CHAPTER NINE

EVEN IN HARSH WEATHER, the Dalton Ranch stable made a cozy winter home for the small, harmless barn spiders. The only animal that Daisy couldn't stand.

"Hold still while I untangle the little beast from your hair," Finn said.

Daisy stiffened, her hands fisted at her sides. "Get it out. Quick!"

Rather than tell her there really was a spider on her head, he removed it from her red hat then tugged on a lock of her hair. She didn't need to know that there really had been a creepy crawly on her.

"Gotcha. Can't believe you fell for that."

Daisy spun on him with an adorable scowl. Her big green eyes flashing. "No fair tricking me like that. You know how I feel about spiders."

He cleared his throat to keep from chuckling. "Sorry. You're making it too easy to mess with you today."

You could use a good spanking, Finn Murphy."

. "It's debatable who needs the spanking." He turned up the wattage on his slow grin. The one that occasionally triggered female giggles.

Daisy's high cheekbones turned a rosy pink as she thrust the red bucket out to him. "Help me out with this, please."

They tended the rest of the horses for a few minutes and managed to avoid any more spider encounters.

"Let's go home, and I'll make another pot of coffee by the fire." He wanted to get out of the stable before Dr. Cameron came back out to chat up Daisy. The idea that his thinking was going in that direction made him frown. He had zero right to keep Daisy from dating anyone she wanted to. Especially since he couldn't be the one who gave her what she was looking for. He could not be her husband or the father of her children.

She hung the bucket on its hook. "I could use the caffeine and the warmth. And Rascal is going to be ready to get out of her crate."

When they got back to his ranch house, he built up the fire. They spent the rest of the day playing with the animals, reading books, eating and napping. The snow turned to sleet and chased away any chance of sunshine. With the conditions even worse, no one would be traveling, and their seclusion was safe from his brothers' return for a while longer.

"I cannot go to bed without a bath or shower," Daisy announced. "I guess I'll have to go to the apartment since it's the only place that has the generator to keep the hot water heater running. I'm sure Dillon won't mind at all."

He was *sure* the doc wouldn't mind. A sharp jab punched him in the gut. After seeing her in the bubble bath, he didn't want her showering with Dillon on the other side of the door. And what if… He shook his head.

She was trying to hide a smile but not doing a very good job of it.

Is she teasing me? Does she know I'm…jealous?

"Seems like a long way to go in this weather," he said.

She laughed. "Because it's sooo far to my place? We can see the stable in the distance from your front yard."

"I mean because of the sleet that has mixed in with the snow. It's slick and more dangerous now." Sounded like a good excuse to him. "I can give you a hot bath right here."

"How?" Her smile was challenging but sweet.

"Remember those two huge pots we used for the crawfish

boil? I can put them on the gas grill on the porch and heat enough water for a bath in the small tub in the hallway bathroom."

"Okay. I'm game for that. Who gets the water first? You or me?"

"While the water heats, we can play a game of cards, and the winner gets the bathwater first."

"Deal," she said.

He let her win because he knew how much she disliked being in cold water, and the bathroom wasn't going to be warm.

When he went into the bathroom carrying the heavy pot of hot water, Daisy was standing there in his black bathrobe. Did she have any idea what she was doing to him? On the counter beside the sink, her pajamas were neatly folded with a pair of red panties on top. He smiled when he saw that his flannel pajamas were stacked neatly beside hers.

She twirled one end of the robe's belt. "I wanted to be ready to jump right into the tub, so we don't waste any of your hard work heating the water."

"Very thoughtful." He carefully poured the second pot of water into the tub. "Have at it, Daisy Maisy."

"I'll be quick."

"Give me a shout when it's safe to come in."

He closed the door and then leaned against the wall to wait. He could hear her splashing and humming. Mother Nature bathing under a waterfall came to mind, and he smiled despite the sexual dilemma he was getting himself into. Only a couple of minutes later, the splashing grew quiet and shortly after, she called out to him.

"Your turn."

He opened the door just as she was cinching the belt of his robe, but her pajamas were still on the counter. Which meant she still wasn't wearing anything beneath. He inwardly groaned.

"It's still hot. I'm going to go make us a snack. Meet you by the fire." She picked up her pajamas and slipped past him.

His self-control was going to be tested tonight, but he was up for the challenge.

While she was in the bedroom talking to her sister on the phone, he used the propane camp stove to heat a coffeepot of water. He made two mugs of hot chocolate and set them in front of the fire to stay warm. He'd set a bottle of rum on the coffee table earlier. Now he grabbed it and added some to his mug.

Daisy entered the room, and as she walked past the dark Christmas tree, she brushed her fingers over its branches. "It still smells good. I wish the Christmas tree lights worked on batteries. I love sitting and staring at the colorful lights."

He'd been wondering what he could do to make their New Year's Eve special, and her wish gave him an idea. He had an AC inverter in the garage that could power the strands of lights. Tomorrow, he would put the inverter in the sun with the solar panel to catch any rays of sun that slipped through and make sure it was charged. He could surprise her with a lighted tree for New Year's Eve.

"The best I can do for you tonight is this fire," he said.

"Oh, I'm not saying the fire isn't wonderful." She sat criss-cross beside him. "I'm just being greedy and want both."

"Nothing wrong with that." She reached for the mug of hot chocolate in his hand—rather than the one on the hearth in front of her. "This one has rum in it," he said in warning.

"Is it the dark sweet rum?" she asked.

"Yes."

"That sounds yummy." She took the mug and sipped. "Mmm. I like it."

He chuckled. "Guess I'll add rum to the other mug as well."

"Good plan."

She was wearing his favorite black flannel shirt over her pajamas. She'd had to roll up the sleeves a few turns but left the top three buttons open enough to tease him, and now he wanted to see her in nothing but his shirt. Just like she'd been in his robe. There was an odd pitching in his stomach. Something…different.

He rubbed his eyes to get himself right, then added rum to the second mug. "I see that you've found one of my shirts to keep you warm."

"I did. Hope you don't mind. It's supersoft." She lifted the collar to her nose. "It smells good too."

For some reason it made him happy that she liked the smell.

"I should be used to you taking my stuff by now," he said with a grin.

"I'll let you borrow my stuff anytime you want to."

They talked and laughed as they drank their hot chocolate and then climbed under the covers.

Finn tucked one arm under his head. Daisy was on her back with her eyes closed, but her face wasn't relaxed enough for her to be asleep. "Are you awake?"

"Yes." She rolled to face him. "I'm just thinking."

"What are you thinking about?" That sounded like something a girl would say, and he mentally chided himself. Plus did he really want to dig into her nighttime thoughts while they were side by side in bed?

"Lots of things."

"Is my shirt still keeping you warm?" He'd meant to tease, but it didn't come out that way. He was flirting with her.

"Not warm enough." And she was flirting right back.

She bit her lip in a way that made him want to nibble on it himself. He lifted the layers of blankets. "Come over this way."

Without hesitation, she slid over to share his pillow.

They were so close. Close enough that he brushed back a long lock of her hair and let his fingers linger on her cheek for a moment longer than necessary. "You smell like flowers. It's nice. I told you that you can be flowery."

"I suppose I can. Cherry blossom mixes well with your leather and warm spices."

"That's a very specific description of my scent."

The dimple on her cheek deepened with her smile. "Don't be too impressed. I read it on your cologne bottle." Her tentative touch moved slowly up his arm, growing bolder with each inch until she curled her fingers around the back of his neck.

Sparks shot to every part of his body, and he groaned. "There are limits to what a man can resist."

"Same for a woman. What should we do about it?"

"I can think of several options worth exploring."

"Are we about to screw up our friendship?"

"Not if we don't let it." His thoughts snapped to her New Year's list.

Sleep with a hot guy.

At the moment, all of his worries and excuses about why they should be strictly friends with physical boundaries seemed useless. Fire was building beneath his skin, burning too hot to stop, and his body was battling with his mind.

Then he remembered the second part of her number one wish.

Brief fun affair.

She wanted hot and brief, and he could give her that. No problem. "If I'm not mistaken, we're both curious. He stroked her cheek with the pad of his thumb. "We could…"

"Scratch that itch?" She ran her tongue between her lips. "Just this once?"

"One time to get it out of our systems?" Thank God they were on the exact same page regarding this. He shouldn't do this. But he wanted to. He really wanted to.

Finn was well practiced and knew how to separate physical intimacy from his feelings. He'd been doing it for years.

But could Daisy handle something like this?

"We can try something simple and see how it goes," she whispered. "Finn Murphy, I dare you to prove you're a good kisser."

CHAPTER TEN

DAISY HELD HER next breath. She had just dared Finn to prove he was a good kisser, and there was no taking it back. Good thing she didn't want to. Sleeping Beauty's delight and Maleficent's you-go-girl cheer seemed to agree.

Am I about to kiss my best friend?

The irresistible grin—that Finn had likely perfected in the cradle—was another vote for yes. The way he caressed her with his eyes made her feel like she was the most beautiful woman he'd ever seen.

He slid his hand into her hair and stroked her cheek with his thumb. "Challenge accepted."

"If we kiss and it's a dud, at least we will have answered the question of who is the better kisser. And I'll be able to tease you forever."

He chuckled. "You sound pretty sure of yourself."

She wasn't. She wasn't sure at all. Long ago she'd learned to keep Finn out of her daydreams, but with their bodies close enough to feel the other's chest move with increasing breaths, there was no way on earth to ignore the crackle of sexual tension.

"Don't be shy," she said with more courage than she was feeling.

Thank you, Maleficent.

The rough pad of his thumb brushed across her mouth, and he made an appreciative rumbling sound before his soft lips caressed hers.

An achingly slow, delicious tease.

Shimmers of longing danced over her skin, and she let her hand explore the solid breadth of his shoulders.

He didn't rush or go where he wasn't invited. He made sure they were both on the verge of molten before moving into a deep, searching, toe-curling kiss.

Cherishing. Savoring.

An ancient rhythm took hold. Their kisses began to explore, and their hands shifted clothing. Checking in with whispered words, they gave and took and shared.

And shared again.

Finn Murphy not only had bragging rights to being a great kisser, but he also had a whole list of delightful talents that she hoped to explore again.

THE COMFORTING WEIGHT of Daisy's upper body was draped across his chest, but Finn kept his eyes closed and replayed last night's highlights in his mind. But where to begin? The choices were plentiful.

He splayed his fingers wider on the bare skin of her back and inhaled against her hair.

He might have started their kiss, but Daisy's enthusiasm had catapulted them into something neither of them had wanted to stop.

Her softness. Her scent. Bodies pressed close. The way she used all of herself to share pleasure and welcome him. His Daisy was a real woman who didn't try to fake anything.

She sighed in her sleep, and her warm breath fanned across his skin. He shivered, and his blood began to surge as memories came to him.

One time had melted into two. Eager and passionate. Slow. Tender.

Their bodies tangled in an exhausted sleep.

His lips curved into a smile. Now that he thought about it, the whole experience had been one big highlight.

Finn opened his eyes to assure himself his mind wasn't playing tricks. Daisy's hand rested over his heart. Her long hair tumbled in a golden cloud around her shoulders, and her creamy skin looked iridescent in the firelight.

The fire had died down and needed to be tended, but he didn't want to move. She was comfortable in his arms, and this blip in their relationship would end soon.

There was no reason to rush it.

DAISY WOKE WITH her cheek resting on the warm skin of Finn's bare chest and his arm curled around her back—that was just as bare as his. The mood of the night had swept her away and there had been no resisting.

What have I done?

Her skin tingled, and she held her breath, trying to figure out if he was awake, or like her, too afraid to move and break the spell.

Please don't let sleeping with him be one of my worst ideas ever.

She'd made mistakes before and lived to tell the tale, but this had the potential to be crushing.

But…she had written down a wish to sleep with a hot guy.

She hadn't even finished writing her list, and she could already check something off. Well…almost. What about the brief fun affair idea she'd subconsciously tagged onto her first wish? Or was one night together as much time as she was going to get?

"I can hear you thinking."

She startled at the sound of his deep, sleepy voice rumbling under her ear. When she started to move off him, he tightened his arm to keep her close against his side. After gathering her wits, she lifted her head to meet his sleepy smile.

"Good morning." Her voice came out an octave higher than normal."

He grinned. "It sure is."

His words eased her worries about his negative reaction to their night together. "So…do we talk about this or pretend it was a dream or never happened?"

"It's kind of hard to pretend at the moment."

She had to agree. She rolled onto her back and pulled the blankets up under her chin. "Our friendship has to survive this, Finn."

With his arms crossed over his chest, he stared at the ceiling for a few heartbeats. "It will survive. This doesn't have to change us. We don't have to make more of this than it is."

That made her flinch. Their night together probably meant way more to her than it did to him. She had to keep in mind that Finn wasn't looking for a relationship like she was. In fact, it was the opposite. He was not an option for the guy she'd spend her romantic life with.

To her, their night had been a fantasy come true, but to Finn... Was she a conquest or just convenient?

"I guess you're right. It won't change us if we don't let it."

He traced his finger along her collarbone. "Since we're still in bed, this technically counts as one time, right?"

She smiled and snuggled closer to him. "Technically, if we continue, it will be our third time, so we already blew the one-time rule."

He wound a lock of her hair around his finger. "You know, it only makes sense for our *one* time to last the amount of time we're snowed in together. For as long as you stay here, we can temporarily explore the physical and satisfy our curiosity."

His promise that their friendship would be safe gave her courage. "Makes sense to me. Instead of only one time, what about one...tryst?"

"Tryst." He tried out the word and grinned. "And that is, what exactly?"

"A brief, fun affair," she said, quoting what she'd written on her wish list. She slid her arms around his neck and twined her fingers through his hair. "Can you do brief and fun, Finnigan Murphy?"

His smile was slow and sexy. "Casual with no strings?"

His words tugged at her heart, and she hesitated, but as he'd suggested, she wasn't going to try and make more of this than it was. "Sounds right to me."

"I can do that. No problem." He cupped her hip in his big

hand. "The question is, can you? Can you separate our friend-ship from a physical relationship?"

Can I?

If she didn't do this, she would always wonder what could have been. She'd gotten through rough times before and could do it again if it came down to that.

Casual and without strings wasn't what she was ultimately looking for in a romance, but it had obviously been on her mind because she'd written down her desire for something brief and fun. Whatever this was with him, it was not and would not be a real romance. Remembering that fact was very important.

"To get myself back into dating, a tryst is actually something I've been thinking about trying."

"Trying a tryst." His lips quivered.

"Are you teasing me?" She pinched his forearm.

"No. That word just makes me want to do naughty things to you. I'm having fun, and according to you, that's a necessary part of a tryst."

"You catch on pretty quick."

"I'm a good student, but practice makes perfect. Plus I bet you're dying to know more details about what that word makes me want to do."

"You know me so well."

"Even better than I did yesterday."

That was certainly true in the physical sense. "I still have a few more secrets to show you. And just so you know, I'm a very tactile learner."

"That's good. So am I." He brushed his fingers over her stom-ach and made her giggle.

He sealed his mouth over hers, and there was no more talk-ing after that.

WHILE FINN WAS outside chopping wood, Daisy sat down at his kitchen table where the sunlight streamed in through the windows. Another perk was the very nice view it provided of him swinging an axe. He brought it down hard and split a log into three pieces.

Now that she knew what those muscles felt like under her hands and against her skin, this was even more entertaining.

Lady pranced in with her bell jingling and hopped up onto Daisy's lap. She stroked the cat's soft fur. "How am I ever going to go back to thinking of him as only a friend?"

She unfolded her wish list and smoothed out the creases in the blue paper. When her electricity had gone out, her second wish had only been partially written.

Should I complete my wish to fall in love or wait until our tryst is over?

Was there a chance putting it on paper could lead to a happily-ever-after? Like a little delayed Christmas magic. Maybe he would change his mind about long-term relationships, or what they had together might develop into more over time.

She stopped overthinking it and picked up her pen to add to her list, but then she stopped right away. If she completed the wish to fall in love, she might be the only one who fell in love and be even more hurt at the end.

She made the decision to complete that wish after their tryst. She drew a fill-in-the-blank line beside the word *fall* and then wrote out several more wishes.

2) Fall
3) Learn a new skill
4) Have an adventure
5) Be a mom

She wrote a number six but then tapped her pencil on the table while considering what it should be.

"Whatcha doing?" Finn asked.

Her heart sprang into her throat. "Nothing. Just a to-do list for later." She refolded the paper and shoved it into her back pocket. He would probably laugh if he saw it.

CHAPTER ELEVEN

FINN KNEW EXACTLY what Daisy had put into her pocket. And he really wished he knew what she had added, but unless it was sitting out in the open, he wouldn't snoop. She was jumpier than normal, and he had doubts that she would be able to go through with their physical relationship.

Was he kidding himself that *he* could do this tryst thing with Daisy?

I do it all the time. I'm fine with this kind of thing.

He told himself this was just like every other time, but it didn't sound convincing—not even to himself.

The other women weren't your best friend, dummy.

She cocked her head and studied him as if she knew what he was thinking. "What's wrong?"

"Nothing. I hope." He moved closer. "I'm just trying to judge how you're feeling. Make sure you're okay. I don't want you to be uncomfortable or feel pressured or—"

She put her fingertips to his lips and smiled. "I want to be here with you. Like this. I'm not feeling any pressure."

He slid his fingers up the soft skin of her inner arm, rubbed his thumb in the center of her palm and kissed her fingertips. "Good. I'm happy you're here."

"Are you finished chopping wood?"

"Yes. Also, Riley called to see if I needed them to try to get home to help me, but I told them to stay in town and not risk getting out on the icy road with tires that don't have snow chains." For once, he didn't want them to come home, and thankfully they'd both decided to stay in town.

"I think that was the right call." She hooked a finger in his belt loop. "For a several reasons."

He pulled her snug against him. "Tell me all about these reasons."

"Want me to show you instead?"

His blood surged and pulsed like a molten river through his veins. Maybe this arrangement was going to work after all.

"Give me all you've got." He clasped her hips and lifted her until she wrapped her legs around his waist. "Hold on tight, Daisy Maisy."

AN HOUR LATER, they lay cuddled skin to skin in front of the fire, silently staring into the mesmerizing flames. The afternoon sun was barely cutting through the storm clouds, but they were cozy.

He played with her hand, letting his fingers trail through hers. "Does Sage have crooked pinkie fingers like you?"

"She does. So did our dad."

"Since we can't go out and no one can get here, our New Year's Eve is going to be a quiet one."

The cat skidded around the corner, jumped across their entwined bodies and then ducked under the coffee table. Astro and Rascal quickly followed.

"I don't know about that," she said. "It might get pretty wild since our only guests will be a bunch of party animals."

He chuckled. "A dog, a cat and a goat walk into a New Year's Eve party…"

She started singing "Old MacDonald." *"E-i-e-i-o."*

Astro howled while Rascal bleated, and Lady hissed before dashing from the room.

THE SUN GLOWED a rainbow of warm autumn colors as it set over the snow-covered landscape. While Daisy was enjoying another bath, courtesy of Finn toting huge pots of hot water, Finn turned on the battery-powered Christmas tree lights he'd rigged up. Now, she would be able to ring in the new year with the colorful lights she loved. He tuned the transistor radio to a Dallas country music station, then poked at the fire, even though it didn't need doing.

With a hand braced on the mantel, he looked at the photographs of him and his brothers. Riley was the sentimental one and had framed a few memories, ranging from when they were scrawny kids to the one they had taken not long ago at a county fair. All three of them, plus Daisy, had crammed themselves into a photo booth. He smiled at the memory of only Jake's head showing up while the rest of him had been on the outside of the curtain. And Daisy fit right in with the whole crazy lot of them.

His heart started to race. *Don't screw this up.*

"You did this for me?"

He turned at the sound of her voice. She was staring at the tree, and her eyes were as lit up as it was. "I thought you'd like it."

"Oh, I do." She joined him in front of the fire and wrapped her arms around his neck. "It's beautiful. Thank you."

He met her halfway for a tender kiss. It wasn't filled with urgent passion like their times in bed. It carried a calming playfulness, but there was also a sensation that sparked a flicker of panic inside him.

He slid one hand up the center of her back to keep her body close to his, hoping it would make the scary feeling go away.

She relaxed against him, and they swayed to the music.

The living room was suddenly flooded with overhead lights. She groaned and he swore, then they looked at one another and seemed to be thinking the same thing.

"Turn off the lights," she said, echoing his thoughts. "I'm not ready for this holiday hideaway to be over."

"Me either. Save my dance and don't forget where we left off." He hurried around turning off lights and met her in front of the Christmas tree.

She finished texting someone and tossed her phone onto one of the recliners and welcomed him back into her embrace. "The power is back on at my ranch too. Oh, I love this song. Dance with me, cowboy."

"Yes, ma'am." He was going to make their last night together as memorable and special as possible.

THEY DANCED AND laughed and toasted at midnight before cozying up in front of the fire where she fell asleep in his arms.

Finn brushed his fingers through the soft strands of Daisy's long hair. It was fanned out between them on the blue pillowcase, firelight dancing among the golden waves, making them multifaceted. Like her.

She looked so young and beautiful. He'd always considered her to be pretty, but now, there was a glow to her. A light that he'd overlooked in the past.

He shifted to ease the pressure on his spine. Three nights on a bed of sleeping bags was taking its toll on his body.

Daisy cracked open one eye. "Are you okay?"

Now that the central heat was working, they could get off the floor and onto a soft mattress. "Let's move to my bedroom."

She raised her head and yawned. "Sounds good to me."

As they climbed into his bed, it struck him that he'd never brought a woman here. He'd kept it as a place all his own. But he'd just changed that.

"Go back to sleep," he whispered, needing a few beats to adjust to the shift.

"Good night." She spooned her back against his chest and was asleep within a minute.

He'd dated a lot of women, but none of them for very long. He was a keep-on-moving kind of guy. Daisy was the first woman he'd ever considered taking a chance on, but she was too important to "take a chance on" and risk breaking her tender heart. He knew full well that Daisy deserved more than him gambling that he could have a lasting long-term relationship. He didn't know what he was capable of giving a woman like her.

She mumbled in her sleep, sighed and smiled.

Was she dreaming about him? He wanted to wake her up with a kiss and make love to her again. But he stopped himself. What if his current feelings of...

He swallowed hard and pressed his fingertips to his closed eyes. A feeling he didn't know how to put a name to.

What if this passion and hunger was just a temporary blip before he reverted to his normal keep-moving response to emotional intimacy? If he didn't navigate this situation carefully and the lust burned away as it always did, this "tryst" had the potential to be the end of a valued friendship.

But for just a little while, he could hold her and imagine what it would be like if he knew how to love a woman.

THROUGH FINN'S BEDROOM WINDOWS, the first glow of sunrise peeked over the horizon, and it was beautiful, but Daisy wished it would freeze in time just for a little while longer. She wasn't ready for their frozen world to melt back into real life. But there was no stopping the dawn to extend their special moment.

Finn was spooned behind her, and he kissed her bare shoulder. "How are you this morning?"

"I'm really going to miss our holiday hideaway. It's been a nice respite from the real world. I'm not ready to go back to the daily grind."

"I know what you mean."

She turned to face him. "Now, I guess it's back to being just friends?" She'd meant for it to come out as a statement, but it had sounded more like a question, and she hoped he hadn't noticed.

"Always friends. You're the only one I can count on for certain kinds of advice." He studied her face as if searching for something. "But what about friends with a few extra benefits for a little while longer?"

Her stomach whooshed like she'd gone over a roller-coaster drop. This was what she had hoped for. More time to see what could develop between them. She tapped her thumb and pinkie together like she often did when she was nervous. "What benefits do you have in mind?"

"Occasionally doing exactly what we are doing right now." He expanded on that explanation by sliding his hands across her bare skin. "Something just between us. When no one else is around."

"A secret?"

"Private."

She liked the sound of that. It was best if their extended tryst remained only between them because she knew it wouldn't last long-term, and then she'd be embarrassed if people knew it had ended and saw him around town with other women. "How do you see this working? Full-time friends and part-time lovers?"

"Yes. Until…" He scratched his head.

"How about a month? We can have all of January because I've always felt like I celebrate the new year for the whole month anyway."

"Good thinking, Daisy Maisy. Since we're both such good students and we're not done learning, we can extend our *tryst.*" He always chuckled when he said that word.

"And to set some limits, it can only happen here at your house." If she kept their romance away from her own ranch, it would hopefully be easier to separate their physical connection from everyday life. She wouldn't have the memories staring her in the face every single day.

"Not at your house or in any of the barns or stables," he added.

"And not in your truck."

He chuckled. "My truck? What made you think of that?"

"Well…" She blushed. "I figured that's why you have blankets in your truck."

He kissed the side of her neck. "Do you have a fantasy about making love under the stars?"

"I do now."

"Too bad the weather isn't cooperating."

"Too bad the truck is on the off-limits list," she said, reminding him.

"Damn. Rules are hard. Even when we are here at my house, it should only be when no one else is home."

"I agree. Otherwise, it won't remain private." And it needed to be, for everyone's sake.

"Because you do get kind of loud in bed," he teased.

She gasped dramatically. "I do not."

"I take it as a compliment, sweetheart."

Daisy's stomach fluttered. That was the first time he had called her sweetheart, but she couldn't allow herself to think it meant anything. She nestled against him with her head under his chin and just enjoyed being in his embrace.

She reluctantly accepted that she'd fallen 90 percent in love, powerless to completely stop it. But the other 10 percent of her love was a safety net for when his aversion to a wife or child eventually tore them apart. The impending heartache was something she would deal with later.

This secret benefits arrangement was probably going to be easy for him, but for her... Not so much.

She would borrow some of Maleficent's inner-badass energy. She was strong enough to do this if she put her mind to it. She would be his full-time friend, just like always, and his part-time lover for a month.

He kissed her shoulder and his hands started to roam. "Speaking of fooling around..."

"Were we talking about that?"

"We are now. Maybe we should take advantage of having the house to ourselves."

"Smart man." She hooked her leg over his hip and pushed him onto his back until she straddled him.

The front door slammed.

Daisy rolled across Finn and leaped from his bed. "Someone is here," she said needlessly.

"My brothers are home."

CHAPTER TWELVE

DAISY'S BARE BOTTOM was the last thing Finn saw before she disappeared into his bathroom. He chuckled and quickly closed his bedroom door.

Why in the hell did they have to come home so early in the morning?

He did not want his brothers to know about them sleeping together. Riley would tell him it was a mistake, and Jake would end up making a joke about it at some point and embarrassing Daisy.

He pulled on a pair of jeans and a long-sleeved blue Henley and then went into the living room. Jake was petting the dog and Riley was taking off his boots. Rascal was kicking up a morning fuss in her crate.

"The roads must be clear," he said to his little brothers.

"For us, yes," Jake said. "For Texas drivers, not so much."

Riley motioned to their bed on the floor. "I remember when we used to sleep in front of the fire."

Finn glanced back toward the hallway, wondering where Daisy was and what she was doing. Hopefully she wasn't freaking out.

Riley got Rascal out of her crate. "Is this little girl still causing trouble?"

"The dog has taken her under his wing and is kind of helping. Astro seems to think she's a puppy, and he is responsible for training her. I'll have to tell you both about the house-training I've been doing with her."

Daisy came into the living room, sporting a smile that was a little too bright. "Hey, guys."

Jake spun to face her. "I didn't know you were here."

"Didn't you see her truck out front, Captain Obvious?" Riley said to Jake.

She ducked her head, and Finn knew she was gearing up to blush.

A band of tension cinched tight around his ribs. If she didn't pull it together in a hurry, she was going to give them away right off the bat. He was starting to doubt the sanity of what they had agreed to. He could do this part-time thing with no problem—well, not much—but in his experience, women were not built the same. Not on the outside or the inside.

The reality of the situation was suddenly hitting him. This was how it was going to be as long as they were sneaking around.

"The electricity went off at our ranch, so I came over here," she said.

"I thought you lost power here too?" Jake asked.

"It did," Finn said. "But not until the next day."

"I stayed because you guys have more firewood." She busied herself folding a blanket that had been tossed on one of the plush, brown recliners. "Riley, I hope you don't mind that I slept in your bedroom, so I'll change your sheets before I go."

"Sure. No problem." Riley sat on the couch and let the goat bounce around from one end to the other.

She cleared her throat. "Okay. I'll go do that, and then I really need to get home." She spun on her heel and rushed back down the hallway.

Jake flopped into one of the recliners and turned on the TV. "What's up with her?"

"I think she's had about all of me she can stand," Finn said. "Guess I shouldn't pick on her so much."

"You two are like a couple of kids." Riley shook his head at Finn, got up and went into the kitchen.

Finn tunneled his hand through his hair. A couple of naughty kids all right. And he hadn't used very good judgment. He'd been blinded by lust.

I'm a fool for thinking this can work without anyone getting hurt.

DAISY SET THE cat carrier on her kitchen floor and then closed the door and pressed her back against it. She was being a total dork and freaking out—exactly like she'd promised herself she wouldn't.

"Meow."

"Sorry, Lady." She let the cat out and watched her race once around the island and then out of the room.

Her kitchen was bright and sunny, but she felt all quivery on the inside. And a bit sick to her stomach. She'd only left Finn's ranch a few minutes ago, but she missed him already.

"Why do I do these things to myself?" She groaned and folded her torso forward over the kitchen island's marble surface. The stone was uncomfortably cold under her cheek, so she pushed herself up and was glad no one was around to see her acting like a child.

They still had the whole month of January, but their uninterrupted time was over. It would never be quite the same as their magical holiday hideaway. Finding time to be alone at his house was going to be a challenge.

She was lonelier now than she had been before her sleepover at Four Star Ranch. What was this achy feeling in her gut? And then she realized what it was. Homesickness.

She was homesick for the bond they'd developed and shared during their time together.

"Well, this sucks even more than I imagined." Daisy started a pot of coffee and stared off into space while it brewed.

It was time to check on the horses, but she needed a few minutes to process her new reality. Ice, snow, power outages and even wild animals hadn't ruined their holiday. It was the best few days she'd had since she couldn't remember. No matter what plan or rules they made, no matter what she told herself or Finn, going back to being nothing more than best buddies in February was going to be a challenge. But she'd always have beautiful memories, even if they hurt at first.

She grabbed a mug, poured in some cream, then added the coffee and watched the colors mix into a creamy goodness. Lady wound around her legs. "Are you lonely too?"

Now she wanted someone she couldn't have. Not truly and fully. Finn would always keep a wedge of one kind or another between them. Just enough to let her know he wouldn't be held down and it wasn't permanent.

After her cup of coffee, she walked out to the stable. The radio was playing a George Strait song, and Dillon was singing along. His voice was surprisingly good. It didn't match the sight of him mucking out a horse stall.

"Happy New Year, Dillon."

He straightened and looked over the black horse's back with a smile. "Happy New Year to you." He rubbed his hand along the horse's flank on his way to the stall door, then stepped out and latched it behind him. "Did you make any resolutions?"

"No. More like wishes and goals."

"That's a good idea. You don't sound very excited about your wishes. Or is it that you drank too much last night?"

"No hangover. Just tired, I guess." Lizzy's horse stuck her head out of her stall, and Daisy put her cheek against Misty's neck as she patted her.

"What's really wrong?" he asked.

She couldn't tell him the truth of her self-imposed romantic pleasure with a side of angst. "Nothing. Really. I didn't get much sleep."

Dillon leaned his back against a post. "Have I ever told you that I have three younger sisters?"

"No, you haven't."

"For some reason they think I'm a good listener, and they always come to me. So, you can't fool me. I can see it on your face."

"What do you see?" She put her hands to her cheeks.

"I suspect there's a man involved, and I have a pretty good idea who he is. I've seen the way you look at one another when you think the other one isn't looking."

"Really?" Her cheeks were flaming now. How was she going to be able to keep their secret? She could not blow it on day one. "Dillon, you cannot say a word to anyone suggesting that there is anything romantic between me and Finn. Please."

His brow furrowed. "Okay. I promise I won't say anything you don't want me to." He braced an elbow on a stall door. "I'm sorry. I didn't mean to tease you. I didn't realize it was a secret."

"You don't have to be sorry. I just didn't know I was being so obvious. And there is really nothing to even talk about."

"You don't have to say another word about it, but I'm here if you ever want to." He tapped the side of his head. "It goes in the vault."

She smiled and sat on the wooden bench beside her. "Are you a vet or a shrink?"

He chuckled. "A bit of both. I couldn't decide when I graduated from high school, and I took a lot of classes."

"Good for you."

"And if you want me to, I'll stop trying to make Finn jealous on purpose."

"You actually do that?"

"Maybe a time or two. I think that's why I've gotten a glimpse into your relationship. He doesn't like having me around you, but he seems to be having trouble recognizing what's right in front of him."

"You think so?"

"All the signs are there."

She tapped her thumb and pinkie together. "On second thought, it won't hurt him to be a little jealous now and then."

Dillon grinned. "Cool."

BY LUNCHTIME, MOST of the ice had melted except for a few patches in the shade. Daisy was too antsy to sit inside, so she went outside to gather the branches that had fallen onto her back patio during the storm. It would make good kindling for her fireplace.

When Finn drove up and parked beside her truck, her heart fluttered. They hadn't spoken since she'd rushed out of his house after almost being caught in bed by his brothers. She hadn't missed his silent pleas for her to be chill in front of Riley and Jake, but she'd been taken by surprise and totally unprepared to publicly hide their January tryst agreement that they'd made only minutes before.

She rearranged her face into what she hoped was a normal expression. His slow smile morphed into a full grin. Calmness settled over her, and she returned his wave.

I can do this. We can do this.

This was her Finn. Not someone she just met and hooked up with. He was one of the few friends she could talk with and laugh with. And bonus, for a limited time, they could occasionally revisit their physical connection. They could get through this, together.

"How is Rascal doing this afternoon?" she called out.

"See for yourself." He lifted the goat out of the truck and set her on the ground. At the end of a purple leash, the tiny animal was buckled into a pink harness.

She laughed as Rascal frisked along beside the tall, sexy cowboy dressed in head to toe black. She pulled her phone from her pocket and snapped a picture of them walking her way.

"What's got you grinning and taking pictures, Daisy Maisy? See something you like?"

"I do. A few things." To resist her urge to kiss him, she knelt to greet the goat. "Hello, sweetie. Where did you get pink and purple items? I know they weren't Astro's when he was a puppy."

"My brothers picked them up in town before they came home. She has taken to wearing it much better than I expected."

"She looks adorable. Almost like a child's toy." The cat ran up to see the goat and started licking her head. "Somebody wants to be friends. Good girl, Lady."

"She's already spoiled." Even though it was still forty degrees, Finn sat in one of the patio chairs.

She took the one beside him. "I was just thinking about calling you. I'm curious if your brothers suspect anything."

"I don't think so. They didn't say anything. And Jake for sure would have. Sorry they blindsided us and we didn't have a chance to say goodbye."

"It was an abrupt ending to our holiday hideaway, but I bet we'll look back on the moment and be able to laugh."

"I already can," he said, and chuckled. "You proved you can spring out of bed every bit as well as Miss Mess here."

Rascal tangled her leash around his foot and kicked up her hind legs.

A car horn honked as her sister's family drove up the gravel driveway.

Her niece Loren was the first one out of the car, and she came running their way. Her long, brown hair was loose and blowing in the wind. "You got a puppy? Oh, wait that's a goat." She hugged Daisy then dropped to her knees to pet her. "She's so adorable."

"Her name is Rascal," Daisy said. "She belongs to Finn."

"Where did you get her?" the teenager asked.

"I kind of came by her on accident when I stopped at the feed store."

Grayson waved to them but went into the house with luggage while Sage headed their way with Rose in her arms. "Finn, you pick up strays just like we do."

Daisy reached out for the baby. "Hello, my sweet Rose. I missed you bunches and bunches." She cuddled her close and straightened her pink hat.

The baby babbled and patted her cheek.

"I have to go check on Mischief," Loren said, and ran toward the barn to visit her horse.

"Did you have a good trip?" she asked her twin.

"We did, but I'm glad to be home. Loren wanted to come out here rather than go to the house in town," Sage said about the house in the Old Town area of Channing that Grayson inherited from his great-aunt Tilly DeLuca.

Her brother-in-law, Grayson, joined them and put an arm around Sage. "Finn, do you have time to look at something with me?"

"I sure do." He stood, picked up Rascal and grinned down at Daisy, a secret smile in his eyes. "I'll see you later."

"Bye." She waved awkwardly.

The men started talking about cattle and headed for his truck.

"Ma-ma-ma," Rose said.

"Let's get her inside out of the cold," Daisy said.

Sage was looking at her curiously—too curiously—so she hurried toward the house with the baby cradled against her chest.

In the kitchen, she put Rose in the playpen near the table.

Sage stopped in front of her and held her by the shoulders, narrowed her eyes and then gasped. "You slept with him."

It wasn't a question, and Daisy palmed her face. "I knew I couldn't hide it from you."

"Spill it, sis. How did this happen?"

"Let's make tea and I'll tell you all about it." She heated water while Sage changed Rose.

Once the tea was ready, they sat at the round kitchen table that had seen countless family discussions. Hours and hours of laughing, crying, secrets and stories.

She told her twin about her snowed-in holiday hideaway and the deal they had made.

"Oh, Daisy. How are you going to do this?"

CHAPTER THIRTEEN

FINN GRINNED AS Daisy moved around her kitchen. She was opening and closing cabinets and the refrigerator while chattering about there being nothing to eat that didn't take forever to cook. He sat back in his chair and sipped his iced tea. She entertained him, and even when she was buzzing around like a bee, she also calmed him.

When he'd brought the goat over on a leash the day before, he'd been unsure about how they should move forward. And second-guessing the wisdom of their intimate time and their January plan. But it hadn't taken long for her nervous expression to ease seamlessly into a genuine smile. The one that told him they would be okay.

She had a way of settling his jumpy nerves. It was one of the reasons he liked being around her so much. She wasn't demanding or too serious. Just his easygoing Daisy Maisy.

I just need to keep things playful and fun. And keep things from sliding into serious.

"Let's go get dinner at the Rodeo Café," he said.

"Excellent idea. I'm starving."

"There's a dress code tonight." He knew his grin told her he was up to something.

"No, there's not."

"There is for you. You'll be wearing a special pair of jeans."

She scowled and crossed her arms. "I'm not hungry anymore."

"Yes, you are. Be a good sport and go get dressed. Unless you don't accept the challenge?"

"Fine."

"Scoot." He patted her bottom.

She spun around and checked to make sure they were alone. "Grayson is in the other room," she whispered, but couldn't hold back her smile. "We're not at your house. And that's against the rules."

He sighed. "Sometimes I hate rules."

She chuckled. "I'll be back in five minutes."

He also liked that she didn't take a ton of time getting ready.

"HEY, LOOK." FINN pointed at the new Italian restaurant. "Antone's is open. Want to try it out?"

"I'm not sure I'm dressed for that restaurant, thanks to you."

"You look beautiful." He wasn't just saying it. He meant it. He saw her differently now.

"Okay. Let's try it out."

He followed Daisy into the restaurant. The handprints on her back pockets shifted as she walked, and it looked like his fingerprints were squeezing her curves. He wanted so much to do it for real that he shoved his hands in his coat pockets.

He needed to find a way to get his brothers out of the house so he and Daisy could have some time alone. He stopped behind her at the hostess stand and looked up when she cleared her throat.

"Has something caught your attention down below?" she said over her shoulder.

He returned her grin. "It sure has."

There was a small bar area in the front corner separated from the main dining room by a wall of photographs. An intricate antique bar stretched across the back, and mood lighting gave it a cozy vibe. They were shown to a table for two near the back of the main dining room.

"I told you this place was too fancy for my handprint jeans," she whispered across the candlelit table. "Most of the other women have on dresses."

"Your ivory sweater is fancy with the beads around the neck." He moved a finger through the air to mimic the scooped neckline.

"I got it out of Sage's closet. And speaking of my sister, she knows about us."

His eyes widened. "Already?"

"I didn't even say a word. She just looked at my face. It's a twin thing."

"I understand. I should've expected that. She'll keep it to herself, right?"

"Definitely. She knows how to keep a secret when it's important."

While they ate, the natural effortlessness of their friendship took over.

"Finn, why don't you want to be a father? Truthfully."

He hated this question but would answer it anyway. When he thought of becoming a father, his palms always began to itch, and his throat tightened. "Because I've already done it with my brothers. I didn't care for it then, and I don't want to repeat it. I don't want to be responsible for anyone but myself. I know that sounds selfish."

She suspected it was a lack of confidence in his own parenting skills and likely a touch of fear. Maybe he just needed time to realize it would be totally different doing it as an adult. "I know better than that. You are not a selfish person. Will you tell me more about being the one who basically raised Riley and Jake?"

"I had to raise myself too."

"You did a good job of it. You're one of the best men I know."

He made a sound in his throat. "Maybe you should ask my brothers about that before jumping to conclusions. I took on the responsibility of feeding them and keeping them safe. I was responsible for pretty much everything."

"That must have been so scary."

"That's one way to put it."

Every few days or weeks, their dad would show up with groceries and a little cash. But the few nights he did spend at home with them, he'd usually been drunk. Jake had always cried when he left again, and Finn had been the one to comfort his youngest brother until he fell asleep.

He'd already done the parenting thing, and it had been extremely hard. The crushing weight of failure when things went wrong. A child carrying an adult's fear. The worry about what the next day would bring their way. It was a miracle Riley and Jake had turned out okay and had lived to tell about it. He couldn't willingly raise another child. He couldn't risk being completely responsible for another person's life.

"Sometimes I would get so mad at one of them when they wouldn't listen and we'd end up wrestling in a pile on the floor."

She covered his hand with hers. "You were a kid, and they are your brothers. Not your children. I would imagine that lots of brothers get rough with one another. Right?"

"I guess. But the stress of keeping them fed and not flunking out of school and…" He took a drink of water. "It was incredibly hard and stressful, and now that they're grown men, I don't want to go through anything like that again."

"I can understand that. Thanks for telling me about it."

On the drive home, Daisy fiddled with the radio. It was dark with only the streetlights occasionally flickering across her face, making her blond hair glisten in the intermittent flash of lights. The truck was filled with the savory scent of leftover lasagna, the sweetness of her hand cream and the peppermint she'd popped into her mouth.

She worked the candy around in her mouth and licked her lips. "Where are your brothers this evening?"

It appeared her thoughts were headed in the same direction as his were. "Probably at home. Unfortunately. But… I could sneak you in through my bedroom window."

She smiled at him. "Didn't we say it could only happen when no one was there?"

Now that they were on the outskirts of Channing, it was darker in the truck. He stopped at a sign, then turned onto the farm road that went past their ranches. "Are you sure? I don't think we said that. I think I would remember."

She laughed. "Selective memory?"

"Only on a case by case basis."

"Rule breaker."

"Rule bender sounds better," he said. "Especially when it benefits both of us and hurts no one."

"You're the one who said I'm loud in bed."

"Grab my phone. My brothers and I have our locations turned on and shared between the three of us."

She opened the share your location app on his phone and softly sighed. "Looks like they're both at home."

That's what he'd expected, and it was probably for the best, but he had hoped. He drove past the entrance of Four Star Ranch and turned in at hers.

They didn't speak as he pressed in the code to make the gate swing open. He drove up her curving driveway that was lined with trees that were all bare branched and skeletal for winter. He pulled through the circular gravel drive near her front door.

"And now it's time to drop you off and say good-night."

He turned to look at her and tucked her hair behind her ear. "It's good practice."

She paused with her hand on the door handle. "Practice for what?"

"For the rest of our lives."

They shared a sad smile, and she got out of his truck.

THE SUN WAS bright when Daisy came out of the stable, so she shielded her eyes to see who was standing beside the corral. A young cowboy had one boot propped on the bottom fence board. There was a large military-style backpack at his feet, and he was stroking the neck of one of their most skittish horses. Hardly anyone could get that close to Cinder, but this stranger was having no problem.

"Hello, there," she called out. When he turned to face her, the expression on his face seemed to flicker through a whole range of emotions. He reminded her of someone, but she couldn't place who it was.

"Hi. I'm Adam Hauser." He extended his hand.

"I'm Daisy. Welcome to Dalton Ranch."

His hand trembled slightly in hers as if he was nervous, and this close, she realized he was only a teenager. He was at least an inch above her five foot nine, and leanly muscled with green eyes and a fringe of light brown hair peeking out from beneath his dark brown cowboy hat. She glanced around for an unfamiliar car or the other people who must be with him, but saw no one. "Are you here with your parents?"

"No, ma'am. It's just me. I heard in town that you're looking to hire a ranch hand."

"We sure are. Do you have any experience?"

"I do." Cinder stretched his neck over the fence and nudged Adam's hat with his nose. He took a step back so he could stroke the horse's neck. "I know a lot about horses."

"Cinder sure seems to like you, and he doesn't like anyone but me or my sister. And occasionally the veterinarian." She patted the other side of the horse's neck.

"My mother boarded and trained horses," he said. "I've been around them my entire life."

"Where does she live?"

He shuffled one boot in the patchy grass that surrounded the corral. "She passed away six months ago, and now it's just me."

The catch in his voice and sadness in his green eyes broke Daisy's heart. "I'm so sorry to hear that. I know this is a hard stage of grieving."

"Yes, ma'am. It is."

She looked around. "How did you get here?"

"I hitchhiked."

She gasped. "That's not safe these days."

"Well, technically, from the bus stop in Channing, I got a ride with an old guy from town right to your gate. So, it wasn't that daring on my part."

"I'm glad to hear you don't make a habit of hitchhiking. How did you get through my front gate?"

"I was standing outside of it when a young woman with long blond hair was leaving. I told her I was here about the job, and she said she was running late for her son's appointment and couldn't show me herself, but she told me to walk up the driveway and find you at the stable."

"That was my niece Lizzy. Can I ask how old you are?"

He straightened his shoulders as if trying to look taller. "I'm eighteen."

"I wasn't much older than you when I lost my mom. My dad was gone before that. What about your father?"

"Never had one. And no brothers or sisters. It's just me, for now."

She liked that he sounded hopeful for his future. "Where are you living?"

"At the moment, nowhere. But I grew up near Houston."

There was another strong tug on her heart. His clothes were clean and of high quality, so he wasn't destitute, but this sad young man needed her help, and she felt an immediate pull to take care of him.

"Grab your backpack and come inside so we can get to know one another and see if you are a good fit for the job." Her gut told her to hire him, but getting to know him better wouldn't hurt.

"That would be great." He hefted the pack onto his shoulders and followed her toward the farmhouse.

"Are you hungry?"

"I had lunch in town at the Rodeo Café, but I could use a cup of coffee to warm up."

They went in through the kitchen door. "There's a bathroom right around the corner if you need it while I make a fresh pot."

"Thanks."

When he came back into the kitchen, Daisy had put a plate of cookies on the table and was pouring coffee. "Do you need cream or sugar?"

"Just cream, please." He took a seat at the round kitchen table.

"That's how I take my coffee too. Those cookies on the table are peanut butter. You're not allergic to peanuts, are you?"

"No, ma'am. I love peanut butter."

"So do I. Please, call me Daisy. I might be almost old enough to be your mom, but I like to pretend I'm not." She chuckled, sat across from him and nudged the plate of cookies his way.

His eyes kept flicking back to her as if he was searching for something in her face. Was he trying to make up his mind about her like she was doing him, or as Finn would likely say, sizing her up to take advantage of her in some way?

It didn't feel that way to her. Nothing about this young man felt dangerous or dishonest. She wasn't nearly as gullible as her protective best friend thought she was.

Adam seemed to realize that he was staring and focused on the cookie in his hand.

"Tell me about growing up around horses," she said.

He swallowed a bite of cookie. "At our ranch outside of Houston, we boarded lots of horses for rich people. Many of the horses were worth a lot of money, so I know what it means to take care of expensive animals. It's serious business and nothing to mess around with."

"Are you familiar with what we do here on Dalton Ranch?"

"Yes, ma'am. I mean Daisy. I looked at your website and know that this is a stud farm."

"That's right. We have several stud horses, but our most famous is Titan. We also do some breeding with our partner Travis. He is married to my niece Lizzy, the woman you met at the front gate."

"You have a niece old enough to be married?"

"I do. I have a much older brother, and I was only ten when Lizzy was born."

"You are lucky to have so much family," he said.

Daisy had to admit that she was.

"I don't know much about breeding, but I know a lot about taking care of horses, and I'm a good rider. Someday I'd like to have my own place, and I would love the opportunity to learn from you." Excitement seemed to make some of his nervousness disappear. "I'd like the opportunity to prove I can be useful."

They talked for a few more minutes. "How did you end up in Channing?"

"I'll show you." He unzipped his pack, pulled out a small photo album and flipped it open.

The first picture was of a beautiful woman with blond hair and a huge smile and a young boy making a silly face. They were standing in front of a water fountain with a horse statue in the center, and she recognized it right away.

"That's Old Town Channing. Is that you?"

"Yes. When I was a kid, we came to Channing on vacation. We stayed at a place on the river, and we fished and canoed. It was lots of fun. My mom always said Channing, Texas, would be a great place to live, and it's where she would move if we didn't have our ranch." He cleared his throat and looked back at the picture.

"So, you decided to make her dream come true, for you. That's really sweet."

He shrugged. "She would like it. I figured while I was looking for a place to start over, this was as good a place as any to check out first."

"What were you going to do if you hadn't heard I was hiring?"

"I was hoping for a cheap motel room. And there are so many ranches in the area, I figured someone would be hiring or there would be a job somewhere around town." He flipped to the next photo and pushed it closer to her. "That's the ranch where I grew up."

"Beautiful. It looks like you had a really nice childhood."

"I did." His throat worked as he swallowed.

Normally, she would talk to her sister before hiring someone, but she had a feeling about Adam. She couldn't send him off to hitchhike around the country and have no one looking out for him. She'd always had a sense about people and was going to go with her gut instinct. "I like what I'm hearing. You sound qualified. We have an apartment behind the stable that has recently become available, and if you'd like, you can live in it as part of your pay."

"I got the job?"

"If you want it."

He sighed and seemed to relax as tension left his shoulders. "Yes, I do. That would be great. Thanks."

"Good." She stood and took her cup to the sink. "Let's go out to the stable and I'll show you the apartment and you can meet all the horses."

They went in through the small side door near the back of the stable. Daisy motioned to her left. "On this side is the tack room, and across from it are the collection room and the laboratory where we get the product ready to ship out."

"I wouldn't mind learning how all of that works."

"I'm happy to teach you." She walked down the aisle between the rooms. "Through this back door is the apartment where you'll be staying."

The one-bedroom was beautiful, because Sage had decorated it. It was an open floor plan kitchen and living area with a small bed and bath off to one side. It had a blue and tan color scheme and comfortable furnishings.

"Will this work for you?" she asked.

"Are you kidding? This is great." He put his backpack on the brown leather couch.

"Good. Let's go meet all the horses."

Back out in the stable, she pointed up to the ceiling as they made their way back past the tack room. "There are cameras all throughout the stable that monitor and record 24-7. The red button on that post will buzz the main house and can be used if there is an emergency."

"Good safety features. That's another thing my mom would appreciate."

"I'm glad to hear it. There are horses in here that belong to every member of the family. You've met Cinder, and next to his stall is Titan." She went down the row and introduced him to the rest of the stud horses, then all the horses the family rode, and the ones that belonged to Travis.

Lifting his hands, he moved them around to encompass the whole space. "It means a lot to me to have a place to stay. You're really going to trust me with all this?"

"Can I?" That he would ask made her believe she was making the right decision.

"Absolutely." He stood tall and put a hand over his heart. "I'll treat every animal and everything here as if I'm part of the family."

CHAPTER FOURTEEN

As FINN DREW close to Daisy, who was standing on her back patio, he followed her gaze to the corral and saw a stranger exercising the feisty stallion that even he had trouble handling.

"Who's that kid working with Cinder?"

She looked over her shoulder and smiled at him. "That's Adam. I just hired him to be our new ranch hand."

"Seriously?"

"Yes. Of course seriously."

"He's just a kid. You should've let me check him out before you hired him."

Her eyebrows popped up. "I don't remember putting you in charge of hiring on my ranch."

He knew when it was time to shut his big mouth and did it in a hurry. They turned at the sound of Riley and Jake walking up behind them.

"What are you two staring at?" Jake asked.

Finn nodded his head toward the stranger. "Daisy hired that scrawny kid to be her ranch hand."

"Hey!" Daisy smacked his arm with the back of her hand. "Be nice. You don't even know him. Adam is smart and knowledgeable, and he recently lost his mom. He's all on his own."

"So, he's a charity case?" Jake asked, echoing Finn's own thoughts.

Daisy scoffed. "No, he's not. He knows a lot about horses

and is really good with them." She motioned toward the corral and started walking that way. "As you can see. I haven't seen any of you three be able to do that with Cinder."

"He looks capable enough to me," Riley said in his deep, quiet voice.

The three of them followed her to the edge of the corral.

"What did y'all come over here for?" she asked. "Other than to pester me about my new employee."

Finn lifted his arm in a new automatic response to being near her, but he stopped himself right before wrapping it around her and shifted his hat instead. It was getting harder and harder to separate the friend from the lover. He watched the kid with the horse. It really did look like he knew what he was doing. "You haven't even put out an ad for the job. Who sent him to you?"

"His mother." Daisy smiled at him as if that settled everything.

A mother's recommendation made him feel a little better about him being here alone with Daisy. "Some of our cattle got out before we could repair a break in the fence, and we could use help rounding them up from the neighbor's place on the other side of us."

"Too bad they didn't get out on my side of your ranch," she said. "I'm happy to help."

The kid slowed the horse and led him over to where they stood.

Daisy propped her arms on the fence. "Adam Hauser, these are the Murphy brothers, Finn, Riley and Jake." She pointed to each of them in turn.

"Nice to meet all of you." Adam held out his hand.

Finn grasped it before either of his brothers could, and he was impressed with the kid's firm grip and use of eye contact.

"Adam, the brothers own Four Star Ranch next door, and they need some help rounding up cattle."

"I can help," Adam said.

"We need a real cowboy," Finn said. Daisy shot him a sharp look and then put a hand on his back and pinched him in warning. He almost laughed. She didn't understand how guys sometimes needed to take a man's measure and also allow him the opportunity to show you who he was.

Adam straightened his spine. "I am a real cowboy."

Finn looked the young man up and down. He had a feeling that he actually was, but another test wouldn't hurt. "What do you think, guys?" he asked his brothers. "Can we make a cowboy out of this kid?"

"I think it's worth a try," Jake said. "How old are you?"

"Eighteen. Almost nineteen."

"Let's see your driver's license," Finn requested.

Daisy mumbled under her breath.

Adam pulled out his wallet and dug out his ID. "I know I look young."

"Is this fake?"

The young man looked at him like he was stupid. "Don't you think if I had bothered with getting a fake ID that I'd make myself at least twenty-one?"

"He's got you there," Riley said.

Finn handed back his driver's license and propped his folded arms on the top railing. "You don't look old enough to shave more than once a week."

"Well, you certainly do," Adam quipped and then tipped up the front of his brown cowboy hat. "So how about it, grandpa? Are we going to round up some cattle or not?"

Jake and Rily laughed, and Daisy ducked her head to hide a smile.

Finn held back his own grin. He could not drop his guard with this teenager. Not yet. "Okay. You can show us what you've got."

"I'll put Cinder in his stall." Adam led the animal away.

He liked this kid's spunk, and later he would make sure Daisy knew why he was giving him a hard time. Every young man his age deserved the opportunity to prove himself. But because Adam would be around Daisy, he planned to keep an extra sharp eye on this young cowboy.

"Adam and I will ride over to your place as soon as we can get the horses saddled."

DAISY TOOK ADAM into the tack room. "For the horse you'll ride, grab that saddle, and I'll get your bridle."

He looked around and lifted the saddle from its stand. "My mom liked to keep a really neat tack room too."

"It makes things easier when everything is organized."

"That's the kind of thing she always said." He followed her out into the stable and down the center aisle between the stalls.

"Please don't let the Murphy brothers get to you."

Adam made a dismissive sound. "They're nothing I haven't dealt with before."

She smiled to herself. This young man was going to fit right in around here. He reminded her of the Murphy brothers. Tough with a little bit of sweetness hiding underneath. He'd proven that while sharing photos from his childhood. "You do seem to be able to hold your own with them."

"Don't worry about me."

"Good to know. You'll be riding Sandy. She's the palomino in the third stall."

Once Sandy and Lou were saddled, they led them outside, mounted up, then rode toward Finn's place.

"How long has this ranch been in your family?" Adam asked.

"My sister and I are the fifth generation to live on it."

"Wow. That must be so cool to be able to say that."

"Can I ask where you were living before you arrived in Channing?"

"With a bunch of other guys. Some of them were bad news, and it wasn't a good fit anymore." He reined his horse around a fallen tree branch.

"I'm glad to hear you got yourself out of a bad situation," she said. "Will you tell me about your mom?" She thought at first that he wouldn't answer, but then he let out a long, slow breath.

"She loved horses like you do."

"So, you inherited your horsemanship skills from your mother."

He studied her for a few seconds before glancing skyward. "I guess I did."

Daisy hoped being here would help heal some of his sorrow.

"This horse wants to run," he said.

"Are you up for that?" She hoped so, because for some reason, she really wanted Adam to impress the Murphy brothers.

"Absolutely. It's been too long since I've been able to ride."

"As soon as we go through the gate up ahead that separates our properties, there is a big flat pasture. It's a perfect place to run the horses."

From horseback, she leaned down to unlatch the gate, and her horse knew the routine of backing up to open it and did the same in reverse to close it. "Let's ride."

They started off at a canter and moved quickly into a gallop. The two of them kept pace side by side.

She was relieved that he was a good rider. For all of their sakes, she hoped Adam would work out as a new hire. She hated the idea of having to fire someone so young and vulnerable and unprotected from the world. Was this teenager the next person the Dalton family would take under their wings?

Finn was watching them as they neared his barn where three other horses were saddled and waiting.

She shared a smile with Finn. A silent I told you so.

Riley told everyone the plan and gave instructions, and Adam didn't have to be told twice. It didn't take the five of them long to round up the cattle and return them to Four Star Ranch, then patch the hole in the fence.

Finn gave Adam a slap on the back. "You did all right, kid."

"Thanks, old man."

Daisy smiled to herself. Maybe these three crazy brothers would be good for this sad young man who suddenly found himself alone in the world.

THAT EVENING, DAISY used an oven mitt to hold the handle of a cast-iron skillet while she cut the corn bread into triangles. A knock on her back door brought her out of her thoughts about the business calls she needed to make tomorrow. She could see Adam's nervous face through the windowpane on the top half of the door, and she motioned for him to come inside.

"You're just in time."

"Thank you for the invitation." He closed the door behind himself.

"Since I know you haven't been able to go grocery shopping yet, the least I can do is feed you."

"I have some snacks in my backpack."

"A growing young man needs better food than trail snacks. I expect you to come to the house for breakfast in the morning."

"Thank you. I appreciate it." He took off his cowboy hat and held it to his chest with one hand.

The movement struck her as protective, as if he needed to shield his heart. But his posture also seemed like a way of showing respect to her. "You can hang your hat on one of those." She pointed to the row of four polished wooden hat hooks that were mounted on the wall under a shelf.

He hung his hat on the far right hook.

"That's the one my dad always used. Most people come in and use the first one." She put the last piece of corn bread in the basket and covered it with a cloth.

He rubbed a hand over the smoothed knob end of one of the empty hooks. "They look old and handmade."

"They are. I believe my great-grandfather made them."

"You have real family history in your house."

"I guess I'm pretty lucky that way." The sadness on his face made her wish she hadn't brought up the family stuff to someone who had no family or home. She wondered what had happened to the ranch where he grew up, but she would wait to ask. It was a question with the potential to be painful. "I'll take you to the grocery store some time tomorrow. But for tonight, I hope you like taco casserole."

"Sounds good." He drummed his fingers against his thigh and tapped one boot heel.

She smiled in the hope of calming him, but instead of returning her expression, his eyes widened, and he rubbed his cheek.

She wasn't exactly sure what his reaction meant, but she chalked it up to him missing his mom.

He turned to study the photos on the front of her refrigerator and pointed to Lizzy and Travis's wedding photo. "That's the lady who let me in your front gate."

"Yes, that's my niece Lizzy. She is an opera singer."

"Oh wow. I like to sing, but I'm definitely not that good."

"You don't even want to hear me sing." She tapped a finger on the photo. "That's her husband, Travis. He partners with us on some horse breeding but is also a part owner of the Four Star Ranch next door, with the three Murphy brothers. And that cutie is their son, Davy."

"He was at their wedding?" Adam said, then grimaced. "Sorry. It was rude of me to say that. I didn't mean to judge. My mom always told me to run a question through my head before letting it come out of my mouth, but I obviously haven't mastered that yet."

"It's okay. No worries. Davy is adopted. He kind of helped bring them together."

"That's admirable of them."

Not for the first time, she noticed the way his speech and manners were a bit more formal than the average Texas cowboy.

"Who is this?" Adam touched a candid shot Sage had recently taken.

"That's my brother-in-law, Grayson, and his two daughters. You're about to meet them."

"Is he a cowboy here on the ranch too?"

"Grayson is an architect and part-time cowboy."

Adam's stomach growled. "What can I do to help with dinner?"

"You can grab that basket of corn bread and follow me."

Daisy used two hot pads to carry the large casserole, and Adam followed her down the hallway to the dining room.

"Come and get it," she called to her family members in the living room.

Grayson entered first, and she introduced the two men.

"You're in for a treat," Grayson said as he took a seat at one end of the table. "I love this meal."

Sage came in right behind him with Rose cradled in her arms.

"Sage, this is Adam Hauser, the new hire I told you about."

Her sister tucked a curl behind her ear. "So nice to meet you. Welcome to the Dalton Ranch family."

"Thank you." Adam looked between them. "You're twins."

"We sure are," Sage said. "And this little one is Rose."

The baby waved her arms and blew a raspberry.

"Hi, Rose," Adam said, and then sat in the empty chair closest to him.

Sage swept around to her chair on the other side of the dining table and buckled the baby into her high chair.

As soon as Daisy sat at the opposite end from Grayson, Loren rushed into the room, and her steps faltered when she saw a stranger. "Hi. I'm Loren. Pronounced like Sophia Loren."

"I'm Adam. But I'm afraid I don't know Sophia Loren."

Her fifteen-year-old niece giggled and took her seat across from their visitor. "That's okay. She's a famous old Hollywood movie star. A lot of people our age don't know who she is."

Daisy smiled at their interaction. "Everyone dig in before it gets cold."

"Are you going to be the new cowboy here on Dalton Ranch?" Loren asked him.

"I guess I am."

Her niece flipped back the cloth and took a piece of corn bread, then held out the basket to their guest. "Soon, you'll meet my cousin Lizzy, her husband Travis and their son Davy."

"I met Lizzy, briefly. And I think her son was in a car seat in the back."

"Davy is two years old and has Down syndrome. He is so smart and so cute. And this is my baby sister, Rose." She leaned to the side and kissed the top of her sister's head. "She is just as smart and cute as Davy."

Daisy and Sage shared a smile. After years of it just being the two of them, it was so nice to have family around their dining room table. When all of them were here, they had to add one of the table extensions to fit everyone.

If I can show Finn that he would make a great family man, we'll need the second table extender.

She bit the inside of her cheek and reminded herself to believe Finn when he said he didn't want a wife or kids. Misplaced hope could lead to greater heartache.

AFTER ADAM WENT back to the apartment and her sister's family left for the ten minute drive to their house in town, Daisy took a long hot bath.

She went into the home office to check the monitor that would show her each of the horses. It was something she always did before bed. Adam was standing in front of Cinder's stall. She couldn't hear what he was saying but he was smiling, and the horse was eating up the attention. He put his forehead against the horse's, and it made her eyes sting with the urge to cry. No matter what anyone else thought, she knew she'd made the right decision hiring him. She watched until he dimmed the lights just like she'd shown him and went into the apartment.

Before climbing into bed, she pulled up her fluffy down comforter. Lady hopped onto the foot of the bed, turned a few circles and settled down by her legs. As she reached to turn off the bedside lamp, a text message came in. It was a sweet photo of the goat and dog cuddling. She replied that it was cute, but rather than responding with another message, he called.

"Good evening, Finnigan."

"What are you doing?"

"I just got in bed."

"I just realized what time it is. I'm glad I didn't wake you."

She snuggled farther down into her soft sheets. "Good friends are allowed to call in the middle of the night—on occasion."

"That's something I've been thinking about a lot lately."

"Calling me in the middle of the night?"

"Our friendship. Even though we have different future family goals, the importance of our friendship is something I think we can agree on."

"Yes, we can." She had a feeling he was about to work on convincing himself of the future he wanted. The one he thought he wanted. But the picture she saw forming had a fork in his road, and although she'd just this evening reminded herself to be cautious, she hoped she could urge him down the right one.

The sound of a television went off in the background. "Ultimately, we want opposite things. You want a kid, and I don't. You want to get married—"

"And you don't," she finished for him. "I'm well aware of your aversion to fatherhood and wedded bliss."

"I've witnessed a lot of the opposite of wedded bliss."

His bad opinion of marriage was sad, and no doubt partially explained his aversion. She might have failed at it in her youth, but that didn't mean she didn't believe in it, and she wasn't giving up on having a husband. "And that's why you don't want to be in a committed long-term relationship."

"In my experience, our curiosity will naturally burn itself out over time, and then we can get back to normal."

Her stomach clenched, and she was glad he couldn't see the look on her face. She understood what he meant, but it hurt to think that he would at any moment just stop desiring her. Most relationships hit a point when initial lust faded, but he'd made it sound as simple as extinguishing a candle.

"You'll meet a guy, fall in love and make it all happen."

He made it sound so easy peasy, like if she loved someone enough the rest would follow, like a wish granted. Her blood surged.

A wish granted.

Both parts of her first wish had come true. She picked up her list from the bedside table. Number two was still unfinished, but she'd decided to wait to complete her wish to fall in love, and she should stick to that decision. That wish would be written in February.

Learning a skill and having an adventure were fairly easy to accomplish. Becoming a mom would be a lot trickier. But just in case wishes really did come true, she now knew what she was going to add to her New Year's wish list.

Find someone who loves me the way I love them. The way I deserve.

Unaware of her tumbling thoughts, he continued. "Even after you're an old married lady, we'll still have our friendship."

"You'll be my cantankerous old bachelor friend."

"That's why we need to keep what we're doing just between us. That way there won't be any weirdness with someone either of us is dating. They won't have to freak out about us being alone together and fooling around. We will have already scratched that itch."

He was really sending her mood downhill. "Did you just call to remind me how much you don't want a family and why we're doomed?"

He was quiet for a moment. "No. Sorry. I didn't mean to get off onto that again. I just wanted to hear your voice...because I miss you."

She smiled as some of her happiness returned. "I miss you too."

Finn was fighting their relationship, and himself, but she could see a few rays of sunlight trying to break through.

CHAPTER FIFTEEN

DAISY AND FINN had always helped one another on their ranches—when needed—but since their holiday hideaway, they'd fallen into a regular routine of working together as if the horse ranch and Four Star Ranch was one large property. Just like this afternoon when she'd helped him find a missing calf.

Finn unzipped his jacket. Today's weather had been mild, but in Texas, who could be sure what the next day would bring. "Thanks for helping me find that calf," he said to Daisy. "You have a knack for it."

"Happy to help."

They walked down the incline to the pond. The sun was just starting to dip behind the horizon, and the water glistened with warm colors. He let the goat off her leash so she could run with the dog. The rowboat had been securely tied so they wouldn't have another goat in a boat incident.

Finn wound up the purple leash and shoved it into his jacket pocket. "What does Adam drive? I didn't see a vehicle."

"He doesn't have a car. He took a bus to Channing and hitchhiked out here from town."

He stopped walking and turned to face her. "Hitchhiked? Where does he live?"

"In the apartment behind the stable."

"Daisy, you don't even know him, and you put him in there with all the horses?"

"What do you think he is? A horse thief or something?"

"Well, not really. He seems like a good kid. But still…" They started walking again.

"There are cameras everywhere, except for in the apartment of course, and Adam knows about them. Last night, I was in the home office and watched him on the monitor. He was out in the stable talking to the horses and all of the animals like him. And that says something about a person. I think he is really lonely, and he's still grieving for his mom. My heart aches for him."

"You have a soft heart."

"Yours is softer than you want people to know, Finnigan."

"Wait a minute. You said his mom was the one who recommended him for the job."

"In a way."

"In what way could that possibly be?"

"Adam's mom used to bring him to Channing on vacation, and she told him it was a place she'd like to live. He showed me photos of them by the horse fountain when he was a kid. He's all alone in the world and trying to start over. He's trying to live out his mom's dream."

He reached down to pet the dog's head before Astro darted off to play again. "I'll admit, I do feel for him. At least I had my brothers to keep me going and to lean on. Maybe Adam should come live at my house until we all get to know him better."

She hooked her arm through his as they walked. "Because you don't want him to be lonely or because you're worried that he is up to no good and don't want him that close to me?"

He shrugged. "A little of both, I guess."

They followed Astro and Rascal up the hill toward his ranch house.

He liked having her arm linked through his. It felt…comfortable. She'd occasionally done it before they'd explored the physical attraction between them, but now, along with the comfort there was a tingle. "Will you do me a favor and go with me to a barbecue tonight? It's a monthly mixer for a group of cattle ranchers that Riley wanted us to join. It has been good networking, but I really need you there."

"You need me to impress people with my witty personality or to chaperone?"

"Both, but actually, more of the second."

She laughed. "I was kidding about that."

"There's a woman who'll be there, and she can't take a hint that I'm not interested in going home with her. She has tried to get me to all three times I've seen her. I don't want to be mean or hurt her feelings."

"She's not your type?"

"Not exactly. I think Dolores is in her late fifties and expecting her first grandchild next month."

She chuckled. "You catch the eye of every woman from one to ninety-nine."

"She's still beautiful, but I think she's interested in only one thing from me."

Daisy was looking at him with a mixture of humor and curiosity. "Not ready to be a grandpa?"

"That's a hard no."

"So, tonight I'll be your what? Pretend girlfriend?"

His pulse jumped. "I hadn't really thought about it exactly, but that could work. I don't think you'll know anyone else there."

"What about your brothers? Won't they be there?"

"We'll just tell them you're going to pretend to be my date for the night."

"Sounds like playing with fire," she said.

It sure did, but it also sounded like a lot of fun.

"Want to know why else I'm happy you're going with me?"

"Can't wait to hear it."

"I'm happy because..." He paused for dramatic effect and grinned. "You're going to wear your handprint jeans."

She stopped walking and snapped her hands to her hips. "I absolutely am not. I already accepted that dare when we went to the new Italian restaurant."

"This time it's for a different reason."

"Why is this time different?"

"Because I like to watch you walk in them." He raised both

hands and made a squeezing motion. "It makes it look like my fingers are cupping your butt."

She laughed and slipped her hands into her own back pockets. "Now I'm definitely not wearing them in public, but I will need to go home to shower and change clothes before we go."

His front door opened, and his brothers came outside, both dressed in their best jeans and boots.

"Are you ready to go?" Jake asked. "I promised to bring ice and need to go into town to get it."

"No, we'll meet y'all there in a little while," Finn said. "Daisy is going to pretend to be my date to keep Dolores away from me."

Jake laughed. "This ought to be good."

"We're taking the new truck. See you there." Riley got in on the driver's side of their silver truck.

The second Jake and Riley drove away, he and Daisy grinned at one another.

"The house is empty," he said. "You said you wanted to take a shower, and I happened to notice that when you left in such a rush the other morning, you left your travel bag of cosmetics in my bathroom."

She tugged on one of his belt loops, then took off jogging. "Race you to the shower."

He whistled for the dog and goat and then followed Daisy inside with a big smile on his face.

AN HOUR AND a half later, they were late to the barbecue, but they were both relaxed and well satisfied. When they'd stopped by Daisy's house for her to change clothes, she had not put on the handprint jeans as he'd hoped. She'd rushed back outside dressed in a pair of slim-fitting black jeans, and a black sweater that fell off one shoulder and was sexy as hell. It was a good compromise as far as wardrobe choices went.

This month the meeting was at the home of the association's president. It was a massive red brick Colonial surrounded by cattle fields, with a big barn behind it. Someday he hoped to be half as successful as this rancher.

He waited for Daisy at the front of her truck, and they went up the brick pathway to the door. "Thanks again for coming with me."

"Let me know when you see your cougar."

"Dolores is not my anything. That's the whole point of this." He swept her hand into his and laced their fingers as they went in through the door behind another group of people.

Daisy gave his hand a squeeze. "Have I ever told you that I wanted to be an actress when I was a kid?"

"I don't believe you have."

"Now is my chance to give it a try."

"Oh, boy. Should I worry?"

She smiled, and there was a gleam in her eyes that hinted at mischief.

Pretend dating is going to be entertaining at the very least.

He introduced her to several people, and they got drinks at the bar. Daisy mingled easily with whoever she met. She seemed to fit in everywhere and was good with people.

Across the room, he spotted Dolores. She was lovely and didn't look at all like a classic grandmother type, and there was a time he would've taken her up on her offer, but lately he'd just needed a break from dating so many different women. Letting this woman down easy was certainly something he could've handled by himself in a perfectly tactful manner, but having Daisy here made it so much easier. He slid an arm around her waist.

Daisy turned to face him and put her arms around his neck as if she knew the reason. "Which one is she?" she whispered.

"The brunette in the red dress," he said against her ear. She shivered, and for added effect, he kissed her forehead.

Over Daisy's shoulder, Dolores smiled at him in a way that was sweet and accepting of their situation. He nodded and smiled back. There was now an understanding between them, but that didn't mean he could stop his pretend date with the woman in his arms. They had to keep up appearances.

"Want to get some food, Daisy Maisy?"

"Yes. It smells really good." She let her hands slide slowly down his chest, and her eyes followed all the way to his belt buckle. "Something I did earlier has given me an appetite."

Before he could respond, she spun away from him, and he

thought he heard her giggle. He hadn't realized until recently what a tease she could be. And he loved that about her.

Riley kept looking at them, and he had a feeling that his quiet brother was suspicious of him and Daisy. But like Sage, he wouldn't tell anyone. His baby brother was a different story.

There were tables set up inside and out, and they chose a standing table on the back deck where it was quieter and there was a good view of the night sky.

"Are you still driving into Fort Worth tomorrow?" she asked.

"Yes. I have a meeting, and I'm leaving at about nine o'clock."

"Can I catch a ride and get dropped off and picked up at the hospital?"

He almost dropped his drink. Panic was the first to hit him with a gut punch.

Oh crap, is she pregnant?

But just as swiftly, his thoughts flipped to worry. For her. He touched her bare shoulder. "What's wrong, sweetheart? Are you okay?"

She tipped her head to the side and grinned. "Yes, I'm perfectly fine. I figured we could carpool and save on gas. My nurse friend called and told me there's a new preemie baby in the NICU who needs some extra cuddling."

Relief made his shoulders drop. "You really like doing that, don't you?"

"I do. There is something so magical about a newborn." She wrapped her arms around herself and glanced up at the starry sky.

He wasn't sure if it was because she was cold or needed a hug. Since they were pretending to be on a date, he pulled her into his arms. What did it matter that there was no one else around to see their display of affection? There was always the chance someone was watching them from the windows. Hopefully not one of his brothers.

She relaxed against his chest, and he let himself enjoy the moment. Everything else would be there to worry about tomorrow.

DAISY SCRUBBED HER hands in the stainless-steel sink in the small room before she could enter the neonatal intensive care unit.

"Hello, ladies," she said to a doctor and her friend Tina. "Who do you have for me today?"

"A beautiful baby boy. He was a month early," Tina said, and motioned for her to follow. "Mom gave birth last night and had a rough time of it after her C-section. Dad is on his way home from a trip overseas, and he should be here sometime today."

"I'm happy to sub in for them. I would want someone to do the same for me." An old familiar ache crept in. Who had held her baby...or babies? She knew she shouldn't think of them as *hers*, but knowing and doing were two different things.

"It's almost time for the baby to eat," Tina said. "After I get you two settled, I'll get a bottle ready."

Daisy sat in one of the rocking chairs and let her friend place the tiny bundle in her arms. The baby was sucking on his little balled-up fist and starting to fuss.

"Hello, little darling. Welcome to the world." Swirls of dark hair topped his head, and his big chocolate-drop eyes blinked slowly as he tried to focus.

Tina came back with the bottle, and she coaxed the baby to drink. While he ate, she let her mind wander from topic to topic, but she kept coming back to Finn.

Finn was such a contradiction. He was good with babies, and she knew he liked them. He'd proven that with the way he was with her niece Rose and her nephew Davy. And yet, he was adamant that he did not want any kids of his own.

From what she'd recently learned about his childhood, it had become pretty clear that it was because he'd been forced to be responsible for his little brothers at an age that was way too young. He didn't seem to understand that it would be different as a grown-up—with other adults around to help out.

She set the empty bottle aside, put the baby against her chest and patted his back. He emitted a soft burp. "That's it, sweetie. Good job."

All she could do was support and encourage Finn to see that he was a good man who could trust in himself and would make a great father. She sighed and rested her head back against the rocker. The last thing she needed was a guy who had a less than zero desire for a wife or child. *I'm too old to waste time.*

Sleeping Beauty sympathized with her dilemma, while Maleficent only shrugged with a mischievous grin.

Who had she been trying to kid that she would be able to keep her heart out of it when she was sharing a man's bed? It had become so much more than just physical for her. But for Finn? That remained to be seen.

Her tentative hold on the ten percent of her love she'd been reserving was starting to slip.

I should've taken Dillon up on his offer to share the apartment during the snowstorm.

At least then she would still have Finn's unblemished friendship, and possibly a tall, dark and handsome veterinarian as a future lover. She groaned. She didn't want to be with Dillon. He didn't give her the delicious tingles that Finn could with nothing more than a heated look or half smile. If she could write her future into existence, Dillon would be the one who remained in the "friend only" category, and Finn would be her...

Everything.

She squeezed her eyes closed. "No, no, no. I'm such a fool."

The baby stretched and grunted as if he was in total agreement with her self-assessment.

How was she supposed to give up her new connection with Finn just because the calendar flipped to a new month?

DAISY WENT OUT into the hospital parking lot and saw Finn's truck at the end of a row. He didn't see her as she approached, and she had to knock on the window for him to unlock the door. She got in and he started the engine. "I hope you haven't been waiting long."

"Not too long. How was the baby?"

She buckled her seat belt. "He was so small and precious. His dad arrived from out of town while I was there and was so happy to meet his newborn son that he teared up. It was so amazing to see his parents experience the moment together. I loved seeing their bond form right there in front of my eyes."

"That's cool."

"What were you thinking about so hard when I got in?"

"Something that keeps popping into my head now and then.

You never finished telling me about how you got your share of the money to save Dalton Ranch."

"It's funny you should ask me about that right now. It's the reason I started going to the hospital to hold babies." She pressed her teeth into her bottom lip.

"It's what made me think of it, too. I get the feeling it has something to do with a child."

"I wasn't a surrogate like my sister, but I did give a part of myself to help another woman be a mother."

"Huh?" He cocked his head and looked at her, clearly not understanding.

"I went to a fertility clinic and gave another woman a chance to get pregnant using my eggs."

"Oh, sweetheart." He reached across the center console and laced his fingers with hers. "That must have been so hard for you."

She took a moment to let the warmth of his touch soak in. "I have no idea if I have a child or children somewhere out there in the world. If I do, they are about Loren's age. Just getting started in high school." Her voice cracked, and she cleared her throat.

"You deserve the chance to have a baby of your own," he said.

That was something they could agree on. She just wished they agreed on the method to make that happen.

FINN'S INSIDES STARTED to twist and cramp. He knew she wanted to be a mom. He also knew her well enough to know she wouldn't start dating anyone else as long as they were sleeping together.

What she'd had to do to save Dalton Ranch years ago went a long way to explain a few things about her. He was wasting Daisy's time and holding her back from finding a good man to start a family with.

She smiled but it faltered around the edges, and she tightened her hold on his hand. "Do you want to stop for something to eat? My treat," she said in an attempt to change the subject.

"You know I can always eat." He kept her hand in his, and she didn't try to pull away. He wasn't ready to let the physical part of their relationship go. Not yet. But soon. He'd have to do it soon.

She was so sweet and kind and real. And deserving of all the happiness life could give her. He should remind her of the incompatibility of their family plans, but she didn't like it when he brought it up, and he didn't want to bring down the mood.

Instead, he wanted to do something that would make her smile.

CHAPTER SIXTEEN

ADAM FOLLOWED DAISY into the kitchen with two bags of groceries and put them on the counter. "That's the last of them."

"Thank you." She made room for the milk in the refrigerator.

"Day-day." Her nephew screeched her name when he toddled around the corner and saw her.

"Hello, angel boy." She scooped Davy into her arms and covered his face with kisses until he was giggling. "Davy, I want you to meet Adam."

Adam smiled at the toddler, and Davy leaned in her arms and reached for the teenager, and Adam didn't hesitate to hold him. "Hey, there, little buddy."

Lizzy came into the kitchen. "Hello, again. I see you've met my son. If he let you hold him this quickly, you must be a good guy. Davy is a good judge of character."

"That's good to know."

"Hey, you only have one dimple," Lizzy said.

Daisy looked over her shoulder. That shared genetic trait was the kind of thing she looked for. Too bad Adam was too old to be hers.

Loren joined them in the kitchen. "Hi, Adam. I didn't know you were here. Do you want to help me read to Davy and Rose before their nap time?"

"Sure, I can do that." Adam shifted Davy to his other hip

and looked at Daisy. "But only if there isn't any work you need me to get done."

"There is nothing pressing right now. Go ahead and help Loren with the little ones."

The teens left the room with Loren chattering away to him about her horse, Mischief.

Lizzy started helping her put groceries away. "He seems like a good kid. I hope it's okay that I let him come in the gate. I probably should've called you, but I was late and rushing."

"I'm glad you sent him my way. I think he needs us more than we need him."

The sound of little boy giggles drifted through the house.

Daisy and Lizzy tiptoed down the hallway and looked into the living room and smiled at the scene.

Adam was sitting on the floor with Davy in his lap. Beside him, Loren held baby Rose. He was reading one of their favorite books and using different voices for each character.

Davy clapped and giggled at the animal sounds.

"That's so sweet," Lizzy whispered.

It sure was. If she never had any kids of her own, at least she had a hand in raising her nephew and nieces.

FINN HAD GONE over to Dalton Ranch to teach Adam how to weld, and he was happy to report that he had picked up the technique quickly. Tonight, all the guys were hanging out at Finn's house, but he didn't want to go home without seeing Daisy. He found her in the home office.

"Hey, Daisy, how's it going?" Her smile was so sweet that he wanted to kiss her.

"Hi. How did the welding lesson go?"

"Good. He's a smart kid." He sat on the edge of the desk.

"I told you he'd be a good addition. Now do you trust my judgement?"

"You have your moments," he teased. "Do you happen to have my watch?"

"I do. I needed to borrow it for the stopwatch feature. It's on the dresser in my bedroom."

"How come you don't take other people's stuff?" he asked.

"I guess you're just extra special."

He couldn't resist tucking a lock of loose hair behind her ear, but then he stood before he did something stupid. Something against the rules. "I'll be right back. I want to ask you about the best saddle brand before I go home."

Upstairs in her bedroom, he saw Daisy's wish list on her bedside table. He started to turn away, but he couldn't resist looking to see if she'd added anything since he'd last seen it. And she had.

Daisy's New Year's Wish List
1) Sleep with a hot guy/Brief, fun affair

They could check both of those off her list. He'd been more than happy to assist with number one

2) Fall

Why hadn't she completed it? What was she waiting on? He had a feeling what her wish would be, but he was dying to know for sure.

3) Learn a new skill
4) Have an adventure

Maybe he should offer to teach her how to weld too. And an adventure was something they could accomplish fairly easily.

5) Be a mom

His skin prickled and he backed away from the list as if it was dangerous. And in a way, it was. He couldn't help her with that one.

Finn went downstairs and found everyone in the living room. Daisy was in her blue chair with a horse magazine, and Sage was in her pink one beside her with baby Rose asleep in her arms. Loren and Adam were playing checkers on the coffee table and trying to keep Davy from taking them while Lizzy tried to get his pajamas on.

"Where did Travis and Grayson go?" he asked everyone.

"They went to pick up your pizzas and said they would meet you at your house," Lizzy said.

"Excellent. I'm hungry. Adam, all the guys are getting together at my house tonight," he said. "Want to hang out with us? We're playing cards, watching a game and drinking beer."

Adam glanced at Daisy as if he needed to ask permission, even though it was after work hours. He seemed to realize what he'd done and jerked his eyes back to Finn. "Sure. I'd like to hang out and get to know everyone."

"Good, because you don't want to hang out around here for girls' night," Finn said. "They might try to give you a makeover."

Loren made a move on the game board. "I keep trying to get Aunt Daisy to let us do a makeover on her, but she always says maybe later."

Finn grinned at her across the room. "Come on, Daisy Maisy. Let your niece give you a makeover."

"Maybe I will." She flipped her blond hair over her shoulder.

He clapped a hand on Adam's back. "Are you bringing beer?"

"Only if they will let eighteen-year-olds buy it in this county."

"Oh, yeah. I forgot you're a kid."

"Whatever, old man." Adam stood up and stretched. "You should get the beer because they won't even bother carding you."

Finn chuckled and winked at Daisy.

She stood and called Finn over to her with the universal finger gesture and dropped her voice to a whisper. "Don't get him drunk, please. In fact, don't let him drink at all."

"That's no fun."

"I know. So sad." She lifted her arms as if she'd put them around his neck the way she did in private but then crossed them over her chest instead. "Thanks for making him feel welcome and part of things."

"I think you get the prize for that." He wanted to lean in

and kiss her, but instead, he tugged on a lock of her hair. "See you tomorrow."

"Y'all have fun tonight."

ON THE SHORT ride to Finn's ranch house, Adam seemed to have something on his mind. "You're the oldest brother, right?"

"Yep. Do you have siblings?"

"No. It was just me and my mom. No siblings, no dad."

"Any other family?"

"An uncle who is a bastard. He wants nothing to do with me, and the feeling is entirely mutual."

"That sucks." Finn opened his truck door and got out. This young man really was alone in the world. Daisy had seen that right away, and he admired her for it. He was probably just too jaded and suspicious of people.

Travis and Grayson came in shortly after them with a stack of pizzas they put on the kitchen counter. Everyone started grabbing slices and opening beers. Travis held out a beer to Adam, and the teenager hesitated but took it.

"You know he's not twenty-one, right?" Finn said to Travis.

"No. I didn't know that. No beer for you then. Now that I'm the dad, I feel like I should say that."

"Your son is two," Finn reminded him.

"But he won't be for long."

"Son of a bitch." Jake plowed his hands through his hair. "This laptop is making me crazy. It keeps doing weird stuff."

"Maybe I can help," Adam said, and took his pizza over to the kitchen table where Jake was sitting. "I'm pretty good with computers. Everybody came to me at school for help."

Finn and Travis left them to it and went into the living room to sit on the couch.

"I don't really know Adam yet, but he seems like a good kid," Travis said.

"It's like Daisy adopted him rather than hired him."

"The twins do tend to take in strays, like me. Sage and Daisy started looking out for me years ago. I'm only where I am today because of them. And I wouldn't have my son if Daisy hadn't taken my Lizzy to the hospital to hold babies. She came home with an orphan, and we became a family. My wife definitely takes after her aunts."

"I see what you mean. And now that you mention it, my brothers and I also worked on Dalton Ranch while we saved up to buy this ranch. Those are three amazing women."

"I might've taken Lizzy off the market, and Grayson did the same with Sage, but as you are well aware, Daisy is single."

"I understand single. I plan to *remain* single."

Travis chuckled and patted him on the back before picking up the remote control to change the channel.

I guess Daisy and I aren't being as secretive as we think.

THE NEXT DAY, Finn was still thinking about what Travis had said about Daisy being single. He couldn't quite get a handle on what he was feeling. It was too many conflicting things all at once. He wanted Daisy to have everything she desired, yet he was hanging on to their tryst longer than he should. January was halfway over, but the lust wasn't fading as he'd expected, and they weren't getting back to normal.

He didn't want to hold her back from the future she wanted and deserved, but there was a problem—he didn't want to give her up either. His plan going forward was to make some hard decisions. Spending some uninterrupted time together away from their ranches and the temptation of his house was step one. And that's what had brought them into town for dinner at the new Italian restaurant in Old Town Channing.

But sitting across from her in a dimly lit restaurant with candlelight flickering on her soft skin wasn't helping to decrease his desire for her. Not one little bit.

"You're quieter than usual tonight," she said.

He looked up from his bowl of baked ziti. "I didn't sleep well last night. I guess I'm just tired. How's your eggplant parmesan?"

"Excellent." She forked up a bite and extended it across the table. "Want to try it?"

He made a face. "I don't think so."

"Scaredy-cat."

He grinned and let himself relax, then leaned forward to let her feed him. "Hmm. That's not bad. It's actually pretty good."

"I've been telling you for ages that it's good."

Finn pushed away his worries and focused on enjoying their friendship, because that was the relationship he needed to nurture and protect.

WHILE HE WAITED for Daisy by the restaurant's front door, a couple of women at the bar caught his attention. They were about his age, beautiful and sexy from their sky-high heels to their red lips and carefully styled hair. Exactly the kind of women he would normally make a beeline to talk to, but his lack of a desire to do so surprised him.

And it wasn't only because he was here with Daisy; he just didn't have the urge to bother.

All he could think about was how they wouldn't be able to walk across his front yard with those shoes on. They would be too afraid of breaking a nail to help him work on the ranch. And he'd bet they couldn't ride like the wind as Daisy had done this morning on her horse.

Was it possible he could give her what she wanted?

What do I want? What do I really want?

His palms began to itch, and his throat tightened like it always did at the thought of being a father. Nope. He couldn't be that man.

DAISY STOPPED TO let a family walk by before making her way to the front of the restaurant. Finn was casually leaning against a cedar post by the front door with one boot crossed over the other. Something in the bar across the way had caught his full attention, and she followed his gaze. A heaviness crowded her chest.

He was staring at a couple of beautiful ladies who wore tight-fitting dresses and high heels. She glanced down at her black jeans and boots. Her periwinkle sweater was old and needed to be replaced. She wasn't anything like the glamorous women who held Finn's complete attention. They were more like her sister than her.

Rather than raid her sister's closet now and then, maybe she should get some new clothes of her own.

Was he starting to lose interest in her like he'd said would happen? What was it he'd said? *Our curiosity will naturally burn itself out over time, and then we can get back to normal.*

The weight hanging from her heart grew heavier. The flame of desire wasn't burning out for her.

When Finn rubbed his eyes and sighed, she made her way over to him. "I'm ready if you are."

And that was the whole problem right there in a tidy little package. She was ready for love and a serious relationship, and he was not.

CHAPTER SEVENTEEN

AFTER WATCHING FINN stare at the fancy ladies at the restaurant the night before, Daisy had been really thinking about the future. She felt like he was drifting away from her. She wanted their future to be shared, so she could either give up and once again bury her attraction to him and move on with her life, or she could try to do something about it.

Daisy stopped in the doorway of the home office where her parents had once worked together at the antique partner desk, face-to-face and laughing much of the time. Now, Sage was set up on one side, and Grayson had architectural plans spread out on the polished oak surface across from his wife. She was so thankful these two had found one another. They were so happy and in love.

Daisy's heart tugged with wanting. She wanted the man she was foolishly falling in love with to love her back in the same way. In the forever kind of way.

Sage looked up. "Oh, Daisy. How long have you been there?"

"Just a few seconds."

Her brother-in-law turned in his chair. "Morning, Daisy. How's it going?"

"Pretty good. Sage, do you have time to go shopping with me?"

Her sister's eyes gleamed. "Makeover shopping?"

"I don't know about a whole makeover, but I do need some clothes and possibly shoes."

"And maybe hair and makeup too?" her twin asked hopefully.

"Maybe."

Sage hopped up from her chair. "Gray, you're in charge of Rosie when she wakes up from her morning nap."

"No problem, honey." He stood, kissed his wife and smiled at Daisy. "You two have fun. And maybe bring home some of that fudge from the new candy shop."

"You got it." They shared one more quick kiss, and then Sage hooked her arm through Daisy's as if she was afraid she'd try to make a break for it.

Fifteen minutes later, they were driving down Main Street in the refurbished part of Channing that was called Old Town. In this area, Main Street traffic slowed to twenty miles per hour. Buildings ranging in age and style from the 1900s to about the 1950s stretched along both sides of the street. There were colorful awnings and sidewalks wide enough for lots of foot traffic. Older but well-tended houses in a variety of styles spread out from this area.

Sage parked her silver sports car in front of Glitz & Glam, the boutique owned by their high school friend Emma Hart.

"Maybe I should get some coffee before we do this," Daisy said. "I'm familiar with your marathon shopping."

"Not to worry. I'll go upstairs to her apartment above the store and make you a cup. You can drink it while Emma and I pick out clothes for you to try on."

"Okay. Let's do this." She moved to open her door.

"Wait." Sage touched her arm. "I hope you know that I don't think you *need* this makeover. You don't need lots of makeup or bling to be beautiful. You are perfect the way you are. I just enjoy doing this."

Daisy smiled. "I know, sis. I think you missed your calling. You should've had a TV program called Makeover Magician."

Sage laughed and opened her car door. "You joke, but I can very easily make a social media video and start a new account. You can be my first client."

"Let me think about it." She pretended to consider it for all of two seconds. "Absolutely not." She followed her sister into the boutique that was decorated in shades of pink with lush velvet curtains framing the plate-glass window. Blingy fixtures hung from the high tin ceiling and artwork featuring flowers gave the place a feminine elegance.

"Hello, ladies," Emma said. "I'm so excited to do this."

"You knew we were coming?" Daisy asked.

"I did. Sage called me."

Her sister put an arm around her shoulders. "It's time to give her wardrobe a boost. But I promised Daisy a cup of coffee before we stuff her into a dressing room."

"That's not helping me want to do this," she said in a singsong voice.

Sage ignored that and tightened her arm around her twin. "Do you mind if I go upstairs to your apartment and make a cup?"

"Not at all," Emma said. "I'll help Daisy look around while we wait."

She should've known she'd have both of them teaming up on her.

Emma hummed along with the song playing softly on the sound system. "I recently unpacked a shipment of new clothes that will look fabulous on you."

"I'll take your word for it." Daisy smiled to herself. She wasn't as opposed to this shopping trip as she was leading them to believe. It was more fun this way. And she liked making Sage happy.

Emma held up a maroon dress with a crisscrossing bodice that plunged into a deep V. "This one will look fabulous on you,"

"I'm not sure I can pull off that look."

"Of course you can."

Her sister returned with a steaming mug of coffee with cream and a homemade chocolate chip cookie. "Now you can't say you don't have any energy."

"Thank you." She grinned, lifted the mug higher and blew steam across the hot liquid.

She sat on a stool behind the counter and drank her coffee while the two of them buzzed around the shop gathering way too many clothes. Daisy even rang up a couple of customers for Emma while she waited for them to fill her dressing room.

Right before she was *stuffed* into the small space, Loren came into the shop. "Hi, Aunt Daisy. When I found out you were here, I walked over from my friend's house to help. But I can only stay for an hour because we're working on a school project."

Daisy hugged her niece. "I'm glad you could join us, even if it's just for a little while. But why aren't you at school?"

"It's a teachers' workday."

"Good timing. Sage, what am I trying on first?"

"Start with the dresses." Her sister rubbed her hands together and looked generally pleased as punch.

Daisy pulled off her shirt and caught sight of her plain, white, serviceable bra in the dressing room mirror. *Boring.* She had no desire to be totally pushed up and out like an offering, but she could certainly do better than this. "I think I might need a new bra," she called out to the girls.

"I'm on it," Emma said. "Same size as Sage?"

"Yes, please." She put on the first dress and was not impressed but stepped out for the judging. To her relief, the dress was vetoed by everyone.

"Try on the green dress next," Sage said.

"Here are three bras to try," Emma said.

The black bra had scalloped lacy edges and gave her a subtle lift that she had to admit was an improvement. The emerald green cashmere dress was ultrasoft against her skin and had a scooped neckline and a skirt that hugged her hips then flared past her knees.

She opened the dressing room door. "I like this one."

"Oh, me too. That's gorgeous on you, Aunt Daisy."

She tried on what felt like a million more clothes and shoes. Daisy left Glitz & Glam with two full bags and wearing the green sweater dress and a beautiful pair of brown suede boots with wedge heels.

"I need food," Daisy said when they made it out onto the wide sidewalk.

"Me too. Let's put the bags in my trunk and then eat at the Rodeo Café."

"Perfect."

Sage looked at her watch. "And then we have one other place to go."

"To the candy shop for Grayson's fudge."

"Thanks for reminding me. Make that two more stops. We have appointments for haircuts at the new spa on the corner."

Daisy laughed. "I should have known."

She only got her hair trimmed, but let them curl it, which was something she rarely did. And she even bought some new makeup and let the beautician apply it for her. She hardly recognized herself and felt a little like she was playing dress up, but she also felt pretty and flirty and feminine. Like a woman who matched her name.

What would Finn think of her new look? The thought was dangerous but her urge to see him was overwhelming. While Sage paid, she pulled out her phone and sent him a text message.

I'm craving pasta. Want to meet me in town for dinner at Antone's?

His response came quickly. Sure thing. What time?

How soon can you get to town?

Thirty minutes. Meet you in the bar area.

She sent him a thumbs-up emoji, then put her phone away. "Sage, when you're ready, can you drop me off at Antone's?"

"Sure. But why?" Her sister grabbed her purse and headed for the door of the beauty shop.

Daisy started to chew her thumbnail but didn't want to mess up her burgundy manicure and snapped her hand to her side. "Because I'm meeting Finn for dinner."

Her twin smiled and grasped Daisy's forearm as they walked down the sidewalk. "Tell me how it's going. You haven't said much lately."

"I think our fling is burning out."

"What? No. Why do you say that?"

"Because that's what he does. He doesn't make long-term or permanent commitments. I went into this knowing that he was not interested in a relationship." She sighed. "And I see the way he looks at other women."

Sage unlocked the car and went around to her side. "But lately I've seen the way he looks at *you*. I thought maybe he was starting to see the error of his ways. Seeing you dressed up like this might stoke the flames."

Daisy's skin heated, and she wasn't sure if it was embarrassment or anticipation. She was about to find out.

What am I doing?

DAISY WAVED TO her sister and then went inside the restaurant to wait for Finn. She stopped in the restroom to swipe on a coat of her new glossy red lipstick, but when she studied her reflection, she wasn't completely sold on the bold look. She almost wiped it off but stopped herself.

"Be bold. Don't be scared to give it a try," she whispered then smiled.

Her red lips reminded her of the live action movie image of Maleficent, and she suddenly felt sexy. There was nothing wrong with mixing a little bit of Maleficent in with the sweetness of Sleeping Beauty.

She found a seat at the small bar and ordered a glass of red wine. She could see a reflection of the entrance in the mirror above the bar. Right on time, Finn came through the door and was standing in the middle of the room looking around. He didn't know it was her. She turned on her bar stool and called his name.

"Finn. Over here."

"Hi, Sage. Where's Daisy?"

She tipped her head to the side and slowly smiled, her single dimple appearing on her cheek. "You've found her."

His mouth went slack. "Daisy?"

"In the flesh. And makeup and heels." She extended one leg to prove the point.

His eyes tracked down to the suede boots that weren't the least bit Western.

Her pulse began to race. She suddenly felt self-conscious and smoothed her skirt. "You don't like it?"

"No... I mean..." He whistled softly and a slow smile made his eyes soften like they did in the bedroom. "You look gorgeous."

Her skin tingled as warmth spread from her center outward. "It's not too much?"

"It's still you. A little extra shine on something that's already beautiful." His smile was the sexy one that she rarely saw in public.

"Sage will be happy to hear that you approve of her makeover. All I asked her to do was help me pick out a few new clothes, but..." She touched her curls then traced her manicured fingers along her body. "It spun out of control."

"Very nice spinning." His gaze went to her lips. "Can I change one thing?"

"Sure. I guess so."

He grabbed a cocktail napkin from the stack on the bar and began to gently wipe off her red lipstick. "There. That's the way I like you." He brushed a quick soft kiss across her lips.

Her breath caught. He'd kissed her. In public.

If his wide-eyed expression was an indication, he was as startled as she was.

"Dalton party of two. Your table is ready," said a hostess.

He put his hand on the small of her back, and neither of them spoke as they followed the woman to a table. But it didn't take long for them to start laughing about something Jake had done and the antics of the baby goat.

Their meal was filled with laughs and teasing and sexual tension that was more delicious than the food.

On the way home, they kept finding excuses to touch one another. A brush of the arm. A caress on her cheek. Any excuse at all.

"Wow. Look at that moon," she said.

He pulled through the gate of her ranch, but instead of driving up the curving road to the farmhouse, he pulled off to the side and turned off the engine.

Without a word, he got out and grabbed a couple of blankets

from the back seat of the truck's cab. "Are you coming? The moon is waiting."

"For once I'm not dressed for this but count me in."

He chuckled. "That's what I was hoping you'd say."

He spread a blanket in the bed of his truck. They climbed onto it and leaned their backs against the cab, and then he covered them with the other blanket.

"You really thought I was my sister?"

"At first. But when you smiled, I knew it was you. Why the change?"

She shrugged and tipped up her face to the moon. "I don't know. My clothes were getting worn out and I needed a few new things. And I guess I'm just experimenting a little bit."

"There's nothing wrong with that." He slowly trailed his fingers through her curls then put his arm around her shoulders and settled her more closely against his side.

The first date vibes kept coming, and she didn't want to admit that she'd longed for this kind of attention from him. Something wobbled inside her, and she sucked in a sharp, cold breath.

Without truly realizing what she'd been doing, had she subconsciously let herself be made over because she'd been testing to see how he would react to her all fixed up? She suddenly felt bad, like she was tricking him into believing she was someone she was not.

"What's wrong?" he asked. "You tensed up. Are you too cold?"

She shifted toward him and rested her hand on his chest. "I'm warm enough."

He'd kissed her in public, flirted through dinner and now held her under the stars. Even though he hadn't liked the lipstick, was it only the addition of the clothes, hair and makeup that were making him be all romantic and breaking the rules?

"Tomorrow, my camouflage will be gone, and I'll turn back into Cinderella before the ball. A cowgirl Cinderella with dirt on her face."

He tipped up her chin and studied her. "Hey, I might have thought you were your sister for a few seconds, but you *are* identical twins." When she started to speak, he pressed a finger to her lips. "It's not camouflage. Even with the changes, I see you. You're beautiful with or without all the extra fluff."

She felt light enough to float. "Thanks for saying that."

"It's true."

"How many of our rules have we broken?"

"Well, a kiss in public and—" he kissed her, soft and sweet liked he done before "—in the back of my truck. So that's at least two."

She touched his cheek and loved the way his beard tickled her fingers. "What do you think about that expression that says some rules are meant to be broken?"

"I think it's true. Want to make out like teenagers?"

"Yes," she whispered against his lips. "I would like that very much."

CHAPTER EIGHTEEN

ADAM TRIED TO get comfortable on the double bed in his apartment, but his head was throbbing, and he was so hot and achy that he couldn't sleep. Now his throat was starting to burn when he swallowed.

He missed his mom more than ever. He missed the way she used to take care of him when he was sick. She'd always made him soup and hot tea with honey. When he'd had a fever, she'd put cool cloths on his forehead. He'd felt safe and protected. And loved.

But there was no one who loved him now.

Adam pressed his fingertips to his aching eyes to hold back tears. His mom had gotten sick, and then been gone so fast. He hadn't had time to prepare. His life had changed so drastically, so fast. From living on an awesome ranch with the best mom ever to being all on his own. With no home.

When he'd learned his childhood home was about to be sold, leaving school and sneaking back inside had been the right decision. It had been a huge relief to discover the things his mom had left for him in their secret hiding place. The discovery had been way more than he'd expected.

Adam swallowed and winced at the pain. He needed medicine. And help. The only person he could think of to go to was Daisy. In a short time, she had become an important part of his life, and even though he probably shouldn't, he couldn't help it. He cracked open his eyes to look at the clock. It was 10:30 at night, and hopefully she would still be awake.

He got up, pulled his coat on over his sweatpants and walked up toward the farmhouse. The lights were on in the kitchen, and he was happy to see someone moving around. The night wasn't that cold, but he shivered and shoved his hands into his pockets. His whole body was chilled and damp with sweat.

He knocked on the kitchen door and went inside when Daisy called out for him to come in. She was wearing purple pajamas, fuzzy slippers and her hair was in a knot on top of her head.

"Hi, Daisy." The bright lights hurt his eyes and he squinted. "Do you have any aspirin or some other kind of pain reliever?"

"Yes, I do." She put another plate into the dishwasher. "Hey, you don't look so good."

"I don't feel so good."

She dried her hands, came around the kitchen island, felt his forehead and gasped. "Adam, you have a fever. You're really sick. Come with me right now."

"Where are we going?"

"Upstairs to my guest room. You can't be out there in the apartment all alone."

"But I might get you sick."

"Don't you worry about that for one second."

Relief washed over him. He didn't have to navigate being alone and sick. He took a step, but his vision wavered, and he braced his hands on the cool marble surface of the island. He had the urge to put his cheek against the cold stone.

An arm slid around his waist. "Adam, if you're going to pass out, let me know."

He shook his head. "I'm okay now."

"Hold on to me just in case." She pulled his arm over her shoulders, kept hold of his waist and guided him upstairs. "I talked to Finn a little while ago and he said Jake is also sick. I guess going to guys' night wasn't such a good idea."

He sat on the edge of the bed and let her help him get his coat and boots off. "I'm sorry to be a bother."

"You're not. Please don't think that way." She pulled down

the blue bedding and waited for him to get under the covers. "Lie down and get comfortable."

He did as she asked and let his head sink into the soft pillow. "Whose room is this?"

"It's the one Sage and Grayson use, unless there are too many people staying here, and then they go stay in that little cabin behind the red barn."

He couldn't imagine having so much family that a house this big was filled up.

"Will you drink hot tea with honey and lemon?"

The backs of his eyes burned with tears. "That would be great. That's just what my mom used to make for me when I was sick."

Daisy brushed his hair back from his forehead. "I'm glad I can be here for you. I'll be right back with meds, water and tea." She hurried from the room.

His throat was tight with more tears he wasn't willing to shed. He wasn't sure if it was because he was sick or because he missed his mom taking care of him or because Daisy was being so nice.

Or because I'm just a runaway kid on a mission who is pretending to be a man.

CHAPTER NINETEEN

DAISY HADN'T EXPECTED to take care of a sick child tonight, but she was glad Adam had come to her. She reminded herself that he wasn't a kid, even though Finn thought so. He was almost nineteen, but being alone while you were sick was the worst.

She'd given him cold and flu medicine and gotten him to eat a bowl of soup and was about to leave him to rest. "Tell me if I'm hovering too much."

"You're not."

He'd said it so quickly that she got the feeling he didn't want to be alone. "I'm going to take these dishes down to the kitchen, and then I'll be back."

"Thanks for taking care of me." He pulled the covers up to his chin and closed his eyes.

When she returned to his room, she carried the rocking chair from her bedroom, and, as quietly as she could, put it down beside his bed. He cracked open his eyes and gave her a weak smile before falling asleep.

There was a new book she'd been planning to read, and now seemed like a good time to start it. She read the first chapter, but her eyes were getting heavy. When she was sure he was sleeping peacefully, she went back to her own bed to get some rest.

Something woke Daisy, but she wasn't sure what it was. Thinking it might have been Adam calling out, she pulled on her robe and went to his room. He was moaning and his face was damp with sweat. His fever was back, and the forehead thermometer read one hundred and two degrees. She touched his cheek, and he opened his eyes.

"Mom?"

Daisy's heart squeezed, and she brushed back his damp hair. "You're okay. Rest your eyes while I get a cold cloth." In his fevered state, did he really think she was his mother?

She went to the bathroom, held a washcloth under cold water and squeezed it out. His eyes were closed when she returned, but she sat on the bed and bathed his forehead and cheeks with the cool cloth.

He blinked open his eyes and moaned.

"Hey, there. How are you feeling?" she asked.

"Crappy."

"I need you to take some more medicine to help with the fever." She helped him sit up.

He swallowed the pills then eased back onto the pillow and wiped a hand over his face. "Is it hot in here?"

"No. I'm afraid that's just the fever. I'll go get you some ice water." She patted his hand and turned to go. Right as she went out the door, she heard him say something.

"Moms always make things better."

She paused and held a hand to her chest. It was just the fever talking, but it still touched her that would think of her in that kind of role. She would take care of him the way she hoped someone else took care of hers.

AFTER FINN FINISHED his share of the morning chores, and picked up the slack for Jake and Adam while they were sick, he went in through Daisy's kitchen door to pick up the chicken soup she'd made for Jake. So far, he and Riley weren't sick, and it would hopefully stay that way.

No one was in her kitchen, so he checked the downstairs rooms, which were also empty. Upstairs, he found her in the guest room standing at Adam's bedside. She was holding a digital thermometer to his forehead, but the teenager was sound asleep.

The rocking chair from her bedroom had been brought into the room, and a couple of books were on the floor beside it along with two empty coffee mugs. She'd been sitting at the bedside of a sick young man. A teenager who had no mother.

A mother who had no child.

His chest tightened, and he pressed a hand to the knot in his stomach. He knew in this moment, without a doubt, that she was meant to be a mother, and he needed to help her reach that dream. Not keep her from it.

Like it or not, their time was limited. He would have to let her go…soon.

She looked up, smiled and held a finger to her lips, then followed him out of the room and closed the door behind them.

"How's Adam?"

She started down the stairs in front of him. "Fever, headache and body aches, but his throat isn't bothering him anymore. What about Jake?"

"Moaning and groaning but about the same as Adam. The girl he went out with a few days ago is also sick. She went to the doctor and was diagnosed with the flu, so now we know where this came from and what it is."

"Sounds like it." She slumped onto the couch like she was exhausted. "I wonder why Adam was the only other one who got sick."

He took a seat beside her. "When he was over at my house the other night, he sat at the table with Jake and helped him work on the computer. I would guess that's how. Did you know that Adam is really good with computers?"

"No, I didn't. But it doesn't surprise me. He learns really fast and is a hard worker." She rested her head on Finn's shoulder. "I'm so tired."

"You've been working hard taking care of him. You need to get some sleep so you don't get sick. After I take the soup home to Jake, I'll come back over here, and you can take a nap. I can look after the kid."

She yawned and lifted her head from his shoulder. "You'd do that for me?"

"That's what friends do."

Her expression flickered with something strange, but she looked away and stood before he could analyze it. "The container of soup is on the kitchen island. I'm going to grab a shower while you take it to Jake. I'll see you soon."

WHEN HE GOT back to Daisy's half an hour later, she was already asleep, so he went into the guest room where Adam was also sleeping. He knew the kid wasn't sick enough to need twenty-four-hour care, but he sat in her rocking chair anyway.

The time had come for him to put enough distance between him and Daisy to ease out of their tryst. He'd granted her first wish, but giving up this closeness was going to be way harder than he'd imagined. She might have written down the words *brief fun affair*, but the brief part was tough. Too bad she hadn't written the words *easy to give up*.

Daisy couldn't be "his" forever. He didn't do long-term commitments—other than friendship and brotherhood. And the thought of being responsible for a child still made his whole body itch.

Adam groaned, brought a hand to his head and cracked open one eye. When he saw Finn, he jerked awake. "What are you doing here?"

"Just came to check on you. Daisy is taking a nap."

Adam cleared his throat. "You know I'm not a little kid, and I don't need constant looking after."

"I know."

He shifted into a sitting position. "I heard Jake is sick too."

"Yep. His date gave him the flu and he gave it to you. I guess that's the thanks you get for helping him with the laptop."

"I feel bad that I'm being a burden on Daisy. I should probably go back to my apartment."

Finn smiled. "You can try, but Daisy isn't going to let you. She's a mama bear about things like this. Just let her take care of you. I'll help her around the ranch while you get better."

"Thanks for that." Adam reached for the glass on the bedside table and took a long drink of ice water. "Did you bring this fresh glass of water to me?"

"No. That would be your fairy godmother."

"Daisy is really nice. She reminds me of the way my mom took care of me when I was sick."

"She does have that quality."

Time's ticking. Finn thought with a twisting sensation in his gut.

Now he felt like he was the one who was sick.

THE NEXT AFTERNOON, Finn walked through his front door and heard the clip-clop of Rascal's hooves and the click of Astro's nails on the hardwood floor as they rushed to greet him. He knelt to let the goat hop up onto his thigh and scratched the dog's head. "What kind of mischief have you two caused today?"

Jake was pacing across the living room from the fireplace to the front windows and back again. His face was scrunched into a confused expression.

"Why aren't you resting? What's wrong?" he asked his sick brother.

Jake stopped moving and looked up. "Dad died."

He was confused by his brother's statement. Was this some kind of weird, delayed reaction to something that happened when Jake was fourteen years old? Was he having some kind of weird fever dream? What had happened to make him bring it up now?

"Do you have fever again? That was a long time ago. What has you thinking about it after all these years?"

"Finn, he died a few weeks ago."

It felt as if he'd been hit in the chest. "What? No way."

"I got a phone call from a lawyer in Montana. He said he sent a letter."

He dropped onto his usual spot in the curve of the sectional and the goat hopped up beside him. He remembered the letter going up in flames in the fireplace. "What about the truck accident years ago?"

"Apparently, he didn't die back then."

"But what about the body in the burned up eighteen-wheeler?" Finn asked. "Who was that?"

"I have no idea." Jake sat in one of the recliners and pulled a blanket over himself. "Dad was living in central Montana and died of heart failure."

"This is nuts. Are you sure it wasn't a scam phone call?"

"It's real. And he left you something in his will."

"Just to me?"

"Apparently so."

"You know whatever it is that I'll share it with you and Riley."

"I know. I'm not worried about that. From how I remember things being, I can't imagine that there was much he had to leave to anyone."

"Who knows? He liked classic cars. Maybe he finally fixed one up." Finn leaned forward as Rascal bounced across the back of the sofa.

"You should call the lawyer. I wrote down his number."

"I'll call him later. Where is Riley? Does he know about this yet?"

"Do I know what?" Riley asked as he came in the front door with an armload of groceries.

"You might want to grab a stiff drink before we tell you," Jake suggested as he pulled the blanket up under his chin.

"Let me put the cold groceries up, and I'll be right back," Riley said, and walked away. Only their calm brother could so patiently wait to hear big news.

Finn leaned forward and rested his head in his hands. "You are absolutely sure this is real?"

"As sure as I can be."

Riley returned and sat in the second recliner.

"Tell him what you told me about the lawyer calling."

They quickly brought their middle brother up to speed, and now all three of them sat there in stunned silence. Their father had not died years ago in a fiery eighteen-wheeler crash. Apparently, he'd been living the life of an unencumbered man with no sons to slow him down.

"Do you think he really faked his own death?" Jake asked.

Finn shrugged. "Looks that way. I'll call the lawyer and see what else I can find out about Dad."

A dad they'd assumed had died years ago. A dad who'd been alive and couldn't be bothered with contacting his three sons, proving that he really hadn't wanted them. Finn's feelings of abandonment hadn't just been a young boy's demons whispering in his ear at night.

How could he have left them alone so often and made them feel like they didn't matter? Sure, their father had barely been eighteen years old when Finn was born, but as far as he was concerned, that was a weak excuse. With the terrible example set, Finn wanted to think he'd be the opposite kind of parent, but what if he took after the old man?

"All these years," Riley said, and absentmindedly rubbed the dog's back. "Who does something like that?"

"You were right," Jake said to Finn. "Dad really was a selfish bastard."

"Finn." Riley shifted to face him better. "You've been more of a father to us than he ever was."

His chest tightened with the compliment. "Are you forgetting the time it was my fault Jake got hurt and almost died?"

Jake waved a hand. "We fought, I ran away and got hurt. It wasn't your fault."

It had certainly felt like it was his fault. The memories made him sick. He'd never forget losing his cool, fighting with Jake and then finding his youngest brother bleeding and unconscious under their old tree house. Giving blood and sitting with him at the hospital had been all he could do. He had done the best he could to take care of his little brothers, but had always felt a sense of never being enough.

That had been the moment he decided he would never willingly become a father. He'd raised his brothers, and it was too risky to be in charge of someone's life in that way.

"You guys okay if I take a walk?" he asked.

"We're fine." His brothers echoed one another.

After pulling on his coat, he put the goat on Jake's lap so she wouldn't try to follow him. "I'll be back in a while."

"Don't worry about us." Riley turned on the TV. "We're having pizza for dinner. Take however long you need."

The sun was setting when he went outside. Finn was feeling raw and confused, his emotions bubbling to the surface, and he absolutely could not fall apart in front of his little brothers.

He'd always had to be the strong one. The one who took care of the little hellions. Feeding them, making them take a bath and getting them to school. All of this from the time he'd been about nine years old, and honestly, much of the time even before their young, free-spirited mom had drowned while boating.

Without consciously doing it, he headed straight for Daisy's house. He craved the peace and calm she gave him and needed to be around her for just a little while.

He sighed and kicked a clump of dry winter grass as he stomped across the cold ground. He could not let himself become too needy.

Maybe if he explained all this to her then she would understand his motives for remaining a childless bachelor.

He shook his head. None of this was fair to her. Plain and simple, he couldn't give her what she wanted. Not as a husband or a father to her children. But that didn't mean she couldn't have her dreams come true. Without him.

He growled at himself and walked faster. When he neared the back of her house, he waved to Sage through the window above their kitchen sink, and she motioned for him to come inside. "Hi, Finn. What's going on with you this evening?"

"Not much," he lied. "Is your sister around?"

"She's upstairs in the nursery rocking Rose to sleep, but you can go on up."

"I'll make sure to be quiet." He went up the stairs, taking care not to clomp his boots on the wooden treads, but he could hear Daisy talking before he got to the doorway of the nursery. She was sitting in a rocking chair with her back to him. She resettled her niece onto her lap. Instead of joining them, he stayed where he was, curious to see their interaction. Rose rooted against Daisy's chest.

"I'm sorry, Rosie Posie. I don't have what your mama does." Daisy's sigh was so sad. "I wish more than you could know that I had my own baby who I could feed from my own breasts, but I'm... I'm not a mom." She kissed her niece's forehead. "But I'm not giving up hope. I think things are moving in the right direction."

Finn's gut twisted and guilt hit him square in the chest with the stab of a thousand knives. He hadn't meant to, but he was leading her on. Making her believe he was going to change his mind about being a family man. She shouldn't have to give up her dreams for him.

The time had come. He had to let her go.

CHAPTER TWENTY

DAISY EASED ROSE into her crib and then startled when she turned around and saw Finn leaning in the doorway. "Hey, there," she whispered, and then tiptoed from the room, leaving the door open a crack.

"I didn't want to interrupt."

He looked so sad, and she instantly knew something was wrong. She couldn't resist reaching up to brush her fingers over the short beard covering his cheek. "Tell me what's wrong."

"Want to take a walk?"

"Sure." Her pulse began thumping uncomfortably, and sweat broke out between her breasts. With the curious way he was acting, she had a bad feeling he was about to end their tryst before the month was over and go back to dating all those much sexier women.

She put on her coat, and they went out the front door. "Tell me what's on your mind."

"My dad died."

She waited for him to continue, but he remained silent. "When you were a teenager, right?"

"No. A few weeks ago."

"What?" She stopped walking and faced him. "How can that be? What about the truck accident?"

He shrugged. "I guess he faked his death."

"Wow. This is…"

"Completely crazy," he said, filling in the blank and then starting to walk again. "I don't know a lot of details yet."

She took hold of his hand and was glad when he held on tight. She'd learned that she could calm him with her touch, and he needed the physical contact as much as she did. Now, if she could just make him see that he would make an amazing dad. "Was your father wanted by the law?"

"Not that I know of."

"Is there a funeral or anything?"

"I assume that's all done. But apparently, he left me something in his will. I don't expect it to be much of anything, but I'll call the lawyer tomorrow."

"I'm here for you. Whatever you need." Finn was a dependable, caring man who rescued animals, but spending time in his arms with only the heat of bare skin between them had been enlightening. She'd discovered a tenderness inside of him that he kept hidden from most of the world. This unexpected news was affecting him more than he'd ever admit.

He remained silent as they walked. There was something else bothering him. Something he wanted to say, but he kept stopping himself. She could feel it.

She'd also learned that he needed time to digest news before he talked about it. The best thing she could do was to give him that time and be there for him. Not to mention, she didn't want to hear him say he was calling an end to their romance.

"We don't have to talk if you don't want to." She squeezed his hand to show her silent support.

THE NEXT AFTERNOON Daisy found out that Jake and Riley had gone to San Antonio with her brother-in-law, leaving Finn home alone. She drove over to his house, but before she could get to his front door, he came out with his keys in his hand.

"Hey, Daisy. I wasn't expecting you." He continued walking, but it was not toward her.

"Going somewhere?"

Rather than meeting her gaze, he looked at his watch. "I'm meeting someone in town. Was there something you needed?"

She bit the inside of her cheek to keep from asking who he was meeting in town, because she knew it wasn't his brothers or Travis. It was difficult to speak around the prickly, foreboding-filled lump that was lodged in her throat, but she forced out a few words. "Nothing that can't wait."

"Cool. I'll talk to you later." He gave her a wave and headed for his truck.

She rushed for hers and got in, unwilling to look any more foolish than she already felt by standing there and watching him drive away. The sound of his truck starting up was like the final bell that marked the beginning of the end of their romance.

Daisy wiped a tear from her cheek. She'd wanted to find comfort and oblivion in his arms, and assumed he would want to as well, but that didn't seem to be at the top of his list.

Her chest felt like it was caving in on itself, and her throat burned. She'd thought that she meant more to him than this. Thought she'd somehow be different than all the other women.

Foolish!

OVER THE NEXT couple of days, he dodged all of her attempts to talk with one lame excuse or another. She stopped trying, giving him space, but more so, giving herself a chance to lick her wounds. His behavior was more than needing time to think. This was avoidance—of her.

He was already tired of her, just like had happened with her ex-husband. The time had come to fall back on what was left of the 10 percent of her love she'd withheld for this very occasion. The impending heartache was becoming a reality.

CHAPTER TWENTY-ONE

DILLON CAMERON'S BIRTHDAY party at the Dalton Ranch was not where Finn wanted to be, but he'd promised to help man the barbecue pit, and that's where he'd started drinking beer. And then switched to whiskey.

The party was in full swing with lots of eating, drinking and laughing. But Finn didn't feel a part of it. He was on the outside looking in as Daisy moved on without him. Staying away from her had been way harder than he'd expected, and it was unforgivable that he hadn't talked to her about the end of their tryst.

Every time he tried, his mouth refused to cooperate, and his brain couldn't convince him otherwise. It refused to give him the right words.

He knew she was hurt by his withdrawal, but at the moment, she looked pretty happy laughing with Dr. Birthday Boy. The other man's hand was on the small of her back, right where *he* liked to kiss the little dimples above her curvy bottom. But that was something he should not—could not—do anymore.

His gut twisted. He'd thought he was ready to be around her without wanting to kiss her, but that was not the case. As he watched her moving around the party, he still wanted to press his mouth to hers and slide his fingers through her hair. This wasn't just lust. This was...

What is this feeling?

He was miserable. And drunk. He looked down into his glass and tossed back the last sip. He grimaced as the burn worked its way down into his stomach. Making this his last drink would be a smart thing to do. He scoffed at himself. Smart was not something he'd been lately.

All of this was a bad combination on a regular day, but the sight of Daisy enjoying herself with Dillon was not helping. In fact, it was kicking his bad mood up to dangerous. A mood that usually got him into trouble of one kind or another.

Daisy's laugh caught his attention again. Of course it was Dr. Cameron who was making her smile when all he'd been doing lately was the opposite. Dillon could give her things he could not. A family. Not to mention the vet was someone whose bank account balance was a lot closer to hers than his was. He would have to get used to seeing her with someone else. Someone who could give her marriage and babies.

Dillon handed a toy to Davy and smiled at Loren who was holding her baby sister. "I can't wait to have kids of my own," he said. "I've always wanted to be a dad."

Daisy ducked her head, and his insides crumpled.

I have to protect her from...me.

Someone called his name, and he turned to see a girl he'd once dated heading his way with a big, bright, lipstick smile. Daisy was also looking his way. Now was his chance—as much as he did not want to—to continue pushing Daisy away. Right into someone else's arms.

His old girlfriend flung herself at him, and he grabbed her up in a hug that lifted her feet off the ground. Daisy scowled and then looked away. Doing this felt so wrong.

He needed to talk to Daisy. He couldn't put it off any longer. On his way over to pull Daisy aside, he bumped into a woman he didn't know. He automatically put out his arms to hold her up.

"Sorry. I wasn't watching where I was going." He'd been laser focused on the woman he had to let go.

The brunette grasped the fabric of his shirt, raised onto her toes and kissed his cheek. "No worries, handsome." She took her time letting go of him.

This time Daisy's scowl was more of a glare, and she turned

her back on the sight of him with another woman in his arms. He had a pretty good idea what she was feeling because he'd felt it when he watched her with another man.

As she rushed from the room toward the stairs, he thought he saw a tear slide down her cheek. He couldn't bear to let her go off so upset without at least talking to her, so he followed her.

"Daisy, wait."

She stopped at the very top of the stairs. "You're drunk," she said under her breath so the whole party wouldn't hear her. "Go home and sleep it off."

He rushed up the rest of the steps and followed her down the hall to her bedroom doorway. "I need to talk to you about—"

She spun on him and jabbed a finger toward his chest. "Finn, stop. Our arrangement is over. We're done. You can go flirt with anyone you want. Forget that we have ever been more than friends."

The full weight of the hit to his heart was so sharp and unexpected that he took a step back. "Shouldn't we talk about this?"

"Oh, *now* you want to talk? After days of silence? Just stop this and go home."

He was starting to panic, and he grasped her hand. "Daisy, please."

"Hey! Stop right there!" Adam snapped at Finn, and then stepped in front of the much bigger man, pressing an open palm against his chest. "She told you to go home. Do not treat her like this."

"Boy, do you realize I could pound your scrawny butt into the dirt?" Finn wouldn't hit the kid for a million bucks, because he knew what it felt like to get slapped around, but Adam didn't know that.

"Finn!" Daisy said, and snapped her hands to her hips.

Adam did not back down. "Standing up for Daisy is worth whatever you do to me. She deserves more respect than this."

The kid was right about that.

She put her hands on Adam's shoulders and urged him back from the other man. "Adam, I've got this. He won't hurt me."

Guilt and shame hit Finn and curdled in his gut. He would never hurt anyone. He was screwing things up left and right tonight. He should've gone home hours ago. He could try to smooth things over and make it up to her, but if they made up and ended up in bed and kept going down this romantic road, he'd only be delaying her from finding a man who could give her what she wanted and needed. A man like Dillon.

"You're a brave kid. Respect. And for the record, I would never hurt either of you."

Daisy patted the young man's back. "Thanks, Adam. It's all good."

He shot Finn one more glare and then went down the hall to the bathroom, leaving them alone.

Finn turned to Daisy and met her furious scowl. "I'm sorry, sweetheart. I'm sorry for everything. I'll go away and give you space. I'm walking home."

"Good idea." She opened her door, went inside and closed it without a backward glance.

"I'm such a screwup," he mumbled, and turned to go.

At least he had the perfect reason to get out of town.

DAISY WAS PEEKING through a crack in her bedroom door when Finn hung his head and walked away. The look on his face broke her heart but she needed him clear headed for this conversation. They would talk tomorrow and work through this mess.

She stepped out a minute later and was surprised to see Adam standing there with a worried expression on his face. "I'm sorry you had to see that."

"Did you break up?"

His question surprised her. "There is nothing to break up." She said it, but she didn't believe it.

"Oh." He shoved his hands into his front pockets. "Until the last couple of days, you both seemed happy, and I thought things were going well between you two."

She leaned against the wall and sighed. "We are good friends who blurred the lines when we shouldn't have."

"I didn't mean to get in your business. I was just worried about you."

"You're sweet, and I appreciate your concern. Finn and I just have something we need to work through. It will be fine.

Don't worry." She crossed her fingers that what she was saying was true.

He nodded. "Okay."

"Let's go downstairs and try to enjoy the rest of the party."

A few minutes later, Dillon made his way over to her. "Everything okay?"

She put on her best smile. "It will be. Sometimes friends... disagree."

"I get that. Want to meet my sisters?"

"Of course."

"There's one of them now." He pointed to a lovely woman with sleek, shiny auburn hair down to her waist. "All three of them came to town to surprise me for my birthday, and now I'll be sleeping on my couch."

His smile told her that he didn't mind a bit.

She met all three of them and did her best to enjoy herself, but when she couldn't fake the smile any longer, she headed for the stairs.

Adam stopped her before she could get there. "Are you going to bed?"

"I am. Will you do me a favor and tell Sage I have a headache and went to bed?"

"Sure." He hesitated and moved from foot to foot. "You know where I am if you need me."

"I sure do. Go enjoy the party and talk some more to that pretty girl who was smiling at you."

He nodded and blushed. "Good night, Daisy."

With a house still full of guests, she grabbed her pajamas and went to take a shower. She stood under the hot spray and let her tears mingle with the water.

Just when she was starting to believe there could be more between them, Finn had to turn into a jerk. "This is my own fault."

She rested her forehead against the tile wall. She should have resisted her attraction to Finn, but she'd thought she could handle a physical relationship. She'd been fooling herself in a big way.

Once she was curled up in bed, her sister knocked on her door and then came inside. "Want to talk about it?"

Daisy shrugged. "Yes and no."

Sage climbed onto the bed beside her and cuddled up to her. "You know I'm here for you."

"What am I going to do?"

"First, you're going to talk it out with me."

She rested her head against her twin's, her tension easing at the comforting contact. "I figured our story was doomed to be a tragedy. This is not an unexpected outcome. I hoped it wouldn't be, but…here we are. An ill-fated romance. Now, I have to deal with the consequences of my actions."

"I'm so annoyed with that man. He has no idea what he's giving up. He can't do better than you."

"I appreciate you saying that, but you're my sister and you have to."

"It happens to be true, no matter who says it. You deserve a great love," Sage said. "You know, it's not a problem with you. It's Finn who won't let himself be happy. Is he punishing himself for something?"

"I don't think so, but it could be I don't know him as well as I thought."

Rose started crying from the nursery, and Sage kissed Daisy's forehead then rolled out of bed. "Get some sleep, sis. I'm just down the hall if you need me."

"Sweet dreams."

BEFORE SHE TURNED out the lamp, Daisy pulled her New Year's wish list from the drawer of her bedside table. Number two still said *Fall* with a blank beside it. It felt like the right time to complete the wish to fall in love. Now that her tryst with Finn was over, she would focus on wishing for the person who was meant for her.

Her sister talk with Sage had also made her realize she needed to write down number six on her list.

6) Find someone who loves me the way I love them. The way I deserve.

CHAPTER TWENTY-TWO

THE NEXT MORNING, Finn woke with a killer headache and a plan. He threw some clothes into a suitcase and then found his brothers in the kitchen. "I'm going to drive to Montana and take care of the legal stuff about Dad."

"Drive?" Jake put down his coffee. "Alone?"

"I could use the time to...figure things out."

The toaster popped and Riley grabbed the hot bagel. "We have to take a load of cattle to the auction the day after tomorrow and need the new truck, and the old one needs too much work to drive that far. Do you think you can borrow one of the vehicles from Dalton Ranch?"

He winced. He had planned to give Daisy the space she wanted and leave without another confrontation, but he had to be an adult about this. "I'll ask."

"What happened with you and Daisy last night?" Jake asked, and spooned up a bite of frosted cereal.

"Nothing good. But I don't want to talk about it."

"Okay," Riley said. "Drive safe and let us know what's going on."

"Will do."

Finn walked next door to Dalton Ranch. He knocked on the back door and then went into the kitchen where Sage was frying sausages, the savory scent making his stomach rumble with hunger pains. Her baby girl, Rose, was asleep in a play-pen near the table.

She narrowed her eyes at him. "Feeling poorly this morning?"

"You could say that."

She mumbled something else under her breath, and it sounded suspiciously like *You deserve it*.

"Is Daisy okay?"

"She's out in the stable with the horses." Sage put down the spatula and leaned against the counter. "I guess you know that she was pretty upset last night."

He hung his head but nodded. "I really hate how things have turned out. The last thing in the world I want to do is hurt her."

"Do you care about my sister?"

"Of course I do. Very much. No question." Recently, in new ways he should not.

"Look me in the eyes, Finn Murphy."

He did as she asked and held her stare, attempting to tele-graph all his feelings—as unwieldy as they were—but he wasn't sure what she saw. Even her nod and drawn out sigh didn't clue him in.

She turned back to the stove and flipped the sausages.

"I know you're mad at me, but I need to ask a favor."

She crossed her arms over her chest and seemed to be considering it. "What is it?"

"I need to make a quick trip to Montana. Our old truck needs repairs, and my brothers need the other one to haul cattle to the auction. Can I borrow one of the Dalton Ranch trucks?"

She softened toward him and pushed a plate of blueberry muffins his way. "Daisy told me about your dad. I'm so sorry. You can use the older red one. We can do without it, no problem. When are you leaving?"

"Today. As soon as I can get on the road." He grabbed a muffin from the plate on the island. "I have to clear up some family legal stuff."

Sage lifted a set of keys from a wooden bowl on the counter near the back door. "Drive safe and let us know if there's anything we can do for you here."

"Will do. Thank you, Sage." He put a hand on the doorknob but stopped and looked over his shoulder when she called his name.

"You should use the time away to do some thinking about how you want the rest of your life to look."

A shiver rolled over him. "That is exactly my plan."

Minutes later he put his suitcase into the back seat of the double cab truck then looked toward the stable. He could go find Daisy or he could take a few more days to think things through so he didn't make things worse and completely screw everything up.

Right or wrong, he got into the truck.

As he drove past the Channing city limits sign, he momentarily thought about turning around and going back to find Daisy. Instead, he pulled off the road and called her. If she answered and wanted to see him, he would go back.

The phone rang and rang and rang.

When she didn't answer, he pulled back onto the road.

It was probably for the best. He needed to get his head straight.

DAISY OPENED THE kitchen door and stepped in out of the chilly wind. "Sage, where is the older red truck?"

"Finn took it."

Just hearing his name made her stomach twist. "Where did he go?"

Sage slowly turned from the kitchen sink with her head tilted and her teeth pressed into her bottom lip. "To Montana."

"Montana!" Surely he wouldn't just leave town—hell, leave the whole state—without a single word. Would he?

"You didn't know he was going?" Sage asked.

But apparently…he had done just that. "No."

"I assumed he'd gone out to the stable to talk to you before he left."

"Nope. He did not." Daisy took her frustration out on a piece of junk mail by ripping it in two, then jammed the toe of her boot onto the trash can's foot peddle. The metal lid clanged against the cabinet. Rose sat straight up and started fussing from the playpen where she'd been napping.

She grimaced. "Sorry, sis. I didn't mean to wake her."

"It's fine. She's been sleeping longer than I should have let her."

Daisy went over to pick up her niece, earning a smile that showed off her new tooth. "Hello, Rosie Posie. Did you have a nice morning nap?"

Rose squealed and grabbed Daisy's hair, babbling away like she always did.

"I'll get her food ready," Sage said.

"Since I woke her, I'll change her diaper." She headed upstairs to the changing table. "Cheer up your old aunt, sweetie. Tell me something good."

Rose did not disappoint. She cooed and babbled and made her smile.

But even the baby's charm couldn't completely keep Daisy from thinking about Finn. He had left town without a single word. He had decided to drive across the country while they were in the middle of a… Not exactly a fight, but they certainly weren't in a great place.

I did tell him to forget we were ever more than friends.

She just hadn't expected him to leave town. She'd thought that sometime today they would hash things out and get back to, well, whatever came next for them.

She snapped Rose's sleeper closed then held the clean baby against her chest and kissed the top of her head. Her dandelion fluff blond hair tickled Daisy's cheek. "I love you, precious girl."

At least she had the joy of helping to raise her niece.

Back downstairs, she buckled Rose into her high chair. "I guess Finn wasn't kidding about his curiosity naturally burning out and getting back to normal. But I don't know how we'll ever get back to our old normal."

Sage wrapped her in a hug. "I'm so sorry, sis. Maybe there can be a new normal between you two. A better one."

"I hope you're right." She let her twin's comfort start to mend some of her heartache. "It was ridiculous of me to think I could turn off my feelings like that."

"Want me to whip Finn's butt the next time I see him?"

"Yes, please," Daisy mumbled into her sister's blond curls. A few tears escaped, and she lifted her head to wipe them away.

"Ma-ma-ma-ma," Rose yelled and banged on her high chair tray.

"Sorry, baby." Sage kissed the top of her daughter's head and spooned a bite of apple sauce into her mouth. "I'm not very happy with Finn at the moment, but don't completely give up on him yet. I think there's something there worth fighting for."

She sighed. "Me too, but now I'm questioning if I'm ready to talk to him yet. He called me earlier."

"What did he say?" She wiped food from Rose's cheek.

"I didn't answer, and he didn't leave a message. I need time to think and make a plan. I'm trying to go through all the scenarios in my mind and figure out what I'll do in different situations."

"You're going to make yourself crazy doing that."

"Entirely likely." She looked at the clock above the table. "I need to get back out to the stable. I have work to do, and later Dillon is coming for a routine check of the horses."

"TITAN IS AS healthy as a horse." Dillon chuckled at his bad joke and patted the horse's flank before stepping out of the stall with his vet bag. "I'm starving. Will you go into town with me for dinner? I hate to eat alone in a restaurant, and I have no food in my refrigerator."

Daisy's initial reaction was to decline so she could eat ice cream in front of the television, but she forced herself to say yes. "Sounds good. I'm hungry too." She was surprised to discover that she actually was.

"How about that new Italian restaurant? It's pretty good," he said.

Her chest ached. She didn't want to go to the restaurant where she and Finn had enjoyed such a romantic evening. "I just had Italian for lunch." She wouldn't tell him it was a frozen dinner she'd popped into the microwave. "Do you mind if we eat at the Rodeo Café?"

"Not at all. I love their fried chicken."

"Give me about ten minutes to change my clothes, and I'll be ready to go."

"I'll meet you at my truck."

The cat followed her into the house and upstairs. In her closet, she grabbed a pair of clean blue jeans and tossed them onto her bed, but when she caught sight of the big blue handprints covering both back pockets, she groaned. Getting away from things that reminded her of Finn was going to be next to impossible.

She placed a hand on top of his much larger print and remembered what it was like to have his calloused palms sliding over her bare skin. Going forward, wearing those would be the only time his hands were on her.

The cat bumped her head against Daisy's hand, and she scratched her under the chin. "You know what, Lady, I'm not wearing jeans tonight. I'm going to wear some of my new dressier clothes. I bought them for me, not for Finn."

At least that was what she was going to continue to tell herself. She picked out a wrap-style dress in a cool shade of blue. She paired it with suede boots that zipped up to her knees and a black angora sweater in case she got cold. She was glad Sage and Emma had talked her into buying all of it.

She dressed before brushing her hair and swiping on a coat of mascara. She leaned in close to the mirror to apply lip gloss.

Was the wish she'd completed last night already starting to work?

She wasn't sure how to feel about that. It would be, it was time to turn her attention to a man who didn't have hang-ups about being a father or a husband. It might not be Dillon who was meant to be hers, but she was going to put herself out there.

I can do this. I don't have a choice.

THE FAMILIAR AND casual ambiance of the Rodeo Café relaxed some of her nervousness. Daisy slid onto one side of a booth near the back, while Dillon slid onto the other.

"I'll have an iced tea, please," Dillon said to the waiter.

"A large chocolate shake for me." At least she was indulging while out in public and not home alone in the dark. She'd count that as progress. She couldn't be expected to get back to her usual self on a dime.

"I'm sorry I didn't get to spend more time with your sisters at the party. Tell me more about them. Or something else about yourself," Daisy said.

"They're younger than me. All three of them are artists, but they're also very different. One is a student, another travels a lot and the third is a journalist. We had a single mom who worked long hours as a surgeon, so they looked to me for a lot of stuff."

"That must be why you're such a good listener. Are you an artist too?"

"I am."

"What kind of art?"

"I like to sketch portraits. Charcoals and pencil mostly."

"I'd love to see some of your work."

The waiter returned with their drinks, and they ordered food.

Daisy was enjoying herself more than she'd thought she could, but she still wasn't getting any tingles from the handsome man across from her.

Dillon leaned back against the red vinyl booth and stretched out one arm. "Do you love him?"

The question startled her, but she sighed and put down her chocolate shake. There was no use denying that she knew what he was talking about. She propped her elbows on the table and her chin on her fists. "I do."

"I thought so. What are you going to do about it?"

She scoffed and flicked a hand in the air. "There is nothing to do. As embarrassing as it is to admit, it's one-sided. We want completely different things."

He shook his head. "It's not one-sided."

She sucked in a quick breath. "Did he say something to you?"

"No. Still just giving me the same old glares whenever I touch you or laugh with you. Hell, even look at you."

"You aren't just saying that to make me feel better?"

"I wouldn't mislead you in that way."

"Even if he does like me, it doesn't change the fact that he and I want completely different things. He never wants to marry or be a father."

"That surprises me."

"Yeah, it does me too. But try telling him that."

Dillon sat forward and lowered his voice. "I'll tell you what. I won't give up on love if you don't."

"Deal."

"You're friends with Emma Hart, right?"

"I am." Now she leaned forward. "Are you interested in Emma?"

"I might be." His smile was adorable. "Will you tell me more about her?"

"I would be happy to." It was a relief that this was not a date. He was interested in someone else, and she was happy to do a little matchmaking. "What do you want to know?"

THE MILES CONTINUED to slip by in a blur, but Finn's foul mood had not improved, and his head wasn't any clearer than when he'd left home without talking to Daisy. The long drive and solitude were not helping as much as he'd expected them to. But it would hopefully give him enough time to sort his unruly emotions and feelings back into their appropriate boxes.

And getting a taste of his old life in Montana would remind him why he stayed away from serious relationships.

He'd left his relationship with Daisy in a messy kind of limbo. It had all turned out just as he feared. He'd hurt Daisy and made her cry.

With every mile, he missed her more and more, and when he stopped for the night, he called her for the fifth time. The phone rang and rang and then went to voicemail. He wasn't completely surprised, but he had hoped that she would want to talk to him by now. She wouldn't answer his calls or texts, and the idea that he had not only lost a lover but also a valued friendship was making his chest hurt.

He still wanted to take her in his arms and press his mouth to hers. Not just in a pleasurable way that made his body burn, but also in an emotional way. Why did his feelings have to get so mixed up with his body? But what he wanted and what was good for the woman he…

His breath faltered and blood whooshed in his ears. The feeling that was swallowing him up from the inside out couldn't be love.

Could it? It was only a touch of panic about losing her friendship. That had to be all it was.

CHAPTER TWENTY-THREE

WHEN HE ARRIVED in Montana, Finn called Brown & Taylor and then drove straight to the law office. He followed the skinny, elderly lawyer into his brightly lit office and took a seat in one of the leather high-back chairs.

"Thank you for coming all this way, Mr. Murphy."

"Sorry I didn't get the letter and it took me so long. What is so important that I needed to come in person?"

Mr. Brown unbuttoned his suitcoat as he sat in the chair behind his desk. "Did you know your father had married again before he died?"

"I did not." Women had always liked him, so he wasn't surprised. "Wouldn't that mean his wife would get anything he had?"

"She would, but they divorced when she ran off almost two years ago."

If it had ended, why had he bothered to mention the marriage? A band of tension around his chest was tightening. Something big was coming. He could feel it in his bones.

"I'm sorry to tell you that there is no money. That all went to medical bills. But there is something." He hit a button on the intercom on his desk and talked to his secretary. "Mary, please send them in now."

Them? This got weirder and weirder.

The office door opened before he could ask what was going on, and an older woman entered with a blond toddler on her hip. She was too old to be the mother, but the child was curled close to her and sucking her thumb. When she saw Finn, the child lifted her head and looked at him with huge blue eyes.

"This little girl is two and a half years old, and she is your half sister, Ivy Murphy."

"Sister?" Finn stood as if he'd been shocked by a cattle prod.

"Yes. Mr. Murphy, you are her legal guardian."

Finn blinked a few times as if that could clear up the bizarre situation that he'd suddenly found himself in. The inheritance was not money—which would've been shocking—or a collection of baseball cards or even a run-down classic car.

It was a child.

The toddler pulled her thumb from her little rosebud mouth with a popping sound. She whispered something he couldn't make out and then leaned out of the woman's arms as she reached for him.

Finn was stunned, but he was used to holding babies around Dalton Ranch, so he moved closer and took Ivy into his arms. She looked a lot like his little brothers had at this age. She looked a lot like all three of them.

The child studied him with confused curiosity, and her lip began to tremble.

The woman stepped forward and rubbed the little girl's back. "It's okay, Ivy. You're safe."

He cradled the back of her tiny head, her riot of blond curls soft under his hand.

"She was a daddy's girl, and you look a lot like your father. I think Ivy sees it."

His throat tightened, and he smiled at the toddler. "Hi. My name is Finn. I'm your big brother. Everything is going to be okay."

But on the inside, he was freaking out in a major way. He couldn't promise everything would be okay and had no idea what to do next. He wasn't even sure how to take his next breath.

Ivy yawned, returned her thumb to her mouth and rested

her head on his shoulder. Since his legs had gone numb, he sat back down.

The woman took the other chair beside him. Her smile was kind, and she was wearing a bright fuchsia blouse and gray slacks that matched her silver-gray pixie haircut. "I'm Sara. I've been taking care of her these last few weeks."

"Tell me more about her. Was my dad actually a hands-on father to her?" Having firsthand knowledge of being his father's son, he was doubtful.

"He was. Especially after her mom left and then lost custody."

This was surprising news, and he wasn't sure how to feel. He was of course grateful that Ivy had been cared for, but that old childhood feeling of abandonment was filling him up.

He looked down at the helpless little girl who was falling asleep on his chest. "And you've been taking care of her?"

"I have. I was your father's neighbor, and since she already knew me, I agreed to look after her until you could get here. But I'm seventy-five and too old to take care of her long-term."

"What happens now?" Finn looked helplessly between Sara and Mr. Brown. "Am I just supposed to be an instant...father?"

The lawyer came out from behind his desk and leaned against the front of it. "You have a couple of options. You can find her a family here in Montana, put her in foster care or you can take her home and be her guardian. You can also make other arrangements for her once you get to Texas." He reached behind himself for a stack of papers. "Here is some paperwork to look through and sign. Don't hesitate to ask any questions you have. Why don't you take the night to look these over and maybe call your brothers."

"I think I'll do that."

"Where are you staying?" Sara asked.

"I'm going to find a cheap motel."

"You'll come to my house," she said. "I have two extra bedrooms, and there is no reason for you to spend money on a hotel."

He started to decline her offer so he could be alone to make some kind of sense out of this, but as he adjusted the two-year-old on his lap, she clung to his shirt as if she never wanted him to let her go.

If only Daisy was here. She would know what to do and say and how to navigate this shocking situation. "Thank you, Sara. I'd like to stay with you."

"Good, because it looks like someone doesn't want to let you go."

Out in the parking lot, he put Ivy in the car seat in the back of Sara's car. She woke up and reached for him, and he knelt to her eye level. "Ivy, you need to ride in your seat, and I have to drive my truck. He pointed to it parked a few spots away. I'll follow you to the house. Is that okay?"

She nodded and hugged an old brown teddy bear.

Sara patted his arm. "It's a small town, so you'll have no trouble following me to my house. It's only a few miles away."

"I'll be right behind you."

He tried to call Daisy as soon as he started the truck. It rang and rang over the Bluetooth speakers, but once again went to voicemail.

"You've reached Daisy Dalton's phone. Please leave me a message." Beep.

"It's me again. Please call me back. I really need to talk to you."

They drove by an area of local small businesses and then into a neighborhood that was old but well-tended. The trip was so quick that he didn't even have time to get his thoughts organized. Sara's house was a midcentury ranch that was painted a soothing shade of yellow. Not the mustard color that Daisy hated. It was surrounded by mature trees, and there was a For Sale sign in the yard of a little white bungalow next door. Was that where his dad had lived?

It was a hell of a lot nicer than the house they'd grown up in.

He parked in the driveway beside her car and met the older woman and the toddler on the small front porch. Ivy stood beside Sara but stared up at him with the most expressive eyes he'd ever seen. He followed them inside and to a guest room where he put his bag. His little sister trailed after him from room to room. When he came out of the bathroom, she was waiting outside the door for him.

"You two can sit in the living room where the toys are while I get supper on the table," Sara said, and turned on the television to a cartoon and then hummed as she made her way to the kitchen.

Finn was still dazed by the day's news and didn't know what to do or say. He wasn't used to kids being this quiet. Davy and Rose didn't let you forget that they were around. "Will you show me your favorite toy?"

Ivy went over to a plastic tub beside a green corduroy chair, pulled out a tattered copy of a book and brought it to him. She climbed up on the couch and settled herself beside him, her tiny red boots not even reaching the edge of the cushion.

Guess I'm reading a book.

He opened it to the first page. She scooted closer and closer as he read about woodland animals.

"Supper is on the table," Sara called to them.

He stood, and this time, he reached for her. "Let's go, little miss."

The corners of her mouth tilted up and then turned into a shy smile, and if he wasn't mistaken, she was batting her long eyelashes.

Aw, man. She's trying to melt my heart. Just like Daisy does.

This was the first real emotion he'd seen her express. He picked her up and settled her in a booster seat at the kitchen table.

He accepted a plate of chicken with rice and green beans. "Thank you. This smells wonderful." It reminded him of something Daisy made.

"Ivy likes it, but you have to make sure to cut everything up really small for her," she said, while demonstrating exactly what size was acceptable.

"Is the house that's for sale next door the one where my father lived?"

"He rented it from me, but having a rental property has become too much work for me alone, and the market is good for selling. Don't let me forget that I have a box of his things in my garage that he wanted me to give to you."

"Okay." He wasn't sure he wanted to look in the box. What other shocking discoveries would he make?

She sprinkled pepper on her food. "You know, he talked about you three boys. He was a complete mess until his wife left. Only then was he able to stop drinking and pull himself together. He said he couldn't bear to fail a fourth child."

"We thought he was dead."

"He told us about that. He came forward years later to clear it all up. That's how my husband met him. He was his lawyer and then later became his AA sponsor when Ivy was born."

"Did he say why he faked his death?"

"He didn't want to drag you down or be a burden on your lives. He didn't want to embarrass you like his father had done to him."

Finn barely remembered his grandfather. He'd thought the old man was funny, but looking back, the man had probably been drunk. Finn's emotions were all over the map, and he made a decision to drink less and maybe stop all together.

AFTER DINNER, FINN went out into Sara's shady front yard to call his brothers.

"Hey, Riley. I have news. Is Jake with you?"

"He's right here. I'll put the call on speaker."

"Hey, bro," his youngest brother said. "What did you discover? Did dear old dad get rich and leave us a fortune?"

"Nope. Dear old dad left us a kid."

There was silence on the line, and he could picture their stunned expressions.

Riley's deep voice broke the silence. "Did you say kid?"

"Dude," Jake said. "He wouldn't leave us a kid."

Finn shook his head when they started arguing. "Shut up, the two of you. Listen. Dad had another child. And he listed me as her guardian."

More silence filled the air. Finn turned toward the house and saw Ivy watching him through the window. Her elbows were braced on the windowsill and her chin was propped on her hands as she stared at him. Her sad little face tore at his heart. He waved to her, and she perked up and waved back.

"Are you putting us on?" Riley asked. "This is a joke, right?"

"No. It's no joke. Her name is Ivy. She's two and a half years old, an orphan and she doesn't want to let me out of her sight. I don't know what the hell to do."

"Do you need us to come to Montana?" Jake asked.

"No. At least not yet."

"We'll be on standby if you need us," Riley said.

Finn walked in a circle around a tree. "I can't just leave her behind. They'll put her in foster care. I know that's not always a bad thing because I've seen the Daltons be great foster parents, but I just can't abandon her here to an uncertain future."

"Agree," they both said.

"You should call Daisy," Riley suggested. "She'll probably know what to do."

He had the same thought, but she wasn't even talking to him.

ONCE IVY WAS ASLEEP, he sat at the kitchen table to read a letter from his dad and to look through the stack of legal paperwork.

Finn,
I hope you get this letter. Let me start by saying how proud I am of the man you have become.

Finn's anger was making his stomach sick. He remembered a few times as a kid when his dad had told him he was proud of him for taking care of his little brothers. Doing *his* job as the parent.

The last time I left you, I went into rehab. I let a drifter I'd met in a bar deliver my last load down south because he wanted to get to that city. I didn't find out about the crash and him being assumed to be me until I left rehab early. Because I couldn't even get through rehab, I knew you three were better off without me in your lives. I've been keeping an eye on you and your brothers all these years, and I'm impressed and proud. Only in the last few years have I been able to pull myself together. And then I found out my heart was giving out on me. Finn, you did real good with your brothers when you were just a kid. Better than I was able to, so I figure you can do it again. Your sister is sweet and very shy and has already had a hard life. I hope you'll consider being a better father to her than I ever was to you. At least find her a good home. I'm sorry I failed you and your brothers. I'm proud of you, son. Dad

He was too numb to know how he felt. This whole situation was so entirely unexpected. The letter seemed like too little too late. What was the proper response? Ripping it up and tossing it away? Getting all nostalgic and forgiving?

He shook his head and moved on to the stack of legal papers. He kept rereading sentences, trying to interpret the legal jargon. And getting more frustrated by the second.

He glanced at his phone on the table beside him. Daisy still hadn't returned any of his calls or responded to any of his text messages. If he didn't hear from her in the next couple of hours, he'd send the SOS message they'd agreed upon to distinguish one of their jokes from a true emergency. And in his mind, his current situation definitely fit the definition of a true emergency. Alarm bells were clanging at a very high decibel.

Sara sat across from him. "Would you like some help? My late husband was a lawyer, and I was his legal secretary."

"Yes, please." He pushed the pages across the table.

She went through it page by page and told him what he needed to know. "Do you know what you want to do? About Ivy."

There was no way he was going to be able to drive away while watching her sweet face get smaller in his rearview mirror. He couldn't bear to leave this quiet little girl behind to an uncertain future. But driving across the country with a toddler seemed too daunting to face alone. The Dalton family knew all about fostering kids. They would help him figure this whole thing out—if Daisy would ever answer his calls or texts.

"I know I can't just leave her here in foster care." He rubbed his eyes to fight the fatigue setting in.

"Go get some sleep, Finn. A decision doesn't have to be made tonight."

FINN LAY ON a mattress that was way too soft, but that wasn't what was keeping him awake. The idea that had been trying to take shape all day would no longer be ignored. He knew the perfect mother for this orphaned little girl. The answer to his problem was obvious.

Daisy wanted to be a mom, and when she met Ivy, she wouldn't be able to resist the cute toddler. This was a way for him to give Daisy one of the biggest wishes on her list while also giving his baby sister a chance at a good life. But he couldn't just spring this on Daisy without careful consideration. Not when they weren't even speaking.

He grabbed his phone from the nightstand and groaned. Still no response. He'd thought their friendship was strong enough to handle the risk they'd taken with it, but more and more he worried that he'd been way off target.

It was time for a Hail Mary.

Maybe a child would help her forgive him for not being what she needed and get over the heartache he'd caused. He crossed his fingers and sent the one text message he knew she would answer.

The cowboy is in the henhouse.

DAISY WOKE WITH a gasp. She was still in the fog of a dream that she couldn't remember, but it had left her wanting to cry.

Her phone chimed from the nightstand.

Finn?

She groaned and covered her face. Couldn't she wake up without him being the very first thing on her mind? Was it her phone or the dream that had awakened her? It was still dark, but there would be no going back to sleep. She had to know who was texting her in the middle of the night, so she rolled over in bed and looked at her phone screen.

The cowboy is in the henhouse.

She sat straight up in bed. It was their SOS message. The one message she couldn't ignore.

She knew him well enough to know he would only send this message they'd agreed on if it was necessary. She called him, and he answered after the first ring.

"Daisy. Thanks for calling me back."

"What's the crisis?" she asked, getting straight to the point.

"I have a little problem, and I could really use your help." His voice sounded tense and slightly panicked. "Can you fly to Montana?"

She swung her feet onto the floor. "Are you hurt or in jail?"

"No. Nothing illegal. I want you to come here and drive back home with me. Please."

Finn was always so confident and self-sufficient. She'd never heard him sound this desperate. "You're sure you don't need bail money?"

He cleared his throat. "I just need you."

Her mind started spinning with what his request could mean. He'd used their SOS because he needed her to come be with him. Did he miss her and want to spend time with her? Was he trying to make things up to her?

"Daisy? Are you still there?"

"Why do you want me to come all that way only to turn around and ride home with you?"

"I'd rather tell you and show you in person when you get here."

Her skin tingled. With time alone to think, had he changed his mind about remaining a single, fatherless bachelor?

She didn't want to work through their issues over the phone. They needed to see one another face-to-face. The long drive would give them the uninterrupted time they needed to talk through everything that had happened between them—in depth. Their true feelings and desires and goals. How they'd move forward. What came next. Even though it would be impossible for her to completely return to her prelove feelings for Finn, they could find a new normal.

"Please, Daisy Maisy. You're the only one I want with me right now." His voice softened and held a note of longing.

And if she wasn't mistaken, a note of panic. "Send me the information about where to fly into, and I'll be there as soon as I can."

"You're the best, sweetheart."

He'd only called her that name a handful of times, and every time it gave her hope that was too risky to have. "I'll see you tomorrow."

WHEN SHE LANDED in Montana and got to the baggage claim area, she spotted Finn over the top of a group of travelers. The other people moved away and...

The breath was knocked from her lungs. An adorable toddler was perched on his hip, clinging to his shirt as if he was the only one who could keep her safe. She was very petite with blond curls and big blue eyes. And she looked a whole lot like Finn.

Daisy's whole body went cold. She remembered the letter he'd accidentally burned the day he'd jumped into the icy pond to save a baby goat. Could that have been about this child? When was the last time Finn was in Montana? She didn't think it had been within the last several years but...

Could this little girl with the same blue eyes be his daughter?

CHAPTER TWENTY-FOUR

A LARGE GROUP of people moved past the baggage claim area, and Finn caught sight of Daisy. His pulse jumped with another powerful flash of that big unnamed feeling. The one that threatened to swallow him up. It made his insides quiver and his brain short-circuit.

He'd left Texas with a goal of controlling his attraction to Daisy and setting his mind to what needed to happen. Not to miss her more every day. He hadn't even realized just how much until he'd seen her gorgeous face in the midst of a faceless crowd.

When did I start thinking of her as gorgeous?

She stared back at him as a myriad of emotions moved across her face, but she remained frozen in place, other people weaving around her.

He made his way over to her. "Hello, Daisy Maisy."

"Finn." She rubbed the base of her throat as if she was having trouble speaking. "Who is this precious little angel?"

"This is Ivy Murphy." He patted the toddler's back. "Ivy, say hello to Daisy."

The little girl tucked her head under his chin and popped her thumb into her mouth.

Daisy looked even more startled than before but forced a

smile. "Hello, sweetie." Her expression wobbled when she met his gaze. "Her last name is Murphy?"

The way her voice rose in pitch on his last name revealed her thoughts. With his free hand, he took hold of hers. "She's not my daughter."

"She's not?"

"She is my half sister."

"Oh." Her shoulders relaxed into their normal easygoing position. She stroked the back of Ivy's tiny hand that clung so fiercely to his shirt. "Ivy, I'm very happy to meet you."

The toddler curled closer to him, and he cradled his sister's head, doing everything he could to make her feel safe. "She's shy."

"That's okay. We can take our time getting to know one another."

He hoped it didn't take too long because he was really counting on the two of them hitting it off. If Daisy didn't want to be her mom, he didn't know what he'd do. He was so unsure about everything to do with taking care of a little girl, and as much as he liked to be in control, this was a very uncomfortable feeling.

"Do you have any luggage to claim?"

"No." She rolled her carry-on bag forward. "Just this."

"Then let's get out of here, and I'll tell you all about it."

As they crossed the parking lot, Daisy got an odd look on her face. "Is she your only other sibling?"

"As far as we know."

"Your father must have been near fifty when he had her."

"Yep. And he had a wife who ran off on them. He lived more years without us than he did with us," he whispered over the top of Ivy's halo of blond curls.

She put a hand on his shoulder, but only gave him an awkward pat. She didn't slide her fingers along his back to massage the tension in his neck or run her fingers up into his hair. He'd lost that privilege when he decided they were over but hadn't had the courage to talk to her about it.

"All this time he let you…" She kept walking, not completing the question he'd been asking himself ever since he'd been to the law office.

Why had their father let them believe he was dead? "There is one more thing. He named me as Ivy's guardian."

Her mouth opened as if she'd speak and then closed again until they stopped beside the truck. "What about her *m-o-m*?"

He shook his head. "Completely out of the picture. Legally and otherwise." He buckled Ivy into her a car seat. "Are you hungry, little miss?"

She nodded and reached for her tattered teddy bear. She hadn't uttered a single sound all day. Not even when Sara had cried and hugged her before they drove away.

There was a box of items on one side of Ivy's car seat that was secured in the center, so Daisy put her suitcase on the floorboard by Finn's bag and then settled on the front passenger seat. "I could eat too."

"I saw a café not far from here." He glanced in the rearview mirror to back out of the parking spot. Ivy was stroking her teddy bear as she hugged it to her chest. Her vulnerableness broke his heart.

"This is all so unexpected," she said.

"That's putting it mildly."

"So..." She swallowed a few times and then cleared her throat. "She is why you wanted me to come to Montana and drive home with you."

There was a note of something in her voice that he couldn't quite place. But as he looked at her, he suspected it was disappointment. He thought about how his phone call and request to come meet him might have sounded from her side of the conversation. Had he led her to believe that he had changed his mind about their future relationship? He felt sick and ashamed.

"Are you mad at me for not telling you about Ivy over the phone?"

She shook her head. "You could have told me, you know. I still would have come to help you."

"It wasn't my intention to trick you. I promise. The thought of driving across the country with a toddler sent me into a panic. And there is no one else I want to make this trip with."

Her sigh was long and drawn out. And sad.

"Daisy, I'm really sorry about that night of the party and the way I've withdrawn. Basically, for my behavior lately."

"What was with all the flirting with multiple women and basically..." She fiddled with a tassel on her purse.

"Acting a fool?" he asked.

"You said it, I didn't."

"But you were thinking it."

"You know me so well."

They shared a smile and a small bit of his tension melted away. He pulled into the parking lot of the café and parked near the front door. It was a rustic building with a covered patio off to one side.

"I like the looks of this place." Daisy attempted to get Ivy out of her car seat, but she wouldn't go to her.

Ivy shook her head and arched toward him, so he once again lifted her into his arms. "You're safe, little miss."

They were seated at a booth with Ivy in a booster seat beside him. His sister hadn't said a word, but he had a feeling that her big blue eyes saw everything.

He scanned the trifold plastic menu. "I'm not even sure what to order for her to eat."

"Let's check our options." She looked at the kid's section. "Ivy, do you want pizza?"

The little girl shook her head and scrunched up her face.

"Do you like chicken nuggets and macaroni and cheese?"

That brought a small smile to her rosebud mouth, but she looked to Finn before nodding.

"I think we have a winner," he said. "Let's get both."

Daisy handed her a red and a purple crayon and the coloring sheet the waitress had put on the table. "So, the three of us are driving back to Texas?"

He lowered his voice. "My choice was either leave her here in foster care or take her with me."

Ivy chose that moment to look up and grin at him with a flirty tilt of her head. He tweaked her little button nose.

"You made the right choice. She's irresistibly adorable. Who has been looking after her?"

"My dad's neighbor, but she is seventy-five years old and only agreed to do it until they got ahold of me."

"Once we're home, what's the plan?"

He met her gaze and saw vulnerability and uncertainty in her eyes. "Honestly, I'm still working on it all out. I'm reeling from the surprise and trying to absorb everything, but you're the only person I want helping me navigate all this."

"I'll do what I can to help you."

"Thank you, Daisy Maisy."

AFTER LUNCH, DAISY got into the back seat with Ivy and read books to her. The fact that she'd so quickly taken on a caretaker role didn't surprise him. It reinforced his decision. It was important to find the right time and the right way to tell her his idea about her raising Ivy. But he also couldn't put it off for too long—like he'd been doing with their conversation about the state of their relationship.

Stop being a chicken.

When she stopped reading, he glanced in the back to see that Ivy was asleep. But even then, Daisy remained behind him. "How's it going back there?"

She climbed into the front and buckled her seat belt. "She is sound asleep. I did get a few smiles out of her while I was reading."

"I knew you two would make friends quickly."

She had nothing to say to that. Their conversation wasn't their normal easygoing banter. It was stilted with long pauses and tension. And he hated it.

They drove for several hours before stopping at a motor lodge in a small Montana town. The kind where your car was parked right in front of the door to your room and one large window looked out over the parking lot.

The woman at the front desk smiled at Ivy. "Your daughter is adorable. She looks just like you."

"Thanks." Finn forced the word through the constriction in his throat. The idea of being a father who was responsible for someone else's life had its usual effect. Panic threatened to burst its way to the surface, and his skin prickled. The stress of looking after his little brothers was something he did not want to repeat.

"Would you like a room with two double beds or one king?"

Finn didn't know what the answer should be, so he turned to Daisy.

"One king," she said, and shot him a don't-even-think-about-it look. "So Ivy can sleep between us and not roll off the bed."

Her message was clear. One bed was not so he could cuddle up to her. She wasn't forgetting or forgiving anytime soon.

He couldn't grant her wish to be her husband or a father to her children, but he did have a way to grant another wish on her list.

CHAPTER TWENTY-FIVE

ROOM NUMBER 7 was small, with a sink and laminate counter straight ahead, and behind a flimsy door was a postage-stamp-size room with the toilet and bathtub. The only piece of art on the wall was a snowy mountain scene that made her think of their holiday hideaway. It instantly made her long for that magical time when they'd felt separated from the rest of the world.

On the airplane, Daisy had convinced herself that this long drive would be a similar bonding experience and help them find their way forward. So much for her hope that he'd seen the light.

She put her carry-on on the floor beside the bed, relieved that the room was clean and that the motel had adopted the practice of wrapping the comforter between two white sheets the way they did at large hotel chains. There was no germy bedspread to deal with.

Finn lifted Ivy from his hip and put her on the center of the bed. "I'm going to go get her suitcase and the other stuff from the truck."

"I'll take her to the bathroom." She held out her arms to the child. "Can I help you go to the potty?"

Ivy nodded, but not quite ready to accept Daisy, she scooted to the edge of the bed and slid off feetfirst. She followed Daisy to the bathroom and let her help with her purple sweatpants and Pull-Up.

"Your Pull-Up is dry. Good job, Ivy. You're such a big girl," she said as she lifted her onto the potty. She received a sweet smile that emphasized the toddler's high cheekbones that were very similar to her three big brothers'.

"Do you want me to order takeout from that hamburger place next door?" Finn said on his way back inside with the last bag.

"That works for me." She propped the child on her raised knee and helped her wash her hands. "I would really like to take a shower, and then I'll give Ivy a bath."

"I'd appreciate that," he said.

Daisy opened her suitcase and pulled out her pajamas. The grime of a day's travel clung to her, and she was exhausted.

"Ivy and I will walk over to get the food while you shower. What do you want?"

"If they have it, a lemonade and a cheeseburger. You know the way I like it. And onion rings, please."

"Got it." He reached out a hand as if he would touch her face but dropped it to his side instead. His attempt at a smile didn't reach his eyes or have the same sparkle as Ivy's had only moments ago. "I'll see if they have anything sweet for dessert."

The toddler peeked over his shoulder and moved her little fingers in a bye-bye wave as they went out the door.

"See you soon, sweetie." Her cuteness made it hard to stay sad.

This dejected mood wasn't productive. On a deep inhale, she raised her arms above her head then slowly let it out as she folded forward to touch her toes. She made the decision to throw off her downer mood, be the best friend she could be and find happiness in every moments that she could.

"I'm choosing to look on the bright side."

They were back with dinner when she came out of the bathroom, and they ate at the tiny round table by the window with the toddler on his lap.

"Guess what I have in my suitcase." Daisy grabbed one of Finn's french fries and handed it to the little girl. "Bubble bath. Is there anyone here who likes to take a bubble bath?"

"Bubble," Ivy whispered so quietly that she almost missed it.

"Oh good. As soon as we finish eating, I'll run your bath."

The toddler dipped the french fry into Finn's puddle of ketchup then smeared it across her cheek on the way to her mouth.

"Good thing the bath is after dinner," he said with a chuckle. "And apparently, I should've ordered more french fries."

Daisy swiped another fry and nibbled the tip of it. "Why do you say that?" She couldn't hold a straight face and giggled.

"Gosh, I wonder."

"I'll share my onion rings with you."

His full lips moved slowly into his bedroom grin. The kind that made her toes curl. It was so hard to keep an emotional distance from this man.

ONCE IVY WAS FED, bathed and read to, she was sound asleep in the center of the big bed. Her hands were tucked under her cheek, and she looked like a cherub.

Daisy wasn't as relaxed, and was sitting in one of the chairs by the window while Finn showered. The thick curtain was pulled back just enough for her to see a sliver of the sky and parking lot. She hated the awkwardness between her and Finn. But they'd had moments throughout the day that gave her hope they would be able to work things out. It might take a while, but they could get there. They had to.

She was unsure of what would or should happen next, but she needed to find out if he planned to be a father to Ivy.

And without getting her hopes up, what he saw her role being, if any.

A cloud of steam escaped the bathroom right before Finn stepped out. In a pair of pajama pants, and no shirt, with wet hair falling over his forehead, he was a treat for the eyes. She flashed back to the moment he'd stepped out of the icy pond in nothing but a pair of boxer briefs.

Daisy put a finger to her lips. "She's asleep."

He turned off the light above the sink and spoiled her view, but her eyes adjusted, and she could see him in the light coming in around the curtain as he pulled on a T-shirt and then sat in the other chair.

"You are so good with her," he said in a low voice.

"I've had lots of recent practice with Davy and Rose."

He worked his mouth around like he'd say something but only slumped down in the chair instead.

The silence was making her want to jump out of her skin. "This is usually something Sage or Lizzy would say, but we're going shopping tomorrow."

"For what?"

"After looking through Ivy's suitcase, I've discovered she needs a few new things. Some clothes, a new pair of shoes and more books and toys so she can entertain herself on the long drive. We're also going to run out of training pants."

"Good point. Today, before you got here, was the first time I was all on my own and completely in charge of her. I wouldn't admit this to many people, but it was kind of terrifying."

Feeling antsy, she put one foot on the windowsill and bounced her leg. "I've watched you with Davy and Rose, and now with Ivy. You are really good with them, and they all adore you."

"I'm funny. Like another kid. Or a big brother."

"I know this is something that was not in your plan, and you're nervous, but you can do this. You are going to be okay. You will be a great dad."

He sat up straight, shook his head and rubbed his palms together. "No. I can't do it, Daisy. I know all about boys, but girls… I don't have the foggiest idea how to raise a little girl. Can you imagine her being raised by her three much older brothers? It would be a disaster."

"Well, she'll know how to hunt and fish and raise cattle and horses."

He groaned. "See what I mean? What about all the pink and the dolls and other girl stuff? Especially when she's a teenager."

"You're not alone in this. I'll be right next door." She wanted to scream at him to see her as a partner. As someone who could be a parent alongside him. As a woman he could love the way she loved him.

He leaned forward and spread both hands on the table like he needed to brace himself. "I was going to wait to say anything until you two got more acquainted and we were on better speaking terms, but I have a way to make one of your dreams come true."

Is he finally seeing what we have together?

"It's perfect," he said. "You can adopt her."

Daisy's heart swelled, and she wanted to throw herself into his lap. Finally. He wanted them to be a family.

"I can turn over guardianship as soon as we get home, and I can be the fun big brother next door, and everyone will be safe."

Her heart that had just soared now plummeted as if all the blood had rushed from her body. He wasn't asking her to build a family *with* him. He wanted her to take a responsibility off of his hands.

Ivy chose that moment to whimper in her sleep then sit up and cry out. They both moved toward her and bumped into one another. Daisy reached out to comfort her, but the toddler turned to Finn. He picked her up and she instantly calmed and settled against his chest.

With a strong aching in her own chest, she went around to her side of the bed, climbed in and rolled to face the wall. He was the most frustrating man on the face of the planet, and she was working hard not to throttle him.

He whispered soothing words to the child, and a few minutes later, she felt Finn put Ivy down and climb in on his side of the bed.

When he whispered her name, she pretended to be asleep. He did not want to hear what she would say to him if she opened her mouth.

If you can't say anything nice...

THE NEXT MORNING, Daisy wasn't feeling much better about the state of things. She knew he had the ability to be a good parent, but *he* didn't believe it. She needed to make him see it. Somehow.

Maybe it was time to review her wish list and make changes. It might be foolish, but it had worked in the past.

They had eaten breakfast, and Ivy was having a morning nap in her car seat while they drove along a rural stretch of highway, but Daisy felt numb and was quieter than normal. With hurt feelings, she didn't know what to say to him, so she answered direct questions and said little else.

But when one question kept spinning around in her mind and wouldn't let go, she finally asked, "Finn, why did you suddenly pull away from me? Was it just time because the excitement wore off?"

He jerked his eyes from the road to her then refocused forward before answering. "No. The excitement did not wear off."

"Just time to date more women?"

"No." He reached across the console and rubbed her arm. "That's not it either. It all kind of snowballed. I knew that our time was limited. Then I found out my dad died after letting us believe he was dead all these years. I started remembering stuff from my childhood. My parents' rotten marriage. Their parenting skills—or lack thereof. Then I heard you talking to Rose about being a mom."

"So, you did hear that. I suspected so."

"I did. And then I saw you laughing with Dillon like you always do and he said he can't wait to have kids of his own. He wants what you want, and you like him. And it all made me realize yet again that you deserve more than I can give you."

She shifted in her seat and stared at him for a moment. "Were you jealous?"

He growled, "Yes. Even though I have no right to be."

"It that why you were flirting with every female at the party?"

"In my inebriated state, I thought it would make you mad enough to push me away and help put needed space between us. I did it to give you a chance at having everything you want."

Something shifted inside her. "You did it to give me a chance to have a husband and a child of my own?"

"As hard as it was, I did."

"Now see—" she put a hand to her chest "—when you go and say things like that, it makes my insides get all warm and melty. Makes it harder to stay mad at you for pulling away without a conversation and running off without a single word."

He smiled, but it was sad. "Does that mean I'm on the road to forgiveness?"

"You really pulled away for my benefit, not yours?"

"Yep."

She studied his profile. "I think if you examine that a little harder, you'll discover it benefits you too. It gets you out of being tied down."

He sighed. "Guess my brothers are right about my ability to be an ass."

"Even so, my heart is urging me toward forgiveness."

"You should probably listen to your heart."

"Maybe you should do the same, Finn."

He glanced in the rearview mirror, and she could tell he was looking at Ivy.

She motioned with her hand. "Oh, pull into that shopping center up ahead on the right. We can get everything we need there."

Ivy refused to sit in the cart and remained securely in her favorite person's arms.

As they made their way through the store, Daisy studied their profiles and could see the family resemblance. "When you met Ivy, did she take to you right away?"

"Yes. I look a lot like my dad," he said.

"He must have been a very handsome man." She picked up a couple of different shirts and held them up. "Which one do you like, sweetie? The pink one or the yellow one?"

Ivy pointed to the pink one.

"Good choice." Daisy put that and several other items of clothing into the cart and then pushed it to the toy section.

Ivy sucked in a breath and leaned from her spot in Finn's arms to grab a toy goat off the shelf. It had a soft, velvety white body, pink satin in its ears and tan leather hooves.

The toddler kissed the toy goat's head and then hugged it to her body. Daisy and Finn smiled at one another.

"I think we've found a winner," he said.

"If she likes this, imagine when she sees Rascal."

"This is a baby goat," he said to his sister. "Can you say goat?"

She smiled at her new toy. "Baby."

Daisy's cheeks hurt from smiling as she watched the two of

them interacting. She was proud of the way he was stepping up to a situation he hadn't expected and never wanted. She could so easily see the three of them as a family. She just needed him to see and want the same thing, and pushing him wouldn't work. Finn Murphy was too strong-headed. This was a realization he needed to come to on his own.

But that didn't mean she wasn't going to help things along.

He just needs time and some gentle prodding in the right direction.

ONCE THEY WERE back on the road, Finn was feeling better about how things were progressing. Daisy sat in the back seat with Ivy and read books to her. Finn listened to their interaction, and although Ivy didn't speak, he heard a couple of soft giggles. The sound made his worries feel just a little bit lighter.

Daisy climbed over the seat into the front and smiled at him as she buckled her seat belt. "Did you hear her adorable little giggle?"

"I did. She's warming up to you quickly."

"She really likes stories about animals."

"We've got enough of those at home."

"Finn, did we just enter Utah?"

"Yep."

"Why are we cutting through the corner of Utah? This is going out of our way."

"To see a few sights. You wanted an adventure, and it's the least I can do to grant your wish," he said, and then bit the inside of his cheek. Had he just given away that he'd read her list?

She narrowed her eyes. "When did I tell you I wanted a big adventure?"

"Can't remember exactly."

"Finn Murphy!"

"Okay, okay. I might've seen your list."

She gasped. "You read it? When?"

"Um…it fell out of your pocket the night I put my handprints on your butt."

"Butt, butt, butt," Ivy said from the back seat.

He looked at Daisy, and they tried not to laugh. "Oops."

"Have you noticed that she likes to say words that start with the letter B?"

"Not until you just mentioned it." They'd heard her say bubble and baby and now one he had not intended to teach her.

"I'm so embarrassed that you read my silly wish list."

"Don't be. It benefited both of us." He grinned but kept staring straight ahead.

She pulled her hair up into a ponytail and secured it with the band she always wore on her wrist. "Is that why we started sleeping together? Because I said I wanted to sleep with a hot guy?"

He rubbed his mouth, trying to hide his grin. "Did that wish come true?"

"I suppose if I really stretch my imagination, you fit that criterion. I bet the part about a brief fun affair caught your eye, didn't it?"

"I can't lie. It did."

"Wait a minute. The adventure wish wasn't written until *after* the handprint incident, yet you know about it."

"It was on your bedside table when I went upstairs to get my watch."

"And your eyes just happened to fall on it?"

"Something like that. It didn't say private or keep out." He grinned in a way that he hoped would make her do the same.

"You are a mess, Finnigan. Hey, look." She pointed to a colorful billboard. "There's a zoo in the next town. We have to stop. Ivy will love it."

He had a feeling both of them would love it. He surprised himself with the desire to go as well. "That sounds like a good idea."

WHEN THEY WALKED up to the zoo and Ivy saw all the animals painted on the entrance, she smiled and patted Finn on the shoulder as if to tell him good job.

Daisy chuckled. "Stopping was a great decision. Let's rent one of the wagons to pull her around in."

"And hope she'll ride in it."

"I bet she will if you put her in it and pull her."

Thankfully, she loved riding in the wagon. They bought snacks and set off toward the bears. Daisy walked beside Ivy and handed her a piece of cookie. And to Daisy's delight, Ivy reached up to hold her hand as she walked along beside her.

Their growing connection chipped away a bit more of the tension that was constricting his ribcage.

When they went through the primate habitats, Ivy was the most excited they'd seen her be. One of the gorillas held her baby upside down and kissed his tiny face before draping him over her shoulder.

Ivy bounced her knees and clapped, her precious giggle making everyone around them smile.

"You like that, little miss?"

She raised her arms for him to pick her up. Finn scooped her up but then held Ivy upside down by her ankles like the gorilla. She laughed harder than they'd heard her yet.

"Daisy, take my hat, please."

She put it on her own head, and he seated Ivy on his shoulders. Her tiny hands clasped the sides of his head as they moved to the next exhibit. At least they were getting a few words out of her. It was all progress. The smiles, the giggles, the hand holding with Daisy. All of it.

"What animal should we see next?" he asked her.

Ivy made a meowing sound.

"I think there's a new lion cub," he said. "Want to go see the baby lion?"

"Baby." She kissed the top of his head with a noisy smack.

"Aww." Daisy put a hand to her heart. "That's the cutest thing ever. You make her feel so safe."

The constriction was back to choke off some of his breath. Keeping her safe was his responsibility.

IN THE HOTEL room that night, Finn opened the bathroom door but paused when he heard Daisy singing a lullaby to Ivy. She didn't have her niece Lizzy's amazing voice, but the way she was using it was beautiful. He pressed the heel of his hand to the center of his chest. Dang it, there was that feeling again.

Ready to engulf him. He waited for the usual foreboding feeling. But it didn't come.

He braced his hands on the sink, closed his eyes and took a few slow breaths. When he opened his eyes, he was looking at Daisy's cosmetics bag. Sticking out of the top was her blue New Year's wish list, now tattered from time and many handlings. Had she left it where he could see it on purpose?

He pulled it out and unfolded it. She had completed wish number two. *Fall in love.* He'd known that's what she'd meant it to be, but what had taken her so long to write it? She had also filled in number six. *Find someone who loves me the way I love them. The way I deserve.*

"Oh, sweetheart." Was it possible? Could he give her what she wanted and deserved?

He put the piece of paper back where he'd found it, stepped out and peeked around the corner. Daisy was curled up on her side with her back to him. Ivy was facing her and staring at her with wonder, kind of the way he liked to do. She was an amazing woman who deserved everything her heart desired.

He watched them until Ivy's eyes fluttered close, and Daisy kissed her forehead. When he went to her side of the bed and sat on the edge, Daisy sat up.

"Are you okay?" She cupped his cheek and brushed her thumb through his beard.

Her touch sent a warmth all the way through to his core. "I'm good. I just wanted to tell you good night before I went way over there onto my side of the bed." He slid his fingers into her hair to cradle the back of her head and brushed his lips against hers.

"Can you be patient with me? Please."

CHAPTER TWENTY-SIX

THE NEXT DAY they only made necessary stops—which were frequent with a toddler—but Daisy was enjoying every minute of it. They were back to their normal easy flowing conversations, and after what Finn had said about being patient with him, she had more hope that he was seeing the light of what could be. Good thing patience was one of her virtues.

She reached into the back seat to hand Ivy a small container of dry Cheerios. "Here you go, sweetie. Do you still have water in your cup?"

Ivy picked up the spill-proof cup and shook it to demonstrate the water sloshing inside.

"Good. We'll get some real food soon."

"My stomach agrees," Finn said. "You know, if we keep driving after we eat, we'll arrive in the middle of the night."

"We need to find a hotel." It was a delay tactic, but one more day on their unplanned adventure would give both of them a little more time to adjust to a new reality. A reality with a child involved. Because as soon as they got to Channing, real life would once again be upon them.

He took the next exit off the highway. "I was just thinking the same thing. Up ahead I see a couple of hotels and a shopping center with restaurants."

"Perfect." They shared a knowing smile. They both knew

the truth of why they were stopping, and she was glad they were in agreement.

The hotel was nicer than the ones they'd stayed in for the past two nights. There was even a playground where Ivy got to run around and get some exercise. But she was still very timid, even around other kids. She made sure she could see Finn and Daisy the whole time, as if she was worried about being left behind. It made Daisy want to gather her up and never let her go. In only a few days, this precious child had stolen her heart. Just like her big brother had.

The toddler climbed up a short ladder with surprising skill, and they moved to the bottom of the slide.

"With those climbing skills, she's going to need to be watched like a hawk," Sage said.

He groaned.

Ivy slid down to them, her blond curls ruffling in the wind and her eyes bright.

Daisy held out a hand to her. "Want to swing?"

Ivy nodded and took hold of her hand, making Sage's heart sigh, right along with Snow White and Maleficent.

Once she was in the baby swing, Daisy stood behind her to push while Finn leaned his back against one leg of the swing set.

A little boy was giggling in the swing beside her. "Mama, higher. Push higher, Mama."

Ivy studied the mother and son then tipped back her head to look at Daisy. When she smiled at the toddler, she received one in return.

"When we get home tomorrow, which one of our houses do you think would be better for Ivy?" he asked.

She pictured his house. Their guest room was full of workout equipment and would take a lot of work to turn into a little girl's bedroom. Paint and furniture and all the little touches to make her feel at home. "There is already a kid's room set up at my house with a crib and a toddler bed, so that makes the most sense. At least to start. But if she is at my house, then you will have to be too."

He put an arm around her waist. "I was hoping you'd say that."

When it got dark, they were all in the hotel room bed watching a movie in their pajamas. Ivy was curled against his side with her head on his shoulder, her tiny fingers twining through his beard as her eyes fluttered closed.

Daisy propped up against the headboard. "Did your dad have a beard?"

"Yes. Sara told me Ivy did this to him too."

"You're a comfort to her. It's so sweet."

"You do the same thing," he said.

"What thing?"

"You absentmindedly run your fingers through my beard when we're lying in bed.

"I guess I do, don't I." She frowned. "At least I did." And if everything fell into its proper place, maybe she would once again.

He settled the sleeping child on the mattress between them and smoothed her curls. Carefully so he wouldn't wake her, he propped his back against the headboard like Daisy. "I miss this. Being in bed with you. Talking and hanging out."

"Just the talking?"

He reached for her hand. "I miss all of it."

"So do I." Whispering made it feel like they were telling secrets.

"Remind me why we have to be friends only," he said.

She shook her head, smiling. "I can't. I might have written that I wanted a brief fun affair, but now that I've had that, I want more. I want back what we had."

"What if I screw it all up?"

"What if *I* do?"

"I can't imagine that. Are you willing to take another chance on a guy who can't get his act together?"

"That depends. Are you putting a time limit on us and planning an end like we did before?"

"No. I'm just…" He brought her hand to his lips and kissed her knuckles. "I don't know how to be away from you. Can we take it day by day, and I'll try to earn it?"

She leaned his way and kissed him. "You've earned a kiss. Want another?"

"Absolutely." He cradled her cheek and kissed her deeply.

THE NEXT MORNING, they started out on the last leg of their adventure. They'd driven through scenery that wowed them and supported the title America the beautiful. Her camera was filled with snowcapped mountain peaks, open valleys where sunshine slanted across the land and pictures of Ivy and Finn.

Daisy looked into the back seat. "Ivy, we're almost to my house. There are going to be a lot of people who want to meet you, but they're all very nice."

"There is another kid for you to play with and lots of animals," he said.

The toddler's smile brightened at the mention of animals, and she hugged her toy goat.

When they pulled up to Dalton Ranch around lunchtime, everyone was gathered on the backyard patio. The Murphy brothers, Sage's family, Lizzy's family and Adam all waved, but because they had warned them of her shyness, they didn't rush over. Except for her adorable nephew. Davy wasn't having any of the staying away and toddled over to Daisy for a hug.

"Hello, my sweet angel boy." She swung him high into the air and made him giggle.

Finn got his baby sister out of her car seat and called his brothers over to join them. Ivy curled against him. When Riley and Jake smiled at her, she raised her head, but she kept her thumb in her mouth and didn't release her tight hold on Finn's shirt.

"We're your big brothers," Jake said. "Welcome to the family."

"I'm Riley, and that's Jake."

"What do you think of that, little miss?" Finn asked. "Now you have three big brothers."

Daisy joined them with Davy on her hip. The little boy reached out to patty Ivy's back. Her thumb popped out of her mouth as she smiled back at him.

"Let's go meet everyone else," Finn suggested.

There was a potluck meal laid out on the patio table, and they all filled their plates and eased Ivy into meeting their extended family group.

The toddlers took to one another right away and played happily side by side on the patio while the cat soaked up their attention.

Davy tugged on Lizzy's skirt. "Mama, mama, mama. Up, pease."

She lifted her son into her arms. "Ready to go inside for a nap?"

He shook his head. "No, no, no. Play."

Ivy stared at them then turned to Daisy and raised her arms, and she picked up the toddler. "Let's go inside and play with Davy until naptime."

"She is so precious," Sage said as they made their way through to the living room. "You have got to catch me up on the status of your relationship."

"I'll give you the highlights. The long version will have to wait until we're alone."

They put the children beside the basket of toys and sat across from them. Davy gave his new playmate a yellow dump truck with a Barbi and Ken doll in the back of it.

Daisy propped her feet on the edge of the coffee table. "The man is making me nuts with his hangups, but he asked me to be patient and give him a chance."

"How patient does a woman have to be?" Sage asked.

"I don't know, but he is wearing on mine."

"But you love him."

"Heaven help me, I do."

THE WHOLE GROUP had been a little overwhelming for Ivy, but now Adam was the only one who remained. He was on the couch watching the end of a movie he couldn't get on the TV in the apartment. Ivy was on the floor beside Davy's toy basket. She looked precious in a new set of pink pajamas with her hair still damp from her bath.

Finn came in the front door with a load of logs in his arms.

"Need help?" Adam asked him, and got up.

"You can get the next load. This is good for now."

Daisy was just happy to be home and relaxing in her comfy blue chair with a glass of white wine. She let contentment spread through her. This was the kind of life she dreamed about. A family of her own. Her dream was within reach and right here for the taking.

Oh, Finn. Why can't you see that you deserve a family of your own?

He just needed to get out of his own way.

He put another log on the fire and closed the screen. His muscles bunched as he put his hands on his thighs and stood in one fluid motion. She inwardly sighed. She loved watching him move. He took a seat in the chair beside her. She grinned at the sight of a cowboy dressed mostly in black sitting in her sister's pink velvet chair.

Adam was focused on the end of the movie, but when Ivy brought him a book and crawled up beside him, he didn't hesitate to turn his attention to her. "Do you want me to read to you?"

The shy little girl nodded and smiled while batting her eyelashes. He was one more person who had fallen a willing victim to her charm.

He opened the book and began to read to her. He used different voices for the characters and made animal sounds that made Ivy giggle and imitate him.

Daisy and Finn shared a smile.

"Someday, she's going to have guys eating out of her hand," he whispered.

"Someday?" Daisy chuckled. "She already does. You, Adam, Riley, Jake and even Lizzy and Sage's husbands. And it's not just men."

"True. I'm so glad I didn't leave her behind, and that she has you in her life."

"She has you too." She reached across the little round table between them and put her hand on top of his. "You know how much she adores you."

His next breath was deep, and his exhale was long and slow as if he needed time to gather his thoughts.

"Finn, because you brought her home with you, she is coming out of her shell and making connections that she will get to keep forever."

When the book was finished, Adam stood. "I have to go back to my own place now, but I'll see you tomorrow, Ivy."

"Morrow?" she asked, and stood on the couch cushion.

"Yes. Tomorrow maybe I can show you the horses."

Daisy followed Adam to the door. "Thanks for being so sweet with her."

"No problem. Thanks for letting me hang out with y'all."

"Anytime. Good night."

"Night, Daisy."

Finn held out his arms. "It's bedtime, little miss."

Daisy went upstairs with them. The nursery had a crib and a toddler bed. The pale blue walls were soothing, and the light fixture looked like a bouquet of brightly colored flowers. The bedding was horse themed and there was a packed bookshelf along one wall that was flanked by crates of toys.

"Ivy, which bed do you want to sleep in?" he asked.

The little girl went over to the toddler bed and climbed on. "You." She pointed at Finn and then to the small bed.

He knelt beside it. "I won't fit in this bed. I'll be in a different room that is just down the hall."

She poked out her bottom lip.

"Let me show you where I'm sleeping, and then you'll know where to find me." He scooped Ivy up but then paused and looked at Daisy. "I didn't ask, but will I be in your room?"

"Do you want to be?"

"Of course."

She turned and smiled over her shoulder. "Then follow me."

In Daisy's bedroom, Ivy climbed up onto the big bed like the little monkey that they'd discovered she was. She lay down in the middle.

Daisy and Finn looked at one another. "This idea might have backfired," he said. "Ivy, this is where I will be tonight. Just down the hall from your room. Now you know where to find me."

She didn't look convinced, but after Daisy rocked her, they eventually got the little girl to sleep in the toddler bed.

When the two of them finally climbed into Daisy's bed—minus a toddler—they were exhausted.

"Adam is so sweet with Ivy," she said. "I knew he would fit in well around here."

"He's a good kid."

"So, you no longer think he's up to something or has an ulterior motive for showing up here?"

"No. He kind of reminds me of myself. Poor kid." He pulled her closer, and she rested her head on his chest.

"Being like you is a positive in my book."

He kissed the top of her head. "Not long ago, you would've agreed with me and teased me."

"You're probably right." She tipped up her face to smile at him. "Give me a few days and I'll be back to teasing you. Promise."

He kissed her. "Thanks for having faith in me."

She could see the changes in him. He seemed a little more settled every day. More open to the kind of life he'd given up on. As she held him in her arms, she remind herself not to rush things, but rather to trust that they would get where they were meant to be.

He nuzzled her neck. "You smell good."

Her body was coming alive under his hands. "You do too."

"Do you think it's okay if we close and lock the door for a few minutes before we go to sleep?"

She chuckled. "I think that's a very good idea."

FINN WOKE WHEN something tickled his ear. When it happened again, he cracked open one eye and immediately grinned. Ivy was at his bedside. Her cherub face was on his level, her chin propped on her hands that were folded on the edge of the mattress.

"Good morning, little miss." He made a big show of stretching and groaning and being silly.

She giggled and clapped for his performance.

Daisy sat up. "Good morning, sweetie. Want to come up here with us?"

She nodded and climbed up with a little help. Instead of settling down between them, she started jumping on the bed. Her blond curls floated about her head as she bounced.

He chuckled and flopped back onto his pillow. "I think she and Rascal are going to get along just fine. And I have a feeling I'm going to have to learn to function on less sleep."

CHAPTER TWENTY-SEVEN

FINN PARKED IN front of his house on the Four Star Ranch and waved to Riley on the front porch. Astro and Rascal were frisking around in the front yard.

"Ivy is going to love this," Daisy said.

They both turned in their seats to look at the little girl who had an old teddy bear under one arm and a toy goat under the other. "Are you ready to meet two more animals?" he asked.

"Yay." She clapped her hands.

As soon as they got out of the truck, the goat saw him and bounded in their direction. Ivy squealed so loudly in his ear that he winced, but her joy made him smile. He knelt to introduce her to the goat and the dog. "This is Astro, and this little girl is Rascal."

"My baby," she said, and plopped onto her bottom to cuddle the baby goat on her lap. She giggled when Astro licked her cheek and Rascal nibbled at the ruffle on her shirt.

Daisy sat beside her, so he went over to talk to Riley while they played with the animals. "Did you have a chance to look through the box of Dad's stuff that I gave you last night?"

"I did. There are some good pictures in there, but I haven't been through all of it yet." His brother crossed his arms over his chest and studied him. "So, are you going to do it? The whole dad, mom and kid thing?"

The question didn't send him into an immediate panic like it would have only days ago. But there was still a level of discomfort that made his pulse jump. "I'm working on figuring out how everything will look. I don't know how to be a good father."

"You idiot," Riley said. "What do you think you've already been doing with Ivy, and the way you teach Adam stuff? What do you think you did with me and Jake from the time you were a kid yourself?"

"Man, when we were young, it was constant stress. I barely got us from day to day."

"But you did. And I didn't turn out so bad."

"That's somewhat true." He slapped his little brother on the back.

Ivy ran across the yard with Rascal on the leash, and Daisy smiled at him. "I have a feeling that little girl and baby goat are going to be hard to separate."

"I think you might be right. If you take the goat over to Daisy's, you'll probably have to take the dog too. Every family needs a dog," Riley said, and chuckled.

Over the next few days, Finn worked on his ranch, helped Adam with some maintenance chores on the Dalton Ranch, worked on his relationship with Daisy and parenting skills with Ivy. All while playing the part of a family man.

While Ivy was with Lizzy and Davy, Daisy, Finn and Adam were getting the horses ready to ride out and check all the fences after a big rain.

"We need to look at every section of fence very carefully," she said. "We especially need to check both locations where the creek cuts through the property."

"Hey, Daisy," Adam said. "I saw an old motorcycle in the red barn. Does it run?"

"No. It hasn't run in many years." She mounted her horse and patted her neck. "It belonged to my older brother. Lizzy's father."

Finn flicked a stone from his horse's hoof then lowered its leg to the ground. "We can pull it out and take a look at it, and I can probably help you get it running."

"That's not a good idea," Daisy said. "My brother got hurt riding that old thing."

Adam swung into the saddle. "It's not just horses that I know how to ride. When I was a kid, I had a motorbike, and I rode it all over our property."

"Well, that old motorcycle is trash. We should've thrown it out ages ago."

"I don't think it's trash," Finn said. "But if you're throwing it out, I'll take it. Adam, do you know anything about working on them?"

"No, but I'd like to learn, if you'll teach me."

"I think we can find some time for that." Finn was now on his horse as well, and they all rode toward the back of the property. "I need to buy some supplies to work on one of the tractors, and we can grab what we need for the motorcycle too. If you'll help me with the tractor, I'll help you."

"You have yourself a deal, old man," Adam said.

She chuckled at his nickname for Finn. The guys started discussing how they would pull the bike out of the barn and look it over so they would know what to buy. They were completely ignoring her safety concerns, but she was happy to see them bonding, and she hated to spoil their fun.

Adam had no family to count on—other than hers. No one to teach him things like mechanics or repairing things around the house or how to be a man. No one to spend holidays and birthdays with. And all of this was no doubt why she felt so protective over him.

Finn and Adam working on something together would build their relationship. And maybe they could help heal one another, because she knew both of them had demons and doubts that they were fighting.

"Put me down as being against the whole motorcycle thing, but I won't try to stop you."

"Cool. Thanks, Daisy." Adam hooked a thumb over his right shoulder. "I'll ride in this direction and y'all can take the other."

"We'll meet you at the front gate," she said, and smiled as Adam spurred his horse."

Finn watched him ride away. "In some ways he seems more mature than his years, and in others…"

"He seems younger," she finished for him.

"There's something about him that I can't put my finger on. Something he isn't telling us."

A FEW DAYS LATER, the motorcycle was close to done. It was getting late, and Finn was hungry, but they'd gotten a lot of work done on it this evening.

"You did good, kid. Let's go get some supper."

Adam walked beside him as they crossed the backyard. He held his left hand against his chest. "Don't tell Daisy that I hurt my hand working on the motorcycle. She might want us to stop before we finish it."

Finn stopped walking. "How bad is it? Let me see."

The teenager held out his hand. There was a scrape across the top from his wrist to his knuckles, and it would surely turn into a bruise. "It's not so bad. Doesn't hurt much."

"Adam, did you break your little finger?"

"No." He wiggled all his fingers to demonstrate their working order. "It's always been like that. They've both been bent for as long as I can remember."

The back door opened, and Daisy stepped out. "Are you two hungry?"

"Yes," they said in unison and followed her inside.

"Go wash up. It will be about ten more minutes until it's ready."

After they had clean hands, they sat at the kitchen table, the savory scents making his stomach growl.

Ivy came into the kitchen with dolls clutched in her arms. She went straight to Finn and handed him the Ken doll. "Daddy."

A rush of emotions hit him, but the toddler wasn't done surprising them yet.

She went over to Daisy and handed her the Barbi. "Mama. Baby," she said, and then hugged the little child-sized doll.

Daisy met Finn's eyes, telegraphing similar emotions to his.

Ivy had just announced what she expected going forward.

The oven timer went off, beeping almost as fast as his heartrate.

Since neither of them were moving, Adam chuckled and went over to the oven. "Is it just me, or does the timing of this alarm seem like a sign that today is the start of something new?"

CHAPTER TWENTY-EIGHT

FINN HAD DISCOVERED that although they'd gotten the motor-cycle running, it wasn't safe to ride until they replaced a part on the front suspension. He'd been looking for Adam so they could go to town to get it, but he couldn't find him. There was one more place to look.

He went into the apartment behind Daisy's stable, but Adam wasn't there either. The kid kept the place clean, as far as floors and the tiny kitchen and bathroom were concerned, but his things were scattered about. Papers around his laptop on the table, clothes hung in layers over a chair and books tossed here and there.

When he turned to go, the toe of his boot caught the corner of a box that was sticking out from under the couch. It slid farther out across the floor, and when it hit the leg of the coffee table, the lid popped off. The first thing he saw was cash. A lot of cash.

"What the hell? Where in the world did he get this much money?" His skin went cold. Were his initial thoughts about Adam right?

He *was* hiding something.

He picked up the box and sat on the couch. It wasn't small bills like you'd have if you'd been saving money over time. They were large bills bundled together in neat, banded stacks. Underneath was a file folder, and when he saw what was written on the tab the hair stood up on the back of his neck.

Daisy Dalton.

He pulled it out from under the cash and flipped it open. An old photo of Daisy was on top. Beneath that were pages of information about her.

"This doesn't make any sense."

Adam didn't seem the grifter type, but his intuition had warned him that something wasn't right when the young man first arrived at the ranch. Adam really was hiding something big, and he had a lot of questions.

"What the hell are you doing getting into my stuff?" Adam shouted.

He looked up into the green eyes of the scowling young cowboy. "Did you steal this money?"

"Hell no! I got it from my mom."

"I thought your mom was dead?"

His eyes narrowed into slits that could shoot arrows, and he stormed closer, once again not intimidated by a much bigger man. "She is, dumbass. She left it for me, and you have no business snooping through my stuff."

Finn instantly felt bad that he'd brought up the kid's mom, but there was a more immediate problem to deal with first. He held up the photo of Daisy. "What about this? Are you going to tell me you got this from your mom too? Why do you have a dossier on Daisy?"

"I don't have to tell you anything, old man. Screw you. I'm out of here." Adam stormed out of the apartment, slamming the door behind him.

Finn jerked off his hat and slapped it against his thigh so he could plow his other hand through his hair. Why did Adam have all this information about Daisy? Was he a grifter here to get her money? Is that why someone his age had thousands of dollars in cash?

Daisy liked this kid so much, and so did he. She'd taken him under her wing. She was going to be crushed when she discovered the truth.

He heard the old motorcycle start up, and his heart leaped

into his throat. He ran outside, but Adam had already taken off down the driveway toward the front gate. If he got going too fast or made any sharp turns, things could go wrong in a hurry.

Finn ran to his truck, jumped in and took off after him. He caught up to Adam right as he pulled out onto the road...

And his heart tried to jump out of his body as he watched the scene play out in sickening slow motion. Adam laid down the motorcycle and slid across the asphalt right in front of an oncoming truck.

Finn skidded his truck to a stop in the gravel along the roadside, threw it into Park and leaped out, leaving his door open as he raced to Adam. Dropping to his knees, he put a hand on Adam's shoulder to keep him still and started checking his head for injuries. "Hold still. Don't move."

"Hurts," he groaned.

"I know, kid. I've got you. Just breathe nice and slow."

A pool of red blood was spreading out from under his pinned leg. He had to see where the blood was coming from and get the bleeding stopped. The rush of adrenaline was making him tremble.

This can't be happening.

The driver of the truck appeared with a cell phone pressed to his ear. "The ambulance is already on the way. He pulled right out in front of me. Thank God I didn't hit him."

Adam groaned and tried to push the bike off himself, but Finn stopped him.

He pulled off his flannel shirt, popping off a few buttons in the process. "Can you lift the motorcycle very slowly so I can see where the bleeding is coming from?"

"You got it," the other man said, and did as he asked.

Finn put his head close to the ground to make sure the motorcycle was safe to move. "Okay, you can lift it all the way off of him." He quickly pressed the wadded shirt to the wound on the teenager's thigh right above the knee.

Adam gritted his teeth and put a hand over his eyes.

"You're doing good, kid. Just hold still, and we'll have you to the hospital in no time."

It was all his fault that Adam had taken off on the motorcycle. His fault he'd been so upset that he'd pulled out onto the road without looking while on an unsafe motorcycle and almost been hit by a truck.

Finn's stomach lurched.

This was way too much like the time he'd carried his little brother who'd been unconscious and bleeding after falling from a tree house. Once again it was his fault that someone was hurt.

This was proof that he should not be a dad.

"Am I going to die?" the teen said through gritted teeth.

"Absolutely not." *Please, God. Let him be all right.*

Adam groaned. "I need Daisy."

"I'll call her. Just let me take care of you first." What was this kid's fascination with Daisy?

"I'm not a thief." Adam lifted his head but dropped it back onto the folded-up towel the other man had put under his head. "It's my money. I promise."

"I know. I believe you. I'm sorry I messed with your stuff."

The ambulance siren grew louder, but before it reached them, Daisy's truck came from the opposite direction. She pulled over, jumped out and ran to them.

"What happened? Oh, my God."

"He's going to be all right," Finn said.

She dropped to Adam's other side and took his hand. "Did you hit your head?"

"Don't think so." He hissed as Finn adjusted the pressure on his leg.

She shot Finn a furious glare that cut to the bone. "Why did you let him ride this stupid motorcycle? I knew something like this would happen."

He should've known too.

His muscles tightened, making him feel as if he was caving in on himself. He didn't answer, because what could he say? This was all his fault.

The ambulance arrived and the paramedics took over.

Time was moving in both hyper speed and slow motion. He held up his hands and looked at the blood. Someone handed him a wet towel, and he cleaned them the best he could.

They got Adam strapped onto a stretcher and wheeled him

toward the ambulance. "There's not much room," said one of the paramedics.

"Can my...mom come? Please?" Adam said, surprising both of them.

A female paramedic patted Adam's arm. "Yes, your mom can come."

She looked at Finn, her wide eyes revealing her emotional state. The kid didn't know what it meant to Daisy to be used as a pretend mom. "You got this," he said. "Go with him."

"Ivy is with Lizzy and Davy." She climbed into the back of the ambulance. "Finn, you're meeting us at the hospital, right?"

"I'll be there." If she wanted him there, he would suck it up and be there. And do his best not to make things worse.

DAISY WAS ABLE to breathe once the paramedics assured her Adam was out of immediate danger. He was woozy from blood loss and drowsy from something they'd given him for the pain, and if she hadn't driven up when she did, he would be going through this all alone.

She wasn't sure why she felt so protective over this young man. He was too old to need her as a mother, but she would be here for him anyway.

At the hospital, they wanted to get an X-ray of his leg right away, so she sat in a small waiting area.

Finn arrived a few minutes later. She had planned to fuss at him about the motorcycle, but he looked so devastated that she just wanted to hug him instead. The problem was, he wasn't getting close enough to touch.

"How's Adam?"

"They're X-raying his leg."

"He took off on the motorcycle before I could stop him." Finn started pacing. "You were right. Working on that old bike was stupid. "

The anguish wafting off of him was palpable. "You were just trying to connect with Adam and teach him something."

Finn came to a sudden stop. "This is the kind of thing that happens when I form a connection with people. Tell him I'm sorry." He turned to go back out of the ER doors.

"Where are you going?"

"I need some air. Before I screw something else up."

She growled under her breath. The last thing she needed right now was him doing his distance thing.

He walked out into the parking lot.

"Maybe he really can't handle fatherhood." She sat in an uncomfortable plastic chair, sick to her stomach and sick at heart.

"Hey, Daisy," Jake said as he sat down beside her a few minutes later.

"How did you know we were here?"

"Finn called me."

"He left. I don't know where he went."

"He's sitting outside. He didn't go far."

Jake handed her a cup of coffee. "It's because of me that Finn is so upset."

She took a sip and waited for him to explain, but he only stared at the wall in front of him. "How is any of this your fault?"

"When I was about ten years old, we got into a fight." He stretched out his legs and tilted his head back. "I can't even remember what it was about, but my usually coolheaded big brother lost his temper. I threatened to run away, he said good, and so I did. I climbed up into an old tree house in the woods near our house. One of the boards was rotten, and I fell. I got hurt pretty badly."

The image made her cringe. "And of course he blamed himself for his little brother getting hurt."

"He said he should've fixed the tree house or kept me from running away or whatever else he could blame himself for."

"You almost died." Finn's voice came from behind them, and they both turned around.

"Can I talk to Daisy alone?"

"Yep." Jake got up and patted his big brother on the back as he walked by.

She stood and grasped his hands. "I'm sorry I made it sound like I was blaming you for the accident. This is not your fault."

He shook his head as if she'd told a lie. "You weren't wrong. It is my fault."

A young nurse walked over to them. "You can follow me to Adam's room. The doctor wants to talk to both of you."

Their discussion would have to wait.

They followed the nurse down a short hallway and into a sterile, white exam room. Adam was in the bed, and a doctor with red hair and wire-rimmed glasses was standing at its foot. "Good afternoon, I'm Dr. Smith. Thankfully, Adam's leg is not broken, but we do need to perform a minor repair surgery."

The nurse opened the door and stuck her head into the room. "Dr. Smith, that call you've been waiting for just came in."

"Please, excuse me for a minute. I'll be back with some paperwork. Since Adam is only fifteen, one of you will need to sign it." He turned in a rush and left the room.

Daisy and Finn shared a shocked expression and then turned their stares to Adam. "Fifteen?" they said in unison.

He winced. "Yes."

"Did you run away from home?" she asked.

"No, I ran away from boarding school."

The ramifications of what this could mean began flashing in her mind. She'd been employing an underage runaway. If only she'd completed the background check. "You have some serious explaining to do, young man."

Finn stopped pacing the small room and stood at the foot of Adam's bed. "Why did you show up at the ranch with a ton of cash and a dossier on Daisy?"

She gasped. "A what?"

"I can explain everything," Adam said.

CHAPTER TWENTY-NINE

FINN BRACED HIS hands on the foot of the hospital bed. "Let's hear it, Kid."

Adam tried to sit up but winced and lowered himself back onto the bed. "It's not as bad as it sounds. I'm not a con man or a thief. After my mom died, my great-uncle who I barely know became my guardian. She had no idea what a big jerk he really is. Instead of moving onto the ranch like he was supposed to do, he sold my home and sent me away to boarding school."

"Where does he think you are now?" Daisy asked.

"Still at school. I'm good with computers and imitating voices, and I might have sent some emails and made some calls. The school thinks I've gone home while my uncle thinks I'm still there."

"Adam!" She momentarily covered her face with her hands. "You're going to get all of us in trouble over this. You should be in school, not working all day on a ranch."

"I'm sorry, Daisy. I promise I'll make it right and make sure you don't get blamed for anything." The teenager moved his leg and hissed with his eyes squeezed tight.

Daisy chewed her thumbnail and sat on the side of his bed. "You traveled to Channing all by yourself?"

"It wasn't hard to do."

Finn hated the worry and distress on her face, so he turned

away. "And what about the folder full of information about Daisy?" he asked from his spot by the window.

"Well... I have a good reason for that too."

The doctor rushed back into the room before he could answer. "Sorry about that. Since Adam has a rare blood type, I wanted to make sure the blood bank has what we might need, just in case."

Daisy's gaze snapped to the doctor. "What blood type?"

"AB negative."

"That's *my* blood type," she said.

Finn looked at Daisy and Adam side by side. He gasped and then cursed under his breath. All the little things that had been spinning around in his mind finally added up. Their shared single dimple. Their laugh and some mannerisms. And now that he knew his true age, it all fell into place.

Adam must be—

"I'm your son," Adam said.

"MY SON?" DAISY'S vision swam and she swayed. Finn was beside her in a moment and put his hands on her shoulders to keep her steady.

"You're my biological mother."

So many feelings and thoughts came at her all at once. Shock. Confusion. Joy mixed with sadness for the time lost. Daisy leaned forward and cradled both sides of his face, searching for some piece of herself in his eyes.

The doctor frowned. "I'm confused. You didn't know that you are his mother?"

"I'll fill you in," Finn said to the other man, then looked at Adam. The hospital is going to need your uncle's phone number."

"He won't care, but it's in my contacts list. I guess there's no way around calling him?"

"Nope. Sorry, kid." Finn picked up Adam's phone from the bedside table. "Pull it up for me."

"We will definitely need to talk to your guardian," Dr. Smith said.

With the information he needed, Finn kissed Daisy's forehead. He might have to slip away to catch his breath now and then, but no matter what happened next, he wanted her to know he was here for her. "You two talk, and I'll go see about what needs to be done."

The men left the room, and Daisy pressed a hand to her pounding heart. "Is this for real? You are really my son?"

"I have a folder full of information and a letter from my mom that says so.

She always told me how I was born, but it wasn't until after she died that I found the information she had on you. She put it with some cash in a secret hiding spot where she knew I would look. I also have a trust fund."

"The fertility clinic had a description of me, but it was supposed to be anonymous. How did your mother know it was me?"

He shrugged. "Maybe because she had a lot of money and knew people? You're not mad at her, are you?"

"No, honey. I'm not mad at all. However she did it, I owe her my biggest thanks." She squeezed his hand. "You've been through so much. You have no idea how long and how many times I have wondered about a child of mine somewhere out there in the world." A tear rolled down her cheek.

"Don't cry. I had a really wonderful childhood. And a great mom."

"I'm so glad to hear that. Is it just you? No brothers or sisters?"

"Just me. And according to the paperwork from the fertility clinic, I'm your only child."

She pressed her lips to his forehead for a quick kiss and couldn't stop the tears. "I'm glad you came to find me."

"I think my mom chose you because of your love for horses."

"I'm overwhelmed." She laugh-cried. "And happy. So happy."

"So, even though I screwed up, I get to stay around?" he asked.

"Well, there is the matter of your guardian and you running away. It won't be simple, but we'll have to deal with all that legal stuff before you get to come back home."

"Home?"

"Absolutely. I want you to think of Dalton Ranch as your

home. Let's just hope we don't have to jump through too many legal hoops to make it happen."

"I'm pretty sure Uncle Pete will be happy to have someone take me off his hands. He has fancy lawyers who handle all that kind of stuff for him."

The crestfallen expression on his face made her chest tight. "Why didn't you tell me who you are when you first arrived?"

"I was worried it would freak you out, and I wanted you to get to know me first. And then maybe you'd..." He shrugged.

"You fit with us from the very first day. As soon as we get things settled, you're going to have to start school. You've already missed too much."

"The same school where Loren goes?"

"It's the only high school in Channing. I can't believe I just found out who you are, and now I have to worry while you have surgery."

His eyes were glazed with pain and medication, but he grinned enough to show his dimple. "Sorry... Mama Daisy. Can I call you that?"

She swallowed the lump in her throat. "I would like that."

A few minutes later, they came to take Adam for his outpatient procedure and left her and Finn alone in the room.

Daisy sat on the bed and let out a slow breath. "Tell me what you found out about his uncle. Is he on his way here?"

"No, he's not. The hospital called him and got permission for the procedure, and then I talked to him. He didn't even seem all that concerned about him leaving boarding school. He was more worried about getting his money back than where Adam had been."

She gasped. "He sounds horrible. Does he want Adam back with him or to return to the boarding school?"

"No. He's eager to hand over guardianship and is calling his lawyer right away to expedite the process."

"That's just what Adam said would happen."

"Since you are a registered foster home, it should make things a little easier. You're going to need to call and talk to him soon, but it looks like things will go the way you want."

She got up and walked his way. "How do you know what I want?"

He met her halfway and opened his arms to cradle her against his chest. "Because I know you."

"It's such a relief that his uncle is getting the process started, but it also makes me want to find the man and smack him." She lifted her head from his shoulder. "Who treats a grieving child like he did?"

"There are those mama bear claws I was talking about. I kind of pity the man."

That made her grin just like he'd been hoping to do.

ADAM'S OUTPATIENT SURGERY went well, and after he woke up, they took him home to the Dalton Ranch with permission from his uncle. With Finn on one side of him and her on the other, they got him upstairs and settled into bed.

Standing in the hallway outside of the bedroom, Finn pulled Daisy into a hug. "You've had a big day."

"One of the biggest."

"I'm going to go over to Travis and Lizzy's to get Ivy."

"Hey, old man," Adam called from the bed. His words were slurred from the anesthesia and pain meds. "Where do you think you're going?"

"Just next door for a few minutes."

"You need to stay here and take care of my mama Daisy." He shook his head unsteadily as if trying to clear his vision. "She cried, and I need a nap before I can take care of her."

Finn moved to his bedside. "You've got it, kid. Close your eyes and get some rest."

Adam was so drowsy that he fell asleep still mumbling something about how he'd make things right.

IN DAISY'S BEDROOM that night, Finn flopped back on the bed and plowed a hand through his hair. "What a day. I can't believe Adam got hurt."

"Want to know what I've noticed?" Daisy asked.

He tucked his hands under the back of his head and stared at the ceiling. "Sure."

"The first time I met Ivy, she was frightened and curled against you. You were looking at me, but you cradled her head in a move so protective and paternal that it melted my heart."

"I did that?"

"Yep. And you've done lots of similar things since then."

He shook his head. "Adam could've been killed because of me. And then you never would've known that you have a son."

"Stop beating yourself up about it, or I'm going to have to give you a spanking."

He chuckled. "I'd like to see you try."

"Mama, where you?" Ivy called from the hallway.

"In here, sweetie."

Ivy peeked around the corner and a smile spread across her face before she ran to them.

Daisy lifted her up onto the bed with them.

"Give me a hug, little miss."

Ivy put her head on his chest and tried her hardest to wrap her short arms around his broad chest.

"That's just what I needed." He kissed the top of her head.

Ivy stood up on the bed and then leaned in to kiss his cheek. "Wuv you."

He sucked in a breath. "I love you, too."

Daisy's tears spilled over once again.

A second later their adorable toddler was jumping on the bed between them.

"I'm going to go check on Adam."

Daisy suspected he also needed to wipe a tear from his eye. She scooped up the toddler and covered her cheeks with kisses until she giggled. "All right, you little jumping bean. Let's go get a bath."

FINN WENT DOWNSTAIRS to check Adam's medication and wound cleaning schedule attached to the front of the refrigerator with butterfly magnets. It was time for his antibiotic and a pain reliever. He put them in a paper cup and poured a fresh glass of water.

When he went into the guest room where the youth was recuperating, Adam was sleeping. Now that he knew the kid was only fifteen years old, he could see it. He could also see Daisy in his features.

Adam had been more alone in the world than he had ever been. But he had faced his struggles head-on. He'd come up with a brilliant scheme to leave boarding school without his guardian's knowledge. He'd traveled alone and found his way to the Dalton Ranch and convinced them he was an adult.

Finn admired this kid's grit. "You're one smart, tough kid," he said under his breath.

Adam opened his eyes and blinked a few times. "I know I am," he said in a quiet, hoarse voice.

"I thought you were asleep."

He winced as he shifted himself up on the pillows.

"It's time for your medication. How are you feeling?"

"I could use one of those pain pills."

"It's in here." He shook the paper cup, poured the pills onto Adam's palm and gave him the glass of water. "Need anything else?"

"A truck would be nice."

"Keep dreaming. First you have to get a driver's license." Finn sat in the rocking chair.

"Are you going to teach me to drive?"

"You really want me to teach you?"

"You've taught me lots of other stuff already."

"Aren't you mad at me for what happened to you?"

"No. I should've said something sooner about who I am. Or been better at hiding my stuff."

"I shouldn't have been looking at your stuff."

"Why were you in there?"

"Looking for you to tell you that the motorcycle needed more work before it could be ridden."

"Oh." Adam grimaced. "It was stupid of me to jump on it and take off."

"I won't argue with that."

Adam shifted again and gritted his teeth. "Thanks for being there with me when I got hurt. You kept me calm when I was freaking out."

The tension in Finn's chest loosened. "I'm glad I was there, too."

He still couldn't help but blame himself for the accident. There were things he could have and should have done to prevent this near tragedy. He could've listened to Daisy and not helped him work on the motorcycle. He shouldn't have come down so hard on him about the money and information about Daisy. If he hadn't been so hot-tempered and jumped to conclusions without really listening, Adam wouldn't have taken off.

While holding Adam's bleeding body in the middle of the road, gripping fear had wound tight around his insides, and he wasn't even his kid.

But he is Daisy's child.

He hadn't known that fact at the time of the accident, but looking back, he should have figured it out. They shared their one dimple, the way they tapped their thumb to their pinkie when they were thinking, and the crooked fingers just like Sage and Daisy. If it hadn't been for the false age thing, he would have put it all together.

It didn't seem to matter whether it was his child or someone else's, he still felt protective. And now he knew there was no escaping connections and relationships. And love.

"You and Daisy are good together," Adam said, interrupting Finn's thoughts.

His head snapped up to look at the young man. "I would've thought you'd want me to stay away from her."

"I used to think that. Until I saw how much you care for her. You'll make good parents for Ivy."

"You think I'll make a good father?"

"I've never had one, so I don't have a comparison, but you seem like a good dad to me."

Finn leaned forward, propped his elbows on his knees and stared at the floral pattern on the rug beside the bed. Daisy had been telling him the same thing, and so had both of his brothers. He'd been fighting all of them. Fighting himself.

He was no longer the scared kid taking care of his brothers when he was just a kid himself. He was an adult. A grown-ass man with a ranch and people and animals depending on him. What difference did a title make? Whether he was a brother or an uncle or a friend, he'd already been taking care of everyone around him.

He could be a dad to Ivy and to this fatherless child beside him. To Daisy's child.

He could be the man Daisy needed him to be.

"Hey, old man. Did you fall asleep on me?"

He sat up straight and grinned at the kid. "Just thinking about some important decisions."

"I could really go for a cheeseburger and french fries," Adam said. "Seems like a perfect chance to get on Daisy's good side and make it up to me."

Finn chuckled. "Is that right? Lucky for you, I was already planning to go into town. I'll pick up some food for you."

"Thanks. Wait, before you go, close the door and hand me that duffel bag."

Finn did as he asked, and put the bag beside him on the bed. The teenager dug around in it, pulled out a ring box and flipped it open to reveal an emerald cut diamond ring.

"This was my mother's ring," he said. "I know she would want Daisy to have it, so if you ever need to use it—hint, hint—you know where it is."

He squeezed Adam's shoulder and nodded but couldn't talk around the lump of emotion lodged in his throat.

If even this kid believed in him, then shouldn't he believe in himself?

CHAPTER THIRTY

WHILE FINN WENT to get the food, Daisy set up a card table by Adam's bed so all four of them could eat together. As Finn headed back into the room with the drinks, he stopped to watch Daisy steal two of his french fries, eat one and give the other one to Ivy. He smiled and a lightness filled him. How had he ever thought Daisy wasn't the sexiest woman in the world?

She was…everything.

He never got tired of her company, she made him laugh and they rarely fought. And when they made love, they were in sync in the best way. What more could a man ask for?

In a spur of the moment decision, he let his heart guide him. He walked forward and sat in the folding chair beside her.

She cocked her head and smiled at him. "What's up?"

"I see that you're teaching the next generation to steal my fries."

"Us girls have to stick together, don't we, sweetie?"

"Girl stick." Ivy giggled and then reached for another one of his french fries.

Daisy kissed the top of her head and beamed a big smile that showed her dimple. Just like the young man in the bed beside her. Her son, who he'd taken under his wing long before he'd known the truth of his parentage. He looked at Adam and a silent understanding passed between them.

He turned his attention back to the woman who held his future in the palm of her hands. "Daisy Maisy, you've not only taken my food and drinks and T-shirts and who knows what else, but you've also taken something much more important." He took her hand across the small card table. "You've stolen my heart."

"Heart," Ivy said, and patted Daisy's chest.

He smiled and stroked her head of curls. "That's right, little one." He put a hand to his own chest. "This heart right here."

"Finn, do you mean it?" Daisy asked with love shining in her eyes.

"Oh, I definitely mean it. I think of you before I fall asleep and when I wake up each morning. I thought I wanted the life of a single, unencumbered man, but you make me see everything in new ways. You came into my life and stirred up my world in a most wonderful way. You are my inspiration and my joy. My conscience. My encouragement. You bring out the best in me and make me see myself as more capable than I gave myself credit."

"It was easy to do. You're a good man, and you have changed my life for the better."

He glanced at Adam, and the teenager tossed him the small box. Finn got down on one knee, making her gasp. "I love you, my sweet stubborn Daisy Maisy. And I have one more thing you can take." He flipped open the ring box. "Will you take my heart? Forever? Will you marry me and build a family with me?"

"Yes. I absolutely will. I love you dearly."

He slipped the diamond ring on her finger. "I had help with the ring, so I can't take all the credit for it."

"It was my mom's," Adam said. "She would want you to have it."

"Oh, Adam. It's gorgeous. That is the sweetest thing ever and so special." She stood and hugged Finn, and Ivy squealed when they squashed her between them. Daisy wiped tears from the corners of her eyes. "We're going to be a real family. You have helped me complete my wish list."

Finn kissed her and then Ivy's rosy cheek. "We've already got two kids, so I think we're off to a good start."

"Two kids?" Adam asked.

"I know you're almost a young man, but I think you could use a dad as well."

"You mean it? You really want to be...my dad?"

"Absolutely. If that's what you want as well."

Adam's grin widened to show his dimple. "Can I still call you old man?"

"Sure thing. But let's retire calling me grandpa...for now."

"Daddy." Ivy got his attention by patting his cheek. "Wuv you."

He cuddled her close and smelled the baby shampoo in her hair. "Love you too, little miss."

Daisy was full on crying now as she wrapped her arms around his waist and whispered in his ear. "I'm so proud of you. I love you."

"Thank you for showing me how to open my heart."

EPILOGUE

EVERYONE WAS AT the Dalton Ranch for Sunday dinner, and Loren was excited about the artwork she'd had framed. She unwrapped the brown craft paper and held the painting of a woman in a garden.

Dillon stopped behind her. "Where did you get this painting?"

"We found it hidden in a secret drawer in our house in town. The house used to belong to my great-aunt Tilly DeLuca. But as hard as I've tried to find out, I don't know who the artist is."

Dillon stepped closer and squinted at the initials in the bottom corner of the painting. "I think I might know. I think it was painted by my great-grandfather James Kenneth Cameron."

"No way! Really?"

"I'm not positive, but I have a sister who knows a lot more about his artwork than I do. Can I take a photo of this and send it to her?"

"That would be great," Loren said. "This isn't the only one. I have more paintings and sketches by the same artist. Do you know the name Tilly DeLuca?"

"I don't think so, but one of my sisters might."

"This is so cool," Loren said. "Hey, Mom. Guess what I just found out." She raced off to spread the news.

A while later, everyone was in the backyard eating and playing and visiting, but Finn stood behind Daisy with his big hands spread across her baby bump.

"Did you feel that?" she asked.

"Was that the baby moving?"

"Yes. Oh, there it is again."

He came around in front of her, dropped to one knee and kissed her baby bump. "Hello in there, tiny one." He looked up at her with a huge smile. "We're going to have three children."

"Can you handle that?"

"Yes, ma'am." He stood, cradled her face and kissed her. He glanced around at their extended family. "With this crew to help out, I know I can."

"The man who never wanted a wife or child is now a husband and soon to be a father of three."

"Isn't it great how things work out?" he said.

"The best."

"Daisy, come sit with me," Sage called over to her.

"I'll go make a plate of food for you while you talk to your sister. You have a baby to feed." He kissed her and headed to the table.

She went over to sit by her twin in a pair of lawn chairs off to the side. "Remember when it was just the two of us here on this big ranch?"

Sage glanced down at Rose who was asleep in her arms and kissed her baby girl's cheek. "How things have changed. We are two lucky ladies."

"I agree."

Ivy's giggles drifted on the warm breeze as Finn lifted her high into the air so she could pretend to be an airplane as he flew her over to her Riley and Jake. Adam was teaching Loren how to rope, and Grayson and Travis were at the grill laughing. Lizzy placed one hand on her own pregnant belly and used the other to wipe ketchup off Davy's cheeks.

"I wish Mama and Daddy were here to see what we've built," Daisy said.

"I think they are. They're up in heaven hand in hand and looking down with smiles."

"Family photo time," Loren called to everyone. "Gather

under the tree, please." The teenager rounded everyone up, set the timer then ran to join the group.

All of them crowded together and smiled for the camera. After they dispersed, Loren went over to check the camera and showed the photo to Daisy. "What do you think? Do we need to take another?"

Adam was making bunny ears behind Loren's head, and Jake was holding Ivy upside down—much to the little girl's delight. Travis and Lizzy were kissing, Finn had one big hand splayed on her stomach and Grayson was making a funny face at his baby daughter. And the cutest thing of all was Davy, who had his back to the camera but was bent over smiling at the camera from between his own legs.

Daisy felt a flutter in her belly and was so filled with love she thought she'd burst. She put an arm around her niece. "It's the most perfect family photo ever taken."

* * * * *

WESTERN

Small towns. Rugged ranchers. Big hearts

Available Next Month

A Maverick's Road Home Catherine Mann
The Cowboy's Compromise Cheryl Harper

....

A Fortune's Redemption Stella Bagwell
Her Cowboy Cupid Sasha Summers

....

LOVE INSPIRED

The Cowboy's Easter Surprise Jill Kemerer
Rescue On The Farm Allie Pleiter

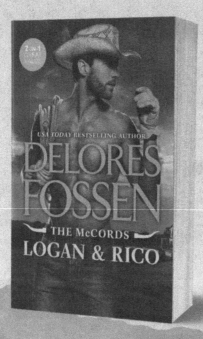